The Air Crash Files:
Jet Blast
A Daniel Tenace Novel

The Air Crash Files
Jet Blast
Copyright © 2017 by Stephen Carbone. All Rights Reserved

No part of this publication may be reproduced, stored in a retrieval system or transmitted in any way by any means, electronic, mechanical, photocopy, recording or otherwise without the prior permission of the author except as provided by USA copyright law.

This novel is a work of fiction. Names, descriptions, entities, and incidents included in the story are products of the author's imagination. Any resemblance to actual persons, events and entities is entirely coincidental.

Cover Art Design by Daniel Carbone

The Air Crash Files: Jet Blast

ACKNOWLEDGEMENTS

To Mary and George – Mary who pushed me forward; she expertly edited my manuscript from the start and checking maintenance items for technical accuracy. George, her husband, a former commercial pilot who kept me on target with flight deck activities and the proper use of pilot/air traffic control lingo. And they don't hold the fact I'm a Yankee/Giants fan against me.

To Penny and Mark – who have always been honest in their opinions and wise in their counsel. I count on them for straight and level-headed advice, no punches pulled, always a mix of humor and common sense.

To my wife – who for 35 years has been my best friend, my life's companion, my greatest critic, my driving force; all that I am and all I'll ever be, I owe to you. Babe, it has been a wonderful journey; I hope I made you proud.

PREFACE

One evening in 1999 I was called out to the flight line ten minutes from departure. At the time I supervised a night shift of thirty-five mechanics for an airline's satellite hub; of my mechanics, one stood out (I'll call him Jonas).

When I entered the flight deck Jonas was signing off the maintenance logbook after fixing the aircraft; the Captain was scowling at him while the First Officer sat shaking his head, smiling. The Captain saw me and started in before Jonas could leave. "I told your mechanic that my Radio Magnetic Indicator was getting a flag and he said ..." He then gestured to Jonas to repeat the offending words.

Jonas looked at me, slid the logbook to the First Officer and said, "I asked him, 'Hey, did Lindbergh need that?'"

I guess the Captain expected me to be shocked, but after all, this was Jonas; I was just amazed he did not accent the question with four-letter adjectives. Instead I shrugged my shoulders and said, "Well, Captain, to be honest ... he really didn't, did he?"

The First Officer chuckled; having known Jonas's history, he anticipated my response and rushed Jonas and me out of the cockpit. Wishing to defuse the angry Captain's pending retort, the First Officer winked and smiled at us, saying, "But if 'Wrong Way' Corrigan had an RMI he might have landed in California instead of Ireland."

Now let me just say something first: the relationships between pilots and mechanics are often perceived as, um ... confrontational? On the contrary, the two groups are more like rivals; like the New York Yankees and the Boston Red Sox: refusing to give an inch to the other, comfortable on their home turf, but they work hard together to further the cause, in this case: Safety. Flight attendants, engineers, fuelers, baggage handlers, air traffic controllers, and all the various aviation industry group members I am honored to know work hard – together – to get the customer from point A to point B – safely.

And in their off-hours, they like to give each other some Jazz.

However, let's get back to Jonas's comment; Lindbergh did not have access to a new-fangled RMI, choosing to stick his head out a window to navigate. To the First Officer's point I think 'Wrong Way' Corrigan was a genius. But if he did have an RMI in 1938 would he have deactivated it just to get to Ireland? I think not.

As an industry, we have made redundancy ... imperative. The airliners of today – and even some general aviation aircraft – have become so complex that to fly without certain instruments could be problematic at best. We're reliant on numerous computers that control every single element of the aircraft's operation.

Some would argue, perhaps, over-reliant.

I've been in aviation since 1981. In my earlier years I worked on B727s, DC-8s, old B737s and an occasional DC-10; airframes that demanded a personal touch, an intimate knowledge. The old analog 'steam' gauges and hard-wired components were like an old friend, trusting you to know when to ask the question and how to find the answer. I've been in aircraft crawlspaces that even the designers forgot about, there to chase a wire or lace a fuel bladder (not a job for the claustrophobic). Truth be known, I miss those days.

By the 1990s the digital age was full swing and fly-by-wire aircraft replaced the analog dinosaurs on the Flight Line. Today, mechanics no longer troubleshoot components at the wing, but instead interrogate one of many system control computers accessed through the flight deck. Pilots fly the computer to keep fuel costs low and meet the manufacturer's selling point for the advanced airliners. In the cabin, flight attendants delegate safety briefings to drop down DVD video players. And now, as we enter a new era, we have NextGen: a marriage of satellites and computers that will ease the burden of an overwhelmed North American airspace system.

These are incredible leaps, technology-wise; the quality of design and the reliability of the equipment are remarkable. To analyze an engine problem from the cockpit and know exactly what component to replace saves money, man-hours, and the stress of meeting a flight schedule. I've watched the first officer punch a button; the aircraft instantly banks left, the rudder barely moves from the centerline, while the throttles advance to add power; all while the pilot attends to other duties. Computers have been designed to serve us, to improve on us, and – in the dawn of technological wizardry – to replace us. Don't believe me? Have you ever heard of a Drone?

At what cost do we buy these conveniences? Are we accepting complacency? Do we blindly trust computerized technology? Can computer programs anticipate every ... possible ... event and crisis? If not, have we as an industry – pilots, mechanics, air traffic controllers – sacrificed so much discipline and tribal knowledge that we cannot remember how to reset the needle when we hear a skip in the record?

I remember the 1973 movie, *Westworld*; about a computer run vacation resort. Its tagline made a good point: an industry run entirely by computers is one 'where nothing can possibly go wrong ... go wrong ... go wro–'

Stephen Carbone, November 2013

DEDICATION

To my inspiration, Christiana Shepherd. I first learned of your passing while investigating the accident that stole you from your family and from a life of hopes and promise. Until that day the casualties were just names, faceless victims still, individuals misplaced in the tragic confusion of the accident. But you were my children's age; your family's grief touched me. You will always be my motivation to make the skies safe.

The Air Crash Files: Jet Blast

"I asked staff to give me a list of accidents that had maintenance involvement, and I got this thousand-yard stare, you know, the glassy-eyed one, 'what are you talking about?'"
NTSB Member, John Goglia

"... a good auto mechanic with grease-stained coveralls can sometimes be as effective and more credible as a design defect expert than an entire stable of GM, Ford, or Chrysler auto design engineers."

Thomas J. Vesper, Seinfeld Syndrome

"Sorry about this. I know it's a bit silly. Just a moment … Just a moment … I've just picked up a fault in the AE-35 unit. It's going to go 100% failure in 72 hours."

The HAL 9000-computer, 2001: A Space Odyssey

The Air Crash Files: Jet Blast

BOOK ONE

FREESTYLE AIR FREIGHT FLIGHT 115

The Air Crash Files: Jet Blast

CHAPTER 01
REVERSE DIRECTION

June 29th

Above the earth, a myriad of stars glows brightly. Constellations normally bathed pale by city lights are out front and on display, their patterns so obvious to the keen-eyed astronomer taking advantage of the dark Midwestern sky. Hercules stands ready for battle; the globular cluster M13 shows clearly in the uncorrupted heavens. Sagittarius takes aim to smite the scorpion – bane of brave Orion. Through the many millennia the stars have moved light years apart and together over great expanses of empty space almost imperceptible to the denizens of Earth.

The humid air of summer lies wearily on the earth; rows of crops form geographic man-made designs that crisscross the floor below. The heat absorbed by the terrain is a reminder of the selfish realm the sun maintains over its third planet, rising in shimmering waves and released nightly, discharged generously into the void. The warmth is given freely; the endless domain of cold space accepts it greedily all through the night.

Almost unnoticeably the Swan's star Deneb flickers momentarily as a hushed roar echoes off the ground. An AeroGalactic KR-450C, registration number N908FS, soars effortlessly across the Nebraska sky at 34,000 feet; its left wing dips as it banks left to meet the course correction initiated by the Autopilot; it is fighting cross winds that gently nudge it from the south. Two engines, one under each wing, and a third mounted in the vertical stabilizer work cooperatively to push the aircraft through the strong winds. Extreme sub-zero temperatures transform the water vapor to ice crystals, leaving a tell-tale sign of the aircraft's westward direction.

Except for the red strobe-effect of the anti-collision lights and the steady piercing radiance of the green and red navigation lights on the wing tips, the KR-450C is invisible against the black of night. The royal blue corrosion preventive paint scheme reflects nothing below. It displays Freestyle Freight Airline's logo – a sweeping capital letter 'F' forms the outline of a bird's wing – itself indiscernible.

Occupying the left pilot seat in the KR-450C is its fifty-five-year old Captain, Richard Grace. A man comfortable with responsibility, he commands this 700,000-pound aircraft through the early morning sky. His look and demeanor are a contradiction; strict to a fault, yet most first officers monitor his trip bids to fly with him. He insists on being called 'Richard,' no variations on the name. A graduate of the Naval Academy, Richard is a professional and the image of discipline with hair cut so short the follicles barely peek out. His sharp chin sits below chiseled cheekbones; an aquiline nose and deep piercing brown eyes cap this scrupulous visage. However, his mouth turns up at the ends in a permanent grin that softens him, and his sense of humor dispels any harshness.

He scans the digital instrument panel on an involuntary schedule that could not be more regimented if he tried; every two minutes on the mark he scans right to left catching the engine readings followed by altitude, air speed, and rate of climb. Satisfied no irregularities exist, he returns to reviewing the destination airport information clipped on the control yoke. Richard clears his throat softly and pushes up slightly on the reading glasses that sit dangerously close to the tip of his nose. He glances right at his first officer, Margaret 'Maggie' O'Neil.

Maggie is deeply engaged in fuel burn calculations; she completes the math prior to entering the data in the flight plan computer. She busies herself with these prosaic duties during these long overnight trips because they fill the tedious moments when conversation drags and the destination seems to move further away with every mile flown.

"How bad?" Richard asked, reaching down for his coffee.

"Actually," Maggie said, after running her numbers for the third time, "you qualify for green pilot of the year, if not just the night. We'll fall short of the calculated fuel burn by several thousand pounds." She stowed the computer in the rack to her left behind the captain's seat where it immediately transmitted data to Freestyle Airlines' maintenance control building in Cleveland, Ohio.

Maggie leaned forward to enter the new fuel data in her Status computer with the back end of her pen. Mounted by her left knee, the Status computer contains the logic memory for the aircraft, gathering data from the various aircraft systems and transmitting it through digital satellite signals to Cleveland.

"We're pretty heavy –" Richard began. Maggie held her hand up as she listened to a transmission.

"Copy Minneapolis, traffic at thirty on a heading of zero-five-zero, Freestyle one-one-five heavy."

Maggie studied her Navigational display to see the air traffic occupying the same airspace as their flight. The detailed instrument that the new satellite system had for portraying all movement in the area impressed her. Maggie liked that Freestyle was always on the cutting edge; they began installing the new Satellite Positioning and Airspace Restructuring – SPAR – air traffic system in the new jets.

A white triangle moved from the top left of the display screen diagonally down to the right; a '4415' displayed next to it with a '30K' below it. The detail of flight 4415 was sharp, crisp; at the same time artificial and simple. An aircraft silhouette represented Freestyle one-one-five pointing straight up on a seeming collision course.

Traffic at this time of night was minimal. Richard was not so impressed by technology, so he glanced out the window. Four thousand feet below and to the left a flashing red strobe appeared from a cloudbank and past swiftly beneath them.

SPAR is the brainchild of the Federal Aviation Administration; an aggressive project designed to address the increasing air traffic threatening to overwhelm the present-day air traffic control system. In cooperation with the FAA, the international aerospace community began investing in similar technologies to increase capacity worldwide.

Based on the principle that computers think and communicate faster than humans, SPAR employs an intricate arrangement of satellites, ground-based transmitters, and computers that track all aircraft in North American airspace, including Hawaii and Alaska. SPAR practically eliminates human interaction between pilots and controllers, communicating directly between land based air traffic computers and aircraft computers. Course corrections, landing approaches, and even airport movements, will be computer-managed with limited input from pilots. The New Age was racing up to meet them.

And Richard did not trust the New Age.

"These STAR graphics are unbelievable," Maggie said staring at the display. "I don't even have to look out the window."

"SPAR, not STAR," Richard chuckled sadly, looking skeptically at his co-pilot. "Sierra-Papa-Alpha-Romeo; like in the wing."

"I don't know where they get these acronyms. It's FAA acronym overload."

Richard scanned his gauges. "It stands for Satellite Positioning ... um, something-something. Actually, it's one of their better acronyms. You see the wing's spar is the backbone of the wing; all loads go into it and wings provide lift. And lift provides job secur–"

"Yeah, whatever boss. Look, I know about your little love affair with the FAA."

Richard snorted.

"I'm assuming," Maggie continued, "that since we have these really cool graphics that Freestyle's modifying the four-fifty fleet first?"

Without looking up, Richard nodded.

"I was playing with this Saturn ... wait a minute, let me see who made this stupid thing," Maggie referenced her training manual. "Here it is; one is a SAT-SPAN Satellite Tracking Computer System; that's part of the satellite fed auto-pilot system.

"And this little baby is my new toy," she said patting an inoperative panel screen to her right. "The Saturn Digamma-Six DATTAM Ground Tracking Computer."

"What does that do, Dale Arden?"

"Who's Dale Garden?" she asked sarcastically. Richard just shook his head.

"Never mind, Captain Old guy," Maggie interrupted, her attention went back to the blank screen. "You can navigate the airport in zero visibility; kinda like infra-red with a seeing-eye dog. I was thinking I'd turn it on before we reach L-A."

Richard's eyes narrowed with doubt. "Will it work?"

"We can find out."

"Just make sure it doesn't interfere with any other systems we may need."

"I already did," she replied, having already anticipated his train of thought. "It's harmless and fully functional. I won't activate it until we're within sight of the airport."

Richard just nodded. "You have too much faith in those things."

The conversation droned on and the cockpit voice recorder caught it, constantly recording while taping on a continuous loop.

Two hours later Maggie scrolled through a series of checklists on her display screen. As aircraft of the past evolved from analog gauges to digital technology, small monitors display various instruments and system alerts/warnings on six primary light emitting diode screens. The information is presented in vibrant colors, usually to highlight the difference in importance or urgency. Two screens for each pilot display all flight information: altitude, speed, and rate of climb/descent. Two shared screens in the center display engine data, systems information, checklists, and messages/alerts.

Color communicates urgency; cyan blue means normal while white conveys 'good-to-know' information. In an abnormal situation, the gauge and message turn amber, alerting the crew to a heightened problem. An emergency will turn a gauge crimson with red warning messages, accompanied by loud aural warnings.

Recently modified text screens were added to display checklists for various phases of flight; these checklists assure pilots complete certain tasks. In emergencies, checklists display critical procedures to follow, thus reducing crew workload; no searching through thick manuals during high stress parts of flight.

Richard pulled up the usual checklist as they descended; they were entering a busy phase of the flight and Richard was organizing. As was Maggie; this was her leg so she put her work area in order, verifying instrument data for the coming landing cycle. She switched on the Saturn DATTAM Ground Tracking screen to her right, but the screen remained blank.

The Digital Airport Traffic and Taxi Alert Map is part of the SPAR system. Its pretentious acronym aside, the DATTAM draws on real time information to display a bird's eye view of the airport, complete with moving aircraft, open gates, and construction. Color technology alerts pilots to the severity of obstacles or unsafe situations. The true advantage: it allows pilots to taxi around an airport without ever looking out the window, permitting movement in heavy snows or fog minus the danger of collisions or incursions.

"Good morning, L-A center, this is Freestyle one-one-five heavy descending through eighteen-thousand for twelve."

"Good Morning Freestyle one-one-five heavy," ATC replied, "turn right heading three-one-zero, descend and maintain ten-thousand."

Richard Grace clicked the push-to-talk switch on the yoke. "L-A center: turn right heading three-one-zero; descend and maintain ten-thousand, Freestyle one-one-five heavy." He turned the altitude selector knob until 1-0-0-0-0 displayed in the window and tapped the window with his finger. "Ten-thousand," he said.

Maggie confirmed the change by reaching over and double-tapping the indicator's window while repeating the words 'ten-thousand'; she engaged the new altitude. The cabin vertical speed indicator registered a change of 1000 feet per minute as the descent continued. Richard retarded the throttles, allowing the aircraft to descend gradually.

Indicated airspeed slowly dropped below 300 knots while the altimeter needle hastened its movement, rotating counterclockwise as it ticked off the descent. Engine vibrations coursing through the airframe diminished; both pilots registering the change subconsciously. There was a mild lurch forward as the aircraft slowed its velocity and the KR-450C steadily descended through sixteen-thousand feet for Los Angeles airport.

For several minutes they descended gracefully, hitting a small patch of unstable air at 12,000 feet. As the

Autopilot leveled the airliner off at 10,000 feet, the DATTAM ground tracking screen to Maggie's right winked on.

"I never liked flying over the pitch-black ocean," Maggie said. She adjusted her seat and focused her full concentration on the landing cycle, settling into the approach. She ran her eyes over the instruments for assurance. Robotically she grabbed the restraining straps over her shoulders and locked them in front. "Always gave me the willies."

"Why? Because you can't see the deck from up here?" Richard teased. He scanned the distance to the right, catching glimpses of California's coastline between scattered clouds.

"You don't find it a bit unnerving?"

"I'll tell you what I find unnerving," Richard swept his eyes across the gauges. "I deadheaded on an Embraer two weeks ago and the two *kids*," he stressed, "flying the ship hadn't even gone through puberty yet; not even a hint of a beard. And they were all about the computer doing this and they don't have to do that because the computer does it." He glanced at Maggie with a pointing of his finger. "You take away their auto-everything and those guys couldn't fly in a straight line. This industry is painting itself into a corner with pilots that are too inexperienced and too dependent."

"I'll take your word for it, my captain." She adjusted her glasses. "Sheesh, your crotchety old side is showing again."

A smile barely showed on Richard's face. "Laugh it up, Miss Maggie May."

Richard displayed the approach checklist on an LED screen between Maggie and himself. A grunt escaped his lips as he saw one of the first items: Set Autoland. Begrudgingly he configured the aircraft controls to the proper profile with the activation of several switches.

All Autoland settings are routed through a device called the Flight Command Computer; quite literally the aircraft's nerve center in flight. The FCC is a computer that monitors and initiates all the routine phases of flight: climb, cruise, go-around, and land. When Autoland is initiated this system takes full jurisdiction of all aspects of the airliner's approach into an airport, including the landing spoilers, wheel brakes, and Autothrottle settings.

"Autoland set," Richard grumbled to Maggie. Under his breath he muttered, "I hate that damned computer."

Autoland, Autobrakes, Autothrottle, auto-freaking stupid, he thought. *They're all the same bad idea.*

As most airlines bring new aircraft models into their fleets, the flight departments require their pilots employ the various computer-driven components they paid good money to have installed. Many pilots worry that these modern technologies keep taking more and more command from them, reducing them to babysitters.

These efforts by the airlines pushed the crews to rely more heavily on automation and less on their experience. In their defense the bean counters applauded the savings; later model aircraft could outpace a human pilot by making minute changes in configuration or engine settings faster and with greater accuracy, resulting in substantial cost savings in fuel, maintenance, and delays.

But it did not guarantee the pilots would like it.

"Freestyle one-one-five heavy: descend and maintain three-thousand, turn right heading zero-one-zero. Maintain present speed."

Richard responded back to Air Traffic. Maggie selected 0-1-0 on the heading selector while Richard turned the altitude selector to 3-0-0-0. They double-tapped the other's selector window, repeating the other's information; a seemingly comical practice that assures each pilot double-checks the other.

As they descended Richard challenged Maggie from the checklist; she looked at each item a second later, assuring proper configuration for the landing cycle. Richard paged forward on the checklist while the altimeter clocked down towards 3000 feet.

"Freestyle one-one-five heavy, descend to one-thousand, turn right heading zero-seven-zero."

Richard responded before selecting 1-0-0-0 in the altitude selector; Maggie adjusted heading to 0-7-0. They tapped the selector windows and Richard engaged the course and altitude changes.

Out on the wings the ailerons followed the FCC's command and the aircraft banked slowly to the right as the Autopilot aligned on the commanded heading. In the cockpit the instruments reflected the changing aircraft's attitude as it leveled off.

"Flaps two, please," Maggie said.

"Flaps two," Richard responded. Reaching over the pedestal, he lifted the flap handle up, rotating it down to the two-degree detent and locking it in. He observed the flight control indicator as a green 'flaps' symbol displayed on the white 'wing' profile. The airliner rose gently as the increased flight surface added lift. The altitude indicator ticked off the airliner's decreasing height. The numbers swept past 1-1-0-0, quickly towards 1-0-0-0.

"Flaps seven." Richard responded by placing the flap handle in the seven-degree detent. On the trailing edges of the wings the flaps extended further back, increasing the surface area of the wings. Slats on the leading edge pushed out forward against the relative wind assaulting the wing, hydraulically locking into place.

Again, the green 'flaps' symbol on the flight control indicator grew as a digital '7' displayed. Maggie's demeanor was all business as she watched the lights of the city of Los Angeles grow in the windscreen. Directly over the nose of the aircraft she made out a series of flashing lights that constantly 'moved' away from the shore. Richard saw them moments before she did.

"L-A, Freestyle one-one-five heavy, we have the field in sight."

"Copy Freestyle one-one-five heavy. You are clear to land seven-right. Contact ground at one-two-one-seven-five."

"Copy L-A, contact ground at one-two-one-seven-five. G'day."

Richard entered the new frequency in the VHF window. Maggie said, "Gear."

Richard reached over and grabbed the gear handle, pulling it out and down. Maggie glanced at the altitude as it slipped below 1-0-0-0.

The altitude continued to decrease.

Outside, the three main and nose gear doors opened. Below the cockpit the nose gear made a clunking sound before swinging aft into position; a harsh roar announced the gears' intrusion into the air stream. Before the main doors opened completely, three main gears began their arced travel to the extended position. As they rotated down, the main gears slowed. The doors slapped shut against the body fairings.

Richard scanned the gauges, noting four gear lights illuminated green, down and locked.
"Four green," he said.
"Flaps fifteen," Maggie said.

Outside on the left gear, a microswitch made contact out of sequence. It received its share of grease and dirt, causing it to stick. By itself, this was not a problem; a bad switch could fault and later be repaired.

But there was another problem down line.

A signal went through paths that did not normally exist in this configuration, through a digital computer gate which interpreted correctly the data received, thus reacting as advertised.

"Holy –!" Richard barked; his peripheral vision caught an amber flicker, a light that did not make sense. Maggie pitched violently against her shoulder straps; sharp pains ran through her shoulders and breasts as the inertial restraints seized, arresting her forward motion. Another sensation took over, 'feeling' it before the instruments could register: the aircraft falling away beneath them; the sudden drop pushed her stomach up towards her throat.

Forward motion was crippled; both wing engines fought a reversing #2 tail engine. With the abrupt drop in speed, the aircraft's weight surrendered to gravity.

"My aircraft!" Richard yelled. Maggie surrendered the yoke.

"Your aircraft," she said calmly. She paged for the emergency checklists.

The #2 throttle automatically advanced calling for thrust; #2 engine spooled up in answer, further hobbling the airliner. The wide body jet plunged towards the ocean, falling through 800 feet for 700.

Richard shoved the throttles for engines one and three forward; altitude was now their only survival, their only hope. The wing engines responded; spooling up and greedily sucking in air to feed the furnace providing thrust. They clawed valiantly to pull the aircraft forward. Although the rapid descent was reduced, the plane still sunk below 600 feet.

In the milliseconds that followed, training and expertise took over as the situation became more chaotic. Richard and Maggie assessed their situation and assumed the roles.

Maggie clicked the mic, "Mayday! Mayday! Mayday! L-A approach, Freestyle one-one-five heavy!"

The radio went silent as every other flight capitulated, silencing all transmissions on the airwaves to their comrades in trouble. A second later, a calm but urgent voice replied in her ear, "L-A approach: what can we do to assist?"

The aircraft's warnings continued blaring, lights flashing, as a scroll of messages littered the screen. Maggie silenced alarms and whoops sounding throughout the flight deck. Computerized voices warned of countless faults threatening the aircraft's existence. Stall warnings, auto-pilot disconnect claxons and terrain alerts blared obnoxiously. Freestyle 115 still sunk towards the dark ocean; the frigid waters of the Pacific stood patiently by as the dying aircraft shuddered towards its cold embrace.

"Pull up the emergency ..."

"I got them," she said methodically.

"Give me the 'Reverser Unlock' list."

"Here it is! Thrust Lever for number two engine, forward thrust!"

He noticed for the first time that the #2 engine reverser knob was in the advanced reverse position. He pulled it back, but it cycled forward again after he released it. The aircraft reacted chaotically from the contradicting commands. Richard slammed the #2 fuel lever down; immediately starved of fuel the #2 engine spooled down. Lights clicked on as the #2 engine slowed its spin; new warning horns sounded, adding to the tension in the cockpit. The altitude indicator hovered just below 300 feet as the lights of the city – now directly in front – grew to an unnerving size.

"Gear up!" he growled. She raised the gear handle driving all four gears back into their wells.

"Freestyle one-one-five, L-A Approach!"

Suddenly the emergency stopped!

The #2 reverser retracted, but the light remained on. The four gear struts continued to rise gracefully into their wells; the reduced drag helped the wing engines pull the aircraft out of its fatal descent. Richard pulled steadily back on the yoke, watching with impatience as the nose slowly pointed up.

For several moments, as they inched back in the air, various warnings persisted in disconcerting chatter. Maggie continued punching buttons. The '#2 REVERSER' indication light flickered and went out.

Richard sat the KR-450C on its tail; the altimeter spun furiously, the numbers racing past 1-0-0-0 and higher. Below the city of Los Angeles fell away; reflections from receding stores and cars reflected off the belly of the KR-450C as it clawed back from the brink, robbing the Pacific of its victims.

"L-A, Freestyle one-one-five heavy. We are presently out of the emergency. We had a number two thrust reverser deployment, but it has retracted. The number two engine is shut down. We are climbing for three-thousand."

"Freestyle one-one-five heavy, climb and maintain three thousand, turn right, heading one-three-zero. Do you wish to vector back around for seven-right?"

Richard ran the math in his head; he did not want to approach over the city in case the episode happened again; too many innocent people. He watched the #2 engine exhaust gas temperature fall safely below 300 degrees before answering. He turned to Maggie. "Tell them we'll take it in again on seven-right."

Maggie relayed the information while Richard flew the aircraft on two engines. The two pilots operated as if with a sixth sense; each one's actions calculated and deliberate: check and recheck.

To avoid overloading Richard with information, Maggie ran through the approach checklist by herself, subconsciously scanning the instruments and maintenance panels, mechanically shutting off all unnecessary systems, finishing off with a double-check.

Richard contemplated the event; it cured itself when one of two things changed ... or two things happened together. First, the Autoland disconnected. He considered this important because on the ground the #2 reverser deploys first when the main wheels touch down, being activated by Autoland. And second, when Maggie raised the gear the emergency immediately dissolved. As he continued the approach he dismissed the first event in favor of the gear.

Now the information that was stored subconsciously surfaced: the reverser deployed when the gear was green: down and locked; then stowed as the gear unlocked. Could these facts about the gear be – coincidentally – tied to the #2 thrust reverser?

For now, they focused on landing the aircraft. Their conversation was subdued, speaking terse challenges and replies, while their senses were honed for any anomaly ready to spring up and catch them off guard.

While waiting for his next flight arrival, the line mechanic read a novel by his favorite author. A radio call came in: Freestyle 115 declared an emergency on final.

He sighed. *Well, that can't be good.*

He keyed his radio, "What type of emergency?"

"They squawked an uncommanded number two reverser deployment in flight. You need to meet the crew."

No, that is definitely not good.

"You got it," the mechanic rejoined. He stepped outside in time to see, rather than hear, Freestyle 115 flare in the distance and touchdown on runway 7-Right.

Within seconds the roar of its reversers could be heard over the early LA morning.

The sun was sending rays of early morning sunlight across the airport when Richard Grace taxied the KR-450C slowly into gate 3. At a hand signal from the marshaller Richard hit the brakes hard, rocking the aircraft forward with inertia. As ground power was activated, Richard cut the fuel to engines one and three while Maggie turned off lights, hydraulic and pneumatic systems.

The mechanic stood near the tail, shining his flashlight up at the #2 engine; he played the bright light back towards the right side reverser. A gap, a mirror image to the one on the left side, yawned between the fan cowl and the reverser, evidence that the reversers were not stowed completely; they were, instead, held in place by the jackscrews that normally powered them back.

As a ground crew rolled the crew stairs up to the aircraft's side, the mechanic and his lead took the steps two at a time, reaching the top as Maggie opened the entry door.

Overlooking protocol, the two men greeted Maggie and ushered her into the cramped cockpit to run through the harrowing events over the Pacific. Together they spoke in detail with Richard and Maggie, their stories supporting each other. Richard drove home the point about the gear instigating the beginning and the end of the event.

After Maggie had been debriefed thoroughly, she excused herself to catch a crew shuttle bus to gate 18. Still running on residual adrenalin, she wanted to make the next return flight to Cleveland. Richard took a few moments to speak to her alone; he wanted to remark on her professionalism, throwing in a comment on the importance of experience over trusting the computer. He shook her hand, holding it longer than normal, reassuring her that he had relied on her skill to get them out of the emergency.

Then he returned to the cockpit; there was a lot to do.

While mechanics in Los Angeles were assigned to troubleshoot, engineers at the aircraft manufacturer, AeroGalactic, were contacted. A conference call was scheduled for 08:00 Pacific time with both the mechanics in Los Angeles and the engineers for Freestyle in Cleveland. Level heads at AeroGalactic determined that an errant main gear ground sense switch had faulted; they recommended replacing it to eliminate it as a problem. As their troubleshooting progressed they concluded that the switch was definitely faulty, somehow activating the reverser in flight.

The KR-450C was to be towed to the hangar where the replacement of the ground sense switch would take place, followed by a gear swing to make the sure the new switch worked properly. Cleveland also ordered both #2 reversers be replaced before the test flight.

"Does it need a test flight?" the oncoming maintenance manager blurted during the conference call.

"Captain Grace pushed for it." The gravelly voice of Freestyle's Director of Maintenance rasped over the telephone speaker. "He's to be present for all repairs.

Call him at the airport Marriott when you have the plane in the hangar.

"And," he continued, a threatening tone bleeding through, "if you have any objections, let me just stipulate – this *will* happen! I will entertain any objections only after they walk the objector out to his car and off the property!"

CHAPTER 02
DAN TENACE (Ten-ah-chā)

Washington – Federal Aviation Administration Administrator, Amelia Varney appeared before the Senate Budget and Finance Committee for Transportation today to lobby for continued funding for the Satellite Positioning and Airspace Restructuring (SPAR) System, the new satellite and computer air traffic control system. SPAR is presently in the sixth year of progress ...

June 30th – Outside Washington, DC

"God, I can't stand this idiot!" Daniel Tenace said under his breath.

Aaron Campo sat discreetly reading his newspaper; a Federal Aviation Administration inspector, he was a quiet man, closing in on sixty and, like his hair, started to see the days to retirement dwindling. He was half-listening over the rumble of the train. Lights occasionally flickered on and off as the car jostled side-to-side. Aaron timed his reading to the on-again-off-again pattern of the lights.

"Which idiot?" he said, focused on his paper.

Daniel nodded his head in the direction of a passenger who just boarded, taking the last seat. The man wore a worn grey suit and in his right hand, a Pepsi can, the aluminum reflecting the alternating lights.

"Wait for it ..." Daniel whispered.

Aaron looked up in mild amusement, glancing back and forth between Tenace and the 'idiot.' He saw humor in everything with a smile never far from the surface.

"Wait ... for ... it ..."

The man popped the top on the can. SPOIT! Foam erupted skyward, hitting the ceiling; soda rained down on unsuspecting commuters angered by the shower. He ignored the comments, oblivious of the looks aimed at him.

Daniel turned to Aaron. "*That* idiot!"

Aaron guffawed and went back to his paper.

"How can anyone drink soda at six in the morning?" Dan asked, shaking his head before returning to his book.

Aaron folded his paper together and looked over his reading glasses. "With all you have on your plate, that's what bothers you?"

Dan Tenace is, for the most part, an unremarkable man sitting on a commuter train. An accident investigator for the National Transportation Safety Board, he has two things most other NTSB aircraft accident investigators do not have: an FAA certification and the experience to go with it.

He sits in the train car, leaning forward with his elbows resting on his knees. He has managed to keep to his normal weight; the strong arms and muscular neck reflect the efforts he puts to this goal. His posture appears relaxed, but Dan has an inherent awareness of his surroundings; a spring with potential energy, he is coiled to react.

His hair is salt and pepper while his beard has gone grey; both are kept trimmed. Dan's eyes are young, penetrating, staring out of an older, wiser face. Years of working long hours in harsh weather are scrawled across his features, but the longing for those days has never left.

To his right is Aaron Campo, an accident investigator for the Federal Aviation Administration. The relationship between the FAA and the NTSB has become adversarial; by rights both men should be sitting apart.

But not these two. Aaron is more relaxed; a southerner who grew up in the rural communities of Mississippi, he is a no-nonsense, take-charge type of man. Never one to pass up an opportunity to rib friends, like Dan, Aaron does not take bureaucrats seriously, but puts his heart into his job of preventing air disasters.

He leans back in his seat, using the hour-long ride into Washington, DC, to absorb his Wall Street Journal. A widower with two adult daughters, Aaron does not fight the battle of the bulge as aggressively as Dan, but he jogs three times a week. His hair is receding but his eyes are clear, laughing, alert where the worries of life have not been harshly evident. Aaron's smile is etched, turning up at the corners; but when his brows knit, the smile takes on a different look, and others may cower from it.

Aaron went on despite Dan's shrug. "How was your trip to San Diego?"

"The engine failure on rollout?" Another shrug. "It was textbook; the lead cargo handler left a metal clip board in the number two engine inlet. The plane rolled out on takeoff and sucked the clipboard into the first stage C-1 fan. Fortunately, the fan blades were harder than the clipboard, so when it got pulled into the engine the board got chewed up and spit back out the front." He paused as he recollected the scene. "You don't realize how much energy there is in throwing a mangled clipboard out the inlet and impaling the forward cargo bay underneath row three in first class."

"What about the engine?"

"Well, even though the clipboard was destroyed, it still managed to do over two hundred thousand dollars' worth of damage."

Aaron put his paper down. "Wait a minute, you said the clipboard sat in the inlet all the way to the runway ... and didn't get pulled in earlier than that?"

Dan inhaled deeply, considering the question. "You're a pilot, Aaron; you know fuel-saving operating procedures for some of these airlines, especially on these quick turns. They push back from the gate and taxi out on one engine. When they get clearance that's when they crank up the second motor and let it idle to get warm. They don't really put the juice to it until they swing around to line up for takeoff."

Aaron resumed his reading. "What happened to the cargo handler?"

"She was devastated. She thought she left the clipboard in her truck; there was so much going on with a broken belt loader that she didn't even remember putting it down to begin with." Dan picked his book back up.

"The first officer had already done his walk around, so nobody came behind her to catch it. They're reviewing the event to see if they'll fire her ... or worse. I don't think it was carelessness; she was just overwhelmed."

"Is that what's going in your report?"

"Not that it matters," Dan replied. "But yeah, that's what I'm putting in there. The airline needs to look at its ramp procedures. Phil's going to make sure they hang her from a yardarm."

Aaron pondered what Dan said. Phil Tulkinghorn was the aviation equivalent of rabble rouser with a bullhorn. "I'll talk to our guys in San Diego." Aaron said into his paper.

"By the way, your boss is a yutz."

Dan never looked up from the pages of his book. "Duly noted," he said.

Twenty minutes later, Daniel was lost in his book when a distinct buzzing came from between Aaron and himself. He looked over at his comrade, who ignored the look in favor of his paper.

"I think your butt's vibrating."

Aaron's concentration never wavered. "It'll stop, Bubba."

The buzzing did stop … and restarted moments later.

"Aren't you even a little bit curious?"

"Nope," Aaron replied, turning the page. "Nothing I can do about it out here."

The pager continued its annoying song. "Come on, Aaron–!"

Aaron sighed and dropped the newspaper. He grabbed the pager off his belt and read quietly to himself, while one eyebrow rose in curiosity.

"Well that bites! In flight, number two thrust reverser deployment on a Freestyle dash four-fifty in L-A last night."

"Reversed on the tail engine? Did it go in?"

"Nope, it's sitting safe and sound in L-A-X."

"Okay, I'll look at it when I get in. Thanks."

"Don't mention it." Aaron went back to his paper, but Dan lost interest in his book, his mind wandering 2700 miles away to L-A.

As the train pulled into the L'Enfant railroad station in Washington, DC, everyone assumed the sardine position at the doors. Dan and Aaron waited for the masses to get out of each other's way before getting up and walking out. As the doors slid open they were struck in the face by a stifling wave of humid air that announced the late June's quadruple-H summer weather pattern: hazy, hot, and hell-it's-humid. The train's air conditioning teased the back of their necks as they stepped out. With a hiss the doors closed on their heels and the train pulled away, increasing speed towards Union Station.

Aaron and Dan walked briskly down the ramp to the Seventh Street, SW, below amidst the organized insanity of everyday Washington, DC. Dan was already sweating through the grey dress shirt he wore. *Damn*, he thought, *can't I even get through until noon without feeling like I didn't take a shower?*

"See you tomorrow, Bubba." Aaron broke left while Dan turned right, making his way south.

"Later," Dan turned down 'D' Street and picked up his pace. He walked to the corner and crossed 'D' Street SW before turning right past the Housing and Urban Development building, an odd-shaped architectural design. Dan scaled the stairs to 490 L'Enfant Plaza two at a time and entered the food court, heading straight for his favorite coffee-and-strudel cafe.

Dan ordered black coffee and the last cherry strudel on the shelf. He began sneaking pastries lately even though his wife, Megan kept a close watch on his cholesterol. However, she was fast asleep fifty miles away and what she did not know …

"Do you think you should be eating all that sugar?"

Dan's head dropped. Chris Wilkerson, aircraft systems investigator, always had impeccable timing.

"What are you, my mother?"

"Why," Chris shot back, "would your father have been attracted to this face?" He ordered coffee, a few chocolate donuts and a lemon tart.

"You should see some of the women my father has dated after my mom died." Dan grabbed his coffee and pastry off the counter. "You'd have been in the front running."

They walked slowly to the elevators that would take them to their offices in the NTSB headquarters. Chris had already finished one chocolate donut while Dan sipped carefully at his coffee.

"Aa-aack!" Dan shuddered, as the coffee burned down his throat, "they gave me the high-test stuff! I specifically ordered–" His face soured in disappointment, "I swear this coffee is so dark, light can't escape it!"

Chris continued to chew his donut, sipping at his coffee. "I like the 'high test stuff.'"

Chris was much younger; even though he recently turned thirty-five, he did not look a day over fifteen. He once had an infectious smile as of one delivering a punch line, but all that remained of that look was a jocular intelligence behind his sharp eyes. Despite this, his pallor was grey, furrowed with worry lines too advanced for one so young. His thin face bore a deep scar on the right cheek, one he never talked about. A thick head of hair always in need of combing also was in desperate need of cutting.

"Did you just get back from Boeing?" Dan asked.

"Yesterday afternoon," Chris took a bite of his second donut. "It was just like old times, you know meeting my old co-workers that is."

Chris towered over Dan by half a foot forcing Dan to always look up at him. Chris's lanky frame moved smoothly, as opposed to his shorter friend's need to step livelier. He checked his stride, not wishing to leave Dan behind.

"How's Karen?"

Chris's smile faded. "She's doing better. She's on a trial medication program, but I think it's making the Cancer worse. Or maybe it's just me." Chris shook his head in frustration. "Anyway, her Mom stayed with her while I was gone." Dan realized he broached a tough subject, but Chris needed the ability to talk about it; Cancer is a cruel disease and his wife was too young. Dan knew this as they approached the elevators.

"Hey, Aaron Campo said a dash four-fifty had an in-flight reverser deployment in L.A." The elevator doors opened and they both stepped in.

"A reverser deployment, hmm?" Then the concept hit him. "In-flight?" Chris went silent, pondering the statement. After several seconds Dan looked up at his friend, who rocked quietly on his heels.

Chris finally responded, "Shouldn't you be talking to–?"

But Dan put his hand up. "I don't want to talk to the Engine guys yet. Hell, I'm not even sure where to start looking."

"All right, all right," Chris said, his smile returning, "I'll swing by with my high-test-stuff coffee and we can review some of those Flintstone tech manuals you got stashed in your office." They went their separate ways, Dan making towards his office.

Dan's office lights came on automatically as he entered. He sat at his desk piled high with reports and printouts, sipping his coffee while his computer warmed up. The white walls reflected light generously. His simple desk was in slight disarray; file cabinets surrounded the desk, overflowing with tech manuals.

"Morning, Dan," said a voice; a familiar mid-west inflection was obvious.

Dan barely saw Connie Brennan rushing past on her way to the morning meeting. Connie managed the Investigators-In-Charge, who were the on-site leads for an investigation. Her natural abilities made her a critically important leader.

"Connie!" Dan called, almost too late. She reappeared with a skeptical look.

"What is it now, Mister Tenace, or do I want to know?"

Using her fingers, she combed her short blond hair back from her forehead. Connie's green eyes had a 'look-through-you' quality, which advertised her ability to extract answers without saying a word.

"Can I meet with Phil today? Aaron Campo said there was an uncommanded reverser deployment in flight!"

She stood straight; her eyes narrowed with concern. "Seriously! Anybody hurt?"

"Not that I know of."

"Dan, you need to ask–"

But he interrupted her. "Aaron said it was a reverser deployment … on a dash four-fifty … *in flight*!"

"Dan, you have to follow the chain of command!"

"Connie …"

"Did you even ask Giv?"

They exchanged a glance; Dan was aware she knew better. "Come on Connie, a reverser deployment in flight? That's a rea-eally bad thing."

She stood chewing her lip.

"Connie," he lowered his voice, "Giv doesn't know what a reverser is, much as less what it shouldn't be doing in flight!"

"Okay, but don't make a habit of this Dan, please. I've gone to bat for you–"

"And I've always proved right."

Connie sighed, "All right, I'll talk to Phil." With that she disappeared, quickening her pace before Dan could assault her with another favor. As she walked, the thought of an uncommanded reverser in flight on a widebody aircraft sent a chill screaming up her spine.

CHAPTER 03
PRIORITIES

It takes years of dedication to one's craft to be considered an expert; whether one is a detective, a surgeon, or an architect. These professionals speak with authority and experience; few could match the skill he or she earned.

However, in the bureaucracies of the Federal government, expertise is measured only by association. A boy raised on the plains of Nebraska may never see a watercraft larger than a bass boat. But as an adult, after winning political office, he could be positioned on the Sea Power and Projection Forces Committee in Washington, making decisions on defense spending or determining what submarine fleet to maintain. He is now a 'naval expert,' answering the nation's questions.

Philip Tulkinghorn is just such an expert; not a political appointee, he is an analyst-turned-bureaucrat who joined the NTSB to conduct safety studies. Relying on inside maneuvering he rose to the position of Director of Aerospace Safety, lording over the entire aerospace division while acting as personal advisor to Ellen Potter, Chairwoman for the NTSB.

Phil is in his late fifties with dark grey hair cut to a precise length. He dresses monochromatically, reflecting the black and white view people have of him. Tall and doughy, his physical stature is not considered threatening. The black rimmed glasses give him a bookish look; they are supported by a large nose nestled between two small calculating eyes, black dots in an otherwise pale complexion, similar to a white shark; the eyes are unnerving for they reflect back … nothing.

Phil subscribes to the leadership style of 'Manage-by-Intimidation'; he looms over all of the aviation division managers like Caligula determining which one to sacrifice next. Though he lacks the inherent and technical skills to satisfactorily oversee the division, his intelligence makes up for what he otherwise lacks.

Phil 'solves' accidents by himself, then filters enough information into the reports to support his position. His reliance on NTSB investigators' input has decreased over the last few years, preferring to favor counsel from airline and manufacturer experts that lobby the Chairperson, often diverting the course of the investigation from the true cause.

Phil is holding court in the meeting room with seven managers sitting warily around the table, waiting for marching orders. The tension at the table is as thick as cold lard; it is suffocating. Phil employs a silent treatment: a mental game that keeps all on edge in anticipation of this next command.

Giv Goosfand is half-sitting, half-slouching in his chair, as if his pants were chafing. An Iranian citizen whose family fled when the Shah was deposed, Giv's light olive complexion and black hair reflect his origins. His facial expression is often distracted, troubled, panicked, portraying intelligence his feelings of entitlement cannot support. Dark brown eyes rapidly move left and right, searching for notice. With a halting English accent, his opinions often run unchecked, awkwardly putting himself into trouble. As Phil's right hand man, Giv arrives at work each day nursing an ulcer that permeates his insides, tendrils of acid scarring his stomach lining. He shadows Phil each day, hating and needing him simultaneously, unable to break away.

Connie sits at ease directly opposite Phil, her legs crossed as she writes in her planner. She commands the room with her silence and no one – even Phil – can ignore the gravitational pull her passive nature creates. Her lips move silently in self-conversation, but she catches every word spoken.

As usual she is dressed conservatively, every detail of her outfit well-thought out to advertise control and confidence. Her short blond bangs fall easily before being swept away again with her hand. Green eyes peek under thin blond eyebrows and a petite nose mellows a harder look. Connie is all-business; if she had the appetite, she could devour any adversary at the table, but she lets her patience do that work for her. An attractive woman – not stunning, yet beautiful – a head turner wherever she goes. Her ten-year marriage, once very strong, has suffered the last few months as the two high school sweethearts find less time together with their demanding careers.

"Giv, what is Tenace doing?"

A smile barely brushes Connie's mouth as she catches Giv peek out from behind another manager, his eyes darting to each attendee. "He isn't assigned to anything," he muttered with a nervous smile, wishing Phil would move on.

No such luck. "So, he has nothing on his desk?"

"He just got back from San Diego," Giv continued smugly, "but I don't have anything else to throw him on. I'll tell him to finish that San Diego report and get it on my desk right away. I'd just as soon keep him out of the spotlight."

A smile creased the ends of Phil's mouth; he liked toying with Giv like a cat 'plays' with a mouse. "Are you saying Tenace didn't hand in his report yet?"

Giv's dark eyes held little white, making them hard to see. They darted back and forth, sensing he was missing something that Phil was aware of. As if on cue his handkerchief came out, wiping vigorously at his nose; he lets loose a prodigious honk, a sign that he is in nervous distress; Giv's nose runs freely under anxiety like an athlete sweats while running a marathon.

"I haven't seen it."

"I have. I told him to blind copy me on your e-mails." Phil continued as if the words galled him. "Approve it and move it up through the proper channels."

Phil continued to hold Giv in a Python's stare, watching him squirm. Connie looked up casually. "If that's the case Phil, I need Dan and Chris Wilkerson to look into something for me."

Phil sensed he played into Connie's hand. Without taking his eyes off the cowering Giv, Phil said, "What does this ... *something* involve?"

Connie leaned forward. "The FAA said Freestyle Air Freight had an uncommanded reverser deployment in flight this morning! We have to look into this."

"Why? Was it an accident?"

The other managers shifted anxiously. Connie sat back casually, her eyes remaining on Phil. "No, however the airliner may never have recovered from the event. In

The Air Crash Files: Jet Blast

other words, a dash four-fifty almost crashed this morning."

Phil asked Giv, "Why didn't you get anything on this?"

Giv's eyes widened, his mouth working like a fish sucking air.

Connie continued, "Look Phil, the FAA will call over. There was no accident, so there's no media attention on it yet."

Phil pursued another tack. "That's a cargo airline? Any fatalities or injuries on the ground?"

Connie closed her eyes and slowly shook her head in disbelief. Phil stared off while doing the 'media-attention' math in his head. "I doubt the press cares about something as trivial as two pilots doing their job."

The Engine supervisor said, "You can't take this lightly Phil. A reverser deployment is a tragedy waiting to happen! And it wouldn't be limited to a cargo airline!"

"Why don't your people look into it?"

"Phil," he continued emphatically, "Connie's right; Systems needs to look at this. We'll support them, but Chris is the best one to investigate."

"Giv, why does Tenace hear about this before you do?" Phil growled.

"Phil, we have to get a handle on this," Connie said, ignoring Giv's panic. "We should put Dan and Chris on with the FAA."

"No," Phil interrupted, "I don't want Tenace anywhere near this. Besides it's probably way over his head."

The Human Factors manager, Quint, sat directly across from Connie. A PhD with impressive qualifications, Quint does not look bookish; the red-haired scholar is a basketball junkie – sans the height; instead he has an Offensive Guard's physique. His deceptively smug demeanor originally puts talented people like Connie off, but his quick wit and razor-sharp tongue always win over those who need an advocate to side with them. If he was with you, Quint was a team player like no other.

Quint glanced at Connie. She nodded her head slightly and he turned towards Phil. "Why not? Dan is the only investigator who's actually worked on commercial airliners. Who better to assign it to?"

"I said, no," Phil grumbled, rapping his knuckles on the table top.

Phil never hid his disdain for Dan; his antipathy traceable to Dan's habit of analyzing accidents correctly. But where Dan's investigatory talents were strong, he lacked political correctness and could not phrase his arguments artfully. Dan's ability to fall back on his experience helped him in proving his case; it just never married up to Phil's 'Ready-Shoot-Aim' approach to investigating.

Quint said, "He's not assigned anything. Giv said he has nothing on his plate."

"I don't expect you to understand; you're just Human Factors."

Quint was stunned. "Really. What'd you do? Research papers?"

"What I do here ... is run *this* division!" Phil shot back, "I've led through many investigations and *I'm* the reason we're successful!"

Quint opened his mouth to retort, but closed it again, recognizing the futility.

"I don't see how this helps anything," Connie interjected. "Quint is right, Phil. We have no choice but to let Dan and Chris look into this. If this blows up down line, we're going to have no excuse for ignoring the obvious signs."

Phil tapped nervously on the table top with a sidelong glare at Quint. He had no problem exacting his authority over anyone, but not Connie. She had a way of reducing his confidence to ashes.

Phil turned to Connie. "Fine, put him on it with Wilkerson … for now! But I want a heads up on *everything* they're doing even before they know they're doing it. Do we need to get the recorders?"

"I'll call the FAA after the meeting," Connie remarked, making a note in her planner. "I'll request the transcripts. I can also get the FAA to reroute the recorders when they're done."

Phil seethed, "Let 'em read it, but I want the transcripts and the recorders."

Connie slowly looked up from the planner and stared across at Phil. He tried unsuccessfully to hold her gaze, but ended up looking down at the table. "Phil, you know we don't have the authority since there was no accident. We can't exceed our mandate."

"I don't care about the–"

"If you don't want another episode like that aircraft battery debacle, then let me handle this."

"What are you going to do?"

"I'm going to keep this quiet," she said as she gathered her papers together. "The last thing we need to do is to make a public spectacle by getting the Chairwoman involved. It took a long time to iron over that mess and until we hear anything different, we should keep a low profile," she casually walked from the room, throwing the last words over her shoulder, "this time."

CHAPTER 04
SEARCHING FOR ANSWERS

June 30 – Los Angeles Airport

Richard Grace entered the hangar with a purpose to his step. He had spent a mostly sleepless night in the hotel running over and over the events of the inflight reverser deployment. Stopping Maggie from flying back to Cleveland was out of the question; she performed admirably, but she needed to report to the Chief Pilot.

After he passed through the office area he urgently made his way to the front of the hangar bay, finding himself standing under the nose of N908FS. Pneumatic tools and electric motors resounded through the entire bay while a stench of oil and diesel fuel permeated through the air. His position as Captain rarely gave him the chance to walk around the KR-450C he flew so frequently; such duties were delegated to the first officer while the captain prepared the aircraft for flight. Standing next to the wide body jet, it still amazed him that it ever got off the ground.

The KR-450C stands alone. The first impression one gets is the non-streamlined look to it, cumbersome and swollen. The fuselage's sides bulge from the nose to the tail ... *like a stick of bologna in a vice*, Richard thought; it is slightly oval when viewed from the front – an odd shape for a modern aircraft. Many critics call it a 'bloated whale' or a 'jet with love handles,' but the nickname that stuck was: 'the slug,' thus named by its competition.

AeroGalactic took the insult in stride, laughing all the way to the bank with a revolutionary design – albeit ugly – that allows the KR-450C to carry more freight and/or passengers than the comparable Boeing or Airbus jet.

At mid-length, two mighty wings sweep out and back from the fuselage, employing a new design that increases lift while limiting drag. From the nose Richard admired the #1 engine, one of two that are wing mounted; the KR-450C uses the massive Sonic S-90V engines which provide over ninety thousand pounds of thrust each; a six-foot man could stand straight up in the inlet with both arms extended up and still not be able to touch the top of the engine's inlet with his fingertips. A third S-90V engine sits nestled within the vertical stabilizer on the tail.

As a pilot he did not often see the engine cowls 'flowered' and he stared curiously at the exposed engine. With the cowls locked in place for flight the engine appears enormous, like a fat bullet. But when the engine is bared beneath the raised cowls, it looks anorexic behind the gigantic fan. Richard chuckled at the sight; he thought, *it's like a huge wheel on a beefy axle*.

There are three sets of cowls per engine and they attach to the pylon above the engine; they spread out and up when open. The fan cowl covers the wide fan case in front while the core cowl encases the exhaust section at the rear. The thrust reverser is in the middle and enshrouds the center of the engine.

When in place for flight they fold down to incase the engine, similar to a clam's shell. Latched at the bottom, the cowls are locked in place to provide protection and make the engine assembly aerodynamic.

"Captain Grace?" Lyle, a hangar manager, caught Richard engrossed in the revealed motor.

"That's right," Richard responded. "Richard is fine."

"Lyle," the manager said, taking a place beside him.

Richard smiled sheepishly, "I don't often get to see the motor like that; all naked, I mean." Lyle laughed and guided Richard towards the rear of the jet.

They stopped near the left main landing gear, the size of which always captivated Richard. A strut descends from the wing root; the lower silver cylinder slides into the wider white cylinder, massive, imposing, and unyielding. It is so thick Richard could barely get his arms around it. In addition to providing the aircraft with movement on the ground, it is a giant shock absorber that consumes the tremendous landing loads when contacting the runway.

The main gear truck at the bottom of the strut resembles a large foot; it consists of four massive tires that rise as high as Richard's chest. The truck itself is huge, as big as a compact car.

Hanging off the gear, the GSS – ground sense switch – was disconnected and evidence of electrical troubleshooting were scattered on a nearby table; wiring diagrams lay marked and grease-stained near fluke meters. Lyle pointed out the ground sensing switch: a small rectangular tan casing four inches long by three wide with three holes for mounting on the strut between the tires. A linkage that normally attached to the upper strut lay immobile on the table waiting for installation.

"It's a simple device for all the trouble it caused you," Lyle raised his voice above the hangar's noise. "As the strut compresses on landing this rod is pushed down.

That action repositions the lever on the GSS from 'air' to 'ground.'"

"The GSS? You mean the ground sense switch?"

"Yes sir, that's the acronym for it."

"You narrowed it down to this?"

Lyle nodded. "We feel the inner workings were bad and corrosion opened the switch early."

"Opened?" Richard shot Lyle a questioning look. "You mean closed the switch, don't you?"

"No, Richard," Lyle remarked, "though you'd think so. This is an AeroGalactic and they do things differently. This particular ground sense switch opens."

Richard took a moment to look the mechanism over. *So, you're what almost killed us*, he thought.

Several mechanics began moving jacks around the aircraft, so Lyle guided Richard out by the wingtips. As they came around to the tail, Richard looked up; he took in the two horizontal stabilizers that spread out from each side like stubby wings. With hydraulic power off, each stabilizer's elevator was 'relaxed', drooping at the trailing edge.

The vertical stabilizer towered high above the ground like a geometrically perfect shark's fin. The swell of the #2 engine blends perfectly into the vertical stabilizer; from the side it is indiscernible, but from the front the engine's bulge is noticeable going from the stabilizer's leading edge to trailing edge.

The Freestyle 'F' logo is presently missing a piece; the left reverser half has already been removed and is being lowered slowly to the ground on a crane. Richard and Lyle walked toward a group of mechanics working on the replacement reverser half. They both approached quietly, not wishing to interrupt the adjustments in progress and stopped six feet away to watch.

"How bad were the reversers?" Richard asked without turning his head.

"The left TC was pretty beat up." Lyle caught himself. "Sorry Captain, force of habit. The translating cowl; TC, for short. It's the outer section that slides back during reverse." Lyle chuckled, "We're all about the acronyms in maintenance, as I'm sure you sky gods are."

"Sky gods?" Richard asked, turning his head with a disapproving squint.

Lyle cleared his throat and continued with the assessment. "As I was saying: the TC was pretty banged up; at least the left side was. You weren't at cruise, but you were flying too fast for a normal deployment."

As Lyle explained Richard looked the reverser half over. From the front it has a crescent moon shape, designed to follow the contour of the engine it covers. The new reverser half was open at the side, in the 'deployed' position; the inner workings exposed.

Richard looked curiously at the two main parts: the inner shroud that hugs the engine and the translating cowl that is attached to the shroud.

For decades aircraft have relied on reversers as one method to slow the aircraft during landing. In normal flight, the jet blast exiting the back of the turbine and fan bypass pushes the aircraft forward. But reversers do just as the name implies: they reverse. They do this by redirecting the jet blast forward and sideways, operating as an air brake.

When deploying on landing, the translating cowl moves aft like a sliding door, riding on both an upper and lower track. These tracks guide the TC so the movement is uniform, smooth. Without the tracks the TC could launch like a leaf in the wind, damaging the engine, the wings or the tail.

Richard turned to Lyle. "How did the jackscrews–?" A sudden squeal drew his attention back; a shriek similar to a screw being drilled into wood surprised him. One mechanic working on the TC retracted it back to check clearances.

"The three jackscrews," Lyle stated, "were in pretty good shape, as were the blocker panels. When the TC retracted after the emergency, all the blocker panels stowed neatly into their recesses in the shroud."

"How many blocker panels are there?"

"Six on each half," Lyle motioned Richard to approach the reverser. The mechanic deployed the translating cowl again; the same screw-into-wood sound filled the air. This time Richard looked in between the TC and the shroud. As the TC ran back, it pulled six square blocker panels away from the shroud; they formed a wall to deflect the jet blast.

Simple genius, Richard thought.

Several hours passed as the two reverser halves were replaced. The cranes at the rear of the plane worked slowly to avoid inducing a spin as each reverser rose to the tail. Once raised above the engine, five pairs of hands guided the three hundred-pound load into place. Richard was impressed by the teamwork of the maintenance crews as they secured the reversers in place and then began raising the plane for the gear swing.

Lyle approached Richard, his attention focused on a cell phone call. He clapped the phone closed as he stepped next to the pilot. "Your test flight is tentatively scheduled for tomorrow at nine o'clock. Weather permitting, you should rotate on time."

"How does the weather look?"

"Pretty good," Lyle said, checking his phone for messages. "We'll yank it outta the barn tonight, throw two ballast pallets on board, and gas her up by morning." Lyle stopped to remember something, "Oh yeah ... your check co-pilot arrives at seventeen hundred from Cleveland. We'll pick him up and you guys can check with each other at the hotel."

"Thanks Lyle, you've treated this 'sky god' very well."

Lyle held his breath a second, expecting the 'sky god' comment to lead to an argument; Richard went on, never cracking a smile.

"I have one more favor."

"Name it," Lyle said.

"The main gear GSS, the bad one. What are you doing with it?"

Lyle shrugged. "It's a consumable part. We don't send it out for repair, so we'll probably throw it out. Engineering didn't request it."

"Fine," Richard said. "Can I please have it? For old time's sake."

Lyle did not say a word but walked over to the workbench and snatched the ground sense switch and a rag from the tabletop. He thoroughly wiped all the grease from the casing and the lever before handing it to Richard without a word.

Richard Grace turned the switch over in his hand; he was intrigued by the simplicity of the device. Visualizing the huge strut this switch was attached to, he saw it as it would look when the aircraft lands; the chrome inner strut sliding into the white painted outer strut, like his car's shock absorber. As the full weight of the aircraft came down on the tires, the rod pushed the GSS lever which announced to the FCC that – at this moment – the aircraft's weight was on the ground.

Richard moved the lever as it would when landing; through his fingertips he felt the almost imperceptible click of the switch through the casing. But he knew there was more to the circuit that activated the reversers than one simple single throw switch.

And a doubt crept into his mind.

Though he trusted the knowledge of the mechanics and engineers, a sour feeling in the pit of his stomach filled him with doubt. Richard took a black marker from his pocket and drew a large 'X' on both sides of the casing. He shook Lyle's hand before stepping into a company van for his ride to the hotel.

During the test flight Captain Grace put the aircraft through rigorous paces with more altitude to play with; N908FS performed normally through all its test trials. Captain Grace noted in the logbook that the test was successful and Maintenance returned N908FS to service.

As the outbound crew took charge that night, they saw the write-up and made a mental note to keep a close eye on that feisty #2 thrust reverser. The crew was wary, but

Captain Grace was highly regarded in the airline and his word was gospel.

Precautionary minds in Cleveland directed maintenance to change out the two FCCs and route them through component repair to check for faults.

The reverser anomaly continued to bother several of Freestyle's engineers; immediately following the incident, the Flight Data Recorder was flown back to Cleveland for analysis of the engine and system data from the aircraft's last two legs. This analysis confirmed the bad GSS on the left gear and gave a reprieve to the two FCCs.

After the test flight a conference call was conducted between Freestyle Air's maintenance group in Los Angeles, Freestyle's engineers in Cleveland, and the engineers at AeroGalactic in Portland, OR. The repairs were reviewed and the three teams exhausted all ideas to assure the anomaly would not surface on a less fortunate crew. AeroGalactic's engineers gave every guarantee that improvements were in the works and the problem experienced by N908FS would never surface again. After all, who would know about the KR-450C sold to Freestyle Air Freight better than AeroGalactic?

But then, N908FS was not *exactly* ... the same airplane AeroGalactic sold to Freestyle Air.

No, not even close.

CHAPTER 05
ALGONQUIAN PREMIERE 1594

Lewistown, MT – Contractors for the Federal Aviation Administration erected a global positioning tower atop Judith Peak today. The tower, which will be used for the Satellite Positioning and Airspace Restructuring (SPAR) system, is one of many located throughout the mountain ranges in both the Appalachians and the Rockies. They provide an uninterrupted link between like structures, completing a net of air traffic control antennas and ground base transmitters for …

July 2nd – Outagamie Airport, Appleton, Wisconsin

The Algonquian Premiere AeroGalactic KR-290B, flight 1594, moved slowly along taxiway Lima-6 to Alpha in Appleton airport on this hot afternoon. The sea-green painted fuselage shimmered dimly in the low overcast hanging like a pall over the city. Two large Pascal QT760 pod engines hung beside the vertical stabilizer – one on either side – while inline and between these two engines was a Pascal QT560.

Algonquian Airlines 1594 was full; the passengers mostly businessmen and women flying to Lexington. Having delivered their safety presentation, the flight attendants took their seats and prepared for the inevitable climb into the Wisconsin sky.

Algonquian Premiere was a small passenger airline that was, among other notables, a forerunner in the SPAR program. The FAA encouraged Algonquian's desire to incorporate SPAR technologies and Algonquian relished the chance to advertise their participation in the new technology. They aggressively equipped their -290 fleet, converting two jets a month into SPAR test beds.

Captain Kelly Tobias taxied flight 1594 down Alpha towards the southern end of Runway three-six. Thoughts of a long day labored in her mind with hopes that nothing intruded on an uninteresting day.

Kelly hated interesting days.

First officer, Tom Elbert followed Kelly's progress on the Saturn Ground Tracking Computer, the white silhouette of their airliner moved fluidly across the screen. Other airliner silhouettes in blue, red, and green stood out against the grey background.

"Copy Ground, taxi to Alpha six and hold short, Algonquian fifteen, ninety-four."

Tom looked over; Kelly nodded her understanding and said, "They're lining up on the approach. Let's do the Configuration checklist." As Tom ran the checklist, they set the airliner's controls for flight.

"Autospoilers, set?" Tom said.

Kelly moved the spoiler handle into the proper detent. "Autospoilers set," she responded, assuring the twelve spoiler panels on both wing upper surfaces were set for a possible rejected takeoff.

Unexpectedly the spoiler handle raced backward to the end of its travel and an irritating takeoff warning alarm blared. On the wings twelve spoiler panels stood up rigidly at a sixty-degree angle.

They were now out of takeoff configuration.

During normal flight the spoilers are stowed flat against the top of the wing, except when turning. Autospoilers are employed during landing to aid in killing lift; they assist the reversers and the brakes in slowing the aircraft by keeping the weight on the wheels for better braking and traction.

While taking off, Autospoilers assist the pilot when rejecting a take-off; they deploy automatically, freeing the pilot during a high stress situation.

If spoilers should deploy uncommanded during take-off, the sudden loss of lift gives the aircraft the flight characteristics of a brick at slow speed, thus providing the aircraft a quick descent to the accident scene.

"Spoilers extended," Tom said matter-of-factly.

Kelly seethed, bringing the -290 to a stop. She disengaged Autospoilers and brought the handle forward. The spoiler indicator showed the spoilers retracted. She called the tower and advised them they were going to hold for a moment. "Let's see what I did wrong, Tom," she half-joked.

They ran the checklist again, staring at the handle in anticipation of it to come back to life. A brief image of the aircraft scattered on the opposite end of the runway played in Kelly's head. She puckered her lips in thought before shaking her head. "I don't like it."

"I concur," Tom replied immediately.

Kelly was impatient with her often chaotic flight schedules, but she never bent the rules or cut corners. She took her responsibilities seriously and the rules she respected most were those crazy laws of physics.

She sighed before calling the maintenance hangar where she requested a mechanic meet them at the gate. She released the brakes and made a wide turn, taxiing back up Alpha. They had not moved twenty yards when the spoiler handle ran backward again and the warning claxon sounded annoyingly in their ears.

"Good call, Kelly."

She called the Operations desk for Algonquian Premiere. After a moment a voice answered, "Operations, go ahead."

"Yeah Operations, this is Kelly Tobias with flight fifteen ninety-four in Appleton. We're returning to the gate with a broken jet. We need an even swap immediately 'cause this flight's running late and I have some connections to drive."

God, she thought, I hate interesting days.

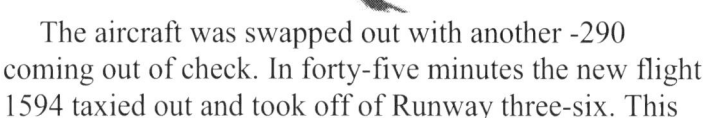

The aircraft was swapped out with another -290 coming out of check. In forty-five minutes the new flight 1594 taxied out and took off of Runway three-six. This time the airplane behaved.

The broken aircraft was towed to the hangar where the lead mechanic suggested swapping out the two flight command computers. The replacement FCCs were absent any SPAR system hardware modifications, but since SPAR was not officially activated the computers were still approved for use on that aircraft. The FCC replacements were followed up with a takeoff warning check, as precautionary. When released back to service the aircraft performed without any flaws. The logbook was signed and the aircraft returned to the gate.

The repair station that restored the FCCs noted no discrepancies in their operation. They performed some integrity checks and returned the computers to Algonquian Premiere two weeks later. Conclusion: they worked as advertised.

The FAA never thought to tie in uncommanded spoiler actuation when they tasked the airlines to report any problems with reversers. Result: an anomaly was overlooked. However, the aircraft made the next flight and the world spun on its axis again. Algonquian Premiere did not alert the FAA about the strange incident.

There is a superstition that says, 'Bad things happen in threes.'

Freestyle was one and Algonquian Premiere was two. If one were superstitious, then another was on the way.

CHAPTER 06
MULTIPLE REQUESTS

Washington, DC

Three days since the harrowing experience over the Pacific, Dan had not been idle. He inundated Aaron Campo with multiple requests for information, giving their friendship a thorough workout.

As an FAA liaison to the NTSB, Aaron assists on accident investigations, greasing the rails by accessing FAA data for the NTSB investigators to determine an accident's cause. His job requires a diplomatic touch, often paving the way for Board investigators with little to no credit for himself. Aaron preferred it that way.

But being a liaison also meant advocating for the FAA and its resources. Normally, Aaron was not required to push Los Angeles for a non-accident, but he trusted where Dan was going and felt it demanded a better analysis than Dan's upper echelons were willing to give it.

The FAA inspectors in Los Angeles delivered to Aaron the interviews conducted with Richard Grace and Maggie O'Neil; this allowed Dan and Chris access to the pilots' stories even before the Cockpit Voice Recorder tapes were transcribed. The personal testimonies gave enormous insight into how the event played out.

"Your metabolism is going to kick into reality mode one day and I hope I'm there to see it."

Chris smiled as he finished another chocolate donut. "What have you got?" He came around Dan's desk to see what Aaron had sent him.

Chris was a talented engineer; one of only five airline-experienced people at the Board and, like Dan, Chris worked for many years at that major airline. When aircraft 'broke' in the field, Chris would fly absolutely anywhere to troubleshoot the broken airliner because of his intimate knowledge of every aircraft in the airline's fleet.

"I got these FAA guys trained." An e-mail from the Los Angeles FAA office was on the screen. Dan dialed Aaron's office; he picked up on the second ring.

"Don't you Board types even break for coffee?"

"I have some on a slow intravenous drip. Listen I got the L-A e-mails. How is the Cleveland CMO coming along with those systems diagrams?" The Cleveland certificate management office is responsible for Freestyle Air; Aaron had their maintenance and flight inspectors jumping through hoops for Dan.

"Do you remember that guy with the soda on the train?"

Dan hesitated before responding, "Yeah ... what about him?"

"Well," Aaron said, "he's the Cleveland CMO manager."

Dan started laughing. "You know I don't doubt anything anymore. This is DC after all."

"Let me make a few calls and I'll get back with you, in ... an ... hour." With that the line went dead.

An hour later Aaron called back. "I got some guys from the Cleveland office on the line." Aaron introduced the two NTSB investigators to several inspectors in Cleveland. "They're sending you copies of the reverser system's fault logic from the Fault Isolation manual. You're also getting Freestyle's thrust reverser maintenance instructions."

"Good deal, Aaron."

"Aaron," a voice interrupted on the telecom, "I'm still not cool with this."

"Chet, I get it," Aaron replied, "but we need to get to the bottom of this."

"Los Angeles did get to the bottom of it, Aaron, and they said it's a good fix." There was a pause in the conversation as voices in Cleveland argued, but Chet's voice came back, "And to be honest, I don't trust the Board after that battery thing."

Chris slowly shook his head. "Are you talking about the aircraft battery?" Dan challenged.

"You know it," Chet steamrolled on, "you guys had no right to get involved. You were way outta line and your leaders made a mountain out of the proverbial molehill."

"That was a bureaucratic decision; we tried to get them to back away but they had their eyes on the headlines."

"Well, that's the real problem, isn't it?" Chet chuckled over the line. "Your bureaucrats don't know squat about aircraft and they got in the weeds dictating to our operators about their business."

"And the FAA's bureaucrats don't?" Dan rejoined. Chet paused, so Dan kept pushing, "Look Chet, we both work for the same political appointees; they have no clue how the industry works and they're only looking to get in the papers. I can't answer for them!"

"But–"

"Are you getting warm fuzzies from L-A's fix?"

There was a pause.

"I'll take that as a 'no'. Do you think there's still something not right about the reversers?"

Another pause as Chet faced the truth. "Yes," he quietly rejoined.

"Then let Chris and I help you. I promise I will never go to the papers, we won't contact the manufacturer, and we'll keep this on the Q-T"

"Chet," Aaron managed, "let them help you with this. Dan and Chris have a good lead on it and they have better resources than you have. And they have no love for their uppity-ups. Your management won't even know."

"The only thing I ask," said another voice in Cleveland, "is that you delete the e-mails after you download the attachments."

"Done," Chris responded.

"Listen," Chet muttered, "we spoke with Captain Grace again. He told us in the strongest terms possible that when the gear was down and locked, *that's* when he noticed the reverser kick in; he was adamant about that! He said a lot was going on, but he's absolutely *pos-i-tive* the gear movement and reverser travel occurred simultaneously."

After the call was over, Dan spoke into the speaker. "Thanks Aaron, I owe you."

"Yeah, I know," Aaron replied.

"Aaron, is the FAA issuing any orders to industry to report any similar anomalies? What about any other reverser problems?"

"Already done, Bubba; we issued it right after it happened. All four-fifty drivers that get unexpected reverser indications have to report to us through their airline's safety programs. Also, there're alerts to modify the dash four-fifty's main gear ground sense switches, to improve the casing's quality." He paused. "Oh, and until that happens and they start making the modifications, all dash four-fifties are forbidden to use Autoland."

Chris said, "Wow, so you guys have been thinking outside the box?"

"Always do," Aaron responded before hanging up.

Within ten minutes the schematics for the reverser systems on the -450C were in Dan's e-mail Inbox. He printed off the schematics before deleting the e-mail. For hours they pored over schematic print-outs. So intent were they that neither one noticed Board member Vince Scalia standing in the doorway.

"So, what did you find out?" Vince asked with a knowing look on his face.

"Hey Vince," Dan replied. "Find out about what?"

"Ri-i-i-i-ight," Vince replied. He looked down the hall and saw Phil heading their way. "If you've got a few minutes," Vince said, "come down to my office. We need to talk."

"We need to talk," Dan whispered to Chris as Vince left the doorway. "I can't think of a lousier four-word sentence."

"How about, 'we're having tuna casserole'?" Chris joked.

Dan did not hear him as he pored over the schematic. His eyes squinted, noticing something similar to the other blueprints; each schematic was revised over six months prior. *It may not mean anything*, he thought, *but what are the odds that all these systems have not been modified – none of them – for six months?*

It would make all the difference in the world.

CHAPTER 07
MECH TALK

Washington, DC

Board Member Vincent Scalia began his professional career working aircraft maintenance for Sky South airlines in Albuquerque, New Mexico. A former conservative from Philadelphia, Vince became active in the mechanic's union, thus cementing his liberal roots for the rest of his life. He was a big man, short but stocky. His manner was a contradiction; he could yell down a charging bear as easily as become teary-eyed at the sight of kittens.

Vince's grey mane made him look noble and unapproachable, while he maintained dress casual: a pair of Dockers and a polo shirt. If you cut Vince, he bled hydraulic fluid and engine oil; all mechanics – whether union or not – were his brothers and sisters for whom he fought the good fight.

Vince Scalia was solely responsible for Dan's appointment and he took great pains to protect his investment. Dan was his first task joining the Board: hiring a real Airframe and Powerplant certificated mechanic; in other words, someone who knew what he was doing when it came to maintenance. And like that charging bear, Vince protected his investment.

Whether Dan knew it or not.

It was late morning when Dan found himself standing in Vince's spacious office. He stared at all the pictures and aircraft models on the walls. The room was a personal collection of aviation memorabilia that the curator at the National Air and Space Museum down the block would salivate over ... and had; it was less office and more aviation archive. Technical publications monopolized the cabinets and cascaded to a floor that was littered with an array of manuals and aviation research books, while assorted collectible traffic fought for available real estate on Vince's desk.

As the sun rose higher in the sky Vince's administrative assistant, Becky opened the blinds in Vince's office despite his insistence that the nasty bright orb remain outside where it belongs. She turned a deaf ear to her boss's rants and welcomed the sunshine that was devoured by the clutter exercising domination over the office.

"Hey, you want some coffee?" Vince practically shouted upon entering the room. Dan jumped at the unexpected arrival; he was about to leave a note saying he would stop by tomorrow.

"No," Dan replied, "I'm good. Do you want me to come back another time?"

"No, take a seat," Vince commanded more than suggested.

Where? Dan thought. He moved to a hidden seat across the room where he took a moment to lift the stack of papers, only to find he did not know where to lay them.

"Organize much?"

Vince ignored the sarcasm and said, "Just throw it on the floor."

Dan was going to remark about not knowing where the floor was, but he stopped himself. He carefully placed the stack on the ground and sat in the vacated seat. Dan waited while Vince took a large draft of his coffee, leaning back in his office chair. His eyes seemed to glow under his thick grey eyebrows in the minimal light of the room.

"I understand you're getting a hard time from that melon head Phil!"

"How – how did you hear about that?"

Vince looked up, gazing at Dan as if he tried his patience.

Dan cleared his throat, "Phil doesn't want me looking into something. Connie went to bat for me …"

"Connie …?"

"Connie Brennan. She's the manager for the I-I-C group."

Vince shrugged. "You're not going to tell me, are you?"

"Would it matter, Vince?"

"It might. Do you want me to …?"

"No … thanks though." Dan leaned forward in the chair. "I have a feeling I may need you to take my side when we make more sense of this." Dan sat back, inspecting his shoes. "You never told me what things were like when I interviewed for the job."

Vince continued to look at Dan under his eyebrows. "Would you have taken it?"

"In a New York second," Dan laughed. "But I would've probably talked over some strategies with you first."

"Good man," Vince guffawed. "Now what's with the melon head?"

Dan sat for a minute. He knew Vince was getting information from the front lines and it bothered him to not know who was informing. He looked suspiciously at the man behind the desk. "Well, apparently you know as much as I do. Why don't you tell me what was the big conundrum?"

Vince glared for a second before roaring with laughter. He and Dan were 180 degrees out of synch with each other politically. Furthermore, Dan was never sycophantic. Vince always relished their discussions; not just for the common histories, but because Dan rarely held back; he was never afraid to tell Vince he was wrong, almost relished it. They rarely agreed, but they truly respected each other.

He waved for Dan to continue.

"Freestyle had a number two engine reverse in flight off Los Angeles two days ago."

Vince's head came up with a shocked look.

"WHAT?"

"Phil doesn't want *me*," Dan emphasized with his thumb, "near it."

"Wait a minute, that issue you're looking at; that was an inflight reverser malfunction two days ago–" He caught his breath. "And I'm only hearing about it *now*?" He stabbed the intercom and yelled, "Becky!"

"I thought you knew," Dan said defensively. "Besides you were in Dallas the last few days."

"Becky!" He yelled as if calling to Becky three counties over.

A voice invaded the office from the other room, dripping with impatience. "I'm on the phone, Vince. Give me a second!"

Dan thought Vince was going to have a coronary. "Honestly, Vince, you weren't even here."

But Vince was intent on finding ... something ... on his desk when he stopped and slowly looked up at Dan. His eyes narrowed; Dan suddenly feared that his chair was conductive to lightning.

Vince ground out the words slowly, "Let me get this straight. Phil doesn't want the maintenance guy looking at it? Is he insane? Is *anyone* investigating it?"

"Well, my friend Chris from Systems and I are," Dan responded, "but Phil doesn't want to pursue it because he feels it's an open and shut case of a bad sensor."

Vince's relief at confirmation the problem was being investigated seemed to have a calming effect. "And you disagree ... because?"

Dan leaned forward. He was not sure how much theory he wanted to voice at this time. Let's just say I think there's more to it. For one thing, they were in Autoland."

Vince took another sip of coffee and leaned further back in his chair. "And you're thinking ... electrical?"

Dan nodded. "My problem is that a ground sense switch ... by itself ... shouldn't deploy a reverser. There's gotta be another input and, yeah ... I think it's electrical."

"What about their maintenance practices?"

"I just started reviewing them. I'd like to talk to the mechanics, but I really think this is something more elusive."

"Does your friend concur?"

Dan said, "He said he needs more time to study the schematics."

It was Vince's turn to nod. "If you think it's the airline, I want to know before you give it to Phil. Just between you and me, like."

"What if we discover that it was some union guy that missed a quality control procedure?" Dan did not really believe that, but Vince held unions in very high regard. Besides, Dan wanted to lighten the mood.

Vince slowly smiled. "I believe that one day I'm gonna get you to buckle under and appreciate the beauty of unions, Mister Tenace. Your archaic conservative ideals never served you when hoping for a pay raise while turning wrenches."

Dan stood up and chuckled. "I think that B, no they probably didn't, and A ... hmmm, I just don't see that day coming in the near future."

Vince was going to respond, but his intercom went off. "Go ahead, Becky!"

Becky's voice came through the intercom, "Vince, Connie Brennan needs to see Dan right away!"

"Okay, he's on his way out." Vince cut off the intercom and said, "I want to be kept updated."

Dan managed a nod before hurrying out the door, where he practically ran into Connie. "Hey Connie, what–?"

Connie stepped quickly, ushering Dan out of the office. She seemed agitated, but started speaking before Dan could get a question out. "There was another deployment in flight," she said urgently. "A seven-fifty-seven had a reverser deployment over the Gulf of Mexico! It departed Houston before the reverser deployed. Phil wanted to send one of the Engine guys, but I convinced him to send you."

Dan was confused, his head spinning with a dozen questions. "It was taking off?" Connie nodded. "How long into the flight was it?"

"Not even five minutes after rotation."

"But–"

"No buts, Dan! Talk while we walk. Your United flight leaves out of Reagan in about two hours!"

CHAPTER 08
NEVER CATCHING A BREAK

July 15th

Just as the winds in a passing storm wane, the urgency to find the cause of a non-fatal event soon loses momentum. Other safety incidents crop up and are placed higher on the list, moving Freestyle 115 to the bottom. Phil leaned heavily on Chris, but more noticeably on Dan, to abandon the 'lost cause' and concentrate on more immediate matters.

Dan was right: Vince's involvement would mean integrity damage to him and political harm for Vince. The Board member managed to push Ellen Potter to allow the investigators to look into the reverser deployment, but he used up a lot of trust with the other three Board members. When Dan and Chris came up empty, Potter embarrassed Vince before the Board and he was forced to capitulate.

And Phil looked better all the time.

Dan and Chris sat in a conference room in the FAA building speaking with Aaron Campo. Several FAA technicians were gathered together to discuss findings from their organizations since the Freestyle incident; the conversations kept returning to the ground sense switch and its integrity during the lifetime of the KR-450C.

"I don't know what to tell you, Bubba," Aaron began, "we've looked at it; you've looked at it; AeroGalactic and Freestyle have been all over it. We're not finding anything beyond the ground sense switch."

Dan did not share his appraisal, but he was confounded. "No, you're right. I looked at the maintenance tasks for the reversers and there's nothing tying them to the switches."

A grin spread across Aaron's face. He said, "So nothing came about from the reverser deployment outside of Houston?"

Dan turned around slowly, his finger pointed at Aaron. "Don't even go there!"

One of the engineers asked, "Was there another reverser deployment that we don't know about?"

The conversation with Phil was still fresh in Dan's mind. "Not a deployment ...

"... it was a departure. The reverser didn't deploy in flight, it departed in flight!"

Dan could swear he heard Phil guffaw over the phone. Dan was calling from Houston, knowing of Phil's desire to divert attention from the Freestyle investigation. The fact it happened at all was fortuitous and Phil jumped on the opportunity. Connie looked at Phil, and did not seem amused.

"What do you mean departed?" Connie asked. "Giv said the reverser deployed."

"Don't blame me," Phil retorted, "if you can't understand Giv. It seems Dan was so convinced, perhaps he heard what he wanted to hear."

"That's not what Giv–"

Phil changed direction, cutting Connie off. "Tenace, what's the difference: deployment or departure?"

"There's a big difference, Phil! The engine nacelles are usually made up of three cowl sections that serve two purposes: protect the engine components and provide a smooth aerodynamic surface for the relative wind to flow over the engines–"

"I still don't see the difference."

Dan knew Phil was baiting him, trying to frustrate him. For the moment Dan felt he should play along or Phil would permanently shut the Freestyle investigation down.

"The three sections are the fan, core and reverser cowls. The fan cowl is along the front and covers the fan section. The core cowl is along the aft covering the turbine section. The reverser is in between the two and it's made up of two parts: the reverser shroud and the translating cowl.

"The reverser shroud protects the center section of the engine. The translating cowl slides back and forth over the shroud to–"

Phil loudly sighed as if bored.

"Get to the point, Dan," Connie said, none too patiently.

"I'm trying, Connie." He paused for a second getting his bearings. "When the translating cowl goes into reverse–"

Phil cut Dan off, "Well, thanks for the familiarization lesson, but that still doesn't explain why the reverser is in the Gulf of Mexico."

"The bottom line is that the mechanics who secured the reverser before flight didn't lock the latches," Dan stated. "When the plane took off, the air stream ripped the reverser off. It damaged the right hand horizontal stabilizer and destroyed its elevator as it cartwheeled past."

Dan coughed. "This was a mechanical failure, Connie; not a system failure. The engine never went into reverse.*"

Aaron placed a hand on Dan's shoulder, his smile never really fading. "You've got the worst luck, Bubba. And to be outplayed by Phil, no less." Then to rub it in, "You do realize that Phil's brain couldn't generate enough spark to light off a room full of gas fumes."

Chris changed the subject, "Aaron, I just want to make sure these are the latest schematics. You're sure there are no technical drawing revisions to the reversers?"

Aaron shook his head slowly. "The revision dates are from April. We double-checked with the Cleveland CMO and those diagrams are the latest and greatest."

One FAA engineer said, "The last aircraft mod was in May during heavy check. Freestyle upgraded the FCC software for the addition of some SPAR components."

"What's SPAR?" Dan asked.

"That's the air traffic systems the airlines are going to," the engineer answered.

"Last I checked," Aaron half-joked, "the towers don't deploy reversers; they still let the pilots do that."

Another engineer piped in. "SPAR can't be the problem. There are so many airliners with the components installed; we would've seen a Boeing or an Airbus do something by now."

Everyone went quiet anticipating another round of discussion, but Dan stood up to go. Everyone else followed suit, heading for the doorway. Dan shook hands all around. "Thanks Aaron, it sounds like you've got it under control, but we're going to keep looking. Can we stay in touch on it?"

"Absolutely, we'll keep at it as well. By the way, how was the Houston flight?" Dan's face went sour and Aaron laughed. "You're not still afraid to fly, are you?"

"I'm not afraid to fly. I just don't like it."

"Oh, you just don't like it."

"What can I say," Dan said over his shoulder, "I'm in the wrong business."

Chris and Dan caught the elevator down to the street level. As they crossed under the CSX train rails overpass on Seventh Street, Dan broke his silence.

"I still think there's a problem."

"Did you find anything?" Connie stood casually at the door to Chris's office looking hopefully at the two investigators. The last few days had been spent running interference for Dan and Chris as Phil used Giv to disrupt their progress.

Chris shrugged before saying, "We've turned these wiring diagrams and technical schematics inside-out. It's taken us this long to trace thousands of wires out through hundreds of possibilities and eliminate them one-by-one. We still can't find a loose thread."

"Not for nothing, Connie, but Giv has been muddying the waters with his *emergencies*," Dan added emphasizing quotation marks in the air, "that have all but derailed our chances of getting in front of this."

Connie nodded, knowing he was right ... and not just about the Houston trip. "Phil is going to press you for anything you've found. It's going on three weeks and it's just a matter of time before he pulls the plug on your investigation."

As if on cue Phil turned the corner with Giv a few steps behind. Phil looked at Connie and cleared his throat, pushing past her to gain access to the office. Connie stepped forward, effectively blocking Giv who tried to nudge past. A look from Connie froze him in his tracks, choosing instead to remain in the hall. His handkerchief sprung free of its pocket, wiping energetically at his nose.

"What progress have you made with Freestyle?" Phil asked.

Dan pointed to the wiring diagram of the Landing Gear system. "We're looking into the different computers. Freestyle's calling us back on some information later–"

"You're done! We can't allow you to waste any more of our time with this."

"Wasted?! What do you mean–?" Dan stopped at a look from Connie. She pushed the door closed behind her shutting Giv out of the conversation and the room.

"Phil, I'd hardly call their project a waste of time," Connie said. "The systems on these aircraft are intensely complex."

"Well, that's not how the Chairwoman sees it." Connie kept her place as Phil moved within inches of her. "She's been on the phone with AeroGalactic since last week getting an earful because these two are scaring the public with nonsense about the incident. She wants the whole thing brought to a halt right now."

Dan moved forward. "We never went public with this!"

"Somebody must have because AeroGalactic is threatening a lawsuit."

Connie's eyes narrowed; she knew a lie when she heard it. AeroGalactic would never sue. The bad press alone would be reason enough to forego any such action. She even doubted that the Chairwoman said anything. In truth, Connie reasoned, Chairwoman Potter knew as much about transportation as a horse knows about beef jerky. Potter did, however, often bow to political pressure from the manufacturers and the airlines, hoping to curry enough favor to ensure herself a comfortable position when her government service ran out.

"So, what do you suggest, Phil? They've come too far to throw it all away."

"Pack it up! I don't care what you do. Just make sure it's cleared up by this afternoon."

Dan and Chris looked at each other. Connie stepped aside as Phil about-faced and opened the door, pausing long enough to rebuke Giv for missing the discussion. She gave Chris and Dan a sympathetic look and watched as they packed up six weeks of analysis and placed it in a box.

"What are you two going to do?"

Dan looked up at Connie and his face was calm despite the anger. "We're not going to *do* anything." Regretting the tone of his answer, he eased back on the sarcasm. "I can't run to Vince, if that's what you mean. That would only make things worse."

Chris continued to gather paperwork. "Dan and I will continue to look at this despite Phil's deflections. If we have to we'll do it on our own time."

Connie nodded. "Well, whatever you need, let me know."

"We can stay under the radar," Dan said. "I appreciate the offer Connie, but if we run rogue ..." He let the last thought hang out there as she walked out.

Chris smiled grimly. "Ya know, God forbid we're right and a plane crashes under similar conditions. If the media finds out that Phil sat on the problem *and* sabotaged attempts to find it, it won't be pretty."

CHAPTER 09
N901FS

The economy plays a major role in the indirect application of circumstances. The flutter of a butterfly's wings may not result in a hurricane on a distant shore, but financial decisions made with the best of intentions may result in unplanned consequences later on.

The same economy can be responsible for the decisions made by the airline industry where the growth and decline of airlines were prescribed by market fluctuations. In some ways the American economy can be blamed for Robert Hermann's decision, which led to the eventual disaster of aircraft N901FS.

August 7th – Cleveland, Ohio

The Freestyle Flight Communications facility building in Cleveland, to look at is not an architectural wonder. The walls are bland, being a sort of wind-blown dullish grey. The roof displays a unique spray of antennas gone wild that sprout outwards like a mad afro, giving the structure an alien quality. These aerial receivers reach out in every direction but down, forming a net that traps all errant radio waves and digital signals bounced off a satellite or beamed through the atmosphere from certain aircraft.

Inside this building, the manager of Fleet Coordination is discussing the feasibility of keeping aircraft N901FS – an AeroGalactic KR-450C – on the fleet list for the following year. N901FS plus four other Freestyle aircraft were drawing close to their scheduled heavy maintenance checks and were the subject of a debate: would it be economically wise to park them in the desert until the American economy recovers?

"We need to put down these aircraft for a minimum of twelve to twenty-four months, depending on the short term economic recovery." He looked down at his notes and glanced back across the table at those assembled. "The Director of Maintenance approved the list I made; it says which jets to park and for how long."

Stephen Woods, Senior Manager for Aircraft Planning, glanced down the list and nodded, comparing it to his own. He ran his hand across his bald head, removed his glasses and looked up. "You do realize we just installed the SPAR components in two of these aircraft, right?"

"Steve we're not spooling up for SPAR for a while."

"I realize that, but if we park some of them it'll delay our testing if we get involved in the Christmas season. I mean the chances of this being a problem are minute at best, but I have to let you know."

"Thanks Steve, I would expect nothing less. Let's make it happen."

Though the work to preserve an aircraft is somewhat involved, it is advantageous. In the case of N901FS and the four other assorted aircraft, the benefits are immediate in the short term. On the surface the gain is somewhat temporary in a begging-from-Peter-to-pay-Paul sort of way. However, in the terms of preserving actually being an asset, results are limited to savings more than profit.

Airlines do not make money from parked aircraft because they only make money from aircraft that fly. The preserving – or 'pickling' – of an aircraft shuts off an outflow of cash; financially, it is less costly to take it out of service.

In the sluggish economy Freestyle's aircraft were not flying full, which in the cargo business is simply a waste of available cargo space. Profits dictate using fewer resources more efficiently until the market recovers enough to return aircraft from storage and bring them back into the game.

The Director of Maintenance's team was tasked with finding aircraft due to go through a heavy maintenance phase check: a scheduled maintenance visit with intense and expensive work assigned. By timing the checks to the schedule, heavy maintenance can be done with less impact on the airline's operation. Five aircraft were chosen for their costly heavy maintenance checks; N901FS was at the top of the list.

Before an aircraft can be parked in the desert it must be 'pickled'; this requires preserving the aircraft against the elements that can cause corrosion, spoilage, or decay. The desert has an arid climate where the dry air impedes corrosion from moisture, such as humidity, even though no environment is totally void of damaging agents from nature.

That is where the 'pickling' process comes in. The aircraft is closed up for the duration; all orifices such as engine inlets, engine exhausts, vents, and most cavities are secured. Landing gear struts may be deflated to prevent blown sand from damaging the chrome finish. Once pickled, the aircraft sits unused on the desert ramp.

N901FS sat on the Cleveland ramp in the warm summer afternoon. Cargo loading equipment that usually hugged this Freestyle workhorse sat dejected to the side. Three mechanics crawled over her making last minute checks. One mechanic stepped up into the nose wheelwell, a cavernous hole that houses the retracted nose gear. Silver hydraulic lines formed straight routes around the sides of the wheelwell, traveling unimpeded through the fuselage to points unseen.

As the mechanic closed an access hatch he failed to notice a crack in the casing of the GSS attached to the nose gear itself, a small grey rod connecting the lower part of the strut to the upper half. The crack in the casing was actually six months old.

It happened during a night sort; a mechanic was servicing the strut when his foot slipped and struck the switch. The strike damaged the switch's casing and opened a small crack to the elements where the integrity of the airtight casing was compromised. Damp air migrated into the once moisture-free interior, often freezing and causing internal damage while at high altitudes.

It could not be blamed on the mechanic who missed the damage; the crack was underneath the switch and one would have to be looking straight at it to see it. Besides, the issue with Freestyle 115 was still months away so no one was the wiser.

As of the day when N901FS was being flown to the desert the switch had not given any problems. Water introduced into the switch from atmosphere had not time enough to corrode it internally. Now it would sit parked in the desert for several months, waiting.

In the world of corrosion and corrosive elements, that is a long time.

The flight to southern California was uneventful and the work to pickle N901FS was about complete. Stephen Woods picked up his phone without even looking at it. "Steve, nine-oh one is parked in the desert. Go ahead and take it off the specs."

"Okay," Steve said into the receiver. "That should be the last one for now. I'll talk to you later. Thanks." Woods pulled up the proper screen displaying the fleet list provided to the FAA, which records what aircraft – by tail or 'N' number – the airline has in service. Woods went to the line showing N901FS as 'in service.' He brought the cursor up and changed the status from 'in service' to 'uncertified,' technically deleting the aircraft from the Operations Specifications, the OpSpec list. After saving the change he sent it to his Director to electronically sign and forward to the FAA where the modified list would become the official record.

He changed screens and went to the Maintenance Program screen. Each airline has their own maintenance program, which dictates how the airline maintains each of its aircraft and then tracks that maintenance. All maintenance procedures are spelled out including how many flight hours each of its aircraft operates in order to properly schedule it for maintenance. Since N901FS was no longer active, maintenance tracking was postponed until the day it was returned to the fleet and put back on the OpSpec list. With a swipe of a mouse Stephen Woods removed N901FS from the flight-hours screen, putting it into a maintenance record hibernation.

The flight to the desert would be the last uneventful flight of N901FS.

CHAPTER 10
FORESIGHT, NOT HINDSIGHT

August 12th – early afternoon

Megan Tenace hated Tuesdays.

It was not up for discussion; Tuesdays were just not her favorite day. This one started out okay; the school was still enrolling students for the new school year, but she managed a day off to ferment on the couch with a book. That was the plan until Dan decided to hunker down for the next ice age.

Her large brown eyes were framed by a clear light complexion. She consciously avoided sunlight lest the freckles materialize magically; a family heirloom of her Irish heritage. She sported a petite nose which supported thick eyeglasses. Megan grew her hair out over the last few years and, despite renegade graying, it draped over her shoulders and upper back with flowing dark brown locks.

Dan and Megan found they enjoyed this concept of 'empty nest syndrome,' a stage of life they originally feared but were now finding to be quite the boon. Since their sons left – Max joined the Army and Patrick was in college – they rediscovered their marital roots, spending as many days together as if they suddenly figured out the other one lived in the same house.

Except for this day. Megan Tenace hated going to the Wholesale store in Manassas on Tuesday and that opinion was still not up for discussion.

The cart was heaped high with all the essentials: various meats, an economy-size package of toilet paper, and a case of bottled water which dominated everything else from the top of the pile. Megan tried to listen to Dan, but news from the older son occupied her mind. Max recently cycled back to Afghanistan, joining up with his platoon in an area consumed in heavy fighting. Even though Max was in his mid-twenties, his mother never surrendered the worrying franchise she had for both her sons.

Dan, on the other hand, had an uncanny talent for putting these cares at arm's length. Meg and Dan had fought many a good fight over the danger to their eldest. It was not that Dan would not give her fears legitimacy; he maintained he could not live vicariously half a world away. Even though she understood his point, it did not make Megan Tenace feel any less desire in hitting Dan over the head with a frozen chicken.

And nothing added to that desire more than spending a Tuesday in Manassas.

As they maneuvered down the many aisles, Megan gave Dan a rundown of the latest news from the Middle East. Usually phone calls from Max were answered by Meg, often interrupted by satellite problems on his end. Meg opined about the insurgent activity and how Max was patrolling, it seemed, more frequently with greater exposure.

On the outside, Dan looked unconcerned; it was, however, tearing him up internally. His strategy was to be her rock; to not allow the appearance that both of them were consumed with worry. Megan interpreted it as being disinterested.

"You're not even listening to me." Meg had stopped walking and stood with her arms crossed.

Dan's chin dropped to his chest as he sensed the 'discussion' coming up again. It was difficult to explain how he did not have the close bond a mother has; that fathers were better emotionally equipped to stand apart from the children and let them live – or, God forbid, die – as they chose to.

"Meg, we've been through this before. I can't do it; I can't be in two places at once."

"But he's out in the middle of the fight!"

"I know," Dan whispered, trying to be consoling.

Meg shrugged him off and walked on down the aisle saying over her shoulder, "But you can't let go of that Freestyle whatever it was. You go on about it every chance you get."

"That's not fair, Babe. Something's going to happen; I know it."

She regretted the jab. Meg looked down at Dan's shopping list, but spoke quietly, "You're usually right about things like that. I don't know why they haven't figured that out yet."

"Well, it isn't like I wanna be right. I hate it when I'm right! Phil still says there's no identical accident, so 'nothing to see here folks, move along.' Giv keeps dropping by my office looking all around for something. The other day I came in early and he's behind my desk, searching. I about gave him a coronary."

"What was he doing in your office?"

"I think he was looking for the AeroGalactic schematics Chris and I are working on. I never saw him move that fast getting out of there." He changed the subject. "What else do you need, Meg? I really don't want to have to come back here again."

Her eyes flashed at her husband. "Me? What did *I* want? Daniel," she began, pointing her pen at his nose, "I've told you before I hate coming here. I'd rather have my teeth drilled with a rusty bit. Now figure out what *you* wanted so we can go home."

They found a line and stood patiently to be checked out. Behind Megan a man was watching the news broadcast on his cell phone; he appeared focused on some chaotic event. Dan half heard a reporter's voice making exclamations of wonder at some horrific incident; the words 'explosion' and 'Memphis' came out. The man's wife went and stood next to her husband, soon becoming caught up in what was so intriguing.

"Why don't we get something for dinner tonight," Dan whispered in Megan's ear, "have a romantic meal, maybe rent a movie?"

"You're assuming I want to spend a romantic evening with you ..."

Dan's cell phone came alive, vibrating in his palm as he pulled the obnoxious device out of the case. He gave Megan a wary look before putting the phone to his ear. His responses were limited to a series of humming noises of agreement. Megan's eyes closed knowing that this was the cell phone the NTSB used to contact him. Any notions of a romantic evening vanished.

Dan clicked the call disconnect button and hit his speed dial. He spoke to Megan while the call connected, "An accident in Memphis; the plane fell hard on the runway and broke up and–" He raised his hand when someone answered.

"Chris, are you going?"

Megan could not hear the reply, but could tell by the way Dan's face relaxed that Chris's wife was spending the week alone.

"Wait ... what?"

Dan was having a hard time with the reception, but he heard enough to say into the receiver, "Hold on; I'll ask her."

Meg looked up; Dan had his hand across the cell phone. "Meg, Chris is launching to Memphis on the go-jet in two hours. Karen's Mom is staying with her, but she's still having a hard time with the new chemo treatments. Can you–"

"Absolutely!" Meg replied. "Tell him not to worry."

He put the phone back to his ear. "She said not to worry. Okay ... okay ... What've you heard?" Dan started to ask before stating, "You're kidding!"

Megan waited patiently as the one-sided conversation continued. Dan looked at nothing in particular. "Yeah, well, I'll probably fly out in the morning. Was it a Boeing or an AeroGalactic–" another pause as Chris responded.

"Well, hopefully not." He closed the phone, staring silently at the floor. He finally looked up and found Meg standing patiently by.

"Like I said – I hate it when I'm right."

The Air Crash Files: Jet Blast

BOOK TWO

NORTHEAST GYRFALCON FLIGHT 427

The Air Crash Files: Jet Blast

CHAPTER 11
DISASTER IN MEMPHIS

August 12th – above northwest Arkansas, late-morning

Northeast Gyrfalcon Airlines flight 427, aircraft registry number N374GY, was making good time flying direct from Denver to Memphis. N374GY, an AeroGalactic KR-350Y is a twin-engine jet with wing-mounted engines. Unlike her older sister, the -450C, AeroGalactic's -350Y is a medium to long range commercial aircraft comfortably seating 250 passengers. Gyrfalcon Airlines strictly flies a -350 fleet; they are the airline's workhorse, providing direct service from Denver to most points west and select points east.

NE Gyrfalcon has its main office and maintenance hub in Denver. The airline has grown steadily for the last two years despite the economic downturn. They will take delivery of one new -350Y every three months for the next four years, adding to their established fleet of one hundred and thirty.

Flight 427 was two hours out of Denver; an on-time departure with expected early arrival in Memphis was good news for those making connections. There were eighty-two passengers and seven flight crew, with two deadheading. The benefit of a light passenger flight was that the flight attendants could ease through the flight while working among the passengers. Due to the emptiness of the cabin, the travelers were able to scatter throughout the cabin and stretch out across seats normally occupied.

Senior flight attendant Doreen Parson maneuvered her petite frame down the single aisle brandishing a smile she found worked best with frequent flyers. She wanted to complete the beverage service early so she could plan out the rest of her day. Luke was pulling the cumbersome beverage cart in front of her; he rolled his eyes as he steered the cart into the armrest of seat 38-D, but the passenger stretched across the seats never woke from blissful unconsciousness.

Luke and Doreen worked smoothly together, often bidding the same flights. His tall wiry frame gives him long reach over seated passengers and his sense of humor made for easygoing flights.

"Doreen," Luke said in between drink orders, "when we get to Memphis let's run down to that Barbeque place in the terminal. If you haven't had their ribs yet, you gotta try them."

Doreen scrunched up her nose in reply.

Luke looked dejected. "Come on! I don't want to go by myself."

Her resistance seemed to soften. "You really oughta go," said the man in 32C. "I know the place he's talking about and it's probably one of the best terminal restaurants around. And I fly to Memphis a lot," he added patting his ample stomach.

"All right," Doreen said, "but we get it as takeout. I hate the food court."

An hour later on the flight deck, Captain Paul Fedow began the descent into Memphis International. During this uneventful flight he had been familiarizing himself with the new equipment recently installed. Gyrfalcon had decided to get on the front end of technology and invest in the SPAR system. Paul was scheduled to run through the new improvements next month, a program that was well under way.

Paul Fedow was not the most proficient pilot in Gyrfalcon. His being at the top of Gyrfalcon's pilot seniority list had more to do with timing than experience. He applied to Gyrfalcon when they opened their doors, at a time most pilots shied away from upstarts. Though his experience level dramatically lagged other captains flying comparable equipment, his seniority assured him a rapid rise in both position and pay.

To Paul's right is first officer Dayton 'Deke' Chamberlain. Deke joined Gyrfalcon three years before, following a 'lifetime' Air Force career; a retired captain who flew every heavy lift aircraft the Air Force owned. Ironically, he has more flight hours as pilot in command than the man in the left seat, a fact Paul was very conscious of.

"That storm has stayed pretty far north of Memphis," Deke said, commenting on the weather radar.

"Okay," Paul mumbled, paging through a manual. As they flew over eastern Arkansas, Fedow was wondering why the new ground tracking screen would not illuminate.

"Do you want me to call Memphis for our gate assignment?" Deke asked, trying to politely nudge Paul back into the approach.

"Gyrfalcon four-two-seven, Memphis Approach. Slow to two-hundred forty knots, descend and maintain ten-thousand," came a voice tinged with a southern twang.

Deke clicked his mic switch. "Copy Memphis Approach, slow to two-hundred forty knots; descend and maintain ten-thousand, Gyrfalcon four-two-seven."

Deke set the altitude in the auto pilot window, tapping it several times before Paul grunted an acknowledgement. Deke pulled the checklist up in the text screen and read through the various challenges. As he ticked off each item he scanned to make sure the systems were properly configured.

"Gyrfalcon four-two-seven, turn right heading one-three-zero."

Deke responded before Paul set the new heading. The aircraft made a slight right bank, lining up on 130 degrees.

The flight deck remained quiet as Paul focused on the upcoming landing. He stowed the SPAR training manual and lifted the microphone out of the holder. "I'm on intercom for a few minutes."

"I've got the aircraft," Deke stated matter-of-factly, aiming his attention on the radio chatter coming across his headset.

"Ladies and gentlemen," Paul spoke into his mic, "this is Captain Fedow. Along with First Officer Deke Chamberlain and your friendly flight attendants, we'd like to thank you for flying this morning on Gyrfalcon. We know you have many choices to reach your destination and we appreciate it when you choose the Gyrfalcon.

"We're descending into Memphis, making our final approach. We should arrive ahead of schedule so I'm afraid you'll all meet your connections. We'll be on the ground within the next ten minutes, so please sit back, relax, and welcome to Memphis." As Paul placed the microphone back in the cradle, he said, "I'm back."

Deke nodded once. "No changes. They called, but they just wanted us to slow."

Paul glanced at the altimeter 'tape' on the digital screen in front of him; the pointer was locked on the center-left side of the screen while the numbers scrolled past it. As '11000' passed the pointer, Paul pulled his seat forward.

Air Traffic called with new directions. Deke answered while sweeping the gauges, "Roger, descend and maintain six-thousand, Gyrfalcon four-two-seven."

Paul reached up and changed the altimeter select in the Autopilot window to show the number 6-0-0-0. He then tapped it twice and Deke said, "six thousand, copy."

As Paul adjusted his seat, his ground tracking screen powered on. Outside the windscreens the available sunlight bleeding through the clouds was barely perceptible to the two pilots. Though it was not raining on the ground, the clouds surrounding the airliner were swollen with moisture. They would no sooner fly out of one dark mass before disappearing into another.

"Autospoilers set."

"Autospoilers set. Let's go to Flaps two," Paul said, adjusting the throttles. Deke placed the flap handle in the two-degree detent and the front display showed the flaps moving back. Deke pulled the throttles back to fifty-five percent N-2.

"Gyrfalcon four-two-seven, descend to two thousand. Turn right heading one-eight-zero."

Deke read back the change in altitude and heading. As he strapped himself in, Deke looked over the glareshield and caught sight of the airport. The clouds that had earlier invaded the skies appeared to back off and make way for traffic. "Airport is in sight," he said. Paul looked forward.

"I see it. Flaps eight."

"Set Autoland."

"Autoland is set."

"Airport in sight, Gyrfalcon four-two-seven," Deke transmitted as he moved the flap handle back into the next detent. Again, the flap illustration enlarged as the flaps sprouted from the display's wing.

"Gyrfalcon four-two-seven, clear to land runway one-eight right. Contact Ground on one two-one-point-six-five. G' day."

Deke replied to the last transmission.

"Flaps fifteen, Deke," Paul said as he watched the yoke and rudder pedals move on their own, lining up more accurately than he ever could. The throttles moved aft as the aircraft slowed to one-hundred and eighty-five knots.

The crew had a steady view of the approaching airport. From this distance aircraft movement was obvious as airliners taxied about. Paul's illuminated DATTAM ground tracking display mimicked the aircraft movements. The outskirts of Memphis were alive below, cars and people moving quickly in the warm day, half anticipating the skies to open up above them and pour rain anew. Little notice was given to the aircraft flying overhead as it lined up on runway 18-Right.

"Flaps thirty, gear down." Paul adjusted his eyeglasses. His eyes scanned the instruments, watching the Autoland for any sudden errors.

Deke lowered the gear handle. A loud clunk echoed through the flight compartment immediately followed by a tempestuous flow of air; the relative wind attacked the dropping nose gear underneath his feet. The gear well directly below the pedestal reverberated with a freight train noise until the doors slapped back into place.

"Gear down and locked, flaps at thirty." Deke, focused on the flap display, caught a brief flash of yellow out of the corner of his eye. The glow was instantaneous, so he could not pick out what the light was for.

"Did you see that?"

The question broke Paul's concentration. "See what?"

"I thought I saw a yellow indication flash, but I don't know what it was." Deke looked up at Paul. "You should go around."

"Five hundred," called out the computerized voice.

"No," Paul said definitively. "You don't know what it was?"

"I couldn't tell. You should go around! Give us some altitude."

"I'll make the call here. Unless you know what the flash was I'm getting us on the ground. If we go around it might be more of a problem."

"I disagree–"

"Noted," insisted Paul. "Let's discuss it on the ground."

"Three hundred ..." the robotic voice announced.

Much as he hated to surrender to a less experienced pilot, Deke knew where he was; this was Paul's aircraft with Paul at the controls. It would be more dangerous to argue on final than to chase a phantom light.

"Two hundred …"

"We'll write it up when we get on the ground." Paul said to appease his co-pilot. Deke was not convinced and stole momentary glances at the indication panel during the remaining approach.

Gyrfalcon 427 had just passed over the western edge of a large cargo facility; a fleet of wide-body aircraft was parked, their shiny white paint scheme reflecting sunlight.

"One hundred …"

The -350Y rocked its wings gently as it descended gracefully in a straight line toward the advancing runway, helical-shaped vortices streaming off the wing tips in the humid air.

As it crossed the end of runway 18-Right, a mechanic working on one of the cargo jets observed the descending -350Y when it was less than one hundred feet off the ground. Instead of flaring, the aircraft leveled off before nosing over hard on the runway. He winced as he watched the nose gear hit first, not convinced of what he was seeing.

At that exact moment he heard a muffled echo, a suspicious roar that overlapped the screaming of metal and a dull explosion. The scene played out in slow motion and he found it impossible to look away.

His radio microphone came to his mouth without thought, and he screamed into it. "A plane just crashed on the runway! Call the emergency trucks!"

Doreen and Luke looked over their passengers anticipating the arrival. Their seats facing aft gave an unobstructed view throughout the cabin. Their backs were to the bulkhead that separated the cabin from the flight deck. "All right, we'll run in and grab some B ... B ... and Q and get right back here."

Doreen laughed at him. "These better be good ribs Luke."

Luke looked at her. "Well, when you eat these ribs, you'll thank–"

And, just then, their routine world collapsed around them.

Paul was anticipating the flare over the runway when Deke saw the light again – two lights; they came on and stayed illuminated. At that moment they were violently forced against their shoulder restraints. They both jolted forward, as if an arresting cable snagged the aircraft from behind. Deke grasped for sense, but the forward momentum was too quick and unexpected; his mind raced to get around the immediate emergency.

As if engulfed in syrup, Deke would never know how quickly he ran through options without even thinking. Over the cacophony of alarms that could pull a pilot in eight different directions, his first reaction probably saved a majority of the passengers.

He pulled back hard on the yoke.

Both reversers had gone into full reverse simultaneously. The resulting force: intense; the direction: forward and down. The nose of the aircraft pushed over. Due to the slow landing speed, lift was lost immediately and the -350Y fell like a rock. If Deke had not retarded the dying aircraft's nose-over momentum by pulling back on the yoke, the airplane would have hit the ground tail up resulting in a more catastrophic crash.

It struck hard on the nose gear, the impact force so powerful that the gear did not collapse; instead it went straight up through the top of the wheelwell, ripping out all attaching structure holding the strut in place. With everything going on, the tortured blast of the gear assembly liberating itself was drowned out; it continued its upward course, deflecting to the left and driving up into the seat that held Paul Fedow. Crushed against the ceiling of the flight deck, Paul was killed instantly.

The torsional load on the aircraft's fuselage ripped the structure completely through in two places. The aircraft's death throe resulted in three independent sections of fuselage separating at the manufacturer splices: one behind the bulkhead at the rear of the flight deck and one aft of the wings' trailing edge.

The liberated flight deck continued its momentum, sliding on its left side off the runway before settling in the grass at a thirty-degree list to the left. Deke was unconscious, his left arm all but separated by the nose gear. He dangled, hanging from his seat restraints over where Paul had been sitting an instant before.

Momentum carried the forward part of the cabin and wings. They leaned right snapping the #2 engine off its pylon where it dug into the runway tarmac; the dying engine ingested the runway surface as it rolled, coming to rest several yards to the right. The right gear collapsed under the excessive side loads, rolling under the fuselage as it continued forward. The right wing threw sparks in every direction, igniting the shower of atomized fuel spraying from the open wound created by the jettisoned #2 engine. The area erupted in a conflagration; a muffled explosion followed an expanding cloud of smoke that ascended ominously in the air; the holocaust embraced the aft section, which came to rest in the midst of the growing lake of spilt fuel and fire.

Several passengers, unfortunate to be sitting where the fuselage's integrity failed, were littered on the runway; several bodies still strapped in their seats were dragged under the sliding structure or were rapidly consumed in the resulting inferno.

Since the nose gear tore free, it had absorbed most of the impact of the flight deck and surrounding structure. Doreen and Luke, sitting just behind the cockpit, received minor injuries. The bulkhead they sat against and the lower fuselage absorbed most of the dying aircraft's kinetic energy, transmitting it to surrounding structure as the stressed areas collapsed underneath like an accordion. The bulkhead dug into the grass, slowing its forward motion.

Both flight attendants watched in horror as the event played out in front of them. When all movement stopped, Luke was too stunned to move, sitting in his seat wondering if he had dreamed the whole thing. After what seemed an eternity, his hearing returned from the explosive noises. The inferno roaring beyond and the heat it generated brought him rudely out of shock, jumping when Doreen placed her hand on his arm.

Doreen was more aware, her training kicking in. When Luke snapped around to face her, Doreen's eyes lost their urgent look and relief crossed her face. "Are you all right?" she yelled over the noise.

Luke nodded vigorously, yet the jolt of the hard landing made its presence known in both their lower backs. Since the flight compartment leaned towards the left, he was above her. She told him to unbuckle his straps before dropping to the soft earth below. He released his restraints and dropped down unsteadily beside her, catching himself with his hand, content that his ankles did not give out.

"We have to get to the passengers," she said, but Luke looked lost. She repeated herself to him, emphasizing with her hand the separated fuselage section beyond, "We have to get to the passengers!"

Confusion continued to play across his face until reality dug in; he motioned for her to lead. Doreen walked quickly to the separated section with Luke beside her. The front end of the forward section was twisted with shards of steel and aluminum jutting in all directions; the silver and grey of the torn metals reflected orange in sporadic displays. The few passengers they could see appeared unconscious – or dead – without any signs of movement. Locating an unobstructed path into the cabin, Luke hoisted Doreen up and inside before carefully picking a path through the jagged metal.

Thick acrid smoke filled the cabin from the back end, but they could hear faint coughing. Looking aft towards the departed tail section Doreen could not make out anything in the smoke except for brief flashes of brilliant flame.

She worried about leading the survivors through the torn metal, so she told Luke to open the two forward entry doors. The left door would not budge. As Doreen went down the aisle, Luke put his weight against the right door; it resisted at first, but soon swung slowly outwards. Metal protested against metal, but Luke forced it open all the way. The automatic slide deployed with a whoosh of air, unfolding into a less cosmetic version of its normal self. He assured the slide's distance from the flames so the injured could be rolled down as opposed to being dropped from the doorway.

Doreen moved conscious passengers towards Luke and located the injured, where she found most had survived, though not all were conscious. Stealing another glance back through the flames, she was convinced that the tail section had not been so lucky. Doreen said a silent prayer for those co-attendants and passengers.

The breached hull at the tail section sat in the midst of a sea of fire; anyone strapped in and unconscious was dead. The temperature inside the tail section soared and all available oxygen was consumed by the greedy flames. All attempts to escape were desperate and short lived; many perishing before action could take place.

Alarms announcing the approach of the Memphis Airport fire department and the National Guard fire trucks forced Doreen back to the situation at hand. She turned her back to the heat and walked forward towards Luke, resigning the tail section's rescue to more capable hands. Doreen moved on, supporting passengers that could not walk and escorting them to Luke, who guided them down the slide the quickest way he could. Like a community effort, rescued passengers formed a fire brigade at the slide to assist their co-travelers away from the flames and off to safety.

Doreen was about to double check when Luke roughly pushed her forward and yelled at her to go down the slide. She protested, but he gestured for her to help those who escaped before he made his way back checking for stragglers. After she slid down an explosion rocked the wing area where Luke was searching. The last thing Doreen remembered of Luke was his determined look with just a hint of a knowing smile.

The combined efforts of both the Memphis airport and the National Guard's fire departments were heralded that day. The team effort overcame the difficult work of the inferno, merging their talents together through the mayhem and the fire was quickly brought under control.

The aft section had two survivors: a 12-year old girl and a young female flight attendant who shielded the other with her body. Miraculously they had escaped death by lying prostrate on the floor of an empty row and sharing a portable oxygen bottle. No one else survived. When the recovery people finally reached the back cabin, they discovered a futile attempt to force the two rear doors open before being overcome by the smoke and heat. The catastrophic forces had jammed the doors closed.

The forward section had all but one survivor: Luke. Both Doreen and Luke's combined efforts were credited with saving all souls up front. Local and national media had a field day spreading the story of the two heroes and their unselfish efforts to care for their passengers. Some in the press preferred to focus instead on the culpability of Gyrfalcon Airlines and the aircraft's manufacturer, AeroGalactic. In the end, attention both wanted and unwanted ran front page for two weeks with interviews of the victims' family members and Luke's parents running neck and neck on page one, long after the victims were buried and mourners returned home.

The total human loss was far below any aeronautical expert could have believed. Final death toll: twenty-six passengers, four flight crew members, though technically Luke died after the crash. The media surprisingly focused on the survivor numbers: fifty-six passengers and three flight crew members. Many survivors suffered severe burns and all had complications from smoke inhalation.

Gyrfalcon flight 427 had not been a terrorist attack, so the question soon spread across the nation: what happened?

CHAPTER 12
SHADES OF GREY

Phil Tulkinghorn looked around the gaudy waiting room belonging to Chairwoman Ellen Potter. A brief sensation of revulsion spread through his gut; the wasteful spending on such garish decorations made him want to dry heave. But that did not equal the aversion he had to these one-on-one meetings her lordship demanded with him. *There is a cornucopia of things I would rather do*, Phil thought, *than have these chats*.

And getting my wisdoms pulled without Novocain was at the top of that list.

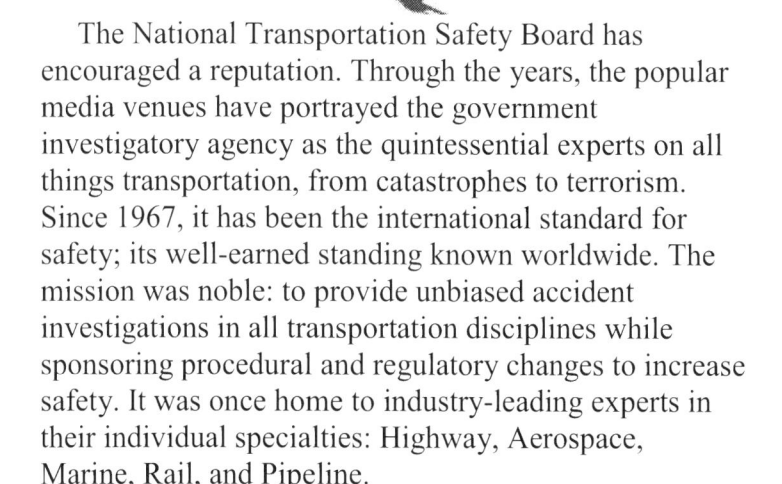

The National Transportation Safety Board has encouraged a reputation. Through the years, the popular media venues have portrayed the government investigatory agency as the quintessential experts on all things transportation, from catastrophes to terrorism. Since 1967, it has been the international standard for safety; its well-earned standing known worldwide. The mission was noble: to provide unbiased accident investigations in all transportation disciplines while sponsoring procedural and regulatory changes to increase safety. It was once home to industry-leading experts in their individual specialties: Highway, Aerospace, Marine, Rail, and Pipeline.

The NTSB was separated from those five specialties it investigates; this detachment assured impartial scrutiny, analysis, and recommendations. Working closely with those regulating bodies the NTSB proposed changes that barely interrupted the flow of commerce, protecting the traveling public by preventing future anomalies. They earned the respect of the international community.

Yet its influence remains one directional; it advises but does not regulate, recommending while detached from the sources, all the time drawing factual conclusions with no power to enact.

But, over time, unsatisfied with performing a limited role, some within the NTSB extended their reach. As accidents declined the media was willing to credit the NTSB for the trend, turning to them to explain what the rise in safety meant and what should be done to maintain it.

Gradually the NTSB assumed a new role, one more cynical. The original objective of the Board became clouded as advising evolved into finger-pointing; recommendations became unrealistic expectations; factual conclusions were replaced by unsolicited opinions. Some personnel began venturing into territory they were unqualified for and its distinct history of shaping safety was now but a grey shade of its greater days.

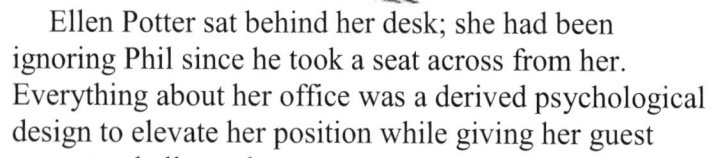

Ellen Potter sat behind her desk; she had been ignoring Phil since he took a seat across from her. Everything about her office was a derived psychological design to elevate her position while giving her guest pause to challenge her.

How predictable, Phil thought. He chose to check his messages.

She finally faced Phil, leaning forward while nervously chewing her pen. "How did we lose control of this?"

Phil raised his gaze, looking into Potter's doe-like eyes; not the eyes of Bambi's mom gazing lovingly at her fawn, but what they would resemble if she was packing heat and turning the tables on the hunters. At first imperceptible, the grey eyes were cadaverous, rimmed in red from lack of sleep. Age lines sprang from the corners like cracks in her temples. The silver that threatened her red hair and the sallow complexion were kept at bay by rouge and red hair dye.

She was probably attractive once, Phil thought, *at one time*.

"We never lost control–" Phil began.

"The accident in Memphis would suggest differently," Potter interrupted. "How many? I heard at least thirty dead!" She said answering her own question. "Do we know if Tenace was right about the reversers in Los Angeles?"

"He was fishing," he replied, brushing off the question. "There's nothing to suggest Memphis is related."

She looked skeptically at Phil, the thin fingers of one claw-like hand drumming on the desktop. Her nostrils flared anxiously and her bright red lips stretched taught. She craved control like a substance addict, and she dreaded unknowns. Chairwoman Potter was indicative of the modern day bureaucratic adulator. In the past, those serving in public office played to the views of the people; today, the push is to emerge high in the opinion of 24-hour news's digital technologies.

"When will we know?' She fell back in her seat, tossing her pen on the blotter. "I have a really bad feeling about this."

"Ron Gebbia is the Investigator in Charge. He should be onsite in Memphis by now," Phil said, looking at his watch. "As soon as he knows, then I'll know. I told him that I have to advise the Board and I need to have everything so the media can be briefed. I see no reason to be concerned." He looked back at her. "What about the FAA?"

"Despite popular opinion, Amelia and I don't get along. I'd rather wait to hear from our people before I lose any credibility with the FAA Administrator."

You can't lose that which you don't have, thought Phil, standing up to exit the room.

"What did you do with Tenace?" Potter asked as Phil walked toward the door.

Phil stopped; he turned slowly, considering Potter with a doubtful look. "He's flying to Denver in the morning."

Potter reacted nervously, "Denver? Why's he going to Denver?"

"He's going to the maintenance facility for Gyrfalcon Airlines." Potter went to protest, but Phil raised his hand to cut her off. *It's time to stop this*, he thought.

"You do understand why he's with us, right?"

Despite the air conditioning, beads of sweat streaked the garish makeup; Potter's face turned deep red. Phil ignored this and kept explaining as if to a child.

"He's our maintenance investigator; the only one we have. So, when we," he said, circling his hand in the air, "have an accident to investigate, Tenace looks at the maintenance issues." He added, "If you have a problem with that, then you need to slap down that imbecile Scalia."

"Don't worry about Scalia. His days are short here."

"But he's with your own political party. How are you–?"

It was Potter's turn to wave away the question. She squinted to clearly see Phil. "How are you," she emphasized with a talon-like finger, "going to keep Tenace from talking to the press?"

"He's gonna be in Denver," Phil said matter-of-factly. "Since the accident is in Memphis, nobody's going to even bother with him a thousand miles away. The press is attracted to sensationalism; he's got the least interesting job in the world."

Potter considered this. "Dick Baeir is the Board Member onsite with your IIC. I'll make sure he runs everything through this office before he even thinks it. But as for the investigation team, I want you–" her fist slammed the desk, "CONTROLLING this.

CHAPTER 13
INVESTIGATION

August 13th – above northeast Colorado

The United 767 slowed as it approached Denver International airport from the west. The flaps sliding out of the wing's trailing edge immediately fell under the assault of air passing over and under. The Autopilot corrected for a momentary roll left while both engines spooled up minutely.

The sun bathed the Earth with an unobstructed spray of warming sunshine. Several brown mountains were spotted with green foliage at the lower altitudes. The view from the airplane gave the Rockies a two-dimensional appearance. Soon they broke over the city from the west and on a direct path to Runway 07.

Before departing Dulles airport, the flight was abuzz with wary passengers wondering if this airliner was the same type as the one that crashed. This was why Dan disliked flying; the paranoia of uninformed travelers; that and the selfishness of this Me-generation.

But, in times like this, it was the paranoia.

For Gyrfalcon Airlines, the financial and public relations nightmare would be temporary, perhaps lasting several weeks; that will be how long before the public realizes every Gyrfalcon jet is not going to fall out of the sky as if on cue.

The accident aircraft, N374GY, was maintained in Denver, Gyrfalcon's hub; its accident in Memphis was a consequence of where it was heading. Dan's specialty dictated that he be where the heavy maintenance was performed, which meant Northeast Gyrfalcon's two large hangars where they conducted most of their maintenance in-house. Dan's objective on arrival was to form his team together, dig through the records for anomalies and interview anyone involved with it to find breaks in the system.

As the Aircraft Maintenance Investigator – the AMI – Dan's responsibilities are unlike the other investigators at the NTSB combing over the wreckage. Instead, he scours through the aircraft's complete history. Although maintenance is considered by the other specialties as grunt work, the investigation stalls without the AMI and his team.

Dan spent several hours the previous evening talking with Chris and Ron Gebbia, the IIC, to discuss what they found in Memphis; the first hours following an investigation team's arrival were crucial, often dictating Dan's own direction. Even before arriving in Denver, he had planned out his strategy.

The 767 crossed the threshold on Runway 07 before the tail dipped slightly in flare. Bleeding off the remaining lift, it settled on the runway, transferring weight from the wings to the landing gear. Tires screeched as the wheels sped up to match the aircraft's speed. A loud whoosh rose in the air as the reversers deployed causing everyone inside to strain against their seat belts and shoulder restraints.

Within forty-five minutes Dan was making his way west on Pena Boulevard to exit five. His cell phone buzzed while driving but he allowed it to go to voice mail as he pulled into the Marriott hotel.

Fifteen minutes later, Dan entered his room and threw his bag on the newly made bed; the room smelled of Febreeze and disinfectant. He closed over the blinds before dialing Chris's number, but Ron Gebbia's call beat him to it.

"Hey, what's happening?"

"Dan, are you in Denver or are you laying over somewhere?" Ron talked over the drone of heavy machinery in the background. He is at the top of Connie's IIC group, the Investigators In-Charge who run the investigation on-site. A former college quarterback with an engineering degree, Ron is a high-energy leader as if operating on straight adrenaline; his professional ambitions were dashed with a hamstring injury, so he stuck with engineering. He still has his athletic good looks, handsome features that women find appealing and only his large nose looks out of place. Ron is all business and runs his investigations like he ran his plays on the field.

Dan spoke loudly into the phone while pacing in his suite. "I just checked into the hotel. I'm heading over to Gyrfalcon's office in about half an hour."

"Great," Ron responded, the background noise receding. "Three of your reps will meet you at Gyrfalcon in about an hour. The other will arrive later in the afternoon."

"Okay, I was going to call Chris. Is he around?"

"He's not with me in the hangar," Ron answered. "You'll have to call him yourself. But listen, there's something important I gotta talk to you about. Did you know the First Officer survived?"

Dan's breathing checked, half-believing what Ron was telling him: the FO survived the crash. "No, I didn't. Did the Captain make it?"

"No, he got the bad end of the landing. He died when the nose gear pushed up through the floor and center-punched him; he never knew what hit him.

"But listen," Ron continued, his words spilling over the phone, "the F-O spoke to Barry. It turns out Barry was at the hospital with the FAA when the guy's doctor approached them. The F-O was in and out of consciousness but wanted to talk to them and Barry called me directly. Now I told the NTSB folks late last night." Ron hesitated, which spoke volumes; there was something wrong. "Now Dan, I was going to call you back after the meeting broke up last night, but Chris told me not to. Instead he told me to wait until today and said, 'ask Dan if he wants to guess what the F-O told Barry.'"

"Why me?" He stopped pacing.

"Chris told me chances are good *you* can tell *me* what the F-O said. If so, we've got a big problem." Ron paused before saying, "Okay Dan, what caused the accident?"

Dan shook his head, remembering his conversation with Meg, yet not fully believing it. "Did the number two reverser deploy?"

"Oh, man," Ron muttered on his end. "You're partly right. Now I have to get Phil involved. This ain't good! It wasn't just the number two, but both of them, just as they were flaring." Ron paused for a second. "Dan, we've got a big problem."

"Ron, do me a favor, keep the team leads from mentioning the reversers to their teams just yet. I know you told them last night, but don't tell the other folks. I need some time to organize my guys before they find out."

"I can't guarantee it hasn't gotten around yet, but I'll try."

Well, Dan thought after hanging up, *the up side is that I know what I'm looking for now.* Usually the flight or voice recorders are read before the teams have a bearing on how to proceed. In some instances, the air traffic tower tapes can give direction; the conversation between air traffic and the aircraft or an emergency called for before impact. But, it appears, none of that will be necessary.

Chances are, Dan thought, *Phil already found out from the recorders what he just learned from Ron.* Either way he doubted Phil would recognize Dan and Chris's efforts to look into the errant reverser deployment on Freestyle's KR-450C. Or maybe worse, they would know. Phil would then rely on a government agency's best friend: Deniability. Bureaucracy and office politics rears its ugly head yet again.

"Did you talk to Ron yet?" Chris asked smugly.

"Yeah, I did." Dan searched his suitcase for a tie.

"Did you make me proud?"

"Ron said he hasn't discussed it with Phil yet. What do you think's gonna happen when he finds out?"

"I bet he already knows," Chris responded off-handedly. "Dan, it's a mess down here, man. We don't normally see survivors, nowhere near this many. Before we got here the ambulances were on the field moving living victims. I mean the media were practically pushing the airport perimeter fencing down.

"That being said, if he knew we could be talking to the media and let it slip that we'd been looking into something similar a couple of weeks ago …"

"Yeah, I'm sure he's working damage control as we speak."

"They're not worried about me because Ron handles the press. You, on the other hand, might have your own platoon of reporters that know you're there–"

Dan's phone buzzed again. He pulled it away and looked at the name. "Hey, Ron's calling me. I bet he got the gag order from Phil. Let me call you back."

Ron did not have time for pleasantries. "Dan, you can't talk about Freestyle's incident in June. Phil just about had a coronary on the phone!"

"Yeah, I figured he would."

"You aren't supposed to see any reporters, are you?" Ron's anxiety oozed over the phone.

"Not yet, but I usually refer them back to Public Relations anyway. But Ron, I'm not your problem ... for now," Dan let the last two words hang out there for a second. "The one you need to worry about ... well, not you, but Phil ... is Vince. He was spring-loaded to the press conference position with Freestyle."

"You told *Vince*?!"

"Come on, seriously Ron? Vince cornered *me*, not the other way around. What was I supposed to do, tell him to take a hike?"

"Well," Ron said, "that's Phil's problem. I wouldn't want the public to know I sat on that information."

Because of the cross-country distance, Dan's 8:00 AM flight lasting four hours, still made for a 10:00 AM arrival. His dislike for flying extended to time zones; the adjustment to another section of the country always reconciled itself just as he headed back to the east coast.

Denver was pleasant, especially in the summer. The temperatures promised to peak at eighty-two, but the dry air in the mile-high city would mean humidity levels were comfortable. He remembered living in Memphis years before and knew the Go-team was not going to have a good time about it; aside from being on his own, this AMI assignment was working in his favor.

Dan picked up coffee at the hotel's courtesy bar, but never touched it. He made his way to Gyrfalcon's Colorado offices in an executive park off East 128th Avenue where he had agreed to meet the team. By practice, the NTSB dispatched their investigators on accidents to head a team made up of participants from the airline, the FAA, the aircraft manufacturer, and the engine manufacturer.

Dan's assigned FAA representative was from the local office. When he pulled into the lot he picked him out right away because of the jacket and tie ... and a look saying Aaron Campo had given him marching orders.

The FAA always supported the NTSB in accidents. However, in major accidents where the fatality count was high or there was a high-profile victim, the FAA supplied one inspector for each NTSB investigator. This amounted to about ten or more teams during each investigation.

As team leader, Dan led the AMI team while other team leaders looked into their areas of expertise. The NTSB investigators had a working knowledge of aircraft, but the FAA not only has an intimate knowledge of the different aircraft, but how the various aviation industries worked. On-site, the NTSB had the power, but the FAA had the experience and knowledge.

Dan exited the car, pulling his computer bag out and donning his dress jacket. He walked slowly towards the FAA inspector, a middle-aged man about Dan's age, with a clean-shaven head. Inspector John Matero looked as if he had been pulled out of the mechanic workforce from any number of airlines. He was relaxed; someone obviously in his element, sporting a lopsided smile. He met Dan halfway, switching his computer bag from his right to his left hand midstride.

"John Matero, FAA here in Denver. I assume you're …"

"Dan Tenace, NTSB," Dan finished John's sentence for him, "Do me a favor, John, give me a second to meet these guys. I need to talk to you."

"Sure, sure," John said releasing Dan's grip. "Have you heard anything?"

But Dan just smiled at him and walked over to two other men near the door. One was finishing off a cigarette, but caught Dan's hand as he extended it. Clay Brinnel was much older and seemed stand-offish; he reeked of old cigarettes. Clay was the AeroGalactic representative, the aircraft's manufacturer; he wore a short-sleeved dress shirt and a black tie from the K-mart collection. His guarded demeanor and averting glance led Dan to trust him, hesitantly.

The second man was dressed unnaturally in a black suit jacket, which he looked as if he wanted to crawl out of. Randy Labosco was the Gyrfalcon Airlines' representative; a lead mechanic in his early thirties. Randy had a full beard and a full head of hair beneath a Denver Rockies baseball cap. He appeared nervous, out of place; but instantly warmed up to Dan when it was clear they shared a common history.

As Randy led Clay inside, Dan put his arm out in front of John and slowed his pace. He waved to Randy to go on ahead before lowering his voice, "I need to ask you to look at the engines and the reverser system, particularly during the last phase inspections." John shrugged his shoulders in agreement.

"The reversers deployed during flare," Dan whispered. "We think that's what brought the plane down."

John looked incredulous. "The reversers deployed early?" Dan nodded. John gestured to where Randy and Clay had been a moment before. "Do you think they know?"

"No," said Dan shaking his head, "that's why I'm talking to you. I need someone I can trust to look for this stuff without skewing the findings. I'm not sure if the deployment was coincidental or systemic, but this is the second deployment we've had during the landing phase in the last few months. The other one didn't make the news."

"Was it on an AeroGalactic? The last one I mean."

"Yeah, but it was on a dash four-fifty and happened below a thousand feet. Aaron Campo had the Portland office overseeing AeroGalactic look into it, but they haven't found anything yet. I need you to look into the systems because Clay or Randy might protect the airline or the manufacturer."

"You got it, Dan," John smiled the lopsided smile again, "Aaron told me to take care of you."

"I appreciate that."

Introductions were made inside. The Director of Maintenance, one or two Vice Presidents and the company lawyers handed out business cards and said a few words. Dan spoke with the Director about interviewing a few of the mechanics who worked the aircraft last; this raised some eyebrows among the lawyers.

Dan suggested a hangar tour to get a feel of the place and also to see if a -350Y was parked inside ... just in case they needed one to crawl around in. When they left the conference room, the lawyers immediately descended upon the executives to discuss strategies. Dan despised being fawned over by upper echelons for answers, though it produced a perk: he now controlled the movers and shakers by insisting on conditions they were loath to originally agree to.

The team was led into a less-than-impressive conference room. Dan, John, and Clay began setting up their computers and logging into their respective systems. An administrative assistant named Francine came into the room, introducing herself to everyone. She explained that she was responsible for the maintenance records for the accident aircraft: N374GY; they had been collected and quarantined in her office. All computer records were locked behind password protection so no unauthorized employees could access anything reserved for the investigators.

Francine was a short woman with the remains of a French accent; Dan believed she played fullback for the Broncos. She stood before the four men with her hands placed firmly on her hips, asserting command over the room with a light-hearted, yet no-nonsense stance.

"Gentlemen," she said as if throwing her voice across the Rockies, "I can be your best friend or," and here she glared strongly at Randy, "your worst enemy. If you need anything, please ask me. If you want copies, please ask me. If you can't find it, I know where it is ... *please* ... ask me."

Dan and the others followed Francine to her office to cart over boxes of aircraft records. Back in the conference room Dan assigned each team member the areas of maintenance they would look into, reserving the reversers for himself and John.

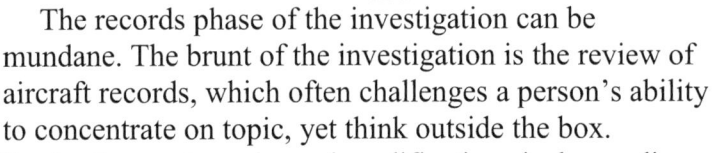

The records phase of the investigation can be mundane. The brunt of the investigation is the review of aircraft records, which often challenges a person's ability to concentrate on topic, yet think outside the box. Evaluating past repairs and modifications is dry reading. Although these records reviews are the main focus of this phase, imagination helps an investigator glean what may have led to the accident.

The Air Traffic and Meteorological groups are grilling the controllers on duty while foraging through the tapes of the fateful day. People from the Airframe, Systems, Engines, and Survival Factors groups are sweeping through the wreckage with full hazardous suits on, moving amongst the twisted debris and burnt structure.

Often, they find human remains, such as limbs separated from the victim; some investigators become immune to the sight, but others move away for fear of losing control of their digestive fluids. However, these are not envied jobs. Dan never missed the spotlight, instead preferring to stay off the grid to concentrate on the aircraft alone.

Dan kept the group's atmosphere light; he found it worked best to prevent missing important information. An easy-going mood cultivated trust; stonewalling or dirty tricks came to the surface. His management experience and rapport with mechanics afforded him a unique view of how his teams worked, often enabling him to clip any deceptive attempts before they became unmanageable.

Clay walked excitedly into the room, stowing his cell phone. "I just heard from my cohort in Memphis. He said the Gyrfalcon plane experienced a double-reverser deployment." John's eyebrows rose but Dan did not react.

"Yeah, I know," Dan said off-handedly.

Clay stared hard at Dan. "Were you going to tell us?"

Dan still did not look up, but kept reviewing the last heavy check N374GY had gone through. "Not really Clay. That's the Systems group's focus, not ours."

"I think we should have been told."

Dan was pre-occupied with the heavy check. He looked up when the silence became noticeable. "Since I couldn't verify the facts I'd rather have everyone look at all possibilities than just the reversers." Dan looked up, his eyes boring into Clay's skull. "I need you guys to look at the entire history, that way you're looking for everything. If there's a pneumatic issue on the airframe side that affected the reversers you might miss it looking for anomalies around the engines. After a thorough review of all the records, we'll focus on specifics. But until I have confirmation on *how* the reversers deployed, we're not getting distracted."

Clay sat down heavily; he scanned through log pages, shaking his head.

"I was hoping our missing team member would be here by now. I arranged for a tour of the hangar." Dan said, walking out the door towards Francine's office.

"He didn't want to tell us about the reversers?" Clay said under his breath. "Who does he think he is keeping information from us?"

John barely looked up, directing his voice to Clay. "He's the boss here, so I guess that's what makes him think that."

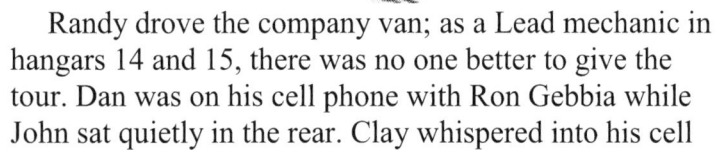

Randy drove the company van; as a Lead mechanic in hangars 14 and 15, there was no one better to give the tour. Dan was on his cell phone with Ron Gebbia while John sat quietly in the rear. Clay whispered into his cell phone with someone in his Portland office.

Randy coaxed the van through the perimeter fence and drove slowly around hangar 14. He made a sweeping circle by the open doors and crossed the threshold, parking off to the side. They each crawled out of the van; Dan was last to exit, closing his cell phone as he stood up and looked around.

"They're still reading out the recorders," Dan said, filling everyone in. "The FDR always takes longer. The CVR caught an interesting comment by the first officer, who says he saw a flickering light just after the gear locks down. Our Operations guy, Barry, said that they were on final and the captain didn't want to interrupt the landing cycle. He said the flicker was momentary but the F-O didn't catch which light it was."

John said, "Did he see it again?"

"Good question," Dan responded. "There's a moment just before the reversers deployed that they get a sharp intake of breath off the F-O's mic. There's no way to know if he was reacting to a light or the captain's landing, but the reversers deployed a split second later. Barry said the F-O told him he saw it but didn't have time to say."

"Are we going to talk to the surviving pilot?" Randy asked.

"We don't talk to the pilots, but the Ops guys will interview him some more," Dan said. "Each investigator focuses on his particular specialty. That's not to say Barry won't ask questions that would interest us. He'll let me know."

Clay asked, "Did they have Autobrakes selected?"

"They haven't finished the FDR readout yet. My friend Chris is combing the wreckage and he says the Autobrakes were selected."

"That would give us a direction to go in if they had it selected."

"Good point, Clay," Dan said turning to Randy. "Why don't you look into Autobrake issues when we go back to the office? In fact, look at Autoland and the flight command computers for issues. Maybe we can get a head start on everybody else if we can rule that option out or verify it without the tapes." He then placed a hand on Randy's shoulder, "Lead on Lead man."

Randy steered them through hangar 14 to the middle bay where a -350Y sat amid a swarm of technicians and equipment. The hangar itself is cavernous; thousands of square feet that, when unoccupied, form a giant empty. The ceiling rises eighty feet above the floor and is crisscrossed with red steel girders that support the roof and sustain several mobile cranes. A contrasting light tan ceiling shows through the various traversing catwalks.

The hangar's uniform floor is an engineering necessity; a level platform is essential for lifting aircraft on jacks where safety is not compromised by an unforgiveable lack of precision. The off-white floor is level to within a degree and spotted with chemical stains from all types of oils and fluids. Running from wall to wall, it reflects the intense lights shining down from the ceiling. Reflective yellow guide lines are painted from the rear to the large front door for positioning airliners in the bays. Technicians meander around the aircraft, performing various repairs or following work card directions. Faint odors of hydraulic fluid and oil hang in the air.

Two hangar doors, nearly as high as the ceiling and together as wide as the longest wall, were open to allow the Denver air to wash in over the work area. Equipment for this particular inspection was positioned around the plane, which resembled a modern-day Gulliver inundated by Lilliputian mechanics. An umbilical power cord ran from a ceiling reel to the aircraft's nose supplying electrical power to energize the various systems.

Randy walked the group around the aircraft, purposely avoiding hazardous work areas. Occasional call-outs were yelled at him, many comments made at Randy's expense – all in good fun. Several mechanics approached John to ask about job opportunities at the FAA.

The team was introduced to the work planners and the floor managers. While Randy led the other team members out to the bay again, Dan spoke to one manager.

John gestured to the aircraft. "Are they doing a phase check?"

Randy walked over to a desk near the right wing. "They're running a J-check, which is done every twelve hundred and fifty flight hours. This phase is basically a visual inspection with some lubrication of the wings."

"Randy," Dan asked, "can we see what's in the other hangar?"

Randy led them through a set of doors leading into hangar 15. Another Gyrfalcon -350Y was parked along the far wall, the unique paint job, dull under reduced lighting. It looked isolated in a hangar bay deprived of the energy so evident in hangar 14.

As the team crossed the empty bays toward the -350Y they noticed five people milling around the plane. Three technicians in jumpsuits of light grey stood over blueprints while two others dressed in Gyrfalcon uniforms focused on the plane.

Dan asked Randy about the jet. "They're completing modifications. They installed the components for that satellite guidance system."

John smiled. "Are you referring to the SPAR system?"

Clay asked, "You're repairing the wing spar?"

"No, not *for* the spar. It's the SPAR system. Satellite," Randy paused. "Positioning and Airspace …"

"Restructuring ... Airspace restructuring. The acronym is SPAR. Dan, that's the new computerized air traffic system."

"Aaron mentioned something about it a few weeks ago. I read a briefing about a ten-year computerized air traffic project, but I didn't know how far it got."

"Don't you Board guys know anything?" John joked. "Look, SPAR enables the aircraft to speak directly with ground computers, thus dramatically reducing the workload of the flight crews."

Dan stared at the aircraft. "You're taking more control from the pilots?"

John replied proudly, "SPAR will revolutionize air travel. The system is basically an independent computer-based system that does several things. One, it reduces communications between air and ground. Two, new technologies that look through cloud covers give the crews an unobstructed view of the runway, all with laser and satellite technology."

For no obvious reason, an involuntary shiver ran up Dan's spine.

"And three, when the aircraft is on the ground, SPAR allows the pilots to navigate around the airport even when they can't see outside the window."

"When did Gyrfalcon start installing them?"

John pursed his lips in thought. "It seems that the launch customers – those involved in the testing of the systems – are installing the last mods in the remainder of their fleets. But I didn't know Gyrfalcon was this far along."

Dan turned to Clay. "Do you know how SPAR interacts with the aircraft's systems?"

Clay looked at the airliner and the three technicians who were shooting worried glances at the team. "I wasn't in on any SPAR stuff. You're better off asking these guys."

"Hey guys," Dan said as he approached with his identification held out. Three sets of eyes locked on the badge slightly hidden from view. Dan hated using the badge, but it did come in handy when you wanted to cut to the chase.

The lead technician cautiously extended his hand to Dan's, his eyes never leaving the badge. "I'm Tim McCreight from Transolutions. I'm the engineer and the liaison between my company and Gyrfalcon."

"Dan Tenace, Mister McCreight." Dan handed him a business card. "This is my team for the maintenance investigation phase of the Memphis accident. You know about the accident?"

Tim nodded his head but gave no other acknowledgement.

"Good," Dan continued, introducing his team.

Tim pointed to the other two Transolutions employees and introduced them. "Is there something wrong, Mister Tenace?"

"No ... not at all. My friend John was just telling me that the SPAR is being installed in several carriers. I was curious, that's all. Can you give us some background?"

Tim led them to a table where schematics were laid out. He flattened the sheets and showed them the installation. "Testing the national SPAR grid won't begin for a few months."

Dan nodded, but John spoke up. "How does the system work?"

"Which part?"

John shrugged his shoulders at the question. "Is Transolutions installing the whole system?"

Tim gestured to his coworkers to return to their work. "Well, no, actually Transolutions is responsible for the route-tracking components and their programming."

Dan and John looked at each other and shrugged. "How about a layman's description of your product and how it interfaces with the aircraft?"

Dan saw Tim relax as he guided the investigators through the SPAR system installation. "Our aircraft components network directly with the corresponding computers in the air traffic stations, orbiting satellites, and ground receiving stations being placed across the country. That's what I meant when I said the national SPAR grid; those combined units make up the grid. What Transolutions components do is tell the aircraft where it is, where to go," Tim started ticking off on his fingers, "how fast, how high to fly at, and basically it cycles aircraft in and out of flight patterns and routes. They do this without any interference from the pilots."

There it was again. Dan felt another chill go up his spine when he said ...

"Interference?"

"Well, interference is the wrong word," John added.

"That's right," Tim continued, "the pilots are fully engaged in the routing of their plane. SPAR is designed to ease their workload and make more economically accurate decisions, faster than a human can."

Dan thought for a minute. "What aircraft systems does SPAR tie into?"

Tim paused to think. "It directly ties into the navigation systems and the flight computers. But indirectly ... well, it can run any system on the jet to facilitate flight controls, climb, descent, approach, departure, even collision avoidance. In other words, if the ATC computer says to climb, then the various systems computers are ordered to follow the ATC commands, like engines, collision avoidance, flight controls, and fuel."

"It can do all that without any input from the pilot?"

Tim gave a curt nod. "That's what it was designed for."

"How about the reversing system?"

John's head whipped around to look at Dan. "You're not implying that—"

"No," Dan assured him. "I just want to know how much control it has."

Tim rocked nervously on the backs of his feet. "I don't think it's designed for reversing. But, that's not to say it couldn't with future modifications." He spoke in detail about the operation of the Navigation system, which was in constant use as long as the engines were running and the aircraft's flight plan was entered into the computer.

"If I need to, can we get together later?" Dan asked. "I appreciate the help, but we have to get back to our records review."

Dan shook his hand, but before he turned to leave Tim said, "I thought you were going to ask me about aircraft three-seventy-four."

Dan slowly stepped sideways. "What about three-seventy-four?"

Again, Tim gave the shoulder shrug. "The accident aircraft, right?"

"What about it?"

But Tim was already looking over his schematics; his elbows were on the table as he made some notes on the installation instructions. He looked up at the group.

"They installed SPAR in three-seventy-four two months ago."

John said simply, "To what operators has Transolutions sold their product to? Do you know?"

Tim stared at the ceiling and rattled off the names of several airlines, not one of them was Freestyle. John looked at Dan, waiting to see the light come on.

"Are you sure that's all of them?" John asked as Tim finished.

Tim simply nodded. "I'm positive; to my knowledge that's an accurate list."

Dan said out loud, "Well that saved us some time. Thanks Tim."

On the walk to the van, John and Dan argued about any connection between Transolutions and the accident.

"But what if SPAR *is* somehow involved?"

"First of all," John said, "SPAR has been heavily tested for two years on active flights, and that's after three years of bench tests. You're saying the first time it does this is now?"

"John, at this point we can't prove that it didn't trigger it."

Dan did not want to go off on tangents, but there was something Aaron did not say about SPAR the other day. When they got back to the office, Dan lagged behind; he speed-dialed Aaron's cell number in Memphis. "Hey Bubba," Aaron said after the first ring. "Whatcha got goin' out there in Denver? Find anything good?"

"I don't know Aaron, but maybe you can help me."

"Well, seeing as you're calling yours truly and not your Double eye-C, I'll assume you don't want him to know about this."

"No," Dan laughed into the receiver, "not just yet. Can you ask your engineer buddies to find out how far Freestyle is from implementing SPAR?"

"SPAR? You're talking at least a year from now, Danny."

Dan winced at the name 'Danny.' He lowered his voice considerably. "Just do me a favor and see what they're doing. And can you get me a copy of the schematics or the wiring diagrams for it?"

There was a small pause. "I'll see what I can do, but they keep their investments pretty close to the vest. I mean everybody does these days."

"I understand," Dan replied, "and maybe I'm wrong. But at this point I'd feel better if I can eliminate something." He turned off his phone and looked across to the hangar thinking: *What happens when the computer makes a mistake?*

CHAPTER 14
BACK IN MEMPHIS

Memphis

Chris was having some problems in the Mississippi River Valley. He called his wife; she was not handling her medication well. The good news was that Megan was on her way over to take command of the patient from his mother-in-law. On that front he could relax a bit.

However, the summer humidity in Memphis was driving his sinuses crazy. A splitting headache had settled in and he felt as though an expanding sphere of pain were placing pressure points on his already raw nerves.

Ron insisted everyone wear their full hazardous – or HAZ – suits, including facemasks; the dark porous material drank in the sunlight, transmitting the suffocating heat to the body.

Chris managed to get to a drug store the previous night where he emptied the shelf of his favorite allergy medicine. Before he put his hazardous mask on he tossed back two more allergy pills and washed it down with half a bottle of water.

Warm and muggy weather intruded on Memphis with a vengeance; the heat index passed one hundred and fourteen degrees with no relief for hours. Working the dark tarmac was akin to trudging through a hot skillet; the humidity settled in over the field and the surrounding city like a hot, damp blanket. A pungent reek of burnt plastic and rubber enveloped the fuselage in the still air; the odor attached itself to everything, seeping into the clothes and pores of the investigators.

Sunlight diffused through the haze, reflecting through the moisture making it difficult for the eyes to see distances, making them ache with the effort. A steady stream of FedEx freighters landed in sequence on the parallel runways 18-left and 18-center. Commuter airliners taxied past, their curious passengers stared wide-eyed, pointing at the recovery through the windows.

As Chris walked toward the center section he noted that Runway 18-right had suffered great abuse during the accident; large scars were carved into the concrete. Normally light grey in color, Runway 18-right now looked like a war-torn path. Burrows were etched out by the violent aircraft breakup as its kinetic energy was exhausted. Black uneven spots spread from the forward and aft fuselage sections marking the aftermath of the inferno.

The different aeronautical investigators crawled around the ruins of the airliner. All small pieces of structure had been identified, removed and their locations marked on a debris field layout. The Engines group finished cataloguing the site and was packing the two engines for tear-down at Sonic's facility.

The two main gears were splayed out in a macabre display, like a headless bird of prey with shattered legs. Chris knew what he wanted to find; he was combing through what had been the left wheelwell in the middle section of the broken airframe searching for the ground sense switch for the left main landing gear. The GSS was not attached to the gear, but had been forcefully separated, nor was Chris having luck in the wheelwell. The switch was nowhere to be seen.

That morning Chris met with his team before dinner to review some drawings he received late in the afternoon for the Autoland system. The team spent several hours locked in the FAA conference room studying exploded views of the schematics. Now, they were looking for components likely consumed by the fire.

Jim Hughes, the Structures investigator, and his team were busying themselves beneath the belly of the nose section. Five people in his group were now taking turns staring up through where the nose gear shoved its way into the flight deck. The AeroGalactic engineer took pictures, for professional reasons, since the catastrophic departure of the nose gear from its mount raised questions. She wanted to determine what AeroGalactic would need to do to reinforce the structure.

As Chris stood up to stretch his back out, he glanced over at Jim standing by the bulkhead where the flight attendants Doreen and Luke sat. Chris liked working with Jim; he never kept his findings secret as some investigators did. It was Phil's practice to cultivate a paranoid work environment at the NTSB, rewarding those who squirreled away the media-grabbing surprises and delivering them to him personally. Chris and Jim believed on the equal distribution of data because fact-checking was just *that* important. Too many times someone delivered their information as a present to Phil only to find that their story was poorly verified, making them infamous in front of the press.

As Chris stared at the nose section, questions from the schematic intruded on his contemplation. The wiring diagram showed the main gear ground sense switch was integral to the Autoland system, but alone would not drive the reversers. It had been so long since Chris had dealt with anything as extraordinary as a reverser deployment in flight that he was not thinking clearly. But now he was dealing with two within weeks of each other. There had to be something else.

As Chris massaged his forehead, he looked up in time to see a FedEx MD-11 flare several hundred yards away. He admired the less-than-graceful appeal of the tri-jet as it floated down to earth. But as the MD-11 touched down it seemed the #2 reverser slid back a split second before the nose gear touched down; the wing engines followed with a similar roar as their reversers deployed.

Why did it do that?

A thought occurred to him, one that had eluded him for the last few hours. *That's weird; it almost looked like the number two reversed first. Why don't the wing engines deploy at the same time as the number two?*

Chris rubbed feverishly at his temples trying to drive the pain back.

Freestyle's number two reverser deployed in flight, but not the wing engines. But technically both of Gyrfalcon's wing engine reversers deployed in flight.

Chris said softly to himself, "Do the wing engines on the four-fifty-C answer to the same ground sensor as the number two engine?"

He slapped his forehead. "We have another problem!"

"Chris!" Artie Sloan, the Gyrfalcon rep on his team called to him as he approached. "Were you looking for this?"

Chris smiled as Artie held out the ground sense switch that, except for some sheared off mount bolts, was in good condition. Half of the upper rod was twisted off and the bottom rod was missing, barring its attach bolts.

"You know I am, Artie. Good find. Where was it?"

"About fifty yards away, over there in the grass. Looks like it departed the gear early on. Good luck for our team now that we have something to look at."

"You got that right."

Chris's attention went back to Jim Hughes at the front section, under the flight deck. He noticed something Jim was playing with; something that caught Chris's interest even from this distance. Without a word to Artie, Chris sprinted to the nose section to ask Jim a favor.

CHAPTER 15
FUEL ON THE FIRE

Denver

At five o'clock the team broke up for the night. Dan made his way back to his room, glad for some time to cycle some ideas. The first day was unproductive; the second day promised to be better, but that was not what Dan had been spending the last forty-five minutes arguing with himself about.

He needed to talk to the mechanics; it was important to establish if maintenance was the cause. He knew Phil would start throwing blame towards someone and the mechanics seemed most likely, in order to divert attention from the Freestyle incident.

The odds that even a mis-adjustment during maintenance could have caused a double deployment were slim. His responsibility as the maintenance investigator: verify the mechanics were not culpable. Phil's job would be to incite a media assault, which would make Dan's job difficult.

Dan's cell began its annoying warble.

"Dan Ten ... ace?" asked a woman's voice over the receiver, pronouncing the 'c' like an 's'. It sounded as if she were trying to read the name off a card.

"Ten-ah-chay, C-H, as in Charlie." Dan corrected the caller. "Who is this?"

"I'm sorry," the voice came back again. "Um, this is Sarah Wallace. I'm the rep from Sonic Engines."

"Miss Wallace …"

"Sarah's fine."

"Okay, are you getting into Denver tonight?"

She cleared her throat. "No, I'm already here. In fact, I'm staying at your hotel. My flight got in an hour ago."

"Excellent. Do me a favor and meet us in the lobby at about six-thirty, 'cause we're going some place to eat."

"Yeah, no problem," came the reply. "I'll meet you in about an hour."

Dan threw the cell on the bed and turned on the news. The attractive news anchor, young and blond, took the hand-off from her co-anchor; she began by opening with the story on everyone's mind today: the aircraft accident in Memphis. She updated her listeners on the latest details surrounding the investigation, cutting to their reporter on scene from their station affiliate in Memphis.

The reporter looked seriously into the camera as he spoke about the afternoon news conference with Board member, the Honorable Dick Baier. It was Member Baier's turn to launch on an accident, he explained. The reporter then prattled on about the NTSB.

Dan saw Chris in the background standing on the remains of the left wing. The picture cut to two older film clips: one showing Ron carrying the black boxes and a second, the fire fighters extinguishing the last flames.

Dan's cell phone rang and he reached across the bed. Chris's name showed up clearly in the display window. "Paisan, what's up?"

Chris was half-listening to something his team members were discussing, before the voice across the country grabbed his attention. "Dan, how're you doing out there?"

"It was kinda slow today, but I'm planning some interviews. Is Ron near you?"

"No, he's at the press conference filling Baier in on the day's discoveries," Chris replied. "Listen Dan, I don't think it was the main gear switch; at least not *just* the main gear switch."

Dan muted the television. "But, isn't the switch what feeds the Autoland?"

Chris walked over to get a clear view of the diagram. The section of schematic that had been faxed to Memphis was enlarged for easy reading. A new wire path was highlighted with a green marker. "We're forgetting this wasn't *exactly* like Freestyle; similar, yet very different." Dan did not respond, so Chris continued. "The number two deployed on Freestyle, but not the wing engines. That tail reverser deployed because it's designed to assist in slowing the aircraft in Autoland, but only with weight on the main gear struts.

"But not the wing engines' reversers." Chris paused for a moment, referencing the schematic. "The wing engine reverser doesn't deploy on a cue from the main gear switch; they respond to the nose gear switch instead. Now, Gyrfalcon didn't have a tail engine; its reversers deployed in flight because they sensed weight on the *nose* gear."

"So, you're saying we may have a dual problem? One with the main gear switch and one with the nose gear switch?"

"So far," Chris said, tracing his finger along the diagram.

"What are the chances the two switches are connected?"

"Not a chance," Chris surmised. "The only common thread is that they both feed the flight command computers when they're activated; first the main gear and then the nose. No, I'd say they're isolated from one another."

Dan considered this; Chris's timing proved convenient. He was confounded by the reverser question himself. "I'm going to talk to the mechanics tomorrow about the last reverser inspection."

"Okay."

"I'm watching you on TV tripping over your own feet. How's the weather?"

"I feel like my head's gonna explode!"

"My sympathies, Buddy. Memphis is unforgiving when it comes to allergies. Will you be on the morning call?"

Chris blew his nose loudly. "Yeah, I'll be on it. I'll talk to you then."

Dan hung up and raised the volume on the news where the accident was still being discussed. He went to flip the channel when the senior anchor cut live to Washington where their DC correspondent was attending Board Member Vincent Scalia's press conference concerning the accident. Dan sat back down, a low moan escaped him.

Dan recognized the hangar interior; the FAA jet sat in the background, having just returned from Memphis. Normally news crews never saw inside of the hangar, but Vince 'the Maverick' Scalia was calling a press conference. Cameras and microphones littered the screen representing all the major networks. It was obvious to

Dan that this press conference was outside the domain of the NTSB.

Vince stood at the podium reading over some prepared notes, his glasses hanging precariously on the edge of his large nose. Dan rubbed at the knot in his stomach and sighed; he admired Scalia's natural presence in front of the cameras. Vince stalled for dramatic effect and the room went silent. Cameras flashed, and Dan was sure he saw a gleam reflect off the Board Member's teeth. Vince whipped off his glasses and stared directly into the center cameras. "I'd like to speak about this horrible accident in Memphis. First, let me say that the condolences of my colleagues and I go out to the victims' families." Again, he paused, referring to his notes.

"I've been analyzing the information collected. As many of you know I have a background in aircraft maintenance, so there's a great interest in this accident from my perspective. Initially, I believed this to be maintenance related. But this situation has been seen before; reversers deploying in flight."

A frenzy of questions followed. Dan knew the conference was going exactly in the direction Vince wanted. He baited the media, testing the waters to make sure they were listening. But Vince did not say things gratuitously; no, he had a point to make ... whatever that would be.

"A previous fatal accident was different in that it was a single deployment on a twin-engine aircraft – one engine deployed, not two. It was also overseas and outside the Board's jurisdiction. I'm exploring the possibility that that accident wasn't a lone event.

"But the data that I have here," he paused again, holding his notes up, "is about the AeroGalactic product specifically. I'm tying this accident to another unreported incident last month. It seems the Board has been sitting on information that may or may not have prevented this accident …" Vince hesitated; sounds of surprise interrupted him. He waited a good minute and then forged on.

"Let me clarify, we're not positive what the cause was, but our maintenance investigator – who is now in Denver – was working diligently on an incident that occurred several weeks ago in Los Angeles. His efforts were interrupted, but they may have prevented this accident."

Dan ran his hand down across his face and sighed deeply. He felt a dry heave rising and tasted the acidic taste of bile on the back of his tongue. He switched off the TV and went about getting dressed for dinner.

The restaurant was typical of the day; a steakhouse offering the common staples with a Hispanic theme. The lingering aroma of cooked steaks and assorted spices wafted through setting all patrons' imaginations into action. The bustle of waiters and diners contributed to the energetic mood within.

John was running late but Randy met them at the restaurant. Dan introduced him to Sarah Wallace, the Sonic engineer, who was about twenty-eight years of age. She had fair skin and red hair that was tied in a ponytail. A conservative dresser, Sarah took her job seriously, even putting Clay on defense out of a fear of being out-engineered.

They were shown to a corner table Dan had reserved; the seating offered some seclusion from the bustling main dining area. Dan took stock of their location, mentally noting the proximity of tables. As soon as everyone was seated the young waitress approached; she took drink orders after passing out menus and was gone.

Dan lowered his voice, addressing everyone at the table. "We need to keep a low profile while we're here. Do you remember those old E.F. Hutton commercials where everyone would stop talking to listen in on a conversation? That'll happen here."

Shrugging, Sarah lowered her voice, "Why? What're we doing that's so secret?"

"It's just best," Dan whispered, "for us not to attract attention."

"Hey Dan," John's voice carried over the diners across the room. He walked up to the table chuckling, "I saw your boss on TV."

He stopped behind Dan's chair; his voice remained loud and clear as he addressed the rest of the team. "Tell me, is there anything Member Scalia won't say when putting the slap down on the NTSB?"

Dan shut his eyes to lock out the sudden attention he acquired; the looks the table now received were mixed with sidebars and finger-pointing from the other patrons. Some more informed patrons recognized the names 'Scalia' and 'NTSB' to mean that Dan was the investigator Scalia mentioned; he was here to investigate the accident in Memphis.

Dan glanced at Sarah, who became painfully aware of the glances and body language of the other customers; conversations at neighboring tables suddenly got quieter as if a juicy detail might slip by unheard.

John was not ignorant of what his performance produced; a wicked smile replaced the usual lopsided grin. He took the chair across from Dan, who stared fuming. It was obvious the FAA inspector had not called all this attention by accident.

"Thanks John," Dan said, gesturing to Sarah, "for making my point for me. You know …" he leaned across the table, "the one about keeping a low profile."

"Don't mention it," John replied impudently. He simultaneously waved over the waitress while studying the menu. "By the way, Aaron says, 'Hey!'"

As dinner progressed, everyone gave a brief history of themselves. John and Randy spoke of getting their education and experience on the hangar work floor; both hired onto an airline straight out of A&P school, turning wrenches for a better part of their career. Though he did not add anything, Dan encouraged them to talk about their past in the airlines so the team could become familiar with each other.

Clay, a graduate of Carnegie Mellon in Pittsburgh, was recruited by AeroGalactic right after receiving his graduate degree; he is responsible for engineering avionic systems improvements and safety modifications.

Sarah had joined Sonic engines after three years with Pratt and Whitney. She was responsible for fuel modifications to the Sonic S-75HB engine, found on the AeroGalactic KR-350Y.

Where Clay danced on the fence between tact and diplomatic recklessness, Sarah kept to herself through dinner; she preferred to find her niche in this, her first accident investigation assignment, by maintaining a low profile.

Dan sipped his iced tea. "Sarah," he said, "you and Clay have experience writing maintenance steps or creating maintenance instruction workcards for mechanics. The problem may turn out to be how the mechanics interpret your data. That's where frequent breakdowns in the system occur."

Sarah asked, "How much emphasis does the NTSB place on maintenance in accidents?"

John said, "A serious look at maintenance is a new game. Mechanics like Dan were never employed by the Board, so the investigators who drew the short straws didn't understand what they were looking at. Since they got serious about maintenance, matters like management, shift schedules, and training are getting a better look-see. I'd say maintenance issues are being taken more seriously."

Dan thought for a moment. "It's according to the accident. I'd say it's equal to the Board's regular go-to blame line: pilot error."

John, a private pilot, physically cringed and waved his hand to ward off Dan's point. Sarah smiled at his reaction. "No, seriously," Dan continued. "The concept of 'pilot error' is a misnomer. How many accidents really apply to pilot error? Maybe one-tenth of one percent? Perhaps higher in your average General Aviation accident and that might be due to a lack of experience." John looked over at Dan, who added, "Present company excepted, of course. Other than one or two major accidents I don't give much credibility to pilot error."

Clay was finishing his steak. "What do you blame pilot accidents on?"

"Well, I think two things: one is unfamiliarity with the aircraft or its performance. And two would be events beyond their control."

Randy asked, "But isn't unfamiliarity pilot error?"

"That's true," John said, "but aircraft have come a long way. These days planes are better designed to fly out of many situations; they have redundant systems that make pilot intervention almost irrelevant, even in general aviation. But, I'm afraid we're designing the pilot out of the aircraft."

Sarah turned back to Dan: "What's beyond the pilot's control?"

"Well, there are a few things such as metal fatigue, system breakdowns and maintenance."

John swallowed the last of his beer and asked Dan after a mild belch. "Are you referring to the accident where the elevators were out of rig?"

"No, but that's a good example." He turned back to Sarah. "A regional airliner crashed because the mechanics mis-rigged the elevators. The pilots tried to force the nose over, but the elevators were hitting against their stops. The aircraft stalled and fell back to earth shortly after takeoff."

"Well, I think we're lucky you Feds are here to fix the problem," Clay said.

Dan and John looked at each other and smirked. Dan shook his head and smiled quietly. "What makes you think government is the answer?"

"Well ... well," Clay stuttered, "that's your job."

John spoke up, "Yeah, we do serve a purpose. But in many ways, it's the government that *is* the problem. We shouldn't tell you how to fix your planes. We should work *with* you to fix it. Industry makes the fixes; we just make sure that industry does it to begin with."

"Look, Clay," Dan said, "I know you think the NTSB is filled with aviation experts who can break any airplane down to the rivet, but that's just not true. The NTSB has limited expertise ... *very* limited expertise. That's why we have you on the team, to fill in the blanks for us."

"But when we find the cause," Sarah asked, "don't the Feds put the fix in place?"

"As for the NTSB, we're a powerless government agency; we make recommendations, but we don't change the rules." Dan pointed at John. "That's what the FAA does; they work with industry to make changes."

John added, "And changes aren't generated by the FAA. I mean we act in emergencies, but industry modifies their products or services." John lowered his voice, "Industry usually makes the changes to what they produce. The FAA enforces those changes on AeroGalactic, Gyrfalcon, Sonic, or even ourselves."

"But why can't the NTSB force industry to change?"

"To begin with, Sarah," Dan replied, "we can only recommend – or advise – nothing more. The problem with the Board is – and I can speak to this – is as I said: the experience level isn't very high. More importantly the Board doesn't work one-on-one with the particular airlines. They aren't involved in the daily ins and outs, and they don't come into contact with people like the FAA does."

"Why can't you write specific regulations?" Randy queried.

John said, "Randy, did you ever teach someone to drive?"

"I taught my younger brother."

"Okay, imagine for a moment writing out those instructions for every single thing your brother did. How detailed would you have to get? And don't get me started on a manual transmission versus automatic, or a Ford and a Maserati; that sort of thing. You'd have to say ... adjust this mirror ... which way to turn the key ... how to put it in reverse, etcetera.

"You know flying an airplane or running an airline is more complicated than driving a car; the different situations are countless. A regulation would have to capture all those situations ... in all those different aircraft ... in all those different airlines."

"But can't you just apply it to the one airline in question?"

"No, because the regulations weren't written for just one or two airlines," Dan interjected. "If the FAA did that there wouldn't be an airline flying that could stay in business. Besides, an airline doesn't make money flying its fleet into the ground, so there's that incentive to be safe."

"But if you feel that government makes the world safer and that we should have more control, then take it from Dan and me when I say," John added, waving for the checks, "be careful what you ask for ..."

CHAPTER 16
MEETINGS AND MARCHING ORDERS

August 14th

Dan had just stepped out of the shower when he heard his pager sing out to him from across the room. As he picked it up he saw Giv's name displayed in the window.

Dan scrolled through the message: a meeting in ten minutes, one he was required to call in on. He rubbed his face in exasperation; a Phil meeting where the micromanager-in-charge would assign directions to each investigator. Phil usually garnered what information he could, then 'solve' the mystery in glorious fashion.

Dan called the communications center in Washington, DC; this was the NTSB nerve center with its collective fingers on the worldwide pulse; it guaranteed first reaction to the next accident no matter which mode it occurred in.

Dan heard a series of tones as his call passed through the microcosms that are the NTSB phone lines. Invisible alleyways opened up and Dan's call came to a screeching halt in the domain of Phil's conference room.

"You're on the conference call," Connie announced into a speaker.

"Hey Connie; it's Dan. How're you doing?"

"Pretty good ... Mister Tenace. How's Denver?"

Uh oh, Dan thought. *She said Mister. That's not good.*

Connie had her own code to alert her IIC group that they were persona non-grata; she used the same code, employing the formal 'mister' only to warn Dan that Phil had it out for him; it was most likely because of Vince's stunt. Dan figured as much.

Before Dan could reply to Connie, she cut him off, "Stand by–"

Ron Gebbia piped in on another line. As the IIC, he represented the gathered investigators in Memphis sitting in a FAA conference room.

The DC conference room noticeably hushed as Phil entered taking his seat at the head of the table. Papers rustled over the sensitive microphones and someone cleared his throat. Phil immediately went after Dan.

"Tenace, are you on?"

Dan did not hesitate. "Right here, Phil."

"Where's that list you were supposed to send me?"

The line went quiet as Dan sat puzzled in his hotel room. Connie knowingly shook her head inconspicuously and a smile creased the corners of her mouth.

"Um ... what list is that, Phil?"

Phil searched across the table for Giv, who averted his eyes. Phil's brow furrowed. "You requested a court stenographer for interviews; did you not?"

"Yes; that's normal procedure."

"Where's the list of candidates you want to interview?"

Dan replied, "I didn't know you wanted a list, Phil. I can get you one, but I need a few hours to speak with their management."

Phil's eyes shot to Giv who melted into his chair. Phil held him in his gaze for a moment before releasing him. "Make it happen, Tenace. I want a list."

"Dan, who are you interviewing?" Connie asked.

"John Matero and I talked about this last night–"

"Who's John Matero? Giv, who's John Matero?" Phil interrupted.

Giv snapped to attention. "I think John Matero is the FAA rep out there. He's assigned to work–"

This time Phil could not refrain from raising his voice, "I don't want any FAA goons running this investigation! This is a Board investigation! Do you understand?"

In Memphis, Ron's head bowed to his chest; several FAA inspectors in the room shifted uncomfortably in their seats. Chris muted the line and said sarcastically, "That's our boss! We apologize; he must be off his medication."

In DC, those sitting around the conference room table moved nervously in their seats – except Connie. She continued to stare casually at her notepad oblivious to anything but what she was writing.

"I asked you if you understood, Tenace?"

"Oh, you were talking to me?" Dan's voice came over the phone with a hint of sarcasm. "I thought you were still yell–, I mean ... talking ... to Giv. What was the question again?"

Phil seethed at the disdain; his mouth worked sideways, grinding his teeth.

"Dan, I'm flying out tonight to sit in with you on the interviews," Quint spoke into the uncomfortable silence. "Is there anything I need to know before I get there or anything I need to bring?"

Phil looked down at the table and inhaled deeply before throwing a warning glance at Quint. The Human Factors division manager ignored Phil but sat still, pen in hand, to write down any needs Dan may suggest. Connie chanced a fleeting look at Quint and their eyes locked for a brief moment. She provided a slight nod of the head and mentally told herself to get with Quint later.

"Why are *you* going out to Denver?" Phil asked tightly.

Quint looked away as he laid out his plan. "I don't have anybody free right now to send down." Phil began to protest, but Quint continued. "I've worked with Dan before. He and I think alike when it comes to chasing questions to the root."

Quint reached over and muted the speaker closest to him, which silenced all the microphones. "I know you don't approve of Dan, but he's really good at what he does. He gets to the core of the maintenance issues like no one else can." Before Phil could respond, Quint turned the microphones on again.

Dan was answering, unaware of the temporary quiet. "I can't think of anything off hand. Quint, I don't think the guys in the hangar are the problem. It seems to me the answers are more ... obscure."

"What do you mean, obscure?"

But Dan raised his voice, "Chris and Ron, are you both on?"

They answered in unison to the affirmative.

"Okay Quint," Dan continued, "I've been over the maintenance instructions for the engine reversers on the dash three-fifty with the systems engineer, Clay Brinnel. Sonic faxed their maintenance procedures for the engines yesterday afternoon. We sat down and compared the task cards against the two manufacturers' approved procedures; they are, for the most part, identical. If we pursue this, implying they didn't follow the procedures as dictated, then it's not Maintenance."

Ron asked, "Why is that?"

"All right," Dan continued, "the engines are serviced in teams of two. That means each engine has two mechanics working the task cards for the reversers. If two mechanics worked the number one engine and then two separate mechanics worked the number two. That means two different people would be dropping the ball for each engine."

"So, then they all messed up when it came to reading the directions," Giv pointed out as he blew his nose, wishing to be included in the conversation.

"Giv," Dan said, "if that were true, how can four different people make the exact same mistake? The odds of that happening rise exponentially the more people you add to the mix. Remember, the reversers reacted simultaneously and in an identical way."

"But," Giv continued, "you said two engines. It's likely to be a coincidence."

"Yeah, but there were four different people," said Quint emphasizing the point by holding up four fingers. "The odds are too great; I see what he's saying. Also, it would be impossible to prove when you get four different stories from over a month ago."

Phil leaned over into the microphone. "Is that the only reason?"

Ignoring Phil, Chris called out, "Satya, is it safe to say that the reversers didn't act alone?"

Satya Gangi, a shy engineer who read the flight data recorders, was sitting quietly next to Connie and was startled from the mental oasis she had relaxed in until hearing her name. Connie leaned over and helped her spread the recorder's readouts across the table where they traced the timeline leading up to and following the accident. Satya found the moment in time and looked at Connie. She turned to Phil and said uncharacteristically loud enough for all to hear, "The ground spoilers also deployed."

Chris repeated Satya's words, "The ground spoilers also deployed."

"So, what?" Giv spat the words out.

Dan continued Chris's thought. "The ground spoiler panels are out on top of the wings. For one, they're in a totally separate system from the reversers. And for two they only lift up together for one reason: to disrupt lift during landing."

"And," Chris threw in, "they react to the same electronic trigger as the reversers. If the reversers were out of rig, the spoilers wouldn't have been affected; they never would have actuated. They don't control each other."

"It isn't limited to the reversers," Quint said matter-of-factly.

Phil leaned in again. "Is that what happened on the Freestyle flight in June?"

Dan responded, "We don't know if the ground spoilers came up."

"So," Phil continued, unable to contain his annoyance any longer, "the issue Scalia made a stink about yesterday on the news doesn't apply here! That whole circus that you and Scalia dreamed up to mock the Board, Tenace, was a mistake! Do you have any idea what damage that did to our office?"

"I didn't dream anything up with Vince," Dan said defensively. "What he did, well ... he did that on his own!"

But Phil was not so easily pacified. "Your history here shows that you go running to him every time you have a problem! You're telling me you didn't plan that with him?"

Connie started to say, "Phil, maybe this isn't the time …" but Phil cut her off with a wave of his hand.

Dan took his time to reply. "I talked to Vince after the Freestyle event because he asked me. I was vague about what happened or what I was looking into."

"You mean to tell me …"

"Look Phil," Dan interrupted, "Don't take my word for it. Go ask him yourself!"

"How do I know you two aren't trying to steer attention away from your mechanic friends? How seriously are you looking at their involvement?"

Ron came to Dan's defense. "That's not fair, Phil! You know Dan hasn't interviewed anybody yet. He's not even done with the records."

Phil stared hard at the microphone as if he could crawl through the wires. He inhaled rapidly, calming himself too late for common sense. Eyes across the table began to catch his; the tendency to look away in intimidation was no longer there.

Neil, the operations manager leaned over the table and said, "Stand by everybody," before muting the phones. "Phil, I didn't come here to listen to you cut Tenace down. Now … if you have issue with him then you better work it out and stop wasting my time." Phil's eyes bulged in indignation, but he swallowed any response.

"Are you done?" Phil managed a nod and the phones were reactivated. "We're back."

"I think I've proved the two events have nothing to do with each other," Phil expostulated.

But Neil countered. "That's not true. The fact that reversers deployed in both cases alone is reason enough to compare them."

"But," Phil continued now looking to win the argument, "what about the ground spoilers? How do you account for the fact that the spoilers didn't activate on Freestyle?"

Chris reiterated, "We don't know the ground spoilers didn't deploy. We'd have to look at the flight recorders to verify it. Ask Satya to review the Freestyle tapes."

Giv, hoping to salvage some of the offensive said, "These are both AeroGalactic aircraft. That being said, the aircraft have similar systems. If the dash four-fifty didn't react like the three fifty then the incidents are unrelated."

Chris said, "Giv, you can't compare them apples to apples. These are two very different aircraft. There are two engines on one aircraft and three engines on the other; therefore, the engine systems themselves are different. We have to look at the disparities and what drives one to act differently from the other." There were several other investigators in Memphis voicing their agreements. "Who knows? There might be something else going on we haven't even considered yet."

Neil sat across from Connie who still sat as if unconcerned with the conversation. He knew Connie rarely got caught up with the discussion until she wanted to. Instead she sat stoically by as the two opposing forces wasted their energies verbally punching each other. For all Neil knew, she was calmly composing her Christmas wish list. Curiosity got the best of him and he asked with a sly grin, "Connie, why are you so quiet?"

Connie was not so much surprised out of her thoughts as annoyed that someone dragged her in too early. She looked left and right, noticing that all eyes were now upon her. Everyone – but Phil – was anticipating her response. She placed her pen carefully down upon the table and allowed the tension to pull in several directions.

"Well, Neil," she paused. "I'd think that Chris is still gathering data from the systems question." She raised her voice, "Chris, is there something else you want to share?"

Ron's laugh came across the speakers as he watched Chris shake his head. Ron said, "As a matter of fact, I think Chris has the most useful information so far. I was kinda hoping, Connie, that you or someone else would ask that question."

Chris said, "The AeroGalactic team member said that the dash three-fifty doesn't deploy reversers and spoilers unless the nose gear is on the ground."

Phil barked, "What is that supposed to mean?"

Chris answered, "They do not deploy when the mains touch the ground. They can only deploy when the nose gear touches down."

Connie spoke evenly, "Just spell it out, Chris."

"Well," he stated, "there's good news and bad news. The bad news is we've got two problems. You see, since the spoilers deployed a bad signal was sent not only through the ground sense switch on the main gear but also through the switch on the nose gear. We have, to begin with, two bad switches on the aircraft."

"When will you be able to confirm this?" Phil asked barely being heard.

Dan responded, "I'll look through the records and see if there's anything on the switches."

"Dan and I are planning tests at the manufacturers in two weeks," Chris said.

"Two weeks?" Giv squeaked.

Dan rejoined, "We're in Memphis and Denver for the next few days. If we leave now we may miss something. Besides it may take some time to set it up. They won't have a comparable aircraft sitting around."

Connie said, "Chris, you said there was good news. What was it?"

"Both incidents occurred while the aircraft was in Autoland; that's a crucial fact."

Neil leaned over the table and winked at Connie. He knew she would get to the root cause while her male counterparts wallowed in chest thumping irrelevance.

Neil cleared his throat and jumped in, "We need to petition the FAA to restrict the use of Autoland on *all* AeroGalactic aircraft until further notice. Autoland must be off the table right now, if not sooner."

"We should ground the AeroGalactic fleets." Phil threw out, "Why limit it just to Autoland?"

Neil shook his head slowly. "Look, we need to restrict use of Autoland until we can figure out where this problem exists. Anything else would be ridiculous. The last thing we need to do is strike fear in the traveling public with frivolous nonsense. We're positive that the airliners involved in both instances were set up for Autoland. I think the only restriction we can add would be to defer the reversers or the ground spoilers until further notice."

Dan's voice resounded over the speakers. "Neil, I don't think you can defer either one. I'd have to look at the Minimum Equipment List, but I'm sure there's no way to defer either both reversers or all the ground spoilers."

Phil pounded on the table. "How do *you* know that?! If the reversers need to be nullified then that's what Maintenance is going to have to do."

The people at the table and those on the phone took a collective breath. Neil, who had gone back to staring at his hand, rose from his chair and quietly exited the room. He directed a statement at Connie as he walked out the door, "Call me when we can have a serious conversation." And he was gone.

Connie discretely made a note, but stayed in her seat as the meeting uncomfortably continued. No one muted the phone before Neil departed. Phil settled back in his seat as the tension began to dissipate.

Ron piped in, "Dan's right. If you can't nullify the reversers and the spoilers then we can't go that route. I know he's got experience in this and I think we should pay attention to what he's saying. There's a method to the madness when it comes to eliminating systems from the normal means of scheduled flight."

Quint asked, "But will deferring the Autoland system prevent a repeat event?"

"I think you'd have to ask Chris about that. By configuring the airliner in Autoland you give it control over the landing systems. If the pilots rely on manual activation then the problem will be prevented. It'll give us time to find out why the gear switches are a problem."

Chris voiced an opinion before Phil could stop him. "My team and I will look harder at the schematics; that includes the system schematics as well as the wiring diagrams. But as of right now, that seems to be where we're focused." He took a breath. "I recommend that we have the Certification offices at the FAA and the AeroGalactic's engineers look at the same things we are and offer opinions within the next two hours. I'd really appreciate their feedback. In the meantime, I suggest we cooperate with the FAA and get the Autoland deactivated immediately."

Phil leaned into the table. "I remind you that this is our investigation and that we need to make the decisions on what needs to be done."

Quint did not care anymore about tarnishing the NTSB image. "I, for one, am not concerned with who makes the decision as long as we get these planes fixed."

Dan took his cue from Quint's comment and pushed on. "I already spoke to Aaron Campo about Chris's concerns with the Autoland. The FAA probably started nullifying the Autoland yesterday. Ron, you should be hearing from him today."

Phil turned a deeper purple. Connie defused any further argument by speaking into the microphone, "Ron, let us know what goes on when you talk to Aaron and we'll get things moving on our end. If there's nothing else, this meeting's adjourned." And before Phil could object she disconnected the outside world from the conference room.

Phil sat deflated; his control now rendered impotent. Although others around the table still did not meet his eyes, their confidence was raised by the dethroning of the king. Connie continued to write on her notepad and Quint began to gather his effects up; with a slight gesture to Connie to call him later, Quint left. One by one the attendees slowly made their way out. Connie sat unaware of the retreating managers as she spoke quietly to Satya, who nodded twice and left. Even Giv chose the heavy calm to exit.

Connie returned to her notes and allowed the silence between her and Phil to speak loudly. If she cared, she would have felt Phil's stare boring deeply into her skull from his ferret like eyes. Finally, she clicked her pen closed and with a sweep of the table gathered her belongings and left. Before departing she said the name 'Phil' in acknowledgement of his presence before turning the corner and disappearing down the hall.

Phil remained seated for a long time.

CHAPTER 17
GROUND WORK

Washington – Two days ago the Federal Aviation Administration released a directive to all domestic airlines and an advisory to all foreign carriers overseas to negate the Autoland systems on all AeroGalactic aircraft until further notice. These actions were taken in response to the Gyrfalcon accident in Memphis, TN. Further research is being conducted into the reliability of the AeroGalactic ground sense switches to determine their integrity. Alerts that speak to these design questions were sent to all AeroGalactic equipment operators advising them of the orders and …

Memphis

The objective in designing aircraft to be self-reliant is safety, driven by economic benefits. The safety theory: aircraft computers respond faster and more accurately to conditions inside and outside the aircraft. They give the pilot more opportunity to manage the aircraft. The economic theory: decrease the number of pilots while streamlining fuel burn and flight times.

The economic benefits – not safety – dictate the discovery of new technologies. The quest for safety is often designed to meet the economic benefits.

In the Gyrfalcon accident there were no warning signs that could be picked up on the cockpit voice recorder aside from first officer Deke Chamberlain's surprised intake of air. Additionally, Gyrfalcon's flight data recorder was not yet programmed to sense when certain as-of-yet unauthorized equipment was being used. Economic benefits dictated there was no need for costly modifications; the recorders would eventually receive the proper software update.

But not yet.

Dan grabbed a cup of coffee at the hotel's breakfast bar and made for the car. He had to speak with the hangar manager about the interviews.

The hangar office was empty except for one mechanic sitting behind a desk with his feet up, sipping coffee. When Dan knocked, he let the investigator in the front door. "Do you know when the hangar manager gets here?" Dan asked, taking a seat.

The mechanic glanced at the clock, as his feet returned to their toes-up position. "Chip gets in about eight, give or take. Can I get you something?"

"No, thanks. Dan Tenace by the way."

"Jay Connelly." They shook hands. "You're investigating the accident?"

"Yeah," Dan said, looking at his watch. "We're going through the maintenance records now."

"Well, you don't think it was something somebody here did, do ya?"

Dan thought the question a mix of caution, morbid curiosity, and fear; Jay was more the second than the other two. "Not at this point," Dan sipped his coffee.

"It's too early to say. It could be manufacturing, but nothing's jumping out at us."

Jay just nodded. He was stocky with a relaxed composure that complimented his self-confidence; a mechanic's mechanic; one who could figure out technical problems just by looking at them. His genial face had a touch of scrutiny to it while sporting a 'gotcha' smile.

The hangar manager, Chip, walked in the front door. Although young by management standards, he held an air of authority. Chip grabbed a schedule off the nearest desk and absent mindedly read through it unaware that Dan was sitting off to the side. "Well, it mustn't be too busy, Jay, seeing as you're spending the time I'm paying you, to do, I don't know ... nothing?"

"I was keeping the Board guy company for ya," Jay responded, removing his feet from the desktop. "You do want me to entertain the Feds while you're grabbin' donuts, right?"

Chip noticed Dan, annoyed that the investigator had been sitting outside his peripheral vision. His shoulders slumped noticeably, but he walked over and introduced himself. "I'm sorry, I usually get swamped with last night's problems, so I ..."

"No problem," Dan began, "I'm not here to check up on you. In fact, I need a favor; I need to interview the mechanics who worked the engines during the last maintenance check."

Chip gestured at Jay. "Jay, didn't you work one of those engines?"

"I think I did. I usually get the engines during the weekends."

I should've known, Dan thought.

Chip put down the schedule and grabbed a pad of paper. "Anything else?"

Well," Dan replied, gathering his notes. "I could use a conference room to conduct interviews in and a time when I can get all of your people together tomorrow."

"Okay then," Chip signaled Jay to get out to the hangar. "I'll get it set up for you. I can give you the conference room down the hall; it should be big enough for you. I'm guessing I should provide lawyers."

"Abso-tively! Call the lawyers, if for nothing more than peace of mind."

There is one area of investigation that can prove most informative, if not more interesting: Interviews. Normally three groups rely on interviews: Maintenance, Operations, and Air Traffic. For the Maintenance group conducting interviews was a new venture and Dan had been perfecting his techniques, providing a cornucopia of information about the airlines themselves.

"A friend of mine is flying in later today." Dan gazed at his team seated around a table off the hotel lobby. "His name is Quint Birnbaum and he's the Human Factors division manager."

John's eyes narrowed. "Why is a human factors guy coming here?"

"Though the five of us are conducting the interviews, Quint has a knack for cutting to the chase. He's the one who taught me the finer techniques of interviewing. Besides, if we need to move against AeroGalactic, I want a manager here."

Clay's head sprang up from his coffee. Sarah asked, "What do you mean, 'move against AeroGalactic'?"

"Well, in case we have to shut them down …"

"What …?"

"Well, now Dan," John interjected, ignoring Clay, "that's actually my job."

"Yeah, but we handle the media; investigator on sight, and all."

"Wait a minute, you can't just shut down an international manufacturer like that! Imagine the lawsuits, the bad press …" Clay launched himself out of his seat. "I have to call my boss!"

Both Dan and John stared evenly at Clay as he clambered to get out of the restaurant. John's arm reached out to snag Clay's wrist as he hurried by. "Excitable, isn't he?"

"Not to mention gullible."

As Clay sat down quietly, reburying his face in his coffee, Sarah asked, "What do you expect to get from the mechanics? I'm not convinced they did anything wrong."

Dan saluted Sarah with his coffee cup. "I agree, Sarah. I'm starting to believe it may be something post-manufacture and post-maintenance. This isn't the first reverser deployment in recent months."

Both Sarah and Clay reacted with surprise, but Dan kept going.

"The failure may not be built into the original AeroGalactic aircraft. I spoke to my office this morning; the theory du jour is it's the Autoland system."

Randy said, "Wouldn't that mean the manufacturer was at fault?"

John shrugged, "Not if the aircraft had been modified since it was built. I think AeroGalactic is definitely still on the table … sorry Clay," he said with a nod to the engineer. "We now have to determine what's been done to the aircraft since it was built. AeroGalactic does incorporate mods … months, even years after the plane is delivered."

"Key-rect!" Dan agreed. "Sarah and John, I'd like you to continue researching the airplane's history today. I'm gonna work with Randy and Clay on any non-warranty type modifications. My friend Chris is researching the GSS for redesigns." Sarah went to ask, but Dan beat her to it, "The ground sense switch; I'm sorry; I keep forgetting you guys weren't on the call this morning. We'll talk about it on the way over. So, if there's nothing else," to which everyone shook their heads, "let's get over to the hangar."

The history of the accident aircraft, registration number N374GY, was not a lengthy one; the manufacturing date was five years prior. As a result, any maintenance facts recorded on the aircraft were limited to heavy checks and occasional modifications brought about by improvements in technology. The boxes of historical maintenance documents were few, so the time to sort through them was cut by a third.

The aircraft's history was peppered with minor improvements that were not uncharacteristic; an airliner goes through many upgrades to keep up with technologies. Sarah made note that N374GY had the SPAR systems installed earlier; each separate component installed with its individual manufacturer's requirements was individually tested to meet FAA standards and installed independently during maintenance checks. The final SPAR component was installed two weeks earlier, in time for the fatal flight to Memphis.

Randy and Clay spent a good portion of the day at Gyrfalcon's engineering division retrieving wiring diagrams that reflected the latest electrical component changes in N374GY. A problem with technologically improving an aircraft is that the paperwork may not marry up with the modified aircraft as it rolls out for its first flight. The time lag between introduction and updating the paperwork rarely becomes an issue.

Except now.

Schematic copies in hand, Randy and Clay headed back to the hangar. "Clay, I don't understand why AeroGalactic doesn't have a copy of these wiring diagrams."

Clay was reviewing a wiring diagram in the passenger seat. "Well, we don't own the Supplemental Type Certificate for the modifications."

"Yeah, I never understood the connection between all these certificates."

Clay rolled the wiring diagram back up. "You see, that's why when a plane crashes, everyone automatically blames the manufacturer." He hung his cigarette out the van's window. "Okay, AeroGalactic owns the *Type* Certificate for the Three-fifty-Y; that's like Ford owning the patent on that sixty-nine Mustang you keep in your garage."

"No, actually I'm a Dodge Charger kinda guy."

Clay glared at Randy for a second, before shrugging his shoulders in surrender. He took a drag of his cigarette. "Okay, I didn't see that coming. All right, you have a Charger and you want to throw in a V-eight or a dual exhaust."

"Already got 'em."

Clay took a final drag before flicking the cigarette into the street. "Okay Randy, work with me. Let's say you install a stereo in the dash; obviously one that wasn't available when the car was built. Do you think Dodge wants copies of the stereo blueprints?"

Randy shook his head. "Well," Clay continued, "the stereo blueprints are like the *Supplemental* Type Certificate, the STC; it's a change you made to the original product. Like this SPAR stuff Tenace keeps going on about, AeroGalactic never designed or installed it; people like those Transolutions guys did. It's their product."

"Alright, I get that, but why doesn't AeroGalactic keep modifications made to its products. Do you just forget about the airliner after it rolls out?"

"We don't need to keep copies of the STC!" Clay leaned forward in his seat. "The big reason is an STC is proprietary. There are numerous STC improvements on every aircraft; they're investments made by companies or individuals with one primary objective: to make lotsa money with a new idea or a much-needed improvement.

"If I design a widget to make an aircraft fly further on less fuel I present my idea to someone willing to back me financially. Money and time are put forth to massage the widget idea, test it, redesign it and test it some more before it's made into a reality.

"Now, I take my new widget and sell it to whoever wants it. That new product belongs to me and my backers; it's ours! We own the STC! It would be unethical for AeroGalactic to expect me to turn over the plans to my idea. What's to stop them from stealing it? That's Capitalism."

When Clay and Randy arrived back at the office they heard Chris on speakerphone. He explained how four years earlier every AeroGalactic main and nose gear ground sense switch was redesigned. A new manufacturer in a third world country provided both switches for AeroGalactic where they were replaced on active airliners and installed during buildup on the assembly line.

Chris found there were problems with the redesigned switches, but nobody had been tracking its use because they were considered 'consumable' items; they were not repaired, but thrown away. In addition, there were problems with the circuits, but no one suspected the integrity of the switches' casings.

Ron Gebbia was required to report all new findings to Connie. Phil insisted on being present during all updates.

When he learned about the ground sense switches being modified, he leaked it to the media, who was hungry for any and all news surrounding the accident. By the next morning, AeroGalactic's switch design was touted as the most likely cause of the Memphis accident. As a result, AeroGalactic took center stage in the accident blame-game.

Phil had assured culpability was deflected from the NTSB and onto someone else.

Vince Scalia's revelation at the press conference was soon forgotten.

CHAPTER 18
INTERVIEWS

News Release: The National Transportation Safety Board has announced today that the investigation into the Gyrfalcon accident in Memphis, TN, has brought to light some early evidence that the landing gear may have been largely responsible for the disaster before impact. The initial analysis shows that a landing gear sensing switch on the gear sent a false signal to a computer on the aircraft that commanded it to deploy its engine reversers. Latest findings in this investigation by NTSB aviation specialists onsite in both Memphis and Denver have discovered that the switch mentioned was known to be faulty, according to initial findings. Further testing will be conducted in the next few weeks, but the NTSB is confident that this switch was the cause.

According to a statement released today by Philip Tulkinghorn, Director of Aerospace Safety at the NTSB, investigators are looking into whether the aircraft had been approved by the Federal Aviation Administration with this known fault. Allegations made by Mr. Tulkinghorn that the FAA has been consistently negligent in their pre-approval testing for aircraft, that the FAA is 'sleeping at the ...

August 15th – Denver

Quint sat slumped in a desk chair with a bad case of jet lag, his eyes sitting recessed in their sockets. A headache threatened his good mood.

While interviewing, Quint is not one to advertise his doctorate; instead he relies on his casual demeanor, less imposing techniques to turn a question, letting the interviewee relax into the interview. His easy-going nature is evident in his face, inquiring eyes coupled with an absurd smile.

"Quint, how do you want to handle this today?" Dan returned to the point.

"What feeling do you get from the hangar mechanics?"

Dan sat down and leaned back, his hands behind his head. "I've only met one or two, but from the paperwork we've read through I'd say they're doing their job.

"I don't think this was maintenance related, maybe the manufacturer ... in some way. But let's face it; I could get something on the airline from these guys if I drill down hard enough, but nothing to do with Memphis."

"You said you spoke to Chris last night. Anything new?"

"He and I don't think this was a switch problem."

"What makes you say that? It sounded like you found the culprit."

"You would think," Dan sighed. "It just doesn't feel right. I started to talk to one of their contractors about these new systems they're putting in. Look, AeroGalactic's had these faulty switches for years. But those switches won't actuate the reversers and spoilers on their own; they take their commands from computers up line. Besides it's too much of a coincidence that similar systems were recently installed on both the Gyrfalcon and the Freestyle aircraft."

"We can talk to the contractors another time. How's your group?"

"My team isn't gelling like usual. John from the FAA is good; Randy is a little closer to the workforce than I'd like. Now Sarah," he said, wagging his finger, "the Sonic rep is sharp, but she's thinking the airframe manufacturer is the bad guy. That leaves Clay, my AeroGalactic rep; I'm keeping my eye on him. If this thing goes where I think, he'll try diverting attention away from AeroGalactic to somewhere else."

"So, he may upset the mechanic interviews?"

"Perhaps, yeah."

"Okay, I'll keep him in mind. When are the interviews?"

Dan looked at his watch. "The interviews start at about nine."

The conference room Francine had reserved for the AMI team was small by standards; it held twelve chairs situated evenly around a large rectangular table made of light brown stained oak surrounded by black ergonomic chairs. The room was painted eggshell; normal conference room décor with a gold and brown carpet. Several pictures of Gyrfalcon's planes hung along the walls.

Francine left to bring in the court reporter; everyone took their places around the table with Dan and Quint positioned at the head of the table. Francine soon led a short gentleman to Dan; he carried a bag with his court recorder equipment inside.

"Ed Condren," he announced. "Where do you want me to set up?" Dan indicated the seat furthest from his and Ed began arranging his microphones.

"Francine," Dan said, "can you show Jay in please?"

Chip leaned near Dan, lowering his voice. "We have a lawyer to sit in on the interviews. It's either him or one of the managers."

Quint responded, "Actually we'd prefer the lawyer. Some guys get tight-lipped when the manager's in the room." Chip nodded knowingly and went to get the lawyer.

Jay Connelly walked in; he was dressed for work, rubbing steadily to remove something grey from his hands.

Chip returned with the lawyer, a young man dressed in a blue pin-striped suit. The man held out his hand, "Lawrence Castle, Mister Tenace. I'm a junior partner in the law firm that's representing Gyrfalcon."

"Do I call you Lawrence or Larry?"

"Larry's fine," he responded. "First names okay with everybody ... Dan?"

Dan nodded as he presented everyone. A microphone slid across the table, stopping in front of John. Dan sat down after gesturing to Francine and Chip to leave the room and close the door.

Once the tape started, Dan introduced the participants and their associated companies or government agencies. "These are aircraft maintenance interviews held at the Gyrfalcon headquarters in Denver, Colorado. My name is Dan Tenace; I'm the maintenance investigatory team's lead. The first interview is Jay Connelly, a hangar mechanic here in Denver. For the purposes of accuracy, we are recording these interviews and having them transcribed later." He looked at Jay. "Do you object to having this interview recorded?"

Jay shook his head. "No."

"Jay, you will be able to verify these transcripts when Mister Condren finishes typing them. You're being represented by legal counsel, Mister Lawrence Castle, who your company has retained for the purposes of these interviews. Larry, you are not yourself being questioned, therefore we ask that you be a silent counsel. You may ask us to stop recording at any time to consult with your client but you cannot answer for your client. I have to make sure you understand this."

"Understood." Larry held up his hand and Dan signaled Ed to stop the tape. "I confess I'm new to the aircraft accident investigation; I was asked to sit in since our senior lawyers were dispatched to Memphis. If I make a mistake in how I represent these mechanics, please forgive my lack of familiarity up front."

Ed sat with his hand on the switch waiting for Dan, who responded, "I appreciate that, Larry. I think Quint will back me up on this when I say these interviews are pretty routine; no hidden agendas. If you feel they get out of hand or you have a question, please feel free to request a break or time to speak off-line. That goes for everyone." He smiled at Larry before continuing. "Besides, we like lawyers." Larry looked confused.

"They taste just like chicken."

Quint shook his head as the others at the table smiled at the comment. Dan then motioned to Ed to start the tape again. "Let me further point out to you Jay how this will work. I'll begin with my questions followed by Quint; we'll then continue around the table to John. Then we'll begin another round, these being follow-up questions to our own or some that may have been raised from one of the others.

"At this point I'm giving you the option to ask that one or more of the people at this table be excused from the questions for any reason you may have, including the FAA inspector. The only ones who can't be asked to leave are Quint and I. Be aware that each person is part of my investigatory team; a copy of your questions and answers will be made available to them. Is there anyone you want excluded from the interviews?"

Jay looked at Larry, who casually shook his head. "No, I'm good," Jay said.

"Okay then, let's begin." With a glance at Ed to assure himself the tape was running Dan started asking generic questions. "Jay, how long have you been working for Gyrfalcon?"

Dan's questions were designed to familiarize the interview panelists with the interviewee. The information gave each member an idea of why Jay had become a mechanic and what his training consisted of. Quint followed up with questions designed to familiarize everyone with Jay's lifestyle; it was important to expose Jay's home environment, to see if there were outside influences on his work or his stress level.

Often a statement Jay made would be broken down by Quint to give the group a better idea of what the person was like; this approach allowed each member to see Jay's work ethic in the hopes of guiding questions to how things actually were instead of how they may be perceived.

Sarah pulled out her phase check notes. Donning her reading glasses, she directed her questions to take in the way the mechanics had accomplished adjustments to the engines' thrust reversers. One question touched on the procedures the mechanics followed while adjusting the reversers. "Did you follow the procedures precisely as written out?"

"Well, no," Jay said, "they aren't written in a progressive manner."

Clay interrupted, "You mean you didn't follow the directions?"

Dan was quick to rein him back in. "Clay, you need to wait your turn." He gestured to Ed to stop the tape.

Jay spoke out, "Oh, I don't mind."

Clay tried to continue, ignoring Dan. "Are you saying–?"

"Clay, it isn't your turn. You need to wait for Sarah to finish."

"But he said he doesn't–"

"Clay, we need to follow the rules here or it turns into a shouting match of questions. The point is to hold your questions until it gets around to you. Jay needs to take the course Sarah is working and satisfy her concerns. If you want, write down your questions and address them when it gets to you."

Clay grumbled under his breath but kept his peace. Ed started the tape.

"Jay," she continued, looking over her notes, "you said you did *not* ... follow the directions as laid out."

Larry looked at Jay as if he would request a sidebar, but Jay was confident in his answer. "The directions, as written on the workcards, are out of sequence."

"Out of sequence?"

"Well, the workcard instructions we use for maintenance are written by Gyrfalcon's engineers from the manufacturer's procedures; our workcards mirror those procedures. Unfortunately, the manufacturing engineers didn't do a good job of checking the procedures. They don't know how difficult they are to follow ... as written."

Sarah looked up from her notes. "But they're written to be followed precisely or have your own engineers get back with the manufacturer for rewriting."

Jay had her attention. "We did that. In fact, I have responses from your company saying that they were looking into the new rewrites."

Sarah placed her hands flat on the table. "Look, Jay, I understand about poorly written instructions, but you do realize that if you don't do what's written and we learn that it contributed to the accident, then you and Gyrfalcon are liable?"

"That's what I was trying to get at," Clay said under his breath.

Jay stared back at Sarah. "Ms. Wallace ... Sarah," he said, knitting his fingers together on the table top in front of him, "I can produce documentation that says we've presented these changes to our engineering department and that they've got your company's buy-in. It isn't a matter of us intentionally blowing off your procedures. It's just that we ... found a better mousetrap."

"Well," she said, mirroring his hand movements, "are you skipping steps or eliminating procedures?"

Jay leaned back and stared at the ceiling. "Skipping steps? I'm not sure I'd ... we may do them out of sequence; so, yes, we skip them in the order as written. But, no, we don't eliminate anything. You have a terrific product, Sarah, I like working the engine. It's just that as we work it we find ways to do the work faster with some

... how can I say this?" Jay sat a second stumped. "We've, uh … streamlined the process."

Sarah was not convinced. She stared at Jay for a few minutes until Dan interrupted her train of thought. "Sarah, do you have anything else?"

She managed a frown and said, "No, I'll wait for the next round. Jay, I'd really like to see the letters back and forth, if you don't mind?"

"You got it," Jay said.

Clay tried to make more of the issue than Sarah. He had a copy of a reverser workcard procured from a -350Y phase check and asked questions about each step of the reverser's rig and check. The questions were tedious, dragged out, Clay breaking down each step down to the syllable. He finally gave up and sat back exasperated and when his next turn came, he waved it off. The questioning continued centering back on Sarah's concern until the subject had been beaten to death.

The questioning of the other three mechanics from Gyrfalcon went a lot faster and ended in the same way. Whether they took a cue from Jay or not, they each answered casually that they had stuck to the maintenance tasks except to move the routine steps around. Clay tried to drag some conflicting information out of the others, but they stuck to the same story. There were no revelations.

After the interviews concluded Clay quietly snuck outside to speak to his office. He had found a way to redirect public pressure from AeroGalactic ... and place it squarely on Gyrfalcon.

CHAPTER 19
REVISITING N901FS: CANNIBALIZATION

August 16th – San Bernardino County, CA

The Canadair Challenger CL-600 soared effortlessly over the Southern California landscape. It banked right, continuing on to the Victorville logistics airport as the city of Barstow slid beneath.

Victorville sits at the southwestern edge of the Mojave Desert in California, almost one hundred miles northeast of Los Angeles. At 3000 feet above sea level, Victorville's motto of 'Key City of the High Desert' speaks to its unique advantage to the aviation community. The arid climate allows minimal water to be deposited in the area in the form of rain and snow, maintaining a low humidity environment. The average annual precipitation is below six inches over twelve months.

Victorville's ideal climate and high altitude offer a premier location for storing aircraft; the dry air protects an airliner waiting patiently to be placed back into service. The economy being what it is, plenty of aircraft – both wide-body and narrow-body – sit grounded.

The Challenger's flight crew advised the two mechanics in the cabin to buckle in. Maynard Cassel snapped his seatbelt together in anticipation for landing while Chaz roused himself from sleep and blinked out the window.

The Challenger – one of Freestyle's five corporate jets employed for its Executive officers – was used conservatively and only when speed was demanded. In this case, a pressing matter: cannibalize parts from a pickled aircraft, transport the parts to Seattle and install them.

During recent post-maintenance tests of a KR-450C in Seattle several problems came up with a wing engine's reverser tracks and several hydraulic components. Searches through the replacement parts system at Freestyle and other KR-450C operators were futile; the parts were not stocked anywhere. Maynard and Chaz were on a road trip to remove the parts from N901FS and install them on the broken aircraft ready to go back into service after the check in Seattle.

After roll out, the Challenger taxied to the fixed base operator: Cal Superior; there it would park and refuel in anticipation of its flight to Seattle. The engines wound down as Maynard and Chaz stepped out into the dry air carrying their portable toolboxes to the maintenance office. Within ten minutes a Cal Superior mechanic joined them; they drove out to the aircraft storage area in a truck with a lift bed.

N901FS sat alone at the northeastern end of the storage ramp; its nose facing away from the rows of narrow-body aircraft behind it. Maynard made out the Freestyle paint scheme as they approached from the airliner's right side. The gold letters on a royal blue background stood out, subliminally suggesting royalty. A sweeping 'F' on the tail surpassed the less ornate tails in the storage area.

Maynard stepped out of the truck and clambered up onto the nose gear to enter the cockpit through a maintenance access hatch. Once inside he took a list from his pocket and began pulling circuit breakers, hanging 'DANGER: DO NOT RESET' tags on the deactivated breakers. Meanwhile Chaz positioned ladders around the aircraft to reach the needed parts.

The sun had coasted across the arc of gentle blue sky when, eight hours later, Maynard and Chaz finished pulling the necessary hydraulic components, capping the lines and wrapping them with plastic before boxing them for the trip to Seattle.

The last items were a reverser track assembly and two blocker doors off the #1 engine.

While Chaz removed the two blocker doors, Maynard climbed up alongside the engine to remove the track. He put all bolts, nuts, and washers in separate parts bags to be left upstairs in the cockpit so as not to get separated from the aircraft.

As he stepped off the ladder, the Cal Superior supervisor approached him; this brief conversation distracted Maynard from putting the parts bags upstairs. Instead, he inadvertently placed the reverser track hardware in his toolbox before accompanying the supervisor back to their office.

Maynard entered all the maintenance work accomplished in the logbook, fifteen items in all. His placement of the track hardware in his toolbox broke the chain of custody; the missing hardware was never accounted for with other bolts from the hydraulic components and, thus, never entered in the logbook.

After removing the necessary log pages for records, the logbook was locked away with logs from the other pickled aircraft. In the rush to get to Seattle, neither mechanic noticed that the entry for the reverser track was illegible and that its hardware was still in Maynard's toolbox.

Within a half hour, the Challenger raced down runway 17. It rotated skyward and the gear retracted into the wells.

Two days later Maynard sat in his supervisor's office in Cleveland with a handful of maintenance log pages where he was trying to enter the information for N901FS in Freestyle's computerized maintenance tracking program.

Unsuccessfully entering the pages, Maynard's computer kept refusing the data with a flashing error message:

```
This aircraft is not registered in the
               Aircraft Listing _
```

After the first attempt to enter the critical information failed, he tried a second and a third entry with the same result. Maynard lacked the authority to override the system and he could not force the maintenance tracking program to accept the information. He did not know that several months earlier, Stephen Woods had removed N901FS and several other Freestyle aircraft from the company's Aircraft Listing; Woods's action denied any access to the maintenance records for those particular aircraft. For the duration these airliners were 'pickled.' It was as if they never existed.

Maynard called Maintenance Control and was given the name of a department to send the paperwork to. He shipped all the log pages to the Data Entry group, promising himself to follow up on it when he came back to work.

Maynard never kept his promise.

That night he and his wife were returning home from a late movie, when a young woman – intent on texting – lost control of her vehicle. Her left front tire hit the median curb causing her pick-up to jump the divider on Interstate 90. It plowed into the front of Maynard's pick-up driving in the opposite direction. The event happened too quickly for him to react to. All three people were killed instantly.

In addition, all knowledge of the missing upper #1 engine reverser track died with Maynard.

CHAPTER 20
HEADING HOME

August 19th – Denver

Dan walked across the busy hangar to where Clay was in quiet conversation with John. The two were sequestered at the far end of the hangar bay to escape the cacophony of noise coming from the aircraft undergoing a maintenance visit.

Clay was still agitated over the interviews, needing to bounce some regulatory questions off the FAA inspector, who sat quietly on the steps of a ladder. Clay's pacing, animatedly gesturing with his arms, contrasted against John's relaxed stance. When Dan approached, Clay abandoned his theatrics, instead shifting back and forth nervously with his hands thrust deep into his pockets.

"Clay, my friend Chris is sticking with your Systems guy out in Memphis." Dan turned to John. "It seems they came across some anomaly yesterday. Chris said they're spending the rest of the day chasing some electrons. It sounds pretty serious."

Reaching for his cell phone, Clay walked quickly away from the two government investigators to call his coworker in Memphis. John and Dan watched indifferently as Clay hastened his pace to increase the distance.

John turned. "There wasn't any call from your friend, was there?"

Dan shook his head, "Nah! I just never get tired of watching Clay freak out."

It was early morning and the group was in the hangar observing the phase check on a -350Y. The paperwork research had been completed late the previous day and Dan was finishing up on his report. As soon as Sarah was satisfied, they would return to the office to finalize their Denver investigation.

John stood up and stretched, bending at the waist to loosen his back up. "What's happening in Memphis?"

"Well, I spoke to my Lead, Ron Gebbia," Dan said, putting his foot up on a water pipe, "and he said they're wrapping up the on-site investigation today. They hit it pretty hard the first few days. Chris wants to get the testing phase going because he's skeptical about the gear switch being the only factor." Dan stared at the aircraft being inspected, but his mind was elsewhere.

"You don't disagree with him." John stared at his team leader for a second and said a little louder than necessary, "DAN!"

This broke Dan's brooding stare. "Sorry, I'm listening. You really took the wind outta my sails the other day. I would've bet that Memphis and the Freestyle incident weren't coincidences and that they had identical SPAR systems." Dan now focused on a braided piece of safety wire lying on the floor.

"You're welcome," John said sarcastically. "I think your reasoning is good, but you can't ignore what the system's diagram says." He paused. "But then, you're not giving up on your theory, are you?"

Dan reached down and picked the safety wire up off the floor, unwinding the twisted braid unconsciously. "Like I said, you knocked the wind out ... but that's good; I appreciate you putting me back on track." He continued to untwist the wire, but with a more focused expression. "And no, I still believe there's more to this than a bad ground sense switch."

Dan spent most of the previous night working on the team's notes. The collection of documents with all the data that told the story of N374GY – from laying the keel beam to its untimely demise – sat in a pile before him; it was the foundation of the AMI investigation report. This batch of observations had been reviewed and verified by the entire team; each member would receive copies before going home.

By ten o'clock, all the team members met in the conference room. "Okay, everyone," Dan said after they all read the final draft of the AMI Investigation report, "I need each of you to sign next to your name on the first sheet." Each member had exact copies of the supporting facts. "I'm asking each of you, is there anything further we need to look at?"

Each member, when asked, said no.

"If there isn't anything else …" Dan let the last word hang as he looked around at his team members, "In that case, please be safe going home. I'll be contacting each of you within the week through e-mail for the testing at AeroGalactic. Clay, you're going to be working with me on that. All right everybody, thank you for your assistance." While Dan visited Chip's office, John drove Sarah and Clay to the terminal.

"It's going to be an empty flight, for the most part," Quint said reaching for his carry-on after checking in.

"We have a two-hour layover in Chicago before jumping down into Dulles. I'll drop you off at Vienna station. Can Meg pick you up there?"

"What time are we getting in?"

Quint looked at the flight schedule. "It looks like around eight o'clock."

Once through security Quint broke off to call his wife and Dan went to the McDonald's stand for lunch. At the gate, he sat down with his cell phone to call Meg. Yes, she would meet him at the Vienna station, just call when you land at Dulles. There was news about Max that she needed to talk to him about. She told him to eat light so he could take her out for a late dinner. He hung up and took a bite of his cheeseburger. *Well, it's a light-weight cheeseburger,* he thought, *it only weighs four ounces.*

"Are you on this flight too?" Sarah had caught Dan chomping on the fries.

"Ah gus sho ..." he managed to mutter.

"Oh, great," she responded, as if she understood him. "I was hoping I'd fly with someone." She sat next to Dan. "I know I'm in the wrong business, but I don't like to fly as much as I used to."

"I know exactly how you feel," he managed.

The airport terminal was alive with travelers consumed in the frenzy of air travel. Flight crews walked at a brisk canter between gates while burdened passengers stood in anticipation of their approaching departures. At an adjoining gate an airliner started an engine, a low thrumming sound vibrated through the observation windows building up to a steady moan as the engine reached idle. Outside, sunlight glinted off various paint schemes advertising different airline identities as each jet joined the dance. Taxiing planes crawled along as a newly airborne jet climbed confidently above the earth, breaking its terrestrial ties.

Within an hour, the United 737 began loading. Quint, Dan, and Sarah fell behind to the end of the line. Since they had assigned seats, the hassle of watching passengers force their too large a carry-on into too-small an overhead compartment far outweighed any trouble of getting to their seats last. Dan did a head count; he figured the flight would be about one-quarter full, each of them scoring an empty seat next to them. They edged down the jetway and into the cabin, waiting patiently for a break in the line to plop into their seats and strap in.

As the Boeing pushed back, the flight attendants accomplished their emergency briefing before sitting down for the take-off phase of the two-and-a-half-hour flight. Shortly the 737 was climbing into the warm Denver afternoon. It gently rose to 1000 feet before banking left during its ascent. As the wings leveled off again, beams of sunlight pierced through the left windows and waltzed across the far end of the cabin.

At cruise altitude Dan was trying to get comfortable when Sarah fell into the empty aisle seat in Dan's row. She brought with her a paperback, but Dan knew she would never crack it open. "Mind if I sit here?" she said, snapping her seat belt together.

Dan looked around. "I'm sure that guy is coming back …"

She took a moment to look over her shoulder, before turning back. "There's nobody sitting here." Dan shook his head.

Sarah pretended to read her book while Dan struggled to get comfortable in the narrow seat. In his peripheral vision, he could see her struggling with something …

"What's on your mind, Sarah?" He said, with a bemused smile.

"I'm sorry," she laid her book down. "I was never on one of these investigations. Can I talk to you about it?"

"Well, if you've never been on one before, I'm sorry you were stuck on mine."

Sarah's face fell, unsure if Dan intentionally insulted her; his face was unreadable. "Did I do something wrong?" she asked. Dan looked at her curiously, his eyebrows knitting in confusion. "You said you were sorry I was on your team."

"No," Dan said, backpedaling, "I said, you were stuck on mine. I meant that you got stuck on my team as opposed to one more interesting, like Systems or Engines."

"Honestly, I cringed when they said they were sending me. I didn't want to see the accident site. I-I don't think I could handle it."

"I know what you mean. The last on-site accident scenes I was at were the three nine eleven sites." His mind wandered back to Shanksville, Pennsylvania, "That was very humbling."

"You were at all three sites? What was it like?"

"Like I said, all very humbling; I can't think of a better way to describe it," he stated quietly, "and each for very different reasons." Dan changed the subject. "So, what did you think of this investigation?"

She placed the paperback between her leg and the armrest. She hoped Dan was in a talkative mood because she had some questions she felt foolish asking in front of the others. "One thing I didn't understand," Sarah thought out loud. "Why didn't Gyrfalcon give us direct access to the records of aircraft three-seventy-four? Why did they have Francine controlling the records?"

"Well, there're two reasons for that. The first reason is proprietary. For instance, you and Clay work for the manufacturer. You would suddenly have access to information that can benefit your companies; Gyrfalcon would want to control that."

"But isn't there an ethics question there? We had to sign a promise to keep all information to ourselves."

"Absolutely, but remember there are a good number of investigatory teams working this accident. Any one team could have someone whose moral compass may be somewhat skewed. Companies have to protect themselves. Look at how the NTSB torpedoed the FAA in the press without any evidence to back it up; guilt by allegation and accusation."

"What's the other reason?"

"Oh," Dan uttered. "When an aircraft crashes, the airline locks all information on that specific plane. That prevents anyone at Gyrfalcon from leaking sensitive information to the press before the investigation. Disgruntled employees can sell that kinda information to the media. The press would have a field day if they found out that the accident aircraft, say, missed an inspection or the last mechanic who worked it was fired for falsification of his timecard. Imagine a lawyer getting that information before anyone's had a chance to analyze it.

"All records have to be presented to the Board before anyone else; the NTSB, for the most part, owns the records. You can't even download the CVR or FDR before the Board gets it. Did you ever see those television shows or movies where some police organization or some renegade former accident investigator assumes command of the investigation from the Board? That's bogus; it doesn't happen."

Sarah thought for a minute. "So, the airline's covering their collective–"

"Well … yes and no," Dan cut her off, "They have to cover themselves; that's survival in the industry. If a Sonic Engine, for instance, broke off an aircraft over the ocean, would you want the press writing stories based on opinions or would you rather the chance to look into it yourself?"

Dan leaned towards her to lower his voice. "I worked an accident off Japan where a jumbo jet fell into the ocean; everyone was killed and the plane sunk in several hundred feet of water. The press said the manufacturer built a garbage aircraft, even though that model flew for thirty years.

"Turns out the airline itself did a lousy repair and it picked that moment to fail. It took weeks to get the recorders off the ocean floor, but by then the lawyers were already fighting it out in court."

Sarah conceded the point. "Do you remember what you were saying before about how the NTSB works by allegation and accusation? Isn't that the same thing?"

Dan sat back in his seat. "The point I was making was it's easier to accuse someone of something, than for that person to defend themselves. Our chairwoman blames others without proof. It doesn't matter what the facts are; once the damage is done, it can't be undone."

"But why do you and John get along?"

The flight attendants started their beverage service. Dan asked for a cup of coffee, which she handed across Sarah. He sipped at his coffee. "Ironically, the people from both organizations work well together. And, I'm not saying the FAA doesn't have their share of troublemakers; they do. The whole media feud is a power play; the NTSB torpedoes the FAA's credibility, making the Board members look like experts.

"Look," Dan continued to Sarah's confused look, "the NTSB doesn't defer in matters they don't understand. The FAA's advantage is they're involved with the aviation community on a daily basis; their knowledge and experience surpass the Board's. If the NTSB consulted with the FAA *before* running to the press with every allegation there wouldn't be such a safety log jam."

She looked at him curiously. "You sound like you work for the FAA."

Dan laughed, "You sound like my boss. One of the guys you'll meet at the testing has been after me to jump ship and go to the other side. Truth is, I feel I'm making a bigger difference where I am. But I don't play games with the FAA. Their front-line guys and ours keep our cards on the table; we talk. And if there's something wrong with the way we do business we work it out. That doesn't happen on the upper echelon side."

Sarah looked doubtful. "Is it really that bad?"

Dan tried to answer without sounding patronizing. "When you've been on a few more of these investigations you'll pick out the nonsense and the facts." He hesitated, "Let me ask you; do you feel the same about the investigation process as you did when you arrived in Denver?"

"Well, no, not really."

"In many ways you're a better investigator than others who've been doing this awhile. Let's take Clay for example; you were more open minded than he was. You took those interviews seriously and followed the course they took. Clay had other ideas on how to question the mechanics. If we all interviewed like he did, we'd be making some terrible mistakes. The reason Clay did that is 'cause he's been bitten; he's learned from experience to cover your butt, because no one else will."

"Is that why you place such heavy emphasis on the interviews?"

"No, not really," Dan said, "the interviews are more of a snapshot if taken as close in time to the accident as possible. When a plane was lost off the coast of Connecticut we set up interviews as soon as possible. The maintenance crews had just worked on the plane, so we talked to them while their memories of the work were still fresh in their minds. I don't do interviews to catch people in lies, but to document the events; by doing that we can find out if a 'T' wasn't crossed and maybe prevent a similar event later on."

"You don't think the interviews went well, do you?"

"I never said that," Dan said. "Truth is they don't always follow a pattern. You never know what may come out of them later. Quint," Dan gestured to his coworker sleeping across the aisle, "likes to meet the mechanics, air traffic controllers, or witnesses as soon as possible, because they have less time to concentrate on the event, messing up the memory. You'd be surprised how many times people remember events differently than how they happened. That's why we try to interview as soon as possible. With Memphis, maintenance didn't really have an effect on the accident."

"But it still helps to interview?"

"Well, it doesn't hurt. If you learn something, well, then so much the better. If not, you haven't lost anything by trying. Anyone who said accident investigation is an exact science, lied."

Sarah shifted in her seat, unsure of how to ask the next question. "Why do you do this?" Sarah blurted the question out quicker than planned.

Dan looked back, puzzled.

"I mean why do you investigate accidents? You said you were making a big difference with the NTSB."

"Oh," Dan said quietly. He glanced over at Quint who shifted in his seat, but maintained a firm foothold in the dream world.

Sarah threw a glance at Quint, then back at Dan. "You don't have to answer if you don't want."

"No, that's okay," Dan said lowering his voice. "I don't usually talk about it, even with my coworkers." He unbuckled his seat belt and leaned toward the window, reaching into his back pocket for his wallet. With a last glance at Quint, he opened the wallet and rummaged through the credit card insert with pictures of Meg and the three boys. In the back, facing his A&P certificate, was a picture of a young girl standing on a front porch.

She was around seventeen with a coy smile. The girl was dressed in jeans, a modest plaid dress shirt, and worn sandals on her feet. The casual pose was calm, but impatient; a look that said, "Come on Dad, take the picture."

"She's pretty," Sarah said looking at the photo. "Who is she?"

Dan did not answer right away.

"I didn't mean to …"

Dan smirked. "No, that's all right. She's Crystal. Crystal Lord," he said. Then he added, "And I never met her."

Sarah asked, smiling, "But why's she in your wallet?"

Dan glanced over at Quint once more. "Crystal was row eight, seat F, and she died at ten-thirty in the morning several years ago."

Sarah's smile slowly faded as she glanced again at the photo.

"She's another testament to fate." Dan just stared at the photo. "Do you remember that regional jet that crashed coming out of that town ... Funny, I can't remember the name. It was in Montana. The aircraft took off but crashed into an abandoned warehouse just outside the airport."

When Sarah did not recall, Dan continued. "Everybody on the plane died and Crystal was one of them. She'd just turned eighteen and was on her way back to college from visiting her family after summer break. Of all the people on that flight who died, her death affected me most of all."

"So, you work on accidents for her?"

"I work on accidents for victims *like* her," he said so quietly Sarah almost did not hear him. "She puts a face to all the other faceless victims we investigate accidents for. She gives me focus.

"Her father wrote our teams a letter thanking us for our efforts. That's when I realized that people like Crystal make this more than just a job. It's a duty; a responsibility that, for me, will always have a face, a name, and a history."

The 737 began its descent into Chicago. The rest of the flight Sarah and Dan hardly spoke, the conversation having ended on a solemn note. Dan fell asleep while Sarah leafed through her paperback; before long she was engulfed in the story.

After landing, the 737 taxied to the gate in O'Hare airport. Quint stood up and stretched in the aisle. Dan and Sarah made their way out to the terminal where they shook hands for the second time that day. Sarah left to catch her next flight.

Dan and Quint caught their connection to Dulles, boarding a packed flight for the two-hour trip. They both nodded off and as the 737 descended into Dulles, the sun was setting over the western horizon where they had just flown from.

CHAPTER 21
N901FS MAINTENANCE TRACKING

As a rule, Eugenia hated coffee. She preferred tea, heavy on the sugar and light on the cream. Her husband gave her a bowl-sized tea cup for Christmas one year with that specific recipe printed on the side so, if she should ever forget, the cup would remind her. The following year he left her for that tart he worked with.

Good tea cup, lousy husband.

Eugenia belonged to the Freestyle Data Entry group in Cleveland where her and her coworkers entered aircraft maintenance information at the hangar. Freestyle felt it unnecessary to have qualified people log the computerized maintenance data.

The data entry group members were not A&P certificated mechanics; they did not possess the technical knowledge necessary for understanding the information they entered. The data – aircraft log pages – came from over four hundred mechanics working several different aircraft types. The use of technically-challenged people spoke to Freestyle's desire to place economy over technical accuracy.

"Here's the latest from the hangar, Jeanie," Eugenia's supervisor said, dropping a heavy envelope on the corner of her desk. The manila envelope bulged at the center, threatening to rupture the sides.

"Thanks," Eugenia muttered, half-heartedly. She tore open the envelope and removed several stacks of maintenance log pages and a smaller envelope from a mechanic named Maynard Cassel; it had a handwritten note attached dated three days prior.

Data Entry Person,
I could not enter these pages. The computer said aircraft N901FS isn't listed in the system. Please enter the pages manually. Aircraft N901FS is pickled in the desert.
Thanks,
M. Cassel

Well, at least he's polite, she thought. *But what does 'pickled' mean?*

As she read from the pages she tried entering the tail number N901FS in the proper field but the number kept showing 'INACTIVE.' A message stated, 'This aircraft does not exist in the active aircraft database.' She searched for the jet's maintenance history, but as far as the computer was concerned, N901FS was never built.

Eugenia tried unsuccessfully to interpret writing on the log page and the computer refused to take the entries so she called her supervisor over.

"Whatcha got, Jeanie?"

"Carol, I'm trying to enter some information for work performed on a pickled aircraft, but …"

"What's a 'pickled' aircraft?" Eugenia shrugged. "What's the problem?"

"I can't enter the information because the tail number doesn't exist. I'm thinking 'pickled' means it's not in the system."

"Call the hangar and get whoever it is over here."

"The problem's not the mechanic who wrote it, but the computer because it doesn't show the airplane in the system."

Carol tried to force the computer to take the entry, but failed each time. "Send the package over to archives. They can put it on disk with the other hard copy files."

By shutting N901FS out of the maintenance tracking system, the policy was to store any log pages in the paper archives, which are separate from the digital archives. These pages would be entered manually at a much later date. It was a small oversight, but small oversights result in larger errors.

When the pages arrived at the archives they were photocopied, stuffed into boxes, labeled with a magic marker, and kept in a records warehouse.

Vital maintenance information pertaining to the airliner's safety of flight vanished forever from the maintenance history of N901FS.

CHAPTER 22
FORCED DECISIONS

An accident investigation is not an exact science; symptoms can be confused with probable cause. The moment an aircraft becomes a statistic, the clock starts running; the Board is under enormous pressure to get answers. The media, surviving family members and political figures give no quarter; self-proclaimed agents of justice throw money and every available resource in an effort to force the cause of the accident to surface. But these efforts produce more confusion than solution.

The probable cause is a golden fleece, the Holy Grail; it is the culmination of hard, exhausting work. But like most goals they have to be found at the end of the journey, not in the middle.

Accident investigating is full of uncertainties, all to be avoided.

August 21st – Bealeton, VA

Megan arrived at the house exhausted. It had been a rough day; the constant bickering of teachers at a planning meeting made her question more times than not who the children were and who was running the asylum.

However, more pressing on her mind was Max. She had not heard from him in days and was worried. She had done some homework, locating Max's base in

Afghanistan. What she read on the Armed Forces' website did nothing to dispel her fears about his safety.

She knew Dan avoided the topic of their son's service. At times she wished she could block the thoughts as well, but her mother's instincts left her empty, dreading. She spent the last two weeks watching TV in the living room while Dan slept. Like it or not, she needed Dan to talk, even if just to put her fears to rest.

But not yet ... not yet.

She pulled the car back into the driveway and stopped as the garage door opened. Dan harped on her to back the car in, saying, 'in his mind it was safer to back into the garage than backing out into the street.' Yeah, yeah, blah, blah; no matter how many times she did it, she could not get used to backing into the tight space. She threw her hair over her right shoulder and turned to back in when she saw Dan's car in one of the two garage bays.

She looked at her watch: 3:20. *Well, that can't be good*, she thought.

She parked the car and opened the door that led into the 'mud' room, making out the distinct muffled rasp of an electric sander. Triggering the garage door to close, she followed the sound towards the back deck where her husband was on his knees, driving a sander across the deck boards. His hair was frosted with spent wood dust, there being more dust than hair. His tan T-shirt was soaked with sweat, which made a paste when mixed with the dust.

Dan had built her the deck several years earlier, claiming she could land a B747 on it. Home improvement was their hobby and she found it helped melt away unnecessary stress from work. During these summer months they concentrated on getting their house in shape with the three S's: sanding, staining, and sore muscles.

She stared at him through the sliding glass doors, searching momentarily for the young Don Quixote she married. Still unnoticed, she went to the refrigerator and grabbed a bottle of beer and a bottle of Chardonnay, which she poured into a tall wine glass. She went back to the glass doors and, trying not to alarm him, tapped on the glass when his sander took a break. He looked up, stumbling over to slide the door open.

She stepped out on the deck and, not for the first time, did Dan's heart do an involuntary somersault. Close to thirty years, he thought, and she still makes me feel like a kid on a first date.

She appraised him with a suspicious eye. "Well," Megan said, leaning against the frame, "you don't appear sick. What brings you home this early?"

Dan took a pull on the beer bottle and sat back on his haunches. "Looks are deceiving. As a matter of fact, I'm quite sick," he grumbled, wiping dust and sweat from his forehead, "of the whole place."

She sat casually several feet away from him and sipped her wine. She looked at him intently. "So, what happened?"

"Well …"

Ron Gebbia was addressing the conference room. Phil sat across from him, peering frequently at his watch.

"We were leaning towards the ground sense switches being the cause," Ron asserted, "but Phil, I don't think we can dismiss the possibility that Dan's correct: that there's more to this accident than simple switches."

The door to the conference room opened and Sweeney Heep walked into the meeting. He took a fast review of the room and took a seat next to Phil. "I'm sorry I'm late," he fretted as he laid down his reference material.

Sweeney Heep is a Systems investigator who began with the NTSB many years before, preferring the company of upper management in deference to his colleagues. By positioning himself with Phil he assumed the role of Systems expert; Phil's NTSB ace to industry, whether Sweeney had the answer or not.

Fifty-five years of age, Sweeney has slick black hair that pastes to the side of his head. His muddy brown eyes peek out from under heavy lids and small rimmed glasses, blinking repeatedly. Sweeney's grey, doleful expression has a disingenuous smile; it marks someone who regularly backs the wrong horse. He is shunned by other investigators for his contemptible habit of stealing investigations from them.

"No problem," Phil assured him, stealing a glance at Dan. "In fact, you couldn't have timed it better."

The conference room went silent. A cloud seemed to settle over the meeting as if someone said something inappropriate; many eyes went from Sweeney to Phil and back again. Phil clasped his hands together on the table while a smile stole across his face. He visibly relaxed, like a coach watching his first-string quarterback take the field.

"Wait a minute," Megan interrupted, "isn't Sweeney that clown who sucks up to Phil all the time?"

Dan just nodded. He painfully stood up; all his joints protesting. "Yeah," he began, "good old Sweeney ..."

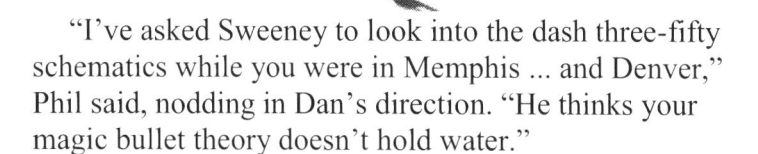

"I've asked Sweeney to look into the dash three-fifty schematics while you were in Memphis ... and Denver," Phil said, nodding in Dan's direction. "He thinks your magic bullet theory doesn't hold water."

"What magic bullet theory?" Dan asked, skeptically.

"There's no reference to a new system installed through the landing gear wiring," Sweeney said, adjusting his glasses.

Dan held out his hand to Sweeney for the schematic, but Sweeney hugged the document to himself. Phil made no attempt to coax him to surrender it.

"Can Ron and I look at that?" Connie said before Sweeney could stow the sheet.

Sweeney gave Phil an imploring glance, but Phil ignored him. As Sweeney surrendered the schematic, Ron asked suspiciously, "But what about Dan's ability to guess the accident results?"

Phil shrugged his shoulders. "A lucky guess."

"Lucky–?" Ron managed, before Connie kicked him.

Connie was poring over the wiring diagram while Sweeney waited impatiently for her to pass it back. She took her time as the conversation continued. The operations manager, Neil, was sitting two seats from Phil. "Are you saying the tests in Portland aren't going to look at the issues Dan brought up? What's the press going to say?"

"Don't worry about the press; that'll be my concern. Besides, Giv and I have already spoken to Chairwoman Potter and explained how the gear sense switch was the deciding factor in the accident and that we suspect Gyrfalcon's Maintenance fouled up the reverser rigging."

Neil's voice rose, "Potter doesn't have any clue how the aircraft works. She's a Presidential appointee with no transportation experience to speak of."

Phil just stared at his hands. "Perhaps you'd like to point that out to her yourself, I mean before the news conference this afternoon."

A hush fell over the conference room. Neil seemed not to react to the challenge. He did not resist taking Phil on out of fear but because he knew that Phil had the Chairwoman's ear and anyone else's opinion was moot. Neil was not a fool; he knew how the political machine worked. Board Members were viewed by the public as experts in the transportation arena, even if one or two Members knew little to nothing about transportation, living instead in a political bubble where title outranked actual know-how.

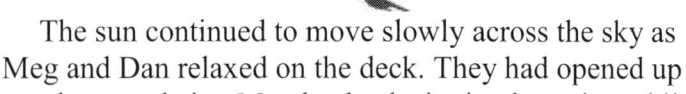

The sun continued to move slowly across the sky as Meg and Dan relaxed on the deck. They had opened up two lounge chairs; Meg lay back sipping her wine while Dan leaned forward, his beer resting on his knee.

"So, Phil has the Chairwoman's ear?"

"He has her ear," Dan answered, "and sole access to her ... period. Even her husband doesn't get that close. But Phil's playing a dangerous game taking on Neil. There isn't a city in this country that Neil can't find a powerful friend."

Meg brushed her hair over her ears, but it fell back in defiance. "So, what happened when Connie read the wiring schematics?"

Dan chuckled, "Oh, yeah. Connie was pretty cool ..."

The Air Crash Files: Jet Blast

Connie moved the wiring diagram to Dan under the table as attention focused on Neil and Phil's confrontation. But Sweeney soon noticed that she was no longer in possession of the wiring diagram. A quick glance at Dan staring down towards the tabletop left no doubt where his schematics were.

"This diagram is bogus; it isn't the latest revision," Dan said during a lull in the conversation. Sweeney regarded Dan with contempt.

Quint raised his voice. "What's wrong with Sweeney's wiring diagram?"

Dan said, "It isn't the latest revision. I mean it's a recent version, but not updated." No one commented. "In other words, this wiring diagram isn't applicable to the accident aircraft."

"What difference does that make?" Phil snarled.

Dan rejoined, matter-of-factly, "The latest components aren't in here. It doesn't apply to Flight four-twenty-seven. Sweeney has the wrong diagram."

"I swear, that guy knows less about aircraft than I know …" pointing at Meg's wine glass, "about Pinot Grigio."

"It's Chardonnay, Dan."

"Whatever," he responded with a shrug.

"Not whatever, Dan. I don't confuse your Budweiser …"

"It's Sam Adams."

"What-*ever*," she said sarcastically.

Dan placed his finger on the bottle's label. "But this says, 'Sam Adams' ... right here. See, it even has Sam offering you a tasty chug-a-lug. What does your wine glass say? Posi-lutely nothing."

"It's all beer to me."

Dan assumed a gruff 'Sam Adams' voice while pointing at the label, "Hey lady, want a beer?"

"Honestly Dan, you're impossible," Megan grinned. "What happened next?"

Connie turned to Ron. "Why don't you lay out your plans for Portland?"

Ron leaned over and grabbed his pad of paper. "We're flying out a week from Friday as a group. I've already made the investigators' reservations. Chris, you're running the tests as the lead Systems invest–"

Phil interrupted him. "Make reservations for Sweeney and me, as well."

Ron stole a glance at Connie, who sat unfazed by the last remark, "Is there a problem with that, Ron?" Phil asked with a hint of threat in his voice.

"Do you think that's wise introducing Sweeney this late into the investigation, Phil?" Connie asked.

"I do," he replied simply, "for one, it's not that late. For two, I want an unbiased view of the tests. Chris allowed Tenace's opinions to affect his judgment."

Dan nudged Chris, who was focused on Sweeney's schematics.

"And, why are you waiting for next Friday to test?" Phil asked.

"I ... I, what do you mean?"

Phil's eyebrows rose at the question. "I thought it was pretty self-explanatory. Why wait until a week from

Friday to start the tests? Isn't there a dash three-fifty in Portland that we can test sooner?"

"Well ... uh, I'm sure, but Gyrfalcon said they had another three-fifty configured exactly like Flight four-twenty-seven and that they'd route it into Portland just so we have a duplicate aircraft."

Phil seemed to rise in his seat; his shoulders squared and his eyes bore down on Ron. "Didn't you just hear Sweeney say that there was no reference to any other systems? The Chairwoman said very clearly, 'get this investigation moving.'" Phil paused for emphasis.

Quint said, "Isn't it worth a few extra days to get a duplicate aircraft as to the one that crashed?"

Phil turned to Quint. "Did the interviews in Denver lead you to think the gear switch wasn't solely responsible?" Quint did not respond; Dan's interviews proved inconclusive.

"Oh, and you," Phil said, pointing at Dan, "need to put in your report that the actions of the Gyrfalcon Maintenance group are under question. Chairwoman Potter wants a full investigation into the Gyrfalcon hangar mechanics."

Dan and Quint looked at each other. "Why is that?" Dan asked.

"That mechanic, Jay Connelly, admitted to disregarding the instructions for rigging the reversers. The chairwoman feels we need to set an example. She may even release a statement in the press that we're focusing on his actions."

"Phil, that's irresponsible," Quint protested. "You can't throw around allegations–"

Phil cut Quint off, "Save it! Potter and I have already decided." He turned to Ron. "I believe you have some organizing to do, Ron. I want those tests to start on Monday." Ron managed a glance at Connie before walking out the door.

The conference room erupted into a debate. "The fact is–" Quint started.

"I don't care about the facts!" Phil said over everyone present, to end the debate, "I just want the aircraft fixed!"

"He said *what*?!"

"He said," Dan laughed, "that he didn't care about the facts."

"What's going to happen to the mechanics in Denver?"

Dan frowned at his beer bottle. "I'm sure Phil and Potter are going to happily throw them under the bus. They'll use the interviews to sell it to the press and hold them up for the world to see. Guilty until proven innocent; that's our motto."

"So, what did Connie say then?" Meg asked shaking her head.

"Is waiting for the other aircraft that important?" Connie asked Dan over lunch.

The noise in the eatery drowned out their conversation. "This trip is a big waste of time. Chris and I think there may be something wrong with ... I don't know, something with this SPAR system. I know that testing this other aircraft like Phil wants will produce just as much misinformation as the Salem witch trials."

"You're right–"

"I sure didn't think it was fair to Chris just because he supported me." Before Connie could object he interrupted her again. "And make no mistake ... Chris was punished for supporting me!" Connie listened quietly as Dan ranted. Phil was sure to do one thing and that was to protect his kingdom. In his mind he was the voice of the NTSB.

"You do know what happened," Connie asked more than stated. "I mean, you two aren't throwing around theories; you have a good direction to pursue on how the plane crashed?" Dan nodded. "Then," she continued, "do what you have to do to prove it and I'll help in any way I can."

Dan looked up from his burger. "Do you mean that?"

Connie found herself pushing a pepper around on her salad. "Why?"

Dan dipped a french fry in ketchup on the way to his mouth. "Chris and I want to try some tests while we're in Portland. Can Ron see his way to get us some alone time with the AeroGalactic mechanics?"

Connie squinted at Dan. "I'll talk to Ron," she said, crunching the pepper in her teeth. "He'll work something out with you."

"At least you have someone there who appreciates you."

"Thanks Babe," Dan said, getting up and offering his wife a hand from her chair. "You always know how to talk me off the soapbox. I may just go out and buy you another bottle of Pinot Grigio."

"It's a chardonnay," she started, but Dan was already laughing.

CHAPTER 23
TESTING

August 24th – Dulles Airport

The flight to Portland made Dan anxious. As a favor, Ron booked the seats so that Dan and Chris sat towards the back, a good distance from Phil and Sweeney sitting behind first class. All the NTSB investigators attending the test were on a direct flight departing Dulles airport in the morning and landing in Oregon five hours afterward.

Meg did something she never did; she dropped Dan off at the airport. She wanted to speak to him about Max, but Chris tagged along for the ride. Meg sat in aggravated silence all the way to the airport.

"Thanks again for the lift," Chris said humbly. "I really appreciate your keeping tabs on Karen and her Mom." Chris leaned forward and lowered his voice. "Don't be shocked if she looks even feebler than before; some of that's from the new medication. She's lost some weight from the vomiting, so you might want, you know ... to be aware. Thanks again."

Megan did not answer, but nodded and smiled out of guilt. She decided yesterday that the car was a great place to trap Dan into talking about their soldier-son; the conversation was put off far too long. However, Chris asked Dan for a ride and he naturally said 'yes.' Megan took her missed opportunity out on Chris.

Dan squatted next to the driver's window. "What's the matter?"

Megan shyly asked, "Was it that obvious?"

"Come on, Meg, what's up?"

"Nothing," she said, shaking her head. "I just needed to–" She kissed him on the lips, saying, "Please apologize to Chris for me. I love you." She drove off before he could push her any further.

"Did I do something?" Chris asked.

Dan watched her drive off, his mind overrunning with questions. "No, Chris, it wasn't you at all. She said she was sorry."

They both lifted their bags and made for the terminal.

The Boeing 767 flew effortlessly through the warm summer morning, banking left to intercept the signal from ground radar. Once captured, the airliner followed it as if being led by the nose. A tail wind promised to shave time off the trek.

Dan stared out the window at the tapestry of American life sliding beneath the airliner and thought about Megan; it had to be Max that was upsetting her. He wanted to say something these past three days when she retreated within herself. It was indicative of her fear of death, but not her own. She acted the same when her brother died.

And then Tyler, he thought.

"Are all your team members showing up?"

Chris's question pulled Dan out of his reverie. Two days before, Dan called Clay, who strangely expected the schedule change; he worked in Portland, so he would arrange everything. John rolled with the punches having participated in investigations before. Sarah had no problem outside of traveling on a Sunday. All associated team members were managed by those who understood that when the Board set up a test, you either jumped through the hoop or you were left out in the cold. No one would miss the tests.

"Yeah," Dan muttered, his mind in Afghanistan, "everybody'll be there."

One of the things that Dan appreciated about working with Ron was that when he told an organization he would be at their place at 8 o'clock, he was there at 7:45 or earlier; first impressions were everything. Ron felt that sticking to a schedule showed they respected that organization enough to be punctual and professional.

Ron directed Phil, Chris, Sweeney, and Dan to meet in the hotel lobby at exactly 7:30 for the ten-minute drive to the plant. Everyone, including Phil, knew the penalty for showing up at 7:31: a long walk to the hangar. In this Ron reigned supreme; he waited for no one.

The rental van showed up at the gate to the AeroGalactic plant with several minutes to spare. The guard at the gate checked identifications while handing out temporary badges that allowed everyone limited access to the grounds.

As they drove along a service road, they saw a -350Y elevated off the ground just inside the closing hangar doors. The securing of the hangar guaranteed a safe environment where stray winds could not threaten to unbalance the raised jet.

Every investigation member found their way in, thanks to Clay's efforts. The Maintenance and Systems team members were met by company vans to get them through security and all gathered in the test hangar's spacious lobby.

Clay reserved the hangar's conference room for the in-briefing and the expected out-briefing. The in-briefing precedes the test phase, allowing for introductions while the specialists lay out the plans for testing. The out-briefing is a conclusion, a chance to get feedback from all present.

Chris's team, who was running the tests, gathered along the head of the table. Dan's team members dominated the back of the room; they would provide technical support and verify that maintenance was not a probable cause in the accident. Ron stood momentarily and presented the manager-types before surrendering the floor to Chris.

"I'd like to welcome everyone here to – hopefully – the only testing phase of the Gyrfalcon four-twenty-seven accident," Chris began quietly. "My name is Chris Wilkerson and I'm the team lead on the Systems group." He introduced his team members and pointed to Dan, who introduced himself and his team. "As you're aware, the purpose–"

"Aren't you going to introduce me?" Sweeney shouted, standing next to Phil.

Chris's eyebrows knitted in confusion as he looked to Ron. Phil impatiently stood up, "My name is Philip Tulkinghorn, the Director of Aerospace Safety at the National Transportation Safety Board." He paused, as if he anticipated an eruption of applause before continuing. "This is Sweeney Heep. Mister Heep is a Systems engineer who has more experience than Chris in these matters. He's here, on my request, to assure me that the investigation moves in the right direction without going off on any tangents."

Dan felt responsible for the public sleight Chris just received from Phil. The Systems group looked at Chris in confusion, wondering if he was being replaced. Chris, however, did not appear fazed by it, taking it in stride.

Almost, Dan thought, *as if he expected it.*

The -350 perched on jacks was unadorned; a test model used for various AeroGalactic modifications. Except for a simple purple line down the aircraft's side, it had no logos. Dan felt the tests were going to be just as unimpressive.

He approached the wheelwell where several mechanics gathered to discuss their roles. As if racing to displace him, Sweeney hurried to the maintenance stand erected inside the wheelwell; he scaled the stand, preventing Dan access in the limited space available. Dan walked up to the stand anyway. "Sweeney, my team is responsible for maintenance and we're going to need anyone else to stay out of the wheelwell."

Sweeney flipped his head up to gesture in Phil's direction. "Phil wants me to stay with the mechanics in the test area. You can talk to him if you want."

"I don't need to talk to Phil or anyone, Sweeney. Your job – according to Phil – is to oversee the Systems side of the investigation. This is maintenance and far outside your area of expertise."

But Sweeney was adamant. "I'm supposed to make sure the tests are done correctly and that means making sure the aircraft is configured correctly. So, get used to me being here."

"Fine," Dan surrendered. He stood off by the side of the engine within earshot of the wheelwell. A.J., a mechanic who Dan met earlier, stepped up to him, accompanied by John Matero.

"Aren't you going to be in the wheelwell with us, Mister Tenace?" A.J. said.

Dan smiled. "It's Dan, and no, I'm not going to be inside the wheelwell, but I'll be nearby."

A.J. spoke with a Minnesotan accent; five-foot-nine and soft-spoken, he looked uncomfortable talking with government investigators. "Who'll be working with us?"

Dan looked at John for a second before continuing, "Sweeney Heep will be working with you." Dan fought the urge to give his opinion of the change in plans, but instead asked, "Will you be okay with that?"

John added, "If you've got a concern, A.J., let us know."

It was as if a light switch was flipped off; A.J. melted away shaking his head. He backed off for about ten feet, turned and trudged to the wheelwell. John just looked at Dan and shrugged. "It seems to me he doesn't know what to say in front of you, Dan. You're with the Board, after all. He may not trust you." They looked after the retreating mechanic. "Either that, or it's your winning personality," he added.

Dan gave John a sidelong glance, before looking for Chris.

Chris spoke with Autris, the lead mechanic, while Dan played liaison to Chris and the mechanics in the wheelwell, keeping a close eye on everything. Most of the participants milled about the test aircraft, giving the mechanics a wide berth, yet maintaining a discrete distance.

"Now, what do you need to do?" Autris asked, looking past Dan to keep an eye on his mechanics. Chris was still editing some of the discarded tests out of the agenda; since Phil had changed the rules, many of the tests Chris was hoping to carry out with the modified equipment installed, were now irrelevant. Chris did not dispose of them, but instead put them to the side, carefully tucking them in a separate folder.

"We need to place these ground sense switches into the nose and main gear; make it think it's in a landing phase." He handed the switches to Autris. Recognizing the parts, Autris walked to the left main wheelwell.

"Where did you get those?" Dan asked.

"Those are the ground sense switches from four-twenty-seven. After all they've been through, I'm hoping they work just like they did at the accident."

Above the noise of the professional gathering, Dan heard the unmistakable sound of Aaron Campo's laugh. With a slight gravelly timbre Aaron was explaining to another pilot about where the tests were supposed to progress to … theoretically. Dan immediately searched the scattered crowds for someone.

"Sarah!" He yelled, acquiring her attention right away; he waved her over with a flourish of his arm. She broke away from the group she was with and walked over.

"Hey boss," she said, "whatcha got?"

"Chris, I'll be right back." Dan led Sarah over to Aaron, who was laughing with the pilot. Dan nodded to the pilot and introduced Sarah to the two of them.

"I'm sorry, but I promised Sarah that she would get to meet you."

Aaron gave her his full attention. "What's your technical specialty?"

Dan sighed, "Can't you give me a second?"

Shaking her hand, Aaron responded, "Waiting for him to make proper introductions is like watching the continents drift."

"Typical pilot," Dan managed in a weak retort.

It dawned on Sarah who Aaron was. "Is this the guy from the FAA you said you get along so well with?"

"Well, up until a moment ago, yeah."

"You said that about me Bubba? I'm honored."

Dan could never keep up with Aaron's pithy exchanges, yet he did not want to surrender the field so easily. However, his concentration was interrupted by a loud disturbance by the wheelwell where the mechanics were configuring the aircraft for the tests. As he walked crisply in that direction, Chris intercepted him, whispering, "Stand by for a change of plans."

The confusion in the wheelwell continued when Sweeney burst forth and headed straight for Phil, who commanded the attention of a group of AeroGalactic's management. Sweeney made a straight line to Phil, his heavy lids drooping in a patronizing gaze, while the corner of his mouth twisted in a half-smirk.

"I think I found a problem in how they do business here," Sweeney announced loudly, standing at attention in front of Phil; an eyebrow rose as if he possessed a secret all would want to know. "I tried to get them to configure the aircraft in a certain way and they totally screwed it up."

Phil gave a sidelong glance at the managers while putting his arm around Sweeney's shoulders. "That's why we have Sweeney here. He's good at finding mistakes made by the manufacturer."

"Show us what A.J. supposedly did wrong," said one manager, skeptically.

Ignoring Sweeney's outburst, Dan walked in the other direction and stepped into the wheelwell. Two other mechanics stood with A.J. as the drama played out thirty feet away. Dan climbed onto the maintenance stand and gave A.J. a sympathetic look.

"What happened, A.J.?" Dan asked.

A.J. gestured, pointing to a switch he was configuring for the tests; he was arranging the wires to Sweeney's specifications.

"That … guy–," A.J. muttered through pressed lips, a finger shaking in the air. "Heep, said to bypass this switch and run these wires here to this point," he said, indicating the wires in question.

"Which is what he did," added one of the other mechanics.

"But when we tested the connection," A.J. continued excitedly, "the circuit didn't work. I coulda told him it wouldn't if he'd asked me. Then he starts spoutin' off," A.J. emphasized with exaggerated movements of his hands, "arguing that he never said nothin' about connectin' it like that – that I didn't know what I was doing!"

It was obvious to Dan that A.J. looked suspect by Sweeney's accusations, saying that the mechanic was incompetent.

"Let me see what he said to do," Dan stated calmly. He motioned to Chris, who stepped quickly into the wheelwell.

A.J. handed over the diagram. Chris and Dan started to run through how it was connected. After verifying that the wiring was exactly as Sweeney had spelled out, Dan turned to Chris. "How is this supposed to look?"

When Sweeney led Phil's contingent to the wheelwell, Chris blocked the stairs. "Chris, get out of the way, I need to show these managers what's wrong," Sweeney said.

But Chris ignored him, instead going over the diagram with Dan, who was hidden from view. Phil pushed past Sweeney and yelled at Chris to move.

"Um … A.J. didn't make the mistake, Phil; Sweeney did." Dan's voice echoed in the wheelwell.

"Tenace, get out of there!" Phil said, his face turning purple with anger.

Chris moved aside and Dan squatted down on the top step, effectively blocking access. "A.J. hooked this up exactly like Sweeney laid it out," Dan spoke loud enough for the managers to hear. "A.J. was right. Chris has the correct diagram and we're setting it straight now."

"Get out and let Sweeney back up there," Phil hissed through his teeth.

Dan did not move. "All things considered, Phil, I don't think that's a good idea."

"YOU ... DON'T–!" Phil began.

"Look," Dan said, raising his own voice, "Sweeney's mistakes wasted enough time already. Now I'm the maintenance guy, so let me do my job. I'll stay here and work with the mechanics so I know the test is done *right*."

Phil turned a darker shade of purple while Sweeney gaped wide-eyed. "I'm sure you'd agree Phil," Dan continued, "our purpose is to find out the cause of the accident, advance the cause of safety. Besides, I'm sure the managers here would prefer having a mechanic who's worked this type of equipment before – like me – to make sure the proper practices are being followed. It gives more credence to the testing, right?"

Phil did not like having the tables turned on him, especially in front of a gathering audience. Sweeney had embarrassed him and he had no choice but to allow Dan to stay. Members of AeroGalactic's management were smiling, exchanging looks that further infuriated Phil. He turned on his heels and led the party back and away from the wheelwell. Sweeney remained for several minutes before moving away, unnoticed.

"I can't believe the Board finally hired a certificated mechanic!" A.J. said.

Dan laughed at the remark, "Oh, I'm certifiable all right. Look," Dan lowered his voice, "don't worry about Sweeney. The truth is, he gets his kicks from pulling these stunts."

A.J. grinned.

Chris said off-handedly, "No seriously; he's the kind of guy who likes to dominate an anthill with a magnifying glass. Vaporizes insects that can't fight back."

With all the equipment connected for testing Chris ran the trials through all of Sweeney's scenarios. But the results were a foregone conclusion: the tests would not duplicate the catastrophic events that brought down flight 427.

Eight hours passed as frustration replaced hopeful speculation. There were clearly too many attendants to the trials; they began to break down into groups of four or five to discuss politics or sports; they grew impatient, longing to be participating more but instead feeling useless as a room full of surgeons with one patient to work on.

All the while Phil stood obstinate, wishing for some response that would justify his faith in Sweeney, but the various configurations that Sweeney's hypotheses played out were proving fruitless; the aircraft was not responding.

"Are you fudging the results?" Sweeney said under his breath to Chris.

Chris turned slowly. "And how do you suppose I could do that?"

"After all this time and testing you're telling me that *nothing* is happening? The reversers aren't even unlocking?" Sweeney was getting nervous; the strain of Phil's displeasure was starting to show its effect.

"What's the matter, Sweeney?" Ron asked across the test bench.

"Heep, I didn't say anything when you shot down my ideas on the tests. I didn't even say anything when you put yourself in charge. But if you want to challenge my integrity, then accuse me of sabotaging this part of the investigation, well …"

Ron stepped around the table and placed himself in front of Chris, gently forcing him to retreat. "Chris, go see if there's anything Dan needs." Reluctantly, Chris walked away towards the wheelwell. Ron turned to

Sweeney. "Your presence here is a distraction. The team can't do their job if you keep this up."

"How dare …"

"Do you want to raise voices? Do you want to draw attention to what's really going on here?"

Sweeney became aware that the remaining participants were watching their exchange. He muttered something under his breath before shuffling away quietly.

The testing was about finished; they had exhausted the whole series of possible causes that a -350 might have gone through during the landing phase. The result: nothing; no spoilers, no reversers, and no reaction outside the norm.

Sweeney pored over his notes, awkwardly trying to avoid Phil's deprecating gaze. He ran his hand across his chin as if it irritated him, looking for anything he may have missed. Phil put the fear into Sweeney; he gave the engineer no mercy as he stood stewing alone, his hands rattling keys and change in his pockets to dispel the nervous energy. Ron glanced every now and then at Dan or Chris, a look that communicated no urgency but instead anticipating some end play they wanted to run.

Autris walked over and began studying Chris's diagrams. "What happens when we leave today?" Chris asked quietly.

Autris scrutinized Chris's face. "We'll put the plane back together and take her off the jacks." He knew Chris would have understood that. "Why do you ask?"

Dan walked over. "Dan," Chris spoke softly, "do you have that wiring diagram from … that other airline?"

Dan walked over to his computer bag and came back with the requested document. Chris dwelled on it for a few minutes, pointing out certain wires to Autris, who scarcely either nodded or shook his head in response. Ron came up on Chris's other side. "What've you got, Chris?"

"Ron, we're going to stay here for a while after you leave. We wanna try something before we shut it down for good."

"Okay." He looked at Dan, saying, "Connie told me you'd ask. Are you going to be able to fake out the system?"

But Chris instead turned to Autris. "How hard would it be to jump some wires in the Autoland system?"

A cannon plug was a unique asset for aircraft. Although it had been designed for other applications, the cannon plug guaranteed an air-tight seal and a firm connection between the wires going into a component – like a computer – and the wire bundle it was attached to.

What Chris and Dan were suggesting was tricky; the computers they would bypass would most likely need repair after the tests, if the circuits survived the unorthodox experiment. Chris and Autris would have to squeeze themselves into some very tight places in a hot electrical equipment bay in the cramped belly of the aircraft.

The downside was that the procedures might cost AeroGalactic thousands of dollars in computer and wire bundle repairs. The only upside was there were no guarantees the attempts would work; there simply were no alternatives.

"You do realize this aircraft doesn't have these components," Autris pointed out.

"I've adapted these diagrams to this dash three-fifty."

Autris nodded. "I could get you behind the computer racks in the lower bay," he muttered. "We can access the wire's pins through the cannon plug backing and hit the circuit you want. But I gotta warn you; there're a lotta wires in that bundle."

Dan piped in, "All we want is a chance. Chris and I believe it's something designed for the aircraft after it was delivered to Gyrfalcon."

Autris looked at his crew and nodded. "We're in; after you stuck up for them before they'd walk on hot coals for you. Besides," he smiled, "I've never known them to turn down the overtime."

"What about the stuffed shirts?"

Autris glanced over at his management and looked over his glasses at Ron. "If you can get rid of the others, I'll work on my management. They want to get to the bottom of this as much as you do."

Ron was quietly listening the whole time, his eyes never left the wiring diagram. "Dan, what do you suggest we do about Phil and Sweeney?"

"Ain't it time you guys broke this test thing up already?" Dan sighed, "We're not getting anywhere."

Ron stared noncommittally at Dan for a minute, his lips pursed in thought. In reality he would not have cared what Phil wanted at this point. "So, I'm assuming you guys won't be at dinner?"

Dan smiled as he picked up the diagram. "Come on, Ron, you know what happens when you assume. You make an ass of outta some guy named Ume."

Chris said, "Isn't that the cute actress?"

Dan responded, "Nah, that's Uma. And you don't make an ass outta her either."

Ron gathered the groups together in the conference room again; Dan and the mechanics who were conducting the tests were missing. Sweeney mentioned this fact; Ron played it down saying Dan was assisting in putting the plane back to the way it was before the tests and collecting the ground sense switches.

Both Dan and Chris had wanted their respective group members around for what they were doing, but that would result in Phil finding out and shutting their impromptu test down. Even some of the AeroGalactic managers were left in the dark. Dan stayed behind in the hangar and worked closely with Autris's mechanics to reconfigure the aircraft's components, working quietly until the visitors left the hangar.

Ron handled the various visiting parties professionally, each leaving the building with those they arrived with. Phil was blind with rage and did not catch on to Dan's absence. Sweeney kept gazing into the hangar bay, suspecting that there was something afoot, but helpless to complain to Phil without receiving some verbal punishment; it was to be a long flight back to Dulles.

Within an hour, everyone departed, making their separate ways to nearby restaurants for a late meal. Some of the more observant may have noticed a pizza delivery van making its way to the hangar from the security shack. The man, who was escorted to the hangar by security in a separate car, dropped off five pizza boxes and four bottles of soda. Dan paid the man in the front office and gave him a generous tip.

Chris and Autris stood hunched over in the avionics bay of the -350; fans hummed loudly nearby drawing hot air out of the bay to keep the computer boxes cool. The light was low, but adequate; the diminished brilliance compared to the hangar afforded enough illumination for Chris to maneuver behind the silver racks. Even though the fans worked frantically to draw out the excess heat, Chris felt like stripping down to his undershirt.

Mild sensations of claustrophobia intruded on Chris's mind as he crowded his tall frame behind the heavy avionics racks. Black computer boxes that managed every aspect of flight stared unsympathetically at him from their uniform positions. All he could see, as Autris squeezed in behind him, were the boxes' backs; he laughed to himself, comparing the view to looking up the computer's skirts.

"It figures you mechanic-types have no problem with stuffing your bodies behind these sardine cans."

Autris chuckled to himself. "How many of you engineer-types actually work in these closets you design?" His right leg was hung up in the tight squeeze, but he angled his knee and the leg disappeared.

"Besides, this is nothing," Autris continued, "try working in a seven-twenty-seven fuel tank with your left knee up around your right ear."

This gave Chris a disturbing mental image. "I'll take your word for it."

"Okay, Dan, we're stuffed into place."

"All right," Dan replied into his walkie-talkie, "let's start with Autoland."

For the next twenty minutes, Autris and Chris coordinated with Dan and A.J. to try different scenarios with the wires. As tight as it was, Chris had little problem probing behind the computers and jumping the wire bundles, thus changing the way the circuit performed. They were careful of not routing higher amperage into a circuit not rated to handle it; if they were not cautious, an expensive control computer could be converted into a useless paperweight. For this reason, Autris was helping Chris; he could not ask one of his guys to take this chance.

Chris asked which wire was next. Dan and A.J., each consuming another piece of pizza, referred to the diagram and relayed the next circuit over the radio. In the limited light, Autris aimed his mini-flashlight at the cannon plug for Chris, who slid the wire into the cannon plug's rubber backing, feeling for the pin. After he was assured contact, he placed the other end of the wire against a power source.

"Chris, try putting the wire across the number one FCC on pin twelve."

Chris nodded his head as he fed the wire into the cannon plug behind the flight command computer, locating pin 12. The static from the walkie-talkie preceded Chris's voice as it relayed his success at finding pin 12.

Dan unconsciously interrupted him by pressing the 'talk' button before he could finish his announcement. As Dan looked over at the aircraft, he had been surprised by a unique sound that caught everyone's attention within hearing distance. The noise was quick and reminded everyone of pneumatic drills driving screws into a wooden board with distinct high-pitched whirs. As suddenly as it started the noise ended, but not before Dan was able to see what had happened. A.J. stared open-mouthed at the left wing of the aircraft as he walked calmly towards it. People from across the hangar were starting to converge on the aircraft sitting several feet above the ground.

Both engine reversers had deployed.

BOOK THREE

DIGITAL CRISIS

CHAPTER 24
GATE THEORIES

Washington – The National Transportation Safety Board announced today that they are focusing on the Aircraft Maintenance division at Gyrfalcon Airlines as the most plausible contributing factor to the crash of Gyrfalcon flight 427 in Memphis on August 12th. The NTSB investigation – under the direction of Chairwoman Ellen Potter – points to interviews conducted after the accident, in which a mechanic stated he chose to ignore manufacturer's instructions when rigging the aircraft's thrust reversers during the last maintenance check. Potter stated today, "The NTSB is taking a hard line with Gyrfalcon; we're centering on this aspect and possible prescription drug abuse one mechanic mentioned during interviews conducted …"

August 28th – Washington, D.C.

"Max is in a place called Camp Yahya Kheyl, in Paktika, somewhere in northern Afghanistan. Megan told me there's a lot of fighting going on there."

"Well, no wonder she's upset, Dan," Chris shook his head. "Don't you talk to her about these deployments? They're obviously tearing her up."

Dan and Chris dominated the old conference room table. Somehow Chris brought the conversation to Max being overseas, but Dan wanted to concentrate on the work at hand. It helped to keep his mind in-country and not twelve thousand miles away.

"Chris, I'm not like her; I can't afford to be concentrating on Max's life."

"But if she—"

"Look!" Dan barked, "It ... it's difficult—!" He took a deep calming breath.

"Max is ... well, he's Max. My son and I are close, but in a different way than I am with Patrick. Max is high maintenance; he's always given me more to worry about. And ever since Tyler di—"

Now he had gone farther than he wanted to; he had told Chris about Tyler, but that subject was no-man's land. The truth is he had not been sleeping lately, mentally commanding the phone not to ring; the military deacon not to telephone.

The dreaded call not to come.

"I'm sorry; I didn't mean to open old wounds." Chris said sheepishly.

"It's alright. I shouldn't have lost it."

"No, I went too far. It's just that Megan means a lot to Karen and me. I didn't mean to bring up Tyler."

"Forget it. I know you're looking out for Meg." Dan stared at the table top, unable to break the uncomfortable silence.

Chris pointed at the scattered diagrams. "What say we look at this NAND Gate?"

Ron found them bent over the conference table with a colorful assortment of highlighting markers scattered in the table's center. Dan pored over the schematics for the

Autoland system, a series of technical prints that showed replicas of the Autoland computer surrounded by a horde of black lines – wires – that ran to other system components. Scattered throughout the schematic were electrical symbols; a chart of wire gauges and symbol identifications occupied the upper left corner of the schematic.

Both men had no idea what they were looking for as they traced the various wires. The -350C was FAA-approved several years before; usually major system anomalies would have presented themselves much earlier.

Chris copied smaller sections of these wiring diagrams before taping them together to form a larger version of the original schematic. Open on the table was a Fault Isolation manual that Dan turned to and referenced every few minutes. As a mechanic, he had used these manuals when diagnosing problems with an aircraft. Like the wiring schematics the diagrams contain a collection of symbols representing various components.

"And why are we looking through these again?" Ron asked, stepping in the room.

Dan looked up for a minute, his reading glasses making his eyes look larger. "The tests proved that the main gear GSS had less to do with this than we thought."

Ron looked confused. "But you told me that you deployed the reversers at least five times after we left. I'd think that would confirm the gear sense problem."

Chris shook his head. "The fact that we got it to work just confirms the problem is down line from the switches, and I emphasize the plural: switches. You've gotta understand, Ron, if Phil hadn't nixed our tests on an identical aircraft we could be putting this to bed. But now, we're crawling through wire diagrams instead of avionics bays. We're armed with highlighting markers instead of voltmeters, without even the benefit of an aircraft to prove our findings."

He held up a portion of the schematic for Ron to see. "The ground sense switches are physically attached to the left main and nose gears where they sense the aircraft's weight on the wheels. Agreed?"

Ron folded his arms across his chest and nodded.

"When this happens, the reversers deploy, the spoilers come up, and the brakes are applied. Right?"

"Yeah, I remember the last eighty times you told me," Ron said, unimpressed.

Chris continued, "You see, so far we're convinced the anomaly isn't *after* the switches because the nose sense switch is sixty feet from the main gear's switch."

Ron shook his head. "Dan said the switches are tied together."

"They are," Chris came back, "because they're connected in the middle. There are two separate paths – one to each switch – where signals are being sent through a confusing series of wires and components to half a dozen computers."

Dan swept his hands out, indicating the pages of schematics. "What Chris is saying is that if there's a problem, it's before the switches. Or–"

Ron closed his eyes, saying, "Or what?"

"Or, a signal is coming in from somewhere else. Chris is right; if Phil allowed us access to an identical twin of the accident aircraft, we'd be a lot further than we are."

"So, you're saying," Ron remarked, "that though the switches gave bad information, they're not what caused the reversers to deploy."

"Correct!"

Connie walked into the room; she quickly viewed the papers and manuals spread out across the table.

"Have you two found anything yet?"

"Well, we've made some progress," Chris began, "and we're trying to …"

"Stop!" Connie practically screamed. "Why don't you start from the beginning and explain it, like I don't know ... because, the fact is, I don't. But I need to understand it so Phil won't catch me off guard."

"You sure you want to do this?" Ron asked with a wry grin.

"From the beginning," Dan began. "From Freestyle's CVR, Satya eliminated any unnecessary sounds or air traffic conversations for the readout. Without the extraneous nonsense, we started tracing the events to find out exactly what happened within a five-second span of time before the deployment to five seconds after the reverser stowed back again. I mean the event happens that fast," he snapped his fingers, "and ends that fast," emphasizing again with another snap.

"It appears Gyrfalcon had a similar cause," Chris said. "We're confident the Freestyle event happened just as the gear locked down, when they were suddenly out on that old creek without a paddle."

"You said before that Freestyle's number two engine 'responded'?"

"Well, Connie, in a normal K-R-four-fifty landing, the number two engine spools up when the reverser deploys," said Dan. "AeroGalactic designed it that way; activate number two reverser while the nose gear is still in the air."

Connie looked confused.

Chris elaborated, "The switch that Freestyle changed out; the main gear's ground sense switch? The GSS?" She nodded. "That alerts the computer ... it's important you understand this ... it alerts the computer that the number two reverser is safe to deploy."

Dan placed a finger on the wiring diagram and then moved it over to the fault manual diagram, bridging the symbols for the GSS in both schematics.

"What if there's an emergency," Connie continued, "and they execute a go-around?"

Dan turned to Chris. "Who said these management-types can't follow through on the basics?"

"My little sister's a JetBlue pilot, remember?"

Dan added, "But obviously can't take a compliment."

Chris smiled at Connie and she grimaced back.

"Good question, Connie," Dan continued, "because that sounded wrong to me too. The answer is: the pilots override the Autoland simply by pushing all three throttles forward to their stops. In Go-Around, they're demanding full power anyway. The throttle computer's digital logic overrides Autoland; it also sends a signal to another computer to stow the reverser. You've got full forward power to go around for another approach."

Connie nodded her understanding.

"All right," Dan said, "when the main wheels touch down, the ground sense switch closes. This closed switch sends power to the FCC to say it's landed."

"The what?" She cut him off.

"The FCC ... I'm sorry, the flight command computer. Every aircraft system, like, say, air conditioning or hydraulics has their own control computer; it makes sure every component of that system is working as designed."

Chris added, "They oversee what each component in that system does and when it does it. They also talk to other system computers; they're the system's data hub. Think of your modem providing internet service throughout your house for all your laptops."

"Right," Dan began again, "now the Autoland computer takes thousands of digital commands, requests, and questions; it directs, redirects, or filters them through the computer's logic. Computers and components talk back and forth the whole flight."

Connie absorbed the information, but just stared at the diagrams.

"And this is where Chris and I get stumped."

Connie looked at Ron, who shrugged his shoulders. She glanced up at the ceiling and rubbed her neck. "So, when you say 'stumped,' you mean you disagree with what the Freestyle mechanics did to fix their airplane in Los Angeles?"

"Not exactly," Chris began, "but we think there was more to the problem."

They felt, more than heard, Phil standing behind them. Giv stood safely off his left elbow still halfway in the hall as if awaiting a command, just out of swatting range.

"Have you found anything?" Phil stated in a droning monotone.

Dan turned around to face Phil, catching sight of Giv standing off in the hall. "We haven't found anything, per se. We think the ground sense switches are related, but there's something not right."

"And what would that be?" Phil slowly moved towards the table. He scanned the diagrams and maintenance documents spread out across the tabletop, but made no effort to ask a detailed explanation. Giv stayed where he was.

Dan continued, "The ground sense switch is a good find because of the corrosion problems. It's part of the Autoland system; it provides a link to deploying the reverser, but it isn't the only one." Dan pointed towards the diagram. "Do you see what I mean?"

Phil's mouth tightened; he knew Dan was purposely answering in technical terms, but refused to be baited into asking for further clarification.

"The system's diagram clearly shows digital paths to the FCC. We think the information was misrouted, but I'm not sure by what or–"

Phil cut him off with a wave of his hand. "So, you don't know and you're only guessing. Is that what you're saying?"

"It's what we're working from right now."

"There's no time for hunches and theories."

"It's more than a theory …" Chris threw in.

But Phil stopped him. "The cargo plane didn't crash, did it?"

He let the last question hang for a second. "I see no reason to continue dragging Freestyle into this. You're supposed to be focused on the Gyrfalcon accident. What we've learned is that Maintenance fouled up. I want your maintenance report to focus on the mechanics not following instructions–"

"Phil, they didn't do anything wrong!"

But Phil continued as if Dan didn't say a word. "And find out about the prescription drugs! But first, clean up this conference room! That goes for you too, Chris!"

Phil walked out of the room and down the hall, followed closely by Giv, handkerchief at the ready as he maintained a close, but safe, distance from Phil's retreating footsteps.

"It's inspiring to see someone like Phil who's so clearly in touch with reality," Chris said. "I wonder when he looks out the window what color the sky is."

"It's rose-colored." Dan said as he collected schematics off the table. "It's like handing a five-year old a loaded pistol and saying, 'Go play cops and robbers.'"

"What are you doing?" Connie inquired.

"I'm cleaning up; you heard him," Dan answered.

Ron glanced down the hall. "Well, the storm's blown over. Dan, finish what you were saying. He's not coming back this way for a while."

Dan looked doubtfully at Ron.

"How sure are you about your theory?" Connie asked quietly.

"Not sure enough to ask you to stake your career on, if that's what you mean. I'm confident this ain't the end, though." Dan lowered his voice, "I'm going to talk to Aaron at the FAA when I get the chance."

Connie stared at her friend for a few seconds and nodded. "Finish what you were saying; I trust your intuitions more than most people's around here."

Dan spread the diagrams, trying to get his bearings. "Okay, we said we weren't sure about replacing the GSS."

"Right," said Connie, "but why don't you think it's the switches?"

"Well, that's simple," he responded. "It's because of the gates."

Connie stared at him, waiting for the other shoe to drop, but Dan never continued; he stood, unconsciously tapping his mouth with a capped highlighting marker. Connie looked over at Chris, who smiled at his friend's eccentricity.

"Dan, what are you talking about when you say the gates?"

Dan stabbed a finger back on the diagram, to the middle of a black outline. It resembled a 'roadmap' of straight lines that connected box-shaped cities. Within the 'map' were many thinner lines representing wires, each connecting numerous symbols.

He raised his eyes to Connie. "What I'm trying to describe is digital technology; *not*," he emphasized by tapping the table, "my strong suit, but I'll do my best."

"If you don't get it," Ron chuckled, "how are we supposed to understand it?"

Dan seemed to ignore the question as he sat in a chair. "As I understand it digital data is represented in ones and zeros, in code. For instance, characters from a Word document, picture colors, or even revised software; they're all a series of ones and zeros."

"You're saying a programmer uses ones and zeros, Dan?"

"Yes, I mean, no ... I mean ... I'm saying that the only way the computer can understand you or another computer is if the data is expressed in ones and zeros," He sat back in the chair. "Your sister sent you a digital picture of the JetBlue plane she flew yesterday, right?"

"Okay."

"The digital picture she sent is composed of ones and zeros. A computer doesn't understand the color red, but if you give it the right series of ones and zeros it 'sees' red."

Both Connie and Ron shook their heads, confused.

Dan looked at Chris for help, then stared back at the diagram. "In the old days, like on the seven-twenty-seven, when a pilot turned an air conditioner on he flicked a toggle switch and power went to the air conditioner; it came on. We used to call the instruments: 'steam gauges,' analog technology. But they were basically hardware; a wire from a power source to a switch, like the kitchen light in your house.

"But today, the pilot presses a button which tells a computer to turn on the A-C. The computer has to first conduct a diagnostic check, which it does digitally. Only then does it trigger the air conditioner on. It sets the temperature and monitors the air conditioner's health; all automatically; no human input beyond pressing a button."

"No hardware?"

"No, that's the point; it's software. The computer does all the controlling."

"Isn't that stealing control from the pilots?"

Dan pointed at Connie with a smile. "Exactly!"

"But Connie," Chris added, "it also steals control from the mechanic who's trying to fix it. Like Dan's seven-twenty-seven, he would troubleshoot the aircraft for problems; he relied on his training to figure out the complication and then he fixed it. Today, the computer tells him where the problem is and how to fix it. Mechanics are becoming parts changers instead of technicians."

"But that's done to save money; less ground time," Ron asked.

"Yeah," Dan said, "but even too much of a good thing is not best. We're encouraging a generation of mechanics and pilots who don't know – rea-eally don't know – the airplane. As a result, we can't even recognize the problems when they go beyond the computer's ability to understand, or worse: the computer thinks what it's doing is right, but it's actually wrong."

"As in Freestyle and Gyrfalcon," Chris concluded. "Did you ever hear of Moore's Law?"

Ron guessed, "Is that like Murphy's Law?"

"No, not even close," Chris said. "Moore's Law – as my instructor interpreted it – says that digital technology will double every two years until 2020, or some such date. That means that digital technology, like SPAR, will outdistance the experience of pilots within the next few years. And SPAR isn't the only thing; the airplanes themselves will out think the pilots, the mechanics, and even the air traffic controllers. These same groups will not have the tribal knowledge, the background, to keep up or know when the aircraft makes a mistake."

Connie's eyes narrowed. "The what knowledge?"

Dan leaned forward in his chair. "The tribal knowledge; it's the experience pilots, mechanics or any professional gains over years of doing their job. What Chris means is, well, take Gyrfalcon for example. When Barry interviewed the first officer, he said he pulled back on the yoke when the reverser light came on, not the captain. Barry checked both of their histories; the first officer had years more experience at the controls under more extreme conditions; the F-O recognized the problem first and reacted by using his tribal knowledge."

"That's quite a stretch, Dan," Ron interjected doubtfully.

"No, it's not, Ron," Dan asserted. "What about Freestyle's crew? The first officer told the FAA that it was the captain's experience that saved the day. She wasn't trying to get on his good side; she repeated that over and over again."

Connie took a seat at the end of the table. Uncharacteristically, she began spinning back and forth in the chair with a contemplative expression.

"What do you think, Boss?" Ron asked.

Her eyes shot to Dan's, holding him in her gaze for a minute. "I think that these two have put me off flying for the near future." She stopped swiveling in the chair and faced Chris. "Can you explain what's hanging you up without killing me with scientific jargon?"

Chris smiled and shrugged. "We'll try."

"Okay," she said, "then tell me what a gate is."

"Dan told you about ones and zeros," Chris stated factually. "A one and a zero cannot share the same space. So, when I say a one, I will call it a one command and the same for zeros; I'll say a zero command."

Connie scrunched her eyes closed. "Why must you do that?"

"Simply put, a computer program is thousands of lines of data," he put his hand up to stop Connie's question. "They're also called commands."

Connie frowned. "Alright, I'll give you some room until you start to lose me."

"Fine," Chris said. He pointed to a symbol in the computer schematic; it resembled a tombstone; instead of its domed surface pointing up, it lay on its side with the flat bottom pointing to the opposite side. There were dozens of other sideways tombstones surrounding it, all with two or more black 'wire' lines going into the flat side. "Do you see that symbol?" Connie just nodded. "Okay, that's an AND gate. This particular AND gate takes a signal from our broken ground sense switch, Autoland, and another input signal that according to this Gyrfalcon wiring diagram is not active."

"Is A-N-D an acronym?"

"No."

"Dan, what exactly is a gate?" Ron asked.

"It's just what it suggests: a gate. It allows signals into or out of a computer." Connie nodded her head while Ron stared blankly.

Chris put it in simpler terms, "Let me put it this way; in the old days a wire ran from a switch to the lights to turn off and on. These were simple circuits. But like we said before, aircraft today are driven by computers." He pointed at Ron. "Do you have cruise control on your car?"

"Doesn't everybody?"

"Right," Chris said, "well, when you want to set a particular speed several things must happen before it works. It's a computer-controlled device and it uses commands to the gates to make it work."

Dan pointed to a legend full of symbols in a corner of the wiring diagram. "Each of these symbols is a basic component, like a light, a fan, or even an air conditioner. The lines represent wires." With his finger he trained their gaze on different symbols inside the wiring diagram. "A component can be as small as a resistor or as large as a hydraulic actuator. If I talk about a particular component, I'll point to it on the diagram and show you what its symbol is. Then I'll explain why it stands out in the explanation."

"That'll work," Connie said simply.

"Do you remember that dream you had when you were little; the one about you and your Prince Charming living in a little cottage with a white picket fence and two-point-five dogs?"

"I never," Connie responded, "ever dreamed about Prince Charming."

"Well, then Jason from the 'Friday the Thirteenth' movies."

Connie turned to Chris. "I always did like the strong silent type."

Dan said smiling, "In the little white picket fence there's a small doorway; it swings in so you and Jason can get through the fence. And we call that …?"

"A gate," Connie laughed. "What do I win?"

"The warm confidence that you're following me so far."

"That doesn't sound like much considering I actually understood you."

Ron leaned over. "Sounds like you got cheated, Boss. I'd settle for a warm confidence," Ron muttered, "because I'm not following them."

"Okay, do you remember the AND gate?" Connie saw where his finger was and nodded. "It needs all the input data to agree. Let's use Ron's cruise control for example; there are two or three input commands coming into the AND gate and they say," Dan started ticking points off on his fingers, "your car is driving over twenty-five miles per hour … *and* … your cruise control is turned on … *and* … you are not using the brake. Now the cruise control will work at fifty-five miles per hour."

Chris said, "On the aircraft, if there's weight on the gear, the flaps are extended as in landing and the throttles are retarded as in landing, then those three things tell the

The Air Crash Files: Jet Blast

number two reverser to deploy, but only those three things for that specific AND gate. Those are three one command signals – no ... zeroes – and all three have to be present.

"In other words, let's say you're one wire, Jason is a second wire, and your dogs are the third wire. You can't open the gate unless only you, Jason, and the dogs are entering at the same time. You can't get in with you, Jason, and your mother; it won't work."

"I'm with you."

"You're sure?"

"I think so," Connie confessed.

"Now, I'll throw you a curve," Dan continued. "There's another gate called an OR gate." He pointed to the schematic again, but this time he showed an arrowhead on its side; two black lines were touching its back.

"In order to get through an OR gate, no two signals can agree; you have to have a one command and a zero command."

"Correct," Chris said. "If you have a radio slash C-D player in your car, can you listen to both at the same time?"

Connie checked to see if Ron would answer before saying, "No!"

"The radio won't interfere with the C-D and vice versa. That's an OR gate; you either listen to your favorite Dee-Jay or your favorite C-D."

Dan considered the point to make before uttering, "Now, if you and Jason arrive home from a good day's haunting innocent college girls who don't have the sense God gave them to run; if you try to get through the gate at the same time, it won't open. Only you ... *or* ... Jason can enter, but not both."

"Airliners don't have C-D players, so it sounds ridiculous. Why would they use OR gates?"

Chris stepped in, "Because you don't always need two or more inputs to make something operate. The electrical computer may choose the number one generator to power the aircraft or it may choose number two, but never both."

"Gotcha," Connie said, "but that wasn't too much of a curve ball."

"That's because now we're going to introduce another gate." Dan pointed to another tombstone-shaped symbol.

"An AND gate, so what?"

"Ah-ah-ah," laughed Chris, coaxing Connie to draw closer to the drawing. At the curved end of the tombstone was a small but obvious circle.

"Allow me to introduce you to the NAND gate," he continued.

Connie rubbed her forehead. "Am I really going to want to hear this?"

Chris laughed quietly, "The NAND gate acts like an anti-AND gate; NAND, which means: not AND."

"I really don't want to hear this," she mumbled, sotto voce.

"Do you want an aspirin?" Dan asked. But Connie just shook her head.

"Chris, give an example where a NAND gate is used."

Chris closed his eyes, lost in thought, finally saying, "The only thing I can think of is a time delay used in a circuit; a command signal is held back until a certain amount of time elapses. NAND gates are used to prevent commands from acting too quickly."

Connie looked to Dan, who said, "Yeah, that sounds about right. Let's say you go from your car to your house but the dome light is still on. You curse and walk back to turn it off, but it turns off by itself. That's a time delay."

He turned back to the diagram. "Now Connie, in the world of ones and zeroes, a NAND gate is opposite of the AND gate, identified by that little circle on the side," he said. "However, it reverses the numbers; ones become zeroes and …"

"I'm not clear on why the NAND gate reverses the inputs?"

Dan looked at Chris, who said, "Do you know what an inverter is?"

Connie shrugged, "I'd have to say it's something that … inverts?"

"Well, yeah," Chris continued. "It's designed to turn ones into zeroes and vice versa. It's supposed to take a positive and turn it into a non-positive. That's why it works on time delays. The intent: take an electrical signal and invert it for a certain period of time, or …" Chris seemed to forget what he was saying, but instead he was emphasizing the point. Connie became annoyed, hanging on his next words.

"… while something's in the middle of a task." Chris looked at Dan and got an impressed nod of the head. "A command may need to be impeded while a generator is on or an actuator is working. The NAND gate allows this to happen, because it's an inverter; AND gates can't and neither can OR gates."

"And, not to belabor this issue anymore," Dan sighed, "but there's several NAND gates in the Autoland system with 'yet-to-be-activated' connections. We don't know if the airline modified them."

"What do you mean by yet-to-be-activated?"

"The wire to the gate is reserved for another system that's not installed yet."

"Do you mean they're going to update the system–?"

"Or they *already updated* it, Connie," said Chris.

"Or," Dan paused. "They routed in a whole new system altogether. That's what these schematics are." Dan became serious. "Connie, even though we've deferred the Autoland, these aircraft are still flying around with the computer equivalent of a brain embolism."

Connie asked, "Is there anything you can do to get a new test going?"

Dan shook his head. "No, we're not even sure if the sensors we used in the first test were shorting or grounding out, like in the accident. The break-up was real violent in Memphis; electronics are real fragile to begin with, without the fire and slamming ... and heat ... and foam."

"What would have been perfect," Chris interceded, "would've been to have that GSS from Freestyle. They landed without a hitch. If there was any way for us to duplicate the conditions, that was it."

"Any chance–"

"No," Dan interrupted her. "The sensor is a consumable item; it isn't saved for any reason like in overhaul. Aaron asked, but the mechanic who worked it said it was missing from the work table, and he said it was probably thrown away."

Connie continued looking at the diagrams for a few more minutes. She looked up at the two of them before heading out the door, talking over her shoulder, "If you two can find a place to work out of view, work on this.

I'll run interference as much as I can." She turned, gesturing for Ron to follow.

"Perhaps an opportunity will present itself in the meantime."

CHAPTER 25
FOLLOWING UP

Almost three months had passed since the accident; many in the media had shelved Gyrfalcon 427 for more immediate national crises. Senators and members of Congress ceased their emotional speeches for public safety, instead turning their attentions to issues that promised constituent votes. Aviation experts – most self-proclaimed – sat nervously by their phones; they anticipated other high-profile accidents or a breakthrough in Gyrfalcon's investigation that would call them out to share their one-dimensional insights.

When broken down, accident investigations are days of adrenaline rushes (immediate response to the accident), followed by weeks of mediocrity (testing and analysis), leading to months of preparation (for the Investigative Hearing), resulting in satisfaction and understanding at the much-anticipated Sunshine Meeting.

The Gyrfalcon 427 investigation was at the end of the mediocrity stage. It takes several months to bridge, the length depending on the severity of the accident. It is a progressive learning phase, where the different investigators touch base, brain-storming without the burden of teleconferences or setting of the sun. These NTSB team leads spend countless hours on the phone or in telecom meetings, aiming to prove or discount one or more hypotheses. Face-to-face with one's counterparts allows for free discourse; revelations come to the surface.

It also provides for impromptu meetings where unasked for directives cannot intrude.

At this stage, two contributing reports are written by each team lead. Each investigator composes these reports to condense the combined years of traceable history of both man and machine into a narrative, a warning to future generations to heed the history so as not to repeat it. They are the foundation for the writing of the Blue Cover Report that, once finished, is finalized by the acceptance of the Board at the NTSB Sunshine meeting.

Why call it a Blue Cover Report? For the obvious reason that all aviation accident reports employ a blue cover.

Though part of a whole, the two contributing reports are decisively different in their makeup. The first is the Factual Report: a report that lays out the facts of the accident. This includes information about, e.g. manufacturers, truthful personal information, documented conditions, and other uncontestable facts; evidences which are stated by subject, with no room for opinion or allegation.

The second report is called the Analysis Report. Here the NTSB staff delves into areas of assertion, spotlighting an investigator's true experience, where their scrutinizing skills take precedence – or fail miserably. The analysis is based on opinion and evaluation. Though directed that this report not be made available to the public, somehow parts often find their way into the open, frequently putting innocent parties on the defensive with only their now-damaged reputations to support them.

The summation of the Analysis Report is the Probable Causes and the Recommendations, which are the meat of the yet unwritten Blue Cover Report. Probable cause allows the investigators to elaborate on what they *think* triggered the accident, based on their supported theories, not necessarily proven. Recommendations are based on the probable causes; they are suggestions to industry and the FAA for preventing future accidents.

Phil collects the submitted probable causes and decides which ones make the Blue Cover Report's final draft, authoring the recommendations to match a certain narrative.

When it comes to his Factual, Dan is a perfectionist; he is fanatical about accuracy, never stating information that he is not absolutely positive about. This single-minded obsession with precision absorbs all his attention. Vince Scalia would ask him for early drafts to hone his own skills on the maintenance issues. The Board Member would correct him for small technical errors, which Dan took and edited it into the report ... after doublechecking Vince's facts.

Even the ability to lock himself in an office did not provide protection for Dan from Giv's constant queries, looking for information to bring back to Phil. Giv's intrusions became frequent and often agitated, arriving at Dan's office unannounced or walking in uninvited, his eyes moving from side-to-side as if hoping to read on the walls what Dan was working on. As a result, Dan kept his work on his computer desktop, accessible only through password security, further frustrating Giv.

During work hours in Washington, Dan and Chris avoided contact as often as possible. Since Phil made it difficult for them to compare notes, they dragged their work into the weekends at one or the other's house. Chris lived in Woodbridge, Virginia, a drive of thirty-five miles from Dan and Meg's house in Bealeton.

November 10

The two investigators stood out on Dan's back deck. Small clouds moved rapidly overhead on an easterly course; the sun fighting to pierce an overcast layer, ten-thousand feet above. It was not cold, but a chilly breeze trickled through several tall trees. The leaves had already vacated the three young saplings Dan had planted; the grass turned tan-brown, waiting tolerantly for another winter to pass.

A lone home-built light aircraft buzzed overhead, its four-cylinder engine droning with lawn mower quality. It soared on fragile wings, reminding ground dwellers more of a misshapen kite than an aerial vehicle. It appeared to battle winds aloft and suddenly turned from a westerly to an easterly direction, spinning like a weather vane.

Dan looked up; he saluted the amateur pilot, shaking his head. Home-built aircraft were numerous in the area, especially in the early fall. Dan respected the pilots he met through his job, but these were a different breed. *Amateurs who often ignored the basic concepts of manned flight; they risked much to themselves and to others*, he thought. *Allowing people who did not feel it necessary to gain the elementary skills of flying was like permitting pogo sticks in a minefield; all it takes is one bad move.*

"Another F-D-G in the making," Dan observed sadly.
"Future Dead Guy?"
"You got it."

Dan guzzled a mouthful of beer and leaned his hands on the rail.

"I called Aaron yesterday. He said he got me the SPAR diagram revisions for both Freestyle and Gyrfalcon."

"Wow, it took this long? Any problems?"

Dan shrugged and said, "Phil was instrumental in slowing the process by telling Gyrfalcon the investigation wasn't focused on SPAR or computer technologies. Giv called them back later and said that the chairwoman wants to focus on maintenance and that Gyrfalcon better get their ducks in a row; that is if he even knows what a duck is." Dan shook his head in frustration.

"Phil also took it upon himself to let Freestyle know they weren't under any pressure to deliver their plans since they weren't under investigation," Dan said. "To add insult to injury, he apologized for my rounding them up in this mess.

"Other than that, just the usual concerns with proprietary issues. Their lawyers are worried that we'll leak their super-duper secret SPAR technologies."

"It's not even theirs. What're they whining about?"

"Gyrfalcon doesn't have a choice because of the investigation, but we weren't checking up on Freestyle. I'm sure they don't want their wiring diagrams plastered on display during the hearing. They're concerned people will associate their aircraft with the accident aircraft."

Chris stared at the bottle in his hand. "That's the least of our problems if we can't find the phantom circuit."

"There's no one at the Board that's better than you at avionics."

Chris shook his head. "I'm afraid that's not saying much."

"Well, unless we find an electronics guru, we're going to go blind going over those systems. I don't know how long I can dodge Phil; he suspects something."

Chris laughed, "Can't Ron run interference for you anymore?"

"Not likely; even Connie can't keep him at bay forever."

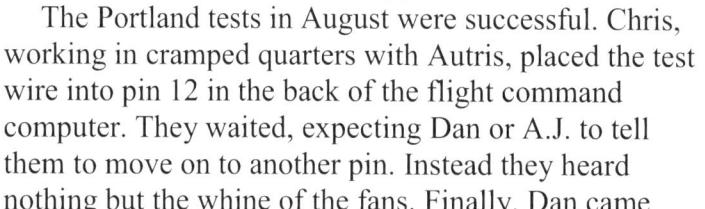

The Portland tests in August were successful. Chris, working in cramped quarters with Autris, placed the test wire into pin 12 in the back of the flight command computer. They waited, expecting Dan or A.J. to tell them to move on to another pin. Instead they heard nothing but the whine of the fans. Finally, Dan came back on the radio to ask them to pull out the wire and put it in again.

Sitting atop the jacks, the test aircraft was kept in a false state of flight after all the other attendees left; all the instruments were 'faked out' into believing it was flaring twenty feet off the ground while moving at 130 knots. In this configuration, Chris tricked the airplane into deploying the reversers. At first the hangar was silent. Soon, rounds of applause broke out, supported by several of the managers asking what they did to figure out the problem.

Chris was not convinced. Instead they stayed in the equipment bay running through the rest of the simulations. By the end of the trial, the reversers deployed five different times by crossing the circuit to different pins.

But the tests were successful. They proved that with the right input the aircraft would mimic the fateful last actions of Flight 427. Furthermore, of the five pins they tapped, four showed a wire going nowhere, not active. The trick now was to find out which input generated the anomaly by digging through countless wiring schematics; each circuit branched off into countless AND gates, OR gates, and NAND gates, which diverged off into hundreds of other circuits and computers. To Dan and Chris, it was akin to finding a needle in a warehouse full of haystacks.

If they could somehow determine which circuit was being stimulated into ignoring its programming they could find the true cause of the accident. The next problem would be to convince Phil and Giv that further tests were necessary before going to the investigatory hearing.

"Well, the public hearing isn't until February. We still have some time."

"Seriously?" Dan asked sarcastically. "You think we've got time? Assuming one of us doesn't get pulled on another accident between now and February, the holidays are coming and trying to find someone to help us won't be easy."

Chris glanced down at the deck boards; his mind traveled through lists of past workers who were good at avionics, but he was drawing a blank. "Well, I've got nothin'. There's nobody I know in industry I can trust with this." He looked around and said, "I'm going in; it's getting cold out here."

Dan followed Chris through the sliding door into the kitchen where Meg sat working a school assignment on her laptop.

"What's the matter?"

"Oh, Miss Chrissy was getting cold outside."

"God, Dan, you can be such a butt sometimes," Meg chastised.

Dan ignored Megan's remark. "I just wish I was more competent when it comes to avionics. I can't think of anyone else either."

"What about 'Sparky' Lyle?"

Chris looked at Meg. "You mean the old Yankees relief pitcher?"

"Of course, Chris, I mean the New York Yankees relief pitcher. He had all those saves and a degree in computer engineering," Megan shot back. "No, Dan knows who I mean."

When Chris looked over at Dan he was looking at nothing, but his mind was having an argument with itself. "Who's Sparky Lyle?"

Still preoccupied, Dan responded, "Gordon, Gordon 'Sparky' Lyle; we called him Sparky … actually I called him Sparky. A 'Spark' was a nickname we gave avionics guys. Gordon came to the hangar when Republic merged back in the eighties. He couldn't throw a baseball, but man, could that guy troubleshoot electrical circuits. That's why I called him Sparky." He paused for a minute. "His last name was Lyle, after all."

Chris muttered, "Yeah, of course; real original of you."

Dan disregarded him. Instead he turned toward Meg. "I can't ask Gordon …"

"You mean Sparky," Chris threw in.

"… 'cause he still works for …"

But Meg cut him off. "He retired two years ago. He's makin' a bunch of money as a maintenance consultant."

"Where does he live now?" Dan asked.

"Honestly, Dan," Megan stood up and crossed to one of the kitchen cabinet drawers, "you are absolutely helpless!" She pulled an address book out of the drawer and threw it on the counter top. "He and Hope moved back to Fort Lauderdale."

"But Meg, I still can't show him the wiring diagrams. They have the airline's information on it. All that stuff's proprietary!"

She reached into the drawer again and pulled out a wide tipped black magic marker. "Use one of these new-fangled magic markers to cover the airline's information. Once you blot it out, there's no problem. Then either send it to him as a scanned attachment or bring it to him." Meg went back to her computer without another word. Chris took a sip of his beer as Dan stood staring between the marker and the address book.

Chris leaned over and whispered. "Don't worry, buddy; I won't tell everybody how your wife just whipped your butt.

"Oh, wait," he said, slapping his forehead, "what am I saying? Of course, I will!"

CHAPTER 26
SPARKY LYLE

November 12 – Fort Lauderdale, FL

Two days later Dan was flying to Fort Lauderdale. He had worked out the details with Ron, who promised to approve his travel in keeping with the investigation; that way Ron had authority over Giv, while keeping Phil at arm's length. In order to keep suspicions down, Dan chose to enroute on a major airline. Normally, reserved for FAA inspectors conducting spot surveillance, Dan's use of the cockpit jumpseat was welcomed to help the FAA perform random inspections. The only downside was that, per FAA rules, Dan had to shave his beard.

Since there was only one observer's seat in the cockpit, Dan flew out of Dulles while Chris flew out of Reagan. They met in the Fort Lauderdale terminal and picked up their rental car; within a half hour they were driving north on I-95 to Coral Springs. Gordon expected them around noon.

"Gordon!" Dan shouted, as he stepped into the small house. Gordon shook his hand warmly, guiding him to the living room. Gordon greeted Chris as well.

"You're the engineer Dan was telling me about?"

"Yeah," Chris responded.

Gordon held Chris in his gaze for a moment, pulling his glasses off to see him better before shrugging his shoulders and remarking, "Well, nobody's perfect."

Gordon 'Sparky' Lyle looked nothing like his Southpaw Yankee's namesake. He was more bookish, with a knack for all things mechanical. His lean frame, thinning grey hair and thick glasses did nothing to hide a sharp mind, an avionics encyclopedia on two feet. Gordon was now in his late-sixties and retired, but had surrendered to the pleas of industry contractors who begged him to design aircraft maintenance programs. His consulting business soon took on a life of its own.

As Gordon made his way behind them he picked up a tray of cold cuts from the refrigerator, some bread and ushered the two investigators out to the screened-in porch.

"Daniel, get the potato salad out of the 'fridge," he ordered, "and Chris can grab the drinks from the cabinet out here."

Soon they were all settled around the table. Dan did not need an invitation while Chris was slower to help himself. Gordon prodded him on by waving a finger at him; the digit was missing the first two knuckles.

"They were never able to save it?" Dan said around his sandwich.

Gordon looked thoughtfully at the maimed finger. "No, the reattachment never took. Besides, it just never looked right."

"What happened?" Chris ventured.

"My finger, you mean?" Gordon asked. "Yeah, we'll save that story for another time."

When they finished lunch, Gordon was all business. Pushing his chair back, he finished off his drink, saying, "Grab your diagrams and let's have a look."

Dan went into the other room and brought back the cardboard cylinder he carried the wiring diagrams in. Pulling off the top, he extracted the heavy roll of paper documents and spread them out on a long picnic table. Along the top, all the information directed at each of the carriers was blacked out. Gordon looked over the paperwork carefully. "Now, you two think there're problems with the Autoland or SPAR system components?"

"We can't prove it, but another episode happened in the summer where Autoland was engaged. The reason I'm thinking SPAR ... and, Gordon, it's nothing but a working theory. But I suspect SPAR because of the timing."

"Has Gyrfalcon started installing SPAR?" Gordon asked, picking his teeth with a toothpick.

Dan and Chris looked at Gordon, who looked back. "Seriously," Gordon remarked, "you didn't think I would figure out who this is? You're thinking the reversers deployed because of Autoland, SPAR, or a combination of either of them, together."

"Gordon, I can't give you that information."

"I understand, but look; I can't work with this," he said pointing with his ruined finger, "and not know the consequences of the problem. And don't worry; I won't take notes about anything proprietary. You can cut off one of my other fingers if I do."

Chris gestured to one of the diagrams that showed the updated wiring diagram of the AeroGalactic -350. "I wrote down which pins deployed the reversers during the test."

"What's this about a NAND gate?"

Dan cleared his throat. "That's the theory we're pursuing; we couldn't be sure if one of the gates had an anomaly, at least it seems to us it might. Anyway, they're in the circuits between the landing gear controller and flight command computer's Autoland systems. This is the only wiring diagram for the dash three-fifty. This other one is for the dash four-fifty," he pulled out the Freestyle wiring diagram. "It had an uncommanded reverser deployment in flight, but it was the number two on the tail."

Chris said, "I've spent years in maintenance engineering support and it still makes no sense that there are so many manufacturers for all these computer systems. Aren't they the same systems?"

"Well, what I'm seeing here," Gordon said, "is a landing gear box for a Boeing, one for an Airbus, and two for two different AeroGalactic aircraft. When somebody designs a system they take into account three things: one, who's the customer? Okay? Two, what do you want the system to do, specifically? For instance, this operator," he said pointing at one of the diagrams, "may not fly overseas, while this one does. So, it's like ordering extras for your car. But they still want the equipment to work with the same ATC system."

"Yeah," Dan said, "but an Airbus isn't built like a Boeing or an AeroGalactic like an old Douglas."

"These systems," Gordon continued, "are supposed to be custom designed for the aircraft they're being installed in. That leads us to three, which is money. SPAR is new; it'll be updated a thousand times before everybody is on the grid. These test bed airlines don't want to lose their investment, so they pay for a system that'll work without putting them in the financial toilet. They want one that will be cost effective in the future."

Two hours later, the three men had barely moved.

"So, what do you think, Gordon?" Dan said with a glimmer of hope in his voice.

Gordon looked up at the two investigators, adjusting his reading glasses. "Are you expecting me to feed you an answer today?"

Dan and Chris exchanged looks. "But," Dan said, "you're the expert."

"Oh well, in that case, let me just rush right through this and get you an answer." He stood straight up and shook his head. "I'm sorry, Daniel, but I can't hit this thing cold and spit out a fix," he continued, snapping his fingers, "just like that!"

"No, of course not, Gordon. How about by tomorrow?"

"How about a week from tomorrow?" Gordon shot back.

"Seriously?"

"Daniel, look at these schematics! I can't go through all these diagrams and give you an accurate analysis right away." He took in a deep breath, letting out a long sigh. "I'll tell you what; you guys get situated and come see me tomorrow for lunch. I'll see what I can gather in that time."

"All right, I'll bring some burgers and we can go over it."

Before they made it to the door, Gordon threw in, "After tomorrow, I'll keep looking into it. I may find something else down line."

The next afternoon Chris parked the car while Dan made his way to the door with lunch. He was hoping to gauge Gordon when he greeted them. When Gordon opened the door, his smile told the story: it was a strained grin.

"How bad?" Dan asked, hesitantly.

"Well, let's just say that I found some possible issues."

Gordon ushered them both into the house where they gathered around the picnic table. "I can tell you this," Gordon began, "I remember why I never felt the calling to be an avionics engineer. The loony houses must be ripping at the seams with these guys and those funny wrap around jackets. You wouldn't believe the intricate paths each system has running in and out of it.

"Take this landing gear computer for instance; I ended up going through ten separate wiring diagrams to get a handle on all the inputs into one pin out of ... oh, I don't know, sixty-two pins on this cannon plug alone. And then for each input, the timing has to be taken into consideration plus time delays, what precedes it, what follows it, and what happens if the inputs aren't there."

"Were you able to get anywhere?"

Gordon pursed his lips and bowed his head over the diagram again. "It doesn't appear to be a malfunction of the landing gear computer."

Dan asked, "Is that the only computer you've been able to discount?"

"I've tried to compare the flight command computers with the other diagrams, but so far I can't find a problem with them. The L-G-C was probably the most questionable, so I looked at it first." Gordon leaned over the diagram for N374GY. "I'm interested in where the information off the gear switches comes in, like here," he said, pointing to the cannon plug, "especially since it figured into the Gyrfalcon accident and the Freestyle incident. So, I spent most of last night poring over the circuits."

Chris ran his finger over the wire lines Gordon was talking about. "You're convinced the L-G-C isn't the problem?"

"It isn't malfunctioning, as far as I can see," Gordon clarified, "but it could lead us to what is supplying the faulty information."

"Well, in your opinion," Chris asked, "if it isn't the L-G-C logic, what's getting the bad info?"

Gordon looked up at Chris with a sly look, anticipating this question. "Chris, that's where you and I part company; I don't think it's getting bad information. In other words," he continued to puzzled looks, "I think the information it's getting is not unlike what the HAL Nine Thousand-computer saw."

Dan stood straight up and slapped his forehead. Chris looked baffled as to the insinuation.

"Did you ever read Two Thousand and One, A Space Odyssey?" Dan asked Chris, who shook his head. "The Heur ... istically programmed ..."

"Algorithmic Nine Thousand-computer," Gordon finished.

"Or HAL Nine Thousand," Dan continued, "the space ship *Discovery*'s main computer; it became schizophrenic and killed almost all the crew. Not for years, until Arthur C. Clarke came out with his sequel, did readers finally understand what happened. You see, HAL received conflicting programming information and acted to prevent a failure to his directive by trying to kill all the ship's crew."

"Are you suggesting the computer purposely killed the crew and passengers?" Chris asked skeptically.

"No," Gordon replied, dismissing the thought. A fearful look crept across his face. "But I can guarantee you this: Whichever one of the plane's computers that caused the accident? It did exactly what it was supposed to do."

CHAPTER 27
N901FS REVISITED

February 5 – Cleveland

Robert Hermann sat across Freestyle's Flight Communications conference table from Stephen Woods of Fleet Planning. Bob read from the list in front of him; the beauty of his job was that he did not have to anticipate the why or wherefore of certain decisions, because upper management decided corporate strategy, even when it made no sense to him at all. But then, again, he did not have the information available to him that the Director of Maintenance or those in international strategic planning had. What seemed to Hermann to be illogical was likely a stroke of genius with the Directors, Vice Presidents and Presidents of the various airline divisions. Freestyle had been a money-making, viable company in an age of financial economic instability. Who was he to question their collective wisdom?

Stephen Woods gave up long ago making sense out of the choices made by company officers; he accepted their decisions without question, acting without hesitation. To be honest, it was not his job to doubt their logic. He often laughed that before retirement there were two things he wanted: to see the Big Picture and to find out who 'They' were.

"As you can see," Bob Hermann began, "we just put nine-oh-one on ice not even six months ago. The Director of Maintenance wants to reactivate her and two other ships. So, how long before we can get them out of the desert?"

Stephen Woods said matter-of-factly, "Well, we can fly nine-oh-one within three weeks, but she goes straight into maintenance."

Hermann shot Woods a look of disbelief, "What do you mean straight into maintenance? They're shouting for it now!"

But Woods stared back unfazed. "I realize that Bob, but don't you remember when we parked her? It was coming up on a heavy phase check. If we pull her out now, we'd have to park her in Seattle for two weeks while waiting for a slot to open at Aero APATech. It's a lot less expensive leaving her pickled until a slot opens. Aero APATech likes our business, but they'll charge what they can to park our planes."

"Is nine-oh-one that close to a check?"

"They're gonna want her for international. Without this heavy check you might get two hops out of her before she rolls over and dies for maintenance ... on the wrong side of the world, no less."

Hermann scratched his scalp; he sighed loudly, his eyes darted up and down the list of aircraft but saw no other recourse. "What about the narrow bodies?"

Woods shifted casually in his chair. "The narrow bodies are good for a few weeks. I can't tell you exactly how many without pulling up their histories, but they've got a few weeks flying domestic before they're due a heavy shop visit."

Hermann sighed, "All right Steve, do what you can. Wake up the two narrow bodies and see if they can get nine-oh-one ready to roll as soon as a slot opens up. I'll break the news to the D-M."

Woods left the room, while Hermann tried to rub the frustration out of his face. He hated telling his boss bad news, especially when it was beyond his control. He just wished he listened to his wife and took that vacation to Florida.

Woods went down the hall to his office where he launched a screen displaying Freestyle's fleet status. He paged forward; it was time to put the three aircraft back on the airline's Operations Specifications.

But before he hit the keys his phone rang. "This is Woods," he stated simply into the phone. He hesitated; the voices on the other end spoke rapidly; Woods played with a pen as he listened to both the Chief Pilot and the DOM on conference call.

"That's right; we're bringing nine-oh-one on line in a few weeks. Uh-huh ... no, we can't." He paused again to listen. "I was going to wait for Bob Hermann to break the news, but nine-oh-one has to go into maintenance straight out of the desert." Woods listened again. "It's due a heavy check be– ... Sir; it's unavoidable.

"Yes, Richard Grace ... Captain ... yes, yes, I know who he is. He was piloting the four fifty that had a mid-air reverse–" The DOM interrupted him. "Mm-hmm, well, I'll call him when the slot opens up, but I don't have a say on who flies it." The conversation dragged on a bit more, the Chief Pilot monopolizing the conversation, talking almost non-stop the whole time while Woods wrote furiously. Finally, the DOM gave Woods a direct instruction: call him and Captain Grace at the numbers given concerning when 901FS was to leave the desert. "I understand, Sir."

The DOM spoke up; Woods made a note to himself: *make a maintenance entry when 901FS was prepped.* "I understand," he said, "I'm to assign some ground sense switch to be installed on nine-oh-one before it leaves. Where will I get it? Okay, you'll send it to me. Won't they have to do a gear swing for that? They're not equipped for that. Mm-hmm, okay, I'll put it on the work release. I'm sorry, you're saying do not put it on the work release? Yes Sir, will do. Goodbye." Woods hung up and shook his head, hoping to shake loose the insanity. He hated talking to the upper management types; case in point.

He turned his attention back to the computer monitor. With a few strokes of his keyboard the three aircraft were re-entered into the Freestyle system. All work performed on the three airplanes during their time in the desert needed to be entered in the computer and reconciled for each individual aircraft's maintenance history; this included the parts removed from 901FS by Chaz Logan and the late Maynard Cassel.

At least whatever records were actually entered.

Back in August.

February 21

Jeff Harper was one of the senior mechanics Freestyle had in its main hangar. Originally from the Ozark Mountains in northwest Arkansas, he got along well with everyone, even though they kidded him about his Southern drawl. *Damn Yankees*, Jeff thought.

"Jeff, you're next on the road trip list for a trip to Victorville," said his lead.

"Victorville? Where is that?" Jeff asked.

The lead mechanic sat across from him at the break room table. "It's in southern California, not far from Los Angeles. A bunch of guys are going there to pull three airplanes out of the brine."

Jeff leaned across the table. "Out of the brine?"

"They're pickled in the desert, Jeff, you slack-jawed yokel," the lead chuckled. "What do I gotta do, draw you a picture? We need six mechanics to go out there, wake them up, prepare them for flight, and ride with them when they're moved."

Jeff never took road trips; too much time away from his fishing. But he had his eyes on a nineteen-foot bass boat and the only way to get his new toy was with money, which made the road trip idea very attractive.

"Count me in," Jeff said, sitting back, "I'll take the trip."

"Okay then, you'll head out tomorrow."

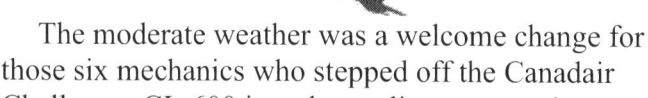

The moderate weather was a welcome change for those six mechanics who stepped off the Canadair Challenger CL-600 into the sunlit ramp area in Victorville. Cleveland suffered under heavy snows since Christmas; citizens had a hard time finding anyplace to throw the white stuff dumped by the never-ending storms across Lake Erie.

Jeff walked as if bent with age, hoisting his toolbox around in his left hand, showing a slight list to port. He boasted being descended from Ozark mountain men, big and brawny with zero fat. A mat of dark brown hair tried escaping from under a John Deere baseball cap and as soon as his boots touched cement, he shoveled a wad of chewing tobacco inside his lower lip. His slate grey eyes said laughter while his demeanor said business. All Yankee/Rebel kidding aside, Jeff enjoyed the undying respect of his peers.

He was working with Trung on N901FS. Trung was a popular mechanic in Cleveland, having learned to be an American better than most honored enough to be born here. Trung and Jeff often pull assignments together, adding to their trust in each other. With two of Freestyle's most reliable mechanics returning N901FS to an airworthy status, no one had any reason to question its safety.

"All right Trung, whatta you wanna hit first?" Jeff asked, reading over the maintenance procedures for taking the aircraft out of storage. Trung looked over his copy of the paperwork and took a long drag off his cigarette. He blew the sweet-smelling smoke over his shoulder where it dissipated in the mild breeze crossing the ramp. He indicated with his finger at the list of items.

"We knock out things they took off the airplane. We then finish getting pickle cleaned up." When Jeff did not respond, he turned to him. "What Goober?"

"I dunno," Jeff laughed, "when're you gonna lose that Eye-talian accent?"

"Stuff it Gomer! When you stop talking like Uncle Jedd?"

"When you stop smoking them cancer sticks," Jeff responded, spitting a brown wet spatter of tobacco juice.

"Yeah," Trung shook his head, "chaw so much better!"

The parts replacing those cannibalized – and recorded – by Chaz and Maynard months earlier were shipped to

Victorville after being repaired, manufactured, or bought; each part had been ordered by the Records Department. Once satisfied all was accounted for, Trung took the sheet into the office and started entering all the missing parts in the aircraft maintenance log.

Using a reference number for each item, Trung opened a new page for recording the maintenance accomplished. The task was tedious, but he assured himself he had not missed anything.

Jeff prepared the truck loaned by Cal Superior. He put their toolboxes on the bed and loaded up cases of oil and hydraulic fluid used to top off any hydraulic reservoirs and engine oil tanks that may have leaked down in the time spent in Victorville. When Trung finished with the logbook, Jeff entered the office wiping his hands of grease.

"How's it comin' along?" Jeff asked, coughing into the crook of his elbow.

"All done here. You ready go out there?"

"It's a shame you can't fly with us up to Seattle."

"Yeah," Trung replied, "my daughter got music recital. She real good, but I gotta stay awake through the rest of it."

Jeff and Trung drove out to N901FS. The airliner still sat where it was parked weeks before, shimmering dully; in the short time it sat in Victorville, the brilliant paint scheme faded under a punishing sun. Both mechanics began the arduous job of bringing the KR-450C out of hibernation.

It took a few days before they finished up. On paper the aircraft was airworthy and stood ready to fly. All cannibalized components were believed to be re-installed and tests were run to assure the replaced items did not bind, leak or malfunction.

Trung and Jeff signed the airworthiness releases in the maintenance logbook; N901FS was airworthy for flight.

CHAPTER 28
THE INVESTIGATORY HEARING

February 22

"Dan," Megan yelled from the kitchen, "pick up the phone and talk to your son!"

Dan ran a brush through his hair, then stuck his head out of the steam-filled bathroom. "Meg, tell Patrick I'll call him from the office. I have to get to the train station."

Meg slapped her palm against the first-floor wall, sending a resounding echo through the house. Dan crossed the bedroom and opened the door. "Meg, I ca–"

"It's not Patrick, Dan. Max is calling from Afghanistan."

A sinking feeling ran shuddering through his gut and suddenly Dan was hesitant to pick up the phone. Max never called when he was home; he did not know whether to count himself fortunate for being home for a call, or whether this dread was foresight.

"Hey Max," Dan found it difficult to speak; he cleared his throat. "What's going on over there?"

There was a four second delay as the words bounced off a satellite and to his son's phone. Both father and son fought the urge to push through the intervals, stepping on each other's words.

"They've increased – r – patrols, Da–," the transmission came broken, forcing Dan to fill in the words. "The in – gents – comi – off the mountain – way too earl – d we're going to have to – beef – p our respon–."

Dan was about to answer, when Max beat him to it.

"I wan – ell – ew and Mom that – ove you guys –"

And then the phone went dead.

Dan stared at the instrument in his hand, unaware that Megan had been standing at the doorway the whole time. Her face went red with anger, realizing that the line disconnected without her having a chance to talk to Max.

"It died on his side," Dan said, regretting the poor choice of words.

"What did he say?" She pivoted from anger to fear.

Dan looked at the phone again, shrugging his shoulders to dispel her anxieties. "His ... um, superiors are pushing them in anticipation of the coming spring," he lied. "They want them ready for the insurgents to come out of the mountains."

"Is he–?"

"He ... he's fine, Meg." Dan replaced the receiver on its cradle. "He wanted to talk to me since we haven't spoken in so long. But he managed to say he loved us before it cut out."

She held him in a riveting gaze, releasing him when she realized he would say no more. She left the room to make breakfast. "Hurry up and get dressed. I'll have coffee for you to go so you don't miss your train."

Dan continued to stare at the phone. For the first time he felt utterly alone.

The Investigatory Hearing is the NTSB's finest hour; very few events in the bureaucratic circles of Washington require more effort. Even though every transportation mode's hearing caters to a large audience of enthralled followers; each being engaged in what is, often, the fantastic causes of accidents, aviation stands out. It draws all types of spectators due to the attention lavished on it by the media. Because investigations can be damaging legally, hearings are never televised. The questioning investigators are not lawyers, but are advised by legal counsel throughout.

Yet, this simple fact does not prevent all television, magazines and newspapers from participating in the feeding frenzy that takes place in the name of sensationalism. Restricted to a quiet room in the Hearing, the print media gather to garner the best view they can in the hopes of exploiting a slip of the tongue to make their story popular, and thereafter into truth.

In a way the Board monopolizes on these fears; they massage this alarm by playing the role of the people's champion, a semblance of hero whose headline stealing breadcrumbs are dropped occasionally so the public will continue hanging spellbound upon every revelation the Board sees fit to release. Since August, the Board has risen unlooked for in the media to remind the public that, though quiet, they are still in control of the situation and will bring justice to the irresponsible parties.

The Investigatory Hearings take place in the bottom floor of L'Enfant Plaza. The large former movie theater was converted to a state-of-the-art conference room. The walls are olive drab, bland; the floor's carpeting worn, unremarkable.

Upon a dais at the far end of the large room, positioned behind a large oak crescent shaped table, sit the five NTSB Board members; their chairs fanning out from the middle where the Chairperson sits dead center.

Behind the table is a blue panel that stands out from the cheerless walls; it steps up from either side to the center, better emphasizing the members. Behind the Chairperson's seat hangs the NTSB seal: an American Eagle on white background, behind a shield adorned with colors of the American Flag. Thirteen arrows are in the eagle's left talon while an olive branch occupies the right. The words 'NATIONAL TRANSPORTATION SAFETY BOARD' encircle the eagle.

To each side of the dais are two twenty-foot wide LED screens, each facing thirty degrees from the back wall; video representations, slides, or evidence acquired from the investigation are displayed here for all to see.

To the Chairperson's far right is where the NTSB investigators and support staff sit; each is afforded a nameplate identifying the investigator with each his own microphone. To the Chairperson's left is the witness seat, dubbed the 'hot seat' by the staff and those who have been seated there.

The contributing parties: manufacturing, airline, and FAA sit below and in front of the dais; their various groups are given their own table. The audience sits closest to the doors and furthest from the front of the dais. To the side of the civilian audience, in a glass-enclosed room, is the media.

In recent weeks Dan hoped Gordon would be able to deliver on his inspection of the wiring diagrams and that the issue would be forced out in the open. Although Gordon was unable to narrow the exact cause down to one element, he was able to eliminate the aircraft's original design as the fault, pointing instead to one or more possible modifications as strong possibilities.

Ron, wishing to convince Phil to allow testimony from Gordon as to the nature of the inspection, had to inform Phil, not only that Dan and Chris were able to duplicate the fault after the tests in Portland but, that there was an outside person with full access to the wiring diagrams. Phil hit the roof; threats of termination resounded in the small conference room where Phil, Dan, Chris and Ron met.

Phil would have been in his right to fire the three of them. No one was sure what allayed Phil's rant, but he settled down, perhaps to bide his time for another occasion. Chris reasoned that if word got out to the media that they were fired looking for a possible cause, then Phil may have suffered more from the attention. At any rate, operating in the shadows was going to be impossible from then on.

The IH was scheduled to begin at nine o'clock Eastern time; Chairwoman Ellen Potter was a stickler for on-time meetings, particularly where inquiries she chaired were concerned. At seven-forty-five the room was a flurry of activity; technicians from the NTSB audio/video office were checking and double-checking each piece of audial and visual equipment.

Computers for all the Board Members and Investigators were tied into the internal NTSB chat room system, providing a direct link between the Board Members and the Investigators; this assured the Members could run their questions past the staff first to avoid making foolish remarks.

Technicians working on the dais offered limited help to the investigators who showed up early. Chris showed up earlier than the technicians; among his many talents was the ability to assure his computer worked and any of the other investigators' as well. The technicians gave him a silent nod of appreciation.

Next to Chris sat George Slade, Survival Factors investigator. He, too, was setting up his computer, making last minute edits to his presentation. A native of Bismarck, North Dakota, George found humor in most things, but was dead serious during investigations. He was slightly over six feet tall, fair-skinned and sported short blond hair. He had grey eyes that held one in place; they laughed easily but were quick to anger. George had wisdom beyond his years; anything he said was well thought out and deliberate, every angle scrutinized.

Presently Chris was assisting both Dan and Ron with their laptops. Ron was still tight lipped following the threats from Phil; he did not blame either Investigator, but he had feelings of regret. He trusted both their professional opinions, but just wished this had not come up on his watch.

"You still sore about the wiring diagram episode?" Chris ventured to ask.

Ron shrugged his shoulders slightly, his eyes darting momentarily at Dan, who paid no attention to the question. "No, not really," Ron lied. "Are you going to ask Vince to push Phil about this avionics guy's testimony?"

When Dan did not answer, Ron added, "Dan?!"

For the first time Dan looked up, his eyes darting back and forth between Chris and Ron. "I'm sorry; what'd you say?"

Ron straightened up as he stood. "I said, are you going to ask Scalia to push for this friend of yours to get on the stand?"

"No," he replied simply.

Chris and Ron looked at each other. Ron said, "Why not?"

"I don't run to Vince every time I've got a problem."

Ron leaned in close in the presence of the technicians nearby. "Well, Phil thinks that you do–"

"I don't give a flying leap through a rolling donut what Phil thinks," Dan said interrupting Ron. "I handle my own battles! Vince may come up to me and take my side with things, but it's not because I ask him to. Besides, everything Vince does is for Vince and Vince alone; just like every other politician in this place. And that includes some non-political appointees, like Phil.

"Look," Dan growled, "Phil expects me to go to Vince. He's got Potter wound so tight she'll stop any action Vince takes. If they don't want to know what brought that airplane down, how can I fight them? Phil's got Potter convinced that the accident was due to maintenance and AeroGalactic's design, not an electrical problem."

"Well, what are we going to do?" Chris asked supportively.

Dan stood up and catching sight of Clay and Sarah entering the room, started to make his way over to them. He stopped a few feet away and responded to Chris. "I'm not sure; hopefully I'll think of something."

Dan extended his hand to Clay as he approached the two, who had just passed through screening. The trio soon settled into a discussion of the upcoming hearing. "You do know that Chris and I were able to get the airplane to deploy the reversers?"

"No," Sarah responded, "Well, that makes a difference; right?"

"I'm afraid not," Clay answered her. "Dan's boss doesn't believe that the test results were conclusive, since they didn't happen in his presence."

"Clay's right, Sarah," Dan said apologetically. "Bureaucracy at its best. Since I couldn't state conclusively that something other than the aircraft's original systems were the culprit, they feel they have no choice but to blame the manufacturer."

"And maintenance," Clay added.

Sarah broke free to greet a friend, but Dan turned to Clay. He gazed at the engineer for a second, recognizing a disturbing look. "Please be careful, Clay."

Dan saw annoyance in Clay's eyes before he went to join his table.

Within an hour, all involved in the hearing were getting seated. At the back of the room, people were filling the audience area. In most cases victims' family members arrived early with their lawyers leading the way to the best seats closest to the action.

Dan could pick the lawyers out from miles away; their legal pads tucked securely under their arms and a fabricated façade of the diligent protector on their faces. They corralled their clients to their seats. Some older family members carried pictures of their lost loved ones, dabbing tears from their cheeks, walking in shock as this hearing intruded on their healing; young children accompanying their elders walked despondently and overwhelmed with genuine grief, often with the lawyer's disingenuous shielding hand on the child's shoulder.

The rest of the audience seats filled up fast. The media area was full; television reporters filmed the only video segments allowed before the cameras were directed to be turned off. The segments were taped in a hurry with many retakes due to other reporters cutting into the screen or talking out loud inopportunely. Before long they took their seats and broke out their individual laptops to record the procedures the best they could.

Most of the Board Members were seated at the dais with Chairwoman Potter absent for the moment. Each Member exhibited a professional demeanor, dressed conservatively with suits and dresses that communicated the solemn atmosphere of the Hearing, while keeping to the authority their position echoed. Vince, his trademark disheveled look despite the new grey suit, was combing his hair in place with his hand.

With ten minutes to go, Chairwoman Potter strolled flamboyantly into the room. Flashes from the media area rapidly played across her as strobes of light. She almost unnoticeably hesitated, allowing all the cameras to take in her entrance. Potter wore a red dress that absorbed all light; brilliant in its presumption. A string of pearls hung flaccid around her neck in an attempt to portray a maternal semblance. She entered from the rear, affording herself the full attention she desired; choosing to forego the hidden entrance in the back specifically installed for Board Members.

Dan sat next to Chris; they shared their notes, unwilling to take the tack that Phil laid out for them. They spoke under their breaths, cursing the circumstances and trying to plan a strategy, but knowing the clock had run out.

Dan wore a dark blue suit, while Chris was comfortable in brown. Other investigators had a knack for dressing as if expecting to be on the news, but some like Chris preferred to make no statement, allowing the searchlight of celebrity to pass unimpeded over his head. He produced a small bowl from his computer bag and, placing it at his side, emptied half a bag of M&Ms into it; the clicking of candies against each other sounded like a small shower of gravel. He placed the bowl on the table by his right hand. Dan clicked his tongue, shaking his head.

"For that, you don't get any."

"You're doing me a favor there, Gumby," Dan remarked, "these days I just rub them right into my sides and save the time it takes to digest them."

Chairwoman Potter took her seat in the center and rapped her gavel three times to bring order to the chamber. As the room fell into a feeble silence, she whispered stern instructions to her assistant, a young lady who seemed to quake in her presence. After this display, she turned her attention back to the audience. Clearing her throat superfluously, Chairwoman Potter welcomed all to the Hearing for Gyrfalcon flight – she checked the sheet at her elbow – flight 427.

"Though we venture to learn against all doubt what transpired that awful day, our hearts and sympathies go to the victims of the accident and, of course, to their grieving families. Let us take this time for a moment of silence ..."

Here a series of flashes sprouted in front of the dais as the Chairwoman took a moment to face the cameras full on. As soon as the barrage of strobes subsided, she continued, "It is the job and purpose of the National Transportation Safety Board to discover these causes and to put the power of our office behind the innocent victims and their families; to take the high road often reserved for those who fight for safety's sake and hold the responsible parties accountable for their lapse in judgment and safety.

"It is also the task before us to hold organizations, like the Federal Aviation Administration, to the fire, providing them with the wisdom of our adjudication; to allow them to benefit from our unlimited experience and insight; to become a better government organization of both oversight and proactive measures that will advance the traveling public."

Dan closed his eyes and shuddered while Chris let out a guffaw.

Chairwoman Potter continued on for ten more minutes. After completing her soliloquy, she looked up in time to watch a sea of cameras snap a myriad of pictures to document her sagacity for all time. Letting the moment last, she finally turned to Philip Tulkinghorn and asked for his opening statements.

"Madam Chairman, esteemed Board Members, NTSB investigators, participants in the investigation, family members, media, and audience observers, allow me to welcome you to the investigatory hearing into the accident investigation of Gyrfalcon four-twenty-seven. It is through this process ..."

As Phil went on laboriously echoing the Chairwoman's sentiments, investigators took the time to finalize any organizing they had for their questioning and evidence. Dan glanced at his computer's messaging page. Vince's name came up with a message:

> We have to talk when this is over. I have something I want you to do.

Dan shot a look over at Vince, but he was focused on the conversation, ignorant of Dan's presence.

With a sweep around the Board Members' table, the Chairwoman concluded no objections to continuing the hearing, and the procedures began. Everyone, from the audience members to the staff, settled in for the duration. Ron Gebbia had opening remarks, presenting a video of the final moments of flight 427.

The computer graphics were incredible; the details of accuracy were well-researched from the precise size and position of the tail N-number to any missing color from the paint scheme. Computer specialists prepared the video's exactitude from recent photos.

The reproduction opened with the words 'Gyrfalcon Flight 427' flashing across the two screens with the NTSB emblem faded in the background. The simulation's view went from watching the aircraft approach over the city of Memphis to a more westerly view of Memphis Airport; buildings on Airways Boulevard dominating the background in proper scale. As the video played out, the words of the tower echoed across the room with subtitles scrolling across the bottom of the screen. The tape ended just as the simulated N374GY appeared to pitch forward with reversers deployed, but before impact to spare family members the unfortunate visual image. Instead the screen faded to the NTSB emblem, center screen.

As the lead Survival Factors investigator, George Slade led the hearing, bringing experts before the Board to answer questions that addressed survivability of the passengers after impact and during the fire.

A composites expert sat in the hot seat. George took the audience through design requirements of these interiors; he explained the need for low weight and approved specifications for minimal toxic fumes and flammability. He was an expert at lightening the mood with his easy-going style; his smooth transition into questioning happened before anyone realized the shift occurred.

After George exhausted his examination, he deferred follow-up questions to the various groups, starting with the FAA, then AeroGalactic, Sonic Engines, and Gyrfalcon. The composites expert stood the test of the hard questioning.

"Mister Tulkinghorn, are we going to hear from the surviving pilot during this hearing?"

Potter's question sounded rehearsed and in response to it, Phil's reply came across scripted. The Operations investigators were informed by Gyrfalcon that Deke Chamberlain was still unable to travel, and answering questions in a public hearing was against his doctor's orders.

Since Phil guided the investigation to be about maintenance, he did not push for the first officer's testimony, explaining that the Operations testimony had little bearing on the findings of the investigation. Gyrfalcon had not argued, wishing to deflect as much attention away from the hearing as possible. All interview material with First Officer Chamberlain was reviewed by Phil, who kept a majority of it out of the Hearing.

Dan pressed Phil to allow the Freestyle pilot, Captain Richard Grace, to be contacted and interviewed for the hearing. Even with Connie supporting his plea, Phil refused, citing that the Freestyle episode of the previous summer was not an accident and therefore Freestyle did not deserve to be dragged into the Hearing against its will.

Despite the fact that only Phil, Connie and Dan were the only ones in the room at the time, somehow Vince Scalia heard about the decision.

CHAPTER 29
SCAPEGOAT

"The investigatory hearing will come to order." Chairwoman Potter welcomed everyone back from lunch with her voice carrying over the throng. She rapped her gavel once; a sharp crack echoed through the already quieting room. Few people still milled about trying to find their previously occupied chairs, but all the room became hushed. "Mister Gebbia, do you have any further experts?"

"Madam Chairman and Board Members," Ron paused for effect, "we are now prepared to turn the remainder of this hearing over to Christopher Wilkerson, the Systems team Lead Investigator and Daniel Tenace, the Aircraft Maintenance and Records team Lead Investigator."

Dan put on his reading glasses, but it was Chris who took the microphone and angled it toward his mouth. "Thank you; Madam Chairman and Board members, I would first like to present the Systems group's simulation that best demonstrates – from the investigation standpoint – what we've been able to determine happened to cause the accident." Without a word, the lights dimmed again. On the two large screens a simulation of the various parts of the aircraft related to the flight's landing phase were displayed; each system took its turn center screen while Chris's taped voice described what the audience was seeing.

The various components were put in motion and other parts of the aircraft were shown in exploded views as their place in the landing phase came into view. As the video progressed people hung on every word recorded-Chris uttered, striving at times to grasp the technical wonder, marveling at the precise workings that normally took place while they sat oblivious in their seats during a flight.

As the simulation ended, the lights rose slowly. Chris waited for the sound to completely fade away before asking the Board for questions. Potter made a comment giving credit to the simulators, made possible by *her* supervision of the Board.

"You may call your first expert," she said, concluding her monologue.

Chris began questioning an aviation expert familiar with avionics systems, a consultant Gordon Lyle recommended. The questions were aimed at clarifying whether what happened with Gyrfalcon 427 was a lone anomaly or is it a precursor to a series of repeat episodes; whether the introduction of new equipment is a concern for future problems. Phil looked down the table at Chris, silently warning him to be careful of where he went; Dan saw the look with his peripheral vision, but Chris simply ignored it.

The rest of the first afternoon was spent with this subject matter expert. Potter concluded the Hearing an hour early to avoid stopping in the middle of the next expert.

The next day, Ron kept talk to a minimum. After Chairwoman Potter welcomed everyone to a second day, he introduced Dan Tenace and his first expert. Dan called Jay Connelly, the aircraft mechanic from Gyrfalcon's hangar. Jay flew in to speak to the maintenance practices employed on N374GY. Dan made several references to the visit in Denver and asked Jay to expand on answers that came out of his interview.

"Mister Connelly," Dan said, "you mentioned in your interview that one of the mechanics in question was on medication during the maintenance phase check."

"Yes, that was me; I was that mechanic."

Dan paused to let the question sink in. "Is there anything unusual about the medication you were on?"

Jay produced a piece of paper, and presented it front forward towards Dan. "The medication was a steroid. My doctor, who signed it here, prescribed it to me for bronchitis. His letter states, it would have no effect on my performance during work."

It was Dan's turn to recite a scripted statement. "Well, it's important to clarify that. I'm not sure how anyone drew a connection between your prescription and this accident, but it's comforting to know the allegations were invalid."

It is NTSB policy to allow the witness to address questionable behavior; Dan had called Jay the week before asking him to provide written proof the prescription was legitimate and that it had no effect on his performance.

Dan's aim was not to divert questioning from the mechanics, but instead to avoid rehashing a thorough, documented interview; that pursuing the hangar work was a dead end. He laid the ground work for this before the questioning went to the individual groups. As his gaze crossed the room his eyes fell on Clay, sitting next to the AeroGalactic representative, speaking in a hushed voice. From his place Dan could see that this would not be good.

Presently Sonic Engines' representative was going over some fine points with Connelly concerning reverser rigging; Jay looked oddly comfortable in the hot seat. The atmosphere became laborious as the audience suffered a feeling of disconnection; people were paying attention, but their interests waned in the uninspiring technical dialogue.

In the world of accident investigation, representatives from airlines, manufacturers, and other industry entities have formed the core of the investigation teams. While there are technical benefits to having these delegates from industry, they can also exemplify the worst in human nature.

An accident's aftermath embodies desperation on the part of most involved; if an aircraft or engine proves to be dangerous or designed with a fault, the manufacturer can go out of business before the lawsuits reach the courts. If the airline itself is culpable – what percentage of the traveling public would feel safe flying on that airline? Within a day, the media, lawyers of the victims' families or even the Inspector General can make the airline a miserable place to work; it is irrelevant that these advocates know nothing of the basics of running an airline.

Before reaching the accident site, the various representatives are working on damage control; it is the rudimentary lesson of survival. While some approach the scrutiny intending to learn and improve, others arrive planning a dangerous game of sleight of hand – or *Hot Potato*.

Unless done right, the deceiving party can bring a worse fate down upon him or his company than originally expected. To succeed, the NTSB team leader must be inexperienced; unable to lead the team through obstacles placed in his or her way.

If successful, the manufacturer or airline escapes all blame by diverting attention to an innocent scapegoat. If unsuccessful, the consequences are disastrous for that person's employer with little to no recovery in the public eye.

Watching Clay, Dan believed he saw the heating up of a hot potato.

"Thank you, Sonic Engines," Chairwoman Potter announced, "AeroGalactic, it is your turn to question."

The AeroGalactic representative, Sid Smith wasted no time; he touched on two minor issues before launching the attack. "Mister Connelly," he started in an oily voice, "I'd like to take a different approach, if I may. According to the transcripts we received from the Denver interviews, you stated that during the last inspection you did *not* follow the maintenance steps for rigging the reversers. Are those your words?"

A hush fell over the room as Jay sat up in his seat, a look of confusion playing across his face. His lawyer leaned towards Jay, but he shrugged him off.

Dan watched several lawyers lean forward in unison, pens at the ready. The attorneys became animated, as if waking from a testimony-induced coma.

"In so many words," Jay responded. "We did not follow the reverser rigging directions on the workcard, to the letter."

"Would you agree then," Sid continued, "that your decision to skip–"

"I didn't skip anything!"

"Shall we say ... performed out of sequence, then?" Sid said, without missing a beat. "That you and your crew ... *performed out of sequence* ... the very important maintenance steps as written, and in the sequence designed by AeroGalactic's engineering department."

Dan leaned into his microphone. "Madam Chairman, this issue has been addressed in the interviews; asked and answered."

But Sid expected this move and countered, "Madam Chairman, we'd like to use the time we're allotted to further pursue this matter. We feel that Investigator Tenace didn't adequately investigate it."

Ron's head spun slowly on his shoulders and fixed Dan an angry look; fears that Phil would use this as a reason to crush all who supported Dan suddenly ran through his mind.

The corners of Phil's mouth curled up ever so slightly. *This was better than he had hoped*, he thought. "Madam Chairman, the Staff sees no reason to prevent this line of questioning. If Investigator Tenace has been remiss in his duties, then this would be a good venue to determine that. I suggest you allow AeroGalactic to continue."

Dan glanced at Jay and felt a warm flush of red run across his face. He sat back helpless.

"AeroGalactic, you may proceed."

"Thank you, Madam Chairman." Sid took a moment to arrange his papers and to adequately draw all attention to this; he was about to throw the hot potato. "Mister Connelly, as I was saying, you decided – you and your fellow hangar crewmembers, that is – to ignore the instructions for the reverser adjustments, to rig them a quicker way. Was this done to save time?"

Jay lifted his head; he took a deep breath and measured his response carefully, knowing full well that each word or inflection would be judged. "We'd decided through trial and error to reorganize the maintenance steps to avoid redundant actions on our part. In this way, we'd accomplish the tasks without having to undo what we did, or rework something we'd already completed."

"By whose authority?"

"Do you mean, who did I ask?" Jay asked.

"I mean, who told you that you could rearrange the steps?"

"I explained that when I was interviewed last August."

"Well, for the benefit of everyone here," Sid said with growing triumph in his voice, "please, restate what you said."

"I told the Sonic engineer, Sarah ... Miss Wallace, that we'd consulted her company about changes to the maintenance instructions, that they were approved."

"Is that your testimony?" Sid droned on when Jay finished.

"Since this isn't litigation, I'll say that's my answer to your question,"

Sid seemed to relish the response; an arrogant smile played across his lips. He pulled a file from under his foot-high stack of notes and books. Sid thumbed through the file as if seeing it for the first time, pulling notes out and placing them accordingly as would a card player when dealt a hand. The lawyers around the room stood ready, pens poised above paper, fingers hovering above keys.

"Mister Connelly," Sid began, pulling a page out of the pile, as if for the first time noticing it among the rest. "Are you aware that the maintenance practices that you and Gyrfalcon tried to revise were not for Sonic Engines to speak to?"

Jay coughed nervously into his fist. "I'm not sure I know what you're talking about," he answered, his voice coming choked in the unwanted attention.

"Well, let me elaborate then," Sid said, with a wink at Clay. "The maintenance steps that you and your coworkers took it upon yourselves to ignore," he put his hand up to prevent the objection, "... or perform out of sequence, then. They were written by AeroGalactic. Sonic has nothing to do with those maintenance instructions; AeroGalactic does."

Jay sat across the room mute, his eyebrows knit in seeming confusion. The lawyers in the audience seemed to hang on every word Sid was saying now. Finally, someone was being brought to task!

"In other words, Mister Connelly, you may have asked permission from Sonic to rewrite the steps for the rigging check, but it wasn't Sonic's jurisdiction to approve those changes; it was AeroGalactic's. You skipped those steps to rig the reversers based on the wrong company's permission."

The room became silent as Jay sat across the room without uttering a syllable; his fingers rubbed silently across the arm of his chair. He was strangely silent, moving as if sitting on a tack. Dan looked on his computer screen at a message sent from Vince:

Is there blood in the water?

Dan looked up from his screen and glanced over at Vince, who returned his stare. They locked eyes for a moment. Dan slowly shook his head before looking back at Jay.

"What do you have to say, Mister Connelly?"

Jay leaned over and consulted his lawyer, who began to fumble through his briefcase in search of something. Sid let the question hang for a moment before pushing the issue again, but Jay cut him off. "Yes, I know that," he said simply.

Confusion took over the faces of all listening. Now it was Sid's turn to stumble over his words. "I didn't quite catch that."

"I said," Jay remarked, "that I knew that. My coworkers and I knew that Sonic wasn't responsible for the instructions."

"But you just said–"

"I *said* ..." Jay paused, before continuing, "that I informed Sonic about the instructions being poorly written and that I wrote Sonic that I wanted the instructions changed. What I didn't say was that we also consulted with AeroGalactic; that we had several letters of correspondence saying that AeroGalactic had miswritten the instructions and that we got approval to change the workcards from ...," and here he took two heart beats to continue, his eyes getting larger in mock surprise, "why … AeroGalactic."

Sid was flustered; his argument deflating. "Did you tell Clay Brinnel this at the interviews?"

"No, I didn't," Jay replied. He took another moment for dramatic pause, "because Mister Brinnel never asked. But I did tell Mister Tenace when we spoke later that day."

Clay melted into his chair. Both Ron and Phil glanced at Dan, who mouthed the words, 'asked and answered' through a knowing smile. Chris just shook his head, while Vince stifled a laugh.

Sid, unfazed, continued to push his point.

"Mister Connelly, we have no record of this *correspondence*," uttering the word with contempt, "you claim you had with our engineering department. All we have is your word that you wrote to AeroGalactic's engineering department, yet there are no authorizations; there is nothing in our records."

"That's correct," Jay riposted, "you won't have any forms from AeroGalactic stating that the changes were allowed. Our engineering guys assumed that when Gyrfalcon four-twenty-seven crashed you'd interrupt any document traffic, but we have something just as good."

"You have something just as good as official agreements from AeroGalactic authorizing you to alter the written instructions?"

"Yes, I do," said Jay reaching down next to his seat. He pulled up a small collection of papers tied with a rubber band around the middle. "I have these e-mails from your chief engineer; it has his e-mail address and is date stamped. It's saying that the changes are being implemented, a revision to the maintenance manual was being written, and that our performing the work – as re-written – was approved."

The remaining questions aimed at Jay were tame by comparison; anyone glancing at Sid Smith could not doubt that this 'simple' mechanic was not to be underestimated. Jay answered all that was asked of him with a sobering voice, allowing no hint of his past performance to bleed through as over-confidence.

The last one to question Jay was the Chairwoman, who chose to abandon any thoughts of corrupting this man in the eyes of those present. Instead she excused the witness and immediately called for Dan's next expert. As Jay stepped down, he gave a slight nod to the Gyrfalcon table, which elicited a similar gesture from Randy.

Dan called Isaac Klein, an engineer for AeroGalactic in their landing systems division. Klein was responsible for the design, testing, and revising of all aspects of the landing gear systems. Dan was particularly interested in what light Klein could shed on why the gear sense switches may have faulted. Isaac brought with him several large books that provided answers to anything thrown his way.

Isaac Klein was seventy-five years old; a man who refused to retire for fear of dying from boredom. He sat his small physique in the witness chair; his balding head barely showing above the table next to him. He was offered legal support, but he felt a lawyer would only confuse things and, being as old as dirt, did not want to be fighting a lawyer while fielding questions from the Board.

Isaac sported a black suit that sat crumpled on his aged frame; a red bowtie complimented his black pants and jacket. His remaining hair consisted of scattered grey tufts that swayed unwillingly under the oppressive breeze of the air vents blowing overhead. The black rimmed glasses were thickly lensed; the eyes that looked out from them were wizened, but appeared to be made for a Muppet character: large and bulbous.

Dan was hesitant to bring this man into the arena, for that is what it was turning into. He did not miss Jay's small gesture to Randy before and Dan feared for the welfare of this old gentleman. A quick glance at the AeroGalactic table confirmed that fear, as the members were visibly agitated to see their own about to take a hit for their actions. Anyone doubting this apprehension had only to ask – where did Clay disappear to?

"Mister Klein, how are you today?" Dan began. This brought a nod and a grin from the expert. "Is there something I can get you before we begin?"

Isaac seemed to ponder that question for a second. "Get something?" He asked in a nasally voice, his head tilting as if unsure. "You can get started with the questions, if you please. I'm not getting any younger, you know."

The audience laughed good-naturedly at the response and Dan smiled in deference to his question.

"I apologize, Mister Klein, I didn't mean to come off patronizing."

Isaac nodded his head and smiled with a knowing look.

"Mister Klein, can you please explain what you do at AeroGalactic?"

Isaac Klein gave a nod again and began to lay out for all attending what his job entailed. For fifteen minutes, his response went on, spattered with light humor, and holding absolutely everyone's full attention; without intending to, he had become endeared to every person present. Dan assured himself with a quick look that

Gyrfalcon's representatives were furiously writing everything he said, looking for the chink in his armor.

"Mister Klein–"

"You should call me Isaac."

Dan looked up and had a sense to laugh again, when he noticed the man was not trying to be funny, but instead was very serious. "Um, thank you, Mister Klein," Dan continued with a shy grin, "but these are formal hearings and we have to speak ... well, um ... formally." He hesitated, having lost his train of thought. Chris reached over with a finger and pointed at the question list in front of him.

"Mister Klein, could you comment on the cause of the accident; more specifically, what do you think happened?"

Isaac got very serious and the small grin faded from his lips as he transitioned into the grave nature of the hearing. "Well, for one thing, I don't think the reverser rigging had anything to do with it." He paused long enough to send a deprecating look at the AeroGalactic table, each representative sinking slightly into his or her seat. "I'm convinced that the error was electrical. There is no doubt in my mind." He took in a breath and continued, "That being said, I'm at a loss as to what went wrong. I've worn my eyes blind going over every inch of those wiring diagrams. I can't find the fault."

"Which wiring diagrams did you use?" Dan asked. Phil leaned forward to get an unobstructed view of Dan, but even if Dan saw Phil, he discounted him.

"I used the original diagrams and a few days ago I went over the diagrams Gyrfalcon sent me. It was from one they had recently released from heavy check."

"Did the diagrams accurately portray any new technologies installed in the aircraft? If so, what new installations did it have?" Dan asked, eliciting a loud clearing of the throat by Phil. Dan continued to ignore him.

"I'm quite sure," Isaac said, "that the new STAR system was installed in the wiring diagrams they sent me. They were making revisions to it; that's why it took so long to send it to me."

"Do you mean the SPAR system?"

"SPAR ... STAR ...," he responded with a surrendering gesture. "I can't follow these acronyms anymore." He took a moment to remember. "But to answer your question, I believe it was SPAR; something to do with air traffic."

Dan looked at Chris, who gestured back to Isaac Klein. "Mister Klein, did you notice anything unusual about the wiring diagrams? Did you have any concerns with the digital computer components like AND or NAND gates?"

"Madam Chairman," Phil interrupted, "I'm going to ask that you instruct Investigator Tenace to stay clear of any questions dealing with SPAR. This is an unfounded theory that he's been trying to sell."

"I, for one, would like to hear this," Vince threw in.

Potter smacked her gavel down and turned to Vince. "I'm going to side with Mister Tulkinghorn on this. We don't have time to go off on tangents. Investigator Tenace, keep your questions limited to the course laid out."

But Vince wouldn't let it go. "I must insist that we–"

"Member Scalia, I will not entertain unfounded theories at this point in time. Investigator Tenace has had ample time to pursue other leads; this is not the time to do so."

Vince took a deep breath and pushed on, "He wasn't allowed to pursue other leads. This investigator's experience with this area is unequaled in the Board. He–"

"Are you suggesting Member Scalia, that I can't recognize a tangible theory?"

Vince was stuck; to embarrass the Chairwoman in public would be political suicide. His momentary burst of bravery was swallowed, along with his pride. Raising his right hand in a gesture of submission, he capitulated; it was obvious to him that Phil and Potter had worked this out before the hearing. Vince glanced at Dan with an apologetic look and sat back in his seat.

But when the Chairwoman turned her attention away from him, he leaned over and spoke in his assistant Becky's ear. She hesitated for a moment, before rising inconspicuously and searching for someone in the audience.

Isaac Klein watched this exchange with great interest. Glancing at Dan Tenace with a knowing look, he guessed at what was happening; the argument became political and solutions took a back seat. He gazed down, but kept his voice level with the microphone.

"Mister Tenace," Isaac began, "I've thought a lot about retiring lately." The little engineer's feeble tone dissipated the room's tension; the room went still as if struck dumb by a hammer blow.

"Excuse me, Mister Klein."

"NAND gates, SPAR, STAR, uncommanded reversers; these are all beyond my time. In with the new, out with the old as they say ... or something like that." He looked up and his eyes locked on Dan's; for a moment they were the only two in the room. "I'm too old for these ... *games*." Isaac's eyelids lowered slightly, as if pushing his last statement at Dan. "I find myself getting lost in the ... technology ... Mister Tenace. Perhaps, I should get out before I'm responsible for hurting others." Isaac then folded his wrinkled hands across his lap and bowed his head in anticipation of the next questioner.

Dan felt the room re-materialize; he relinquished his questions to Chris who worked hard to insert their gate theories without actually using the terms. Phil recognized the attempts but was powerless to block Chris's pursuits seeing as he would not give Phil an opening.

When Chris asked all that he could, he turned the interrogation over to the different groups. The blood was in the water again, this time the little engineer appeared vulnerable; he was inundated with accusations and questions to his skill in properly looking into the problem.

The attacks were not as antagonistic as what was laid on Jay Connelly, but Isaac Klein was up to the challenge, occasionally laying to waste most of the detractors of his ability. When the questions ended, the lawyers had pages of notes either rolled to the back of legal pads or saved to their hard drives. The group representatives took deep breaths after each volley, each reeling from the crippling blows delivered by Klein.

As Chairwoman Potter exhausted all her questions, she asked if the staff had anything further, then each group followed by the Board Members; each had either hoisted the white flag or simply had no point to make.

Dan laughed to himself; *I guess I was worried for nothing,* he thought. As Isaac stepped down from the hot seat, he looked straight at Dan and winked. This time Dan did laugh, just a little.

Chairwoman Potter turned to Phil. "Mister Tulkinghorn, does your staff have anything further to add to these proceedings?"

Phil pushed his glasses up and gazed across the table; he was greeted with several people shaking their heads. Keeping to protocol, he asked each individually, to which the response was: No.

"Then I thank all the participants of this hearing," Potter began, "I know I speak for the staff when I say, that we now have reams of information to sort through before we complete our report on this accident.

"May I emphasize, again, the Board extends its sympathies to all the family members who lost loved ones and I offer my personal promise that the cause of this accident will be discovered from the information brought to the surface here and the evidence we've recovered. No one will again suffer the pains you have for these reasons.

"This concludes the investigatory hearing proceedings. Again, I would like to thank everyone who participated; Good night." And with that she brought her gavel down again with a crack.

Everyone moved at once; the group representatives stood simultaneously and milled about looking for a place to gather and assess damage control; their eyes searching for reporters to know in what direction to avoid them. The FAA representatives stood quietly, shaking hands with each other and moving about. The various Board Members sought out media personnel; Potter had already cornered her own favorite reporter and gave an interview while ignoring family members who stepped forward to thank her.

Dan turned slightly to Chris and whispered, "Thanks." Chris gave him a pat on the back before disconnecting his computer and raveling up the cords. The NTSB technicians swam through the throng of humans; dissecting the wiring running to and from the equipment, oblivious of the crowds.

Dan looked for Vince, but the chair was empty. He shook his head; Vince was obviously on his soap box with the reporters; he was, after all, their favorite maverick Board Member.

Ron came over to Dan and shook his hand; an apology escaped his lips for Phil stonewalling him. Dan shrugged his shoulders and smiled, pushing the issue to the past. He saw over Ron's shoulder Vince talking very animatedly with Phil. To his right, Dan saw Potter attracted to the discussion and walking swiftly over to find out what the situation was. Soon all three were engaged in a subdued argument that contradicted the voice level. Dan became aware of a gentleman standing off Vince's left; he seemed amused at how the discussion was progressing.

The man stood about six-foot even and his hair was cut so short that it was almost non-existent. He had a rigid stance, as if born at attention. He appeared as no stranger to discipline, his eyes piercing through Phil and the Chairwoman. The only feature that conflicted with the rest of him was his mouth, that showed a consistent easy-going smile.

Dan dismissed the heated dialogue as nothing until he heard distinctly over the buzz of the crowd his own name.

"Investigator Tenace, isn't it?"

Dan pulled himself from his eavesdropping and looked over the end of the table into the eyes of Isaac Klein. The wizened little man was smiling up at him with his hand extended; Dan reached out and grasped it firmly.

"Mister Klein, I apologize for that. I didn't realize they were going to–"

But Isaac Klein was shaking his head and smiling. "Now, please call me Isaac." He pointed his finger comically at Dan. "We are not so formal now, you and I."

Dan laughed, "Point taken; please call me Dan. I am sorry though."

Isaac waved off the apology. "I'm a big boy, Dan. This isn't the first time I've been called before the Board," he said tapping his own chest. "The nerve of them going up against Isaac Klein. Besides, I made most of them tuck their tails between their legs."

"That, you did," Dan agreed. "Mister Klein," the little engineer gave a disapproving look; Dan changed direction, "Isaac then … I hope you weren't serious about retiring. The industry needs your experience."

"Dan, did you ever see those shows where a ghost haunts a house; someone who didn't know they died and ended up staying?" Dan looked confused, but Isaac continued. "The thought of me dying in the AeroGalactic building and spending an eternity walking the halls ... well, well, well, that would be awful."

Dan sensed there was something underneath these words. "I understand."

Isaac caught Dan's eye again and nodded his head. "I would appreciate it if you gave me a call. I'd like to talk to you about this NAND gate theory of yours. I confess; I didn't look that far into it." He handed Dan a business card; Dan fished around in his pocket for a card of his own, which he handed to Isaac.

"Until then, Dan."

"I look forward to it, Isaac."

Isaac gave his little wink and was soon lost in the crowd.

"Dan, I want to introduce you to someone." This time Dan's head swiveled left and he found himself looking at Vince and the man from the argument. Over Vince's shoulder Dan saw Potter and Phil stewing, looking angrily at Vince. *I guess I can figure out who won that argument*, Dan thought.

"Daniel Tenace, this is Richard Grace." Dan went to proffer his hand when he hesitated. He looked stupidly, his arm half-extended.

"It's a pleasure to finally meet you." This woke Dan from his reverie and he clasped Richard's hand, but his mind was not in it. Richard laughed at the absent-minded look. Vince was about to reproach Dan, when Richard cleared the air.

"You may not remember me, but I fly for Freestyle."

Vince added, "This is *Captain* Richard Grace. Number two thrust reverser deployed in flight."

Dan slapped his forehead as the name registered. "Captain Grace, I'm sorry; it's great to put the face to the name. What are you doing here?" He said, completing the handshake.

"Well, Vince here asked if I could attend the hearing. He seemed to feel – as do I – that you'd be interested in a proposal."

Dan was looking around for Chris, when the end statement hit him. He looked back and forth between Richard Grace and Vince, finally looking skeptically at the pilot. "What kind of proposal?"

Richard glanced at Vince, who deferred to the pilot. "My company is intrigued by your gate theory–"

"Actually, it's Chris Wilkerson's and my theory."

"Understood," Richard acknowledged, "however, I can only extend this offer to one of you. I'd prefer it be you since you have a maintenance background."

Dan did not answer but came around the table to talk face-to-face.

"Freestyle Airlines," Richard continued, "is bringing a dash four-fifty out of the desert and putting it back into service. Since we use the four-fifty on the international runs, they're anxious to find out what happened with my flight and why Gyrfalcon crashed. Naturally, they don't want to see it happen to one of their own. I've been authorized to ferry and perhaps test the aircraft while flying to Seattle for a heavy check in a few days. I want to know if you'd like to ride with us."

Dan stood speechless for a moment. "Are you allowed to ferry an aircraft with a known fault and turn it into a test flight?" He lowered his voice. "Is that what you're suggesting?"

Richard smiled and nodded. "All right, you caught me; so much the better. Allow me to clarify my previous statement. We're not, exactly," Richard said, teeth gritted, as if trying to find a word on the far wall, "*ferrying* … the aircraft, as the term suggests." His easygoing smile returned as he looked Dan in the eye. "It's still legal to fly maintenance-wise but we're … repositioning it, from the field in Victorville to a maintenance base in Seattle.

"But, as far as I'm concerned, we aren't conducting a test flight; we're just moving it from Point A to Point B. However, if the aircraft faults in flight you'll be there to witness it and maybe see what goes wrong. Besides, my co-pilot and I will be a lot more prepared for any emergencies since we now know what to expect. I swear Maggie and I aged ten years each the last time."

Vince added with a laugh, "You'll have to shave your beard again."

Dan laughed somewhat nervously as the prospect hit him.

"So, what do you say, Dan," Richard asked, leaning in, "you wanna take a ride?"

The Air Crash Files: Jet Blast

BOOK FOUR

FREESTYLE AIR FREIGHT FLIGHT 399

The Air Crash Files: Jet Blast

CHAPTER 30
MORE THAN EXPECTED

February 27

Dan fought an urge to yawn. He caught a direct flight to Los Angeles, hoping to catch a nap on the trip but the couple seated behind wore noise suppression headphones; their eight-month old screamed non-stop, while their son kicked Dan's seat out of boredom. It taxed his patience while he skated close to the edge of losing his religion.

Richard Grace wanted Dan to accompany the pilots on Freestyle's Challenger Jet, but government policy strictly forbade anything that could be misinterpreted as a 'gift' or 'favor,' thereby skewing the investigator's impartiality. It did not apply here, but rules are rules and, under the circumstances, Phil would make sure Dan followed the rules.

It was late morning in Los Angeles when he arrived, the temperature promised to peak at around 72 Fahrenheit. The sun was playing peek-a-boo with the clouds; a good day for Victorville. Dan checked in with the unnecessarily pleasant front desk attendant, went to his room and fell asleep without even removing his shoes.

Phil made sure Dan's departure did not go without some sort of warning; he waited until the majority of personnel left for the night, before walking into Dan's office unannounced and shutting the door. The Director did not afford any pleasantries, but bent over the desk with his finger inches from Dan's face.

At first, Phil could barely utter anything, but a series of strangled noises. Finally, he commenced in an incomprehensible lecture. "I'll begin by pointing out that you went behind my back for the last time! I don't like being taken to task by that slob, Scalia. I really hate you using him like your personal muscle every time things don't go your way!" And so on for ten minutes. Dan's hopes of catching his train were dashed along with his patience.

As Phil paused to take a breath, Dan calmly fired back. "I didn't ask Vince to take my side; I don't even know what you're talking about. I haven't talked with Vince since the Freestyle incident last summer."

Phil's face blossomed into a scarlet mask and Dan feared he would explode grey matter all over his desk. But Phil reined it in and leaned back. "How do you explain Scalia knowing about the tests in Portland? He *knew* you made the reversers deploy after we left."

Images of people ran through Dan's mind; only four persons knew about that, other than him: Chris, Ron, George, and Connie. Chris has no patience for Vince while Ron feared for his job, even with Vince. George? Rubbing elbows with Vince was just not George's style.

Connie? *No way. That didn't make any sense*, he thought. *But, how else could Vince have learned about certain things?* Dan decided he would never throw Connie under the bus. *She is, after all, the anti-Phil; the only one with any spine to push back.*

"I can't explain it," Dan said in surrender. "but it wasn't me!"

Dan woke to the loud blare of the phone. Half his face was buried in the pillow, but he managed to bare one eye to look incredulously at the noisy device. It announced its urgency again. Consciousness fought to regain control of the mind, as reality rose from a soup of conflict; he fought to wake from where dreams refuse to play.

"Huh-low?"

"Mister Tenace, is that you?"

"Hmm-mmm," he responded.

"Daniel, this is Richard Grace. I'm in room three-twenty-two. We're going to dinner, so come join us."

Dan sat up in a very dark room and brought his legs over the edge of the bed. "Captain Grace," he managed, stifling a yawn. "I'm sorry, but I had a bad flight. Can you give me about a half-hour and I'll meet you in the lobby?"

"We'll meet you in the lobby at eight-thirty."

Dan looked at the clock: 7:57. *How generous*, he thought, *a whole three minutes extra.*

"Daniel, this is my first officer, Mitchell McNally," Richard Grace said when Dan entered the lobby. Mitch stood up and shook Dan's hand.

"It's just Mitch, Dan." No stranger to the Boston marathon, Mitchell McNally was roughly Dan's height; he wore his hair short, but not as severely as Richard. His young face was clean shaven with a mischievous smile, a perfect foil for Richard. Mitch knew how to cross the chasms that separated pilot and mechanic; a workplace barrier he despised, for he respected another professional for what they did, not how they dressed for work.

"And this is Jeffrey Harper. He works in the hangar in Cleveland and he's a wiz with the four-fifty." Jeff shook Dan's hand and pointed him towards the front door. The two pilots preceded them outside.

"Just call me 'Jeff,'" he said. "It's good ta meet ya ... even if you do talk like a Yank."

The four of them sat around the table and drinks were brought. Richard waited for the waitress to take their orders and depart before he grabbed a piece of bread. "We're glad you could make this, Dan." Richard scrutinized Dan before saying, "Bad flight? You didn't sound good before."

Despite the shower Dan was still shaking off the jet lag. "Do I look that bad?" All three nodded. "Let's just say, I've had better flights in my life."

"Fair enough," Mitch laughed. "I think it's safe to say we've all been there. But if I was to wager a guess – and I'm not a betting man–," he threw in for good measure, "I'd say, hmm ... middle seat, crying infants, or snoring guy on the aisle."

Jeff took a pull of his beer. "Nah, that's way too easy. I'll go with brat kicking his seat and two women yakkin' it up."

Dan shook his head with a grin. Richard added, "My guess is that the sleeping pill didn't kick in and ... and ..." looking for his next guess on the ceiling, "his headset had dead batteries."

Dan pointed at Mitch. "I had a window, but the crying infant was one thing." He then pointed at Jeff, "No to the yakkin', but yes to the brat with restless leg syndrome."

"And mine?" Richard said after swallowing his bread.

"I was surprised Richard; you had the right guess, but the wrong person. The headsets – and I emphasize the plural – worked fine. However, they belonged to the brat and the infant's parents, who had a pleasant flight, thank you very much."

All three laughed sympathetically; they then lifted their glasses and toasted to the success of their flight in the morning. Richard said, "Dan, we need to fill you in on a few things. I also want to give you a chance to back out if you want."

Dan's hand went up to negate Richard's offer. "No, I'm in; I've been looking for an opportunity just like this. I'd be lying if I said I wasn't originally reluctant," he added honestly, "because, if I understood you, this is a hunting trip; we're looking to make this happen. So, unless you specifically," he pointed at Richard, "want me to sit this out, I'd really like to go."

Richard nodded approvingly. "Good deal, you're in."

Dan added, "I just wish we had the ground sense switch from your L-A flight, Richard. So far, we've had trouble duplicating the results, but that switch would've been the perfect test subject."

Jeff opened his mouth, but Richard cut him off with a stern look. "We'll see if we can work around that, Dan. We're really going to need your help on this ..." he frowned at the metaphor, "hunting trip. I was already putting things in motion before Vince Scalia called me."

"Vince called you? How did he know?"

But Richard shrugged his shoulders. "All he said was that he shared my concern following the incident in L-A. I don't know how he got my name or anything beyond what you told him at the time–" Dan went to interrupt, "Dan, I – I don't know, you're going to have to ask him."

"You need to help us fill in some blanks," Mitch said, cradling his ice water. "I mean we're not really sure what your theories are."

Jeff added, "Me and Trung configured the aircraft as close to the other dash four-fifty from last summer. Your being a mechanic will help us out, since Trung couldn't make it," Jeff spread his hands in supplication, "I'm gonna need somebody to hold the flashlight."

"I haven't been trained–"

"You don't need to be," Jeff interrupted, "everything's set up. All you gotta do is help us with the scenarios and watch for fireworks. Richard was there last time and no one's better. Mitch is a test pilot and can make that plane do tricks the builders never intended. And me," Jeff said, with a smile, "well, I'm simply the best there is."

"If not the most modest," Mitch laughed.

Dan leaned across the table. "If you don't mind me asking, but why isn't the L-A first officer here?"

Mitch fielded the question, leaning forward and lowering his voice, "For one, Maggie's keeping her flight schedule; we couldn't pull her away. Second, she isn't qualified as a test pilot. With what Richard here is proposing, it'd be wiser to have someone trained to handle these situations. Is there a reason you need her?"

"Well, to be honest," Dan uttered, reaching for the butter, "I wanted to pick her brain about anything she may have been testing out that night." Richard went to object, but Dan stopped him. "I'm not suggesting she did anything wrong, but did she say anything to you about using the SPAR system? I couldn't catch anything from the CVR."

Richard closed his eyes, reviewing the flight so many months ago. "Oddly enough, Maggie was talking about SPAR. We went over the flight detail by detail later that morning. Whatever was turned on, it wasn't on the checklist."

"Are you sure she turned something on, Richard?" Mitch asked.

"No, I'm not pos–"

"What," Dan stated more than asked.

"She'd been talking about the new equipment, specifically the ground tracking computer. She wanted to monitor them to see how they worked because she'd just completed the training."

"Can you call her?"

Richard looked at his watch. "No, I think she's flying back from San Diego right now." He turned to Mitch. "That transits through Denver, right? I can leave a message for her to call me when she gets to Cleveland."

"So," Dan generalized, "either she never had it on or she didn't remember turning it off. What do you suggest?"

"I'm pretty sure she turned the ground tracker on."

Jeff mused, "Can we play while we're up there?"

"We're going to have to," Dan suggested, deferring to Richard's authority, "if that's okay. It's the best information we've got. I do know that the Gyrfalcon plane used a Transolutions Satellite Tracking System; you guys use something called SAT-SPAN."

"Has this shown up with Boeing or Airbus?"

"Not from what we've seen," Dan answered. "My management was stuck on AeroGalactic because they're the only manufacturer showing these glitches so far. They're convinced it's the aircraft manufacturer."

"But you're not."

Dan made an effort to smile. "Is it that obvious?"

The next morning Jeff and Dan were at the airport three hours before scheduled departure; Jeff wanted to make sure N901FS was ready. After accessing the ramp, both he and Dan pushed the crew stairs up to the entry door.

Once inside, Dan looked toward the back of the empty fuselage, scattered fragments of light gained ingress through the four windows in the back. The sunlight did nothing to give perspective of the spacious interior.

Then Jeff switched on the power; a series of bells and claxons immediately shrieked at the two from within the aircraft's belly and speaker system; gauges powered up while cooling fans hummed. Within seconds, the cavernous view of the enclosed empty captured Dan's attention. The thought of a bowling alley came close to the description of space; an endless enclosure with nothing but air. The long fuselage visually narrowed as it approached the tail.

As he walked in the cargo area, Dan stepped up onto one of two neon-yellow ballast pallets – each weighing six thousand pounds. They were low profile concrete slabs encased in aluminum plating and bolted to flat aluminum sheets. Sprouting out of the flat tops were tubular aluminum bars that the ramp crews use to maneuver the pallets around. Both pallets were locked in place on the upper cargo floor. Dan knew the purpose of the pallets was to balance the -450 while in flight.

"How much more freight can you carry with this unusual oval shape?"

Jeff replied, "The paper-pushers say sixty thousand pounds of extra freight."

As they reached the tail Jeff pointed up, "The number two-engine starts here," he said indicating with his finger to a spot just before the aft pressure bulkhead. "The engine is lower than the M-D-eleven, but they've reinforced the engine nacelle with light-weight Kevlar bands which are supposed to contain a compressor break-up."

They went forward to the cockpit where Jeff ran the three engines one more time. He then showed Dan around the aircraft, pointing out differences and similarities to other aircraft that Dan worked. As they made their way, Jeff opened panels, checked fluids, and verified the integrity of all the components he could.

Mitch and Richard stepped out of the taxi and went through Cal Superior's security measures. While Mitch conducted last minute weather and flight plan paperwork, Richard walked around the aircraft, accomplishing his visual inspection.

Jeff and Dan had stopped their tour by the left gear. Dan glanced at the left main ground sense switch noticing a black 'X' across its tan housing. He said over his shoulder to Jeff, "Why the black 'X'?"

"That," Richard answered, "is the ground sense switch from the L-A flight."

Dan stood straight up, pointing at the switch. "You found the actual switch?"

Jeff was smiling behind Richard, who said, "I never found the switch. I asked for it, specifically, when they swapped it out. You could say, I saved it from being lost." Here he lowered his voice, "I had Jeff install it."

Before Dan could reply, Richard turned to Jeff. "How does she look?"

"Fit to fly in every meanin' of the term," Jeff replied. "Fluids are good, we ran the motors ... oh, I mean, engines, for you piloting-types. We should have a smooth flight. That is, if you guys can avoid beatin' up my airplane with any barrel rolls."

Richard gave his signature grin, nodding at the engines jab. "We'll try to avoid any aerobatics; I know how sensitive you mechanic-types are. The fueler will be adding about ten thousand pounds of fuel, so keep an eye on him for me, will ya?"

"You got it," Jeff replied. He turned back to Dan, his left eyebrow arching. "Do ya want to back out now?"

Dan grinned. "No way, José."

Jeff headed for the cockpit, but Dan's phone began to warble. He stepped aside; recognizing the number, he answered it on the second ring.

"What is it, Babe?"

"Dan," Megan started, "You've gotta come home now!"

"What's the matter?"

"I called the family support group in Fort Campbell–"

"What? Why'd you call?"

"I haven't been able to shake this feeling–! The woman there transferred me to an officer who said that

Max's unit hasn't checked in. They were in a heavy fire fight!"

"Megan, I can't leave here!"

"Dan! Your son is missing and you need to get back here."

Dan held the phone against his chest. Muffled cries of, 'Dan! Dan!' could be heard coming from the receiver. He felt out of place; he was needed by his wife.

He spoke into the phone, "Meg, even if I left now and ran to L-A, I would never beat my Seattle flight back to Washington. I really have no way of getting there faster!"

"But, Dan–"

"Babe, I'll be there as soon as I can! Didn't Patrick come home today to visit?"

The line went dead; in frustration, Meg hung up on him.

A knot the size of Wichita formed in his stomach; a large section of his mind was thousands of miles away in Afghanistan, and a smaller part in Virginia. He felt wretched, miserable, as if he betrayed his wife and his son.

But Max would understand, he reminded himself. He would resent my shirking my responsibility to head home, to wait in futile misery. If he knew anything about his sons it was that they were unselfish; they knew what he was doing was important.

Max trusted him to do what was right, just like he would.

With a near-paralyzing sense of despair he headed for the cockpit.

Within an hour N901FS was ready to depart. Richard took his place in the left seat with Mitch to his right. Jeff occupied the first observer's seat, just behind and to the left of Richard's captain's seat; Jeff needed to sit here where his knowledge of the aircraft and its systems would be most beneficial to the flight crew in an emergency. Dan sat in what was originally designated, per the original design as, the second officer's seat.

Richard accomplished a last minute pre-flight meeting for what he called Freestyle flight 399 heavy, where he pointed out for the CVR that this was a repositioning flight, worked out any emergency procedures, and tabled any questions. When all four people were satisfied, Richard asked the last question: "Does anyone wish to back out?"

Everyone simultaneously responded to the negative.

Jeff and Trung did everything to guarantee the airworthiness of N901FS. Only clairvoyance or the ability to peer inside of hard plastic could have enabled them to see the damage incurred over a year prior by a careless step; a mechanic servicing the nose gear strut accidentally cracked the casing. Time, atmospheric pressure variations, and moisture worked together to introduce a short in the circuit within the seemingly undamaged casing. The occupants of N901FS innocently believed that the main gear sense switch was the only problem purposely introduced into the aircraft.

However, they were blind to the damaged nose gear ground sense switch.

"By the way, Dan ..." Richard turned to see Dan staring out the window without actually seeing anything. "Dan?"

Jeff nudged Dan, and he spun his head around. Jeff pointed to Richard, who sat with a grin on his face.

"I'm sorry, Richard. What did you want?"

"Are you okay?"

"Yeah, go ahead with what you were saying."

"I spoke to Maggie last night; she called about eleven o'clock. She said she was testing the satellite tracking computer and something called the Digamma Six Ground Tracking Computer, which follows ground traffic. I remembered talking about it. She suggested the satellite tracking as a possible culprit. What do you think?"

"I'm sorry Richard, but I wouldn't discount anything."

"We'll see," Richard replied before he triggered the mic switch.

"Ground ... flight; we are ready for pushback. Standing by to release brakes."

The distorted voice came back over the pushback tug's diesel engine's rumbling, "Copy flight; chocks are pulled and steering bypass is pinned; release brakes."

Richard released the brakes by pressing on the top of the rudder pedals with his toes, easing the pedals back. "Brakes are released. Push back, tail west."

"Copy, brakes off, tail west."

The four in the cockpit jolted forward as the aircraft started to move in reverse. A distinct diesel roar escalated over the normal quiet announcing the pushback tug had been accelerated to meet the demand for power. "Clear to start engines."

Mitch looked up at the instruments for engine start. He placed the selector switch in START and switched another selector to ENG ONE.

"Copy, clear to start," Richard said into his headset. He turned to Mitch. "She's all yours, Mitch."

"Starting one."

Mitch pressed a T-shaped switch in; it lit up upon activation. Almost immediately a whoosh could be heard through the frame of the aircraft; pressurized air was delivered from the Auxiliary Power Unit, itself spooling up to meet the demand.

"Pressure drop," Mitch observed.

While the aircraft continued its backward push, a distinct moan advertised the starting of the engines; a low 'woo-woo' sound blended into a steady hum as each engine in turn reached idle power.

Ten minutes later, N901FS turned left off taxiway Echo-1 onto runway 17. Clearance was given and the -450 rolled down the runway gathering speed for flight; Mitch set the throttles for climb.

"V2, rotate," Mitch said. Richard pulled gently back on the yoke; the aircraft defied the captain's input for several seconds. Slowly the runway slid below the nose; in its place, the sky looked a scattered grey overcast with patches of blue peeking out of place in its midst. Richard banked the -450C right towards the Pacific Ocean. Dan saw the ground momentarily before leveling off for the short trip past the Los Angeles skyline.

As flight 399 climbed confidently into the California sky, observers on the ground may have noticed how the thickening clouds spread ominously over the airliner. Flight 399 banked right again, climbing into the disheartening heavens; a beam of sunlight pierced the grey, touching the aircraft's tail like a caress.

Patrick Tenace picked the phone up on the second ring. "Hello?"

"Hi," the slightly congested voice said in response. "How are you doing, Dan?"

"I'm not my father," Patrick responded in a monotone; he never liked being mistaken for Dan, even over the phone. A younger version of his father, Patrick Tenace had driven up from school to visit his parents. "This is his son, Pat."

"Oh ... I'm sorry. My name is Gordon Lyle and I'm a friend of your father's. Is he home or at work?"

"No, Mister Lyle. Actually, he's in L-A looking at an airplane for that Memphis accident." Pat considered giving out Dan's cell phone, but he did not know the caller. "Can I get a message to him?"

"That's alright. I have his cell number; maybe I'll give him a call tonight." A feeling of unanticipated foreboding came across Lyle as he thought of what to say. *After all*, he thought, *they've taken precautions*.

He started to say goodbye when he felt compelled to add, "Listen Pat, if your father calls you, please tell him I need to talk to him. I've been looking at the Gyrfalcon Airlines problem all wrong. The aircraft manufacturer does things differently; the switches operate differently ... You know what, never mind, just please ask him to call me tonight."

"Are you sure?"

"Yes," Lyle said, "it's not an emergency. Goodbye"

Gordon hung up the phone, unable to get the feeling out of his head. As Freestyle 399 paralleled the Oregon coast, he would not know how wrong he was about it not being an emergency.

Two hours and twenty minutes into the flight, Freestyle 399 began a gradual descent from an altitude of thirty thousand feet. Weather up the Pacific coast had been uneventfully clear.

The conversation had been light on the flight deck; Jeff was curious about the directions Dan's investigation had taken. He had brought with him the wiring diagrams for the -450 plus any SPAR systems he could get his hands on. Together, he and Dan passed the time scouring through the pages.

As flight 399 passed the airspace outside of Oregon, Richard was busy communicating with the ground. The altimeter skated past sixteen thousand feet, heading for fifteen thousand.

Dan said, "I noticed Richard, you go out of your way to avoid the technology."

"How so?" Richard asked.

Jeff turned to look at Dan, while Mitch half-listened, reviewing his airport diagrams. "Well, the other crews I've flown with are always checking the digital readouts. But you on the other hand, always look at the standby gauges; the old analog back-up instruments." Dan could see Richard smile from the angle he had, behind and to the right. "Are you verifying the analog gauges?"

Richard seemed to relax into the seat in a physical sigh, "You know Dan, I've flown the most advanced aircraft – both military and civilian – so I've seen it all.

But with all these gauges and illuminated buttons and computerized wizardry available, I still find myself wanting to look out the window. But to answer your question, I don't trust the technology to do my job for me–" He put his hand up to stop further conversation.

"Copy Seattle," Richard said aloud, "contact Approach on one-two-five-decimal-nine, Three-nine-nine heavy. G' day."

Mitch dialed in the new frequency and triggered the mic, "Seattle Approach, this is Three-nine-nine heavy at fifteen descending for twelve."

"Good afternoon, Freestyle three-nine-nine heavy. Descend and maintain ten thousand. Slow to two-five-zero, turn right heading zero-nine-zero."

Richard responded with the proper reply, adjusting the Heading selector knob until the numbers 0-9-0 were displayed in the window. Mitch tapped the indicator with his finger, verifying silently the numbers in the window matched the assigned course. Richard pressed the Autopilot and the aircraft banked right to line up on the new heading. He sat back for a few seconds counting to himself. When Dan was pre-occupied with the diagrams, Richard turned to Mitch. "Did you see that?"

"Yeah, I did," Mitch said matter-of-factly. He glanced over his shoulder at Jeff who nodded his head grimly.

"I saw it too," Jeff said sardonically. "Whatta coincidence."

Dan's head turned left and caught the three men looking casually at the data display page on the forward computer screen. His eyes immediately gravitated to the monitor as well, but there was nothing unusual displayed. "Saw what?"

Richard keyed the mic, ignoring Dan's question. "Seattle Approach, Three-nine-nine heavy, we've got an indication here we wish to check out before continuing our descent."

The worried controller's voice came back, "Freestyle three-nine-nine heavy; are you declaring an emergency?"

Richard's voice was laced with confidence. "Negative Seattle, there was an indication anomaly. Requesting to vector west off the approach."

"Copy Freestyle three-nine-nine heavy, contact Seattle Center at one-three-five-decimal one-five. State the nature of the indication."

"One-three-five-decimal-one-five. Three-nine-nine heavy."

As Mitch dialed in the new number, he shook his head slowly and said through gritted teeth, "Well, we're committed now."

Richard took a deep breath and blew it out slowly. He turned towards Dan for a second and winked at him. "Seattle Center, Freestyle Three-nine-nine heavy."

As Richard spoke with Seattle Center, Mitch planned out the upcoming diversion. Jeff consulted a troubleshooting manual for last minute references and direction. Meanwhile, Dan sat, feeling like Zeppo Marx, the only brother left out of the gag.

"Copy, Seattle, turn left heading two-seven-zero, maintain fifteen, Three-nine-nine heavy."

And with that the large jet banked to the west, heading further out over the ocean.

Seattle Center routed flight 399 west of the air traffic and safely away from the coast. This prevented them from interfering with slower moving general aviation, allowing them to check their systems far from the civilians on the ground. The deviation gave the crew of flight 399 a section of sky that was unimpeded with traffic or obstacles, making it easy for them to concentrate on the problem at hand.

The space allotted was a 450-cubic mile area, 80 miles west of Seattle; Richard could maneuver the aircraft through this airspace, thousands of feet above the ocean surface. During normal maneuvers this block may be considered generous. However, altitude is a pilot's best friend.

And in an emergency, there is never enough altitude.

When they traveled on a heading of 270 degrees for twenty minutes, Richard turned to Mitch. "Grab the hard copy pages for the approach checklists."

Mitch reached over and started rummaging through his flight bag. Richard turned around and looked at Dan, who sat skeptical in his seat.

Dan mouthed the words, "There was no flicker, was there?"

But Richard just shook his head for the benefit of the cockpit voice recorder; he pointed up to the microphone and waved his finger at Dan, who nodded his head in response.

Mitch said casually, "Richard, I've been running this SATSPAN since we took off. Did you want to see what it does while we're out here?"

Richard nodded his head in understanding. "Sure Mitch, but I'd also like to see that Ground Tracking Computer, if we have some time."

Now it was Mitch's turn to nod his head in understanding. As they descended slowly towards ten thousand, all eyes were glued to the status page while Richard kept his fingers on the fuel shutoff for the #2 engine. Jeff glanced periodically at the fuel and hydraulic quantities.

"Flaps two," Richard said. Mitch reacted by placing the flap handle in the proper position. As the aircraft continued to descend, Richard called for flaps seven and armed the Autoland. As they broke through nine thousand feet, Richard called for gear down.

The empty airliner amplified the noises vibrating through the massive airframe. The sounds of rushing wind echoed through the plane as all four-landing gear broke out of their covered wells and violated the air stream; the noise that emanated from the nose well was not unlike a howling banshee, driven with madness. Dan's eyes shot to the front panel and saw all four gear lights go from red in-transit to green, down and locked.

And they all held their breath.

But nothing happened.

As the altimeter approached five thousand feet above sea level, Richard called for gear up. He gently pushed the throttles forward to claw back up into the sky. He disengaged Autoland and signaled to Mitch to raise the flaps.

"So much for Maggie's suggestion," Richard said, stating the obvious.

Mitch leaned close and murmured, "we can give it one more go." He turned on the DATTAM Ground Tracking Computer and allowed it to warm up. As they passed eight thousand feet of altitude, Richard and Mitch looked at their designated screens and saw the outline for Seattle airport materialize out of a grey background.

The airport looked alive; 'airplanes' moving on the ground in a variety of colors danced across the screen as if choreographed to music. "That's pretty neat," Mitch said sarcastically looking at the monitor, "I haven't taken the training yet, but I assume these colors designate an aircraft's either in motion or static and a bunch of other super-zoomie stuff?"

Jeff looked away from the monitor, "Don't look at me. You guys get all the good training before we ever see it."

Dan went back to reviewing the diagrams just as flight 399 casually passed through ten thousand feet of altitude. Jeff, Richard, and Mitch focused on other instruments as the Ground Tracking winked out, the screens going completely grey.

Richard leveled off at thirteen thousand feet. Disappointment played across everyone's faces; the failed test crushing their resolve.

As the -450C cruised along a southeasterly course, both pilots configured flight 399 for the landing procedure again. As they descended, Richard pulled back on the throttles, bleeding off unnecessary airspeed.

Dan committed himself to studying the revised wiring diagrams provided by Jeff, looking for anything that stood out as unusual. He momentarily glanced at the main gear ground sense switch and saw something he never saw before.

"Jeff," he whispered, "is this diagram right?"

Richard and Mitch busied themselves trying to duplicate the L-A incident. Jeff looked over. "Why do ya ask?"

"I never noticed this before, but if this diagram is correct, the main gear ground sense switch opens on landing."

"Yeah, so?"

Richard, despite Dan's whispering, overheard the question. "I gotta tell you, Dan, that was my question too. Every Boeing or Airbus I ever flew the ground sense switch closes on landing. When they fixed the plane in L-A, the manager there told me the switch on the AeroGalactic opens."

Dan caught Jeff's attention, a serious look crossing his face. "We've been trying to find a bad digital gate on the assumption all ground sense switches close on landing. Boeing and Airbus; the switches close."

"No," Jeff said casually, "AeroGalactic likes to be different. I remember from class that the switch opens on landing."

"Is it like that with all AeroGalactic planes?"

"I'm not sure, but I would think so."

Dan started looking at the wiring diagrams again. A feeling of anxiety overcame him; he and Chris had been working under the wrong information; it was, all the while, right under their noses.

Meanwhile flight 399 slowly descended.

Jeff monitored the jet's systems, diligently staying ahead of the curve. He wanted to keep track despite the fact he was not flight crew. Richard knew Jeff was an extra set of eyes; that he was checking the aircraft's status.

And flight 399 slowly descended.

Richard watched as the altimeter slowly scrolled downward, incrementally seeking a lower altitude than previously attained; the numbers showed eleven thousand, dropping agonizingly slow towards ten thousand. He asked for flaps two as the jet slowed. The vibration from the engines receded, giving the -450C over to the hesitant active force of drag. Mitch displayed the reverser unlock emergency procedures again on the status page.

Richard armed the Autoland system one more time. With the press of a button, the system activated; current was directed through the proper computers, standing by for the next command.

"Flaps seven," Richard said. Mitch reached over and brought the flap handle down yet another detent. On the front panel a digital display showed a representation of the flaps growing from a thin to a wider rectangle. A configuration warning sounded but Richard silenced it.

And flight 399 slowly descended.

As they fell below ten thousand feet of altitude, both pilots' Ground Tracking Computers came alive again. Nobody noticed the visual displays, except Dan who caught Mitch's monitor out of the corner of his eye.

"Flaps fifteen."

With the wiring diagram book open, Dan tried one more time to find the evasive; he turned the page to the Ground Tracking Computer page, following the lines with his finger to the Autoland computer. A wire/line intercepted the computer box with a note next to the computer's outline.

"We're coming up on eight thousand and descending," Mitch said.

"Drop the gear," Richard said.

Dan read the note in the wiring diagram: '< Ten Thousand Feet' ... below ten thousand feet. *What happens below ten thousand feet?* He looked down at the diagram again. The wire/line went into the flight command computer where it met two separate lines coming from ... both gear sense switches. Dan realized he had not been listening.

What altitude were they at?

Mitch reached forward and pulled the gear handle out and back, moving it down; he let it slide forward when the handle was in the 'DN' position. A 'chunk' sound echoed through the flight deck. The gear in-transit lights went red as the gear broke out of their wells and started to rotate out into the air stream. Richard's right hand hovered near the fuel shut-off switch for the #2 engine. His eyes were plastered to the status page, anticipating the amber reverser light.

Dan looked at the front panel and noticed the red lights announcing that the four gears were on their way out. The noise coming from the nose gear exiting its well below into the relative wind was unmistakable.

What's our altitude? Dan thought to himself; he looked over his shoulder at the instruments. The digital displays on the front monitor showed the various indications: airspeed, artificial horizon, engine monitoring ... and altitude.

Eight thousand feet! A chill ran up Dan's spine as he watched the gear in-transit lights on the front panel.

"Here we go, guys!" He said out loud, unconsciously checking his harness.

The four down and locked lights on the front panel illuminated green.

Then the airplane plummeted to the ocean below.

CHAPTER 31
DEPLOYMENT

Dan had no sooner uttered the words, "Here we go, guys," when everybody was violently thrust forward. The aircraft abruptly fell like a runaway elevator; everyone gravitated off their seat cushions, shoulder harnesses painfully digging in; the KR-450C nosed over, pointing towards the ocean. Ears popped agonizingly as the cabin pressure controller tried to keep up.

Richard's hand slipped away from the fuel shutoff lever. Mitch pushed off the forward panel, watching the altimeter scroll downwards at a stomach-wrenching rate.

Richard grappled again for the #2 fuel shutoff lever; his fingers located the switch lock, but Mitch's left hand stopped him. "We've got three reverser deployments! Ground spoilers deployed!" Mitch stated factually, staring at the status page.

Time slowed; Richard's experience kicked in. He glanced at the altimeter as it raced past four thousand feet.

"Gear up! Now!"

Mitch pulled the gear handle out and up. Immediately, the four gear in-transit lights went red. Inertia stopped, releasing everyone back in their seats. Richard shoved the throttles forward and eased back on the yoke. Forward momentum restored, the airliner slowly advanced.

"Spoilers retracted," Mitch said.

The #2 and #3 reverser lights extinguished.

"Number one reverser is still deployed!"

Dan fought the bile rising in his throat; he turned to Jeff, "It's the Ground Tracking Computer! That's the bad signal!" Mitch looked to his right and switched off his ground tracker. Jeff opened two circuit breakers, killing power to the ground tracking computers.

The aircraft yawed left; the nose, at a negative angle, giving everyone an unobstructed view of the approaching ocean. Richard reached over and cut off the fuel to the #1 engine. They felt, more than heard, the engine quit and fall behind the other two.

In that time, the gear lights extinguished one-by-one as the four gears stowed in their wells. The uncontrolled descent slowed; as the altimeter approached 3000 feet, it leveled off while the Pacific Ocean waited patiently below. Engines #2 and #3 rotated faster; they spooled up to maximum power; their hungry fans pulling air in and pushing it back.

Flight 399 – reluctantly, at first – started to climb. Richard compensated for the aircraft veering to the left. Slowly at first, then gradually, the -450C nosed up and rose gently into the sky. Mitch 'cleaned' the airplane, withdrawing the flaps and slats that eased sluggishly into their retracted positions. The Pacific Ocean receded beneath and soon the waves were indiscriminate from the dark blue surface.

"Freestyle three-nine-nine heavy, Seattle Center, what is your status?"

"I got this," Mitch said. "Seattle, Three-nine-nine heavy, Mayday! Mayday! Mayday!" Mitch clicked off the mic and pointed at the #1 reverser light. "Richard–?"

Seattle interrupted Mitch's question. "Freestyle three-nine-nine heavy, state your emergency!"

Richard looked at the indication and said, "Dan, I need you to run back and see if you can tell what's going on with the number one reverser!"

"I'll go–"

"No Jeff, I need you here! Dan doesn't know the airplane better than you."

"I'm on it," Dan said, unbuckling his restraints. "Number one reverser is still deployed." He opened the cockpit door and disappeared into the back.

"Seattle, Freestyle three-nine-nine heavy," Mitch said calmly, "We've had three reverser deployments and lost over five thousand feet of altitude. Reversers two and three retracted, number one remains deployed, number one engine shut down."

"Copy Three-nine-nine heavy. At your discretion climb and maintain one-two thousand."

"Seattle, climb and maintain one-two thousand. We are verifying a hung number one reverser, Three-nine-nine heavy."

"Understood."

Behind the cockpit, Dan climbed back over the ballast pallet. Within a few seconds he was standing in the doorway of the cockpit, slightly out of breath. "Richard, from what I can see your inboard number one reverser is still deployed; I can see the translating cowl fluttering. I saw your outboard translating cowl over the front of the pylon; as far as I can tell, it's retracted."

Richard turned to Jeff. "Do you know why?"

Jeff did not hesitate, "The only thing I can think of is the inboard hung up and the outboard didn't. The halves are independent; if one binds during retraction or extension, the independent drive units allow one to drive without the other."

"What's the purpose of that?" Mitch asked.

"It normally happens after landing when the plane is moving slow. That and deferring one half is easier and faster; less turnaround time. Why it's hangin' in the breeze is beyond me. I know it's impossible to remotely retract it."

"What problems can we expect," Richard asked, "flying with it like that?"

"It'll 'fect your speed, mostly, and yer yaw," Jeff responded. "I dunno how much damage there is, which means you might launch it off towards the tail."

Richard and Mitch looked at each other. "Nice," Mitch said.

Flight 399 had been directed almost one hundred miles off the Seattle coast to give them room to maneuver, but now that distance was working against them. Richard maintained the aircraft's climb rate to gain as much altitude as he could.

"Jeff," Richard calmly said, alternating attention between different instruments. "Keep an eye on the fuel for us. If my math is correct we've got enough, but I want you to watch it anyway."

"You got it, Cap'n," Jeff responded.

The inboard #1 reverser's translating cowl was buffeted in the 230-knot air speed; it twisted further out into the air stream with each second of abuse. The only things preventing the translating cowl from separating from the reverser half were the battered jackscrew transmissions, six blocker doors and the remaining bottom track. With nothing to support them, the blocker doors – designed only to deflect slower air – absorbed the greatest punishment, trying to restrain the convulsing, 150-pound translating cowl.

"Seattle Center, maintaining one-two thousand, heading one-five-zero, Three-nine-nine heavy."

"Three-nine-nine heavy, what are your intentions?"

"Request landing at SEATAC."

"Three-nine-nine heavy, turn left, heading zero-four-zero."

Richard concentrated on level flight. Both pilots' movements were fluid and the gravity of the situation never showed. Jeff knew they would need the Air Driven Alternate Motor – A. D. A. M. – as they approached the airport. Richard would use all his options and ADAM could handle hydraulics or electrical.

Dan went to the back to keep an eye on the deployed reverser and report any additional problems. Before he left, Richard ordered him to get belted in his seat when they approached for landing.

"Heading zero-four-zero," Mitch said before tapping the HEADING display window. Richard double-tapped the HEADING display in response. He hesitated, reluctantly engaging the Autopilot.

The jet took a few seconds before it responded, dipping left ten degrees in response to the new heading. But, as the -450C entered its left turn, three blocker doors broke free of the deployed reverser half; they slid under the raised left inboard aileron and directly into the #2 engine inlet. They immediately intercepted the eight-foot wide fan turning at more than 3600 rotations per minute.

Much of the #2 engine's compressor disintegrated; the remarkable kinetic energy of the fan's blades smashing into the rigid blocker doors was catastrophic. One hundredth of a second later the shattered fan blades and chunks of blocker door were ingested into the inner engine core, stripping out all the internal workings of the compressor and turbine sections; the engine ate itself from the inside.

Most of the expelled fragments were captured by the fan shroud. Many metal shards escaped, propelled with great force back out of the inlet in various directions.

Vomited from the rear of the #2 engine were various internal components that scattered in the slipstream; glittering flakes that fell unmarked into the ocean, never seen again. Black smoke billowed; pressurized fuel vented from breached lines, vaporizing in the atmosphere. The engine shaft ground to a stop.

A metallic rainstorm oscillated through the airframe; intense vibrations, low rumblings, high frequency shrieks, echoed through the hull. As the cacophony ebbed, banging noises rang through the structure, followed closely by two more hard tremors; the aircraft's nose began dipping slightly on its own.

Everyone anticipated a fatal dive for the ocean that never came. Warning indications filled the cockpit with conflicting alerts. Forward momentum faltered as #2 engine failed. The #3 engine strained under the load as the nose pivoted left.

"Drop ADAM!" Richard commanded as he disengaged the Autopilot. Mitch lifted a door behind the pedestal; he reached into the hole it covered and pulled up a red handle. Immediately, a familiar low din resounded through the cockpit, followed by the low rumbling of a propeller. A gauge with the word ADAM came alive on the upper instrument display and began reading RPM. Mitch clicked the selector to HYDRAULICS.

"Yer losin' number one hydraulics, Richard!" Jeff yelled.

"You mean number two–"

"You'd think," Mitch countered, pointing at the quantity indications. "It's definitely number one. System two is holding steady."

Dan stood at the doorway again. "You just lost the inboard number one reverser half and it sounds like the hull's been breached near the tail,"

Richard killed the cross pump for #1 hydraulics; he spoke loudly at Dan, "Go back and see how bad the damage is!" He turned to Mitch. "Start number one." Richard clicked the mic, "Seattle Center, Freestyle three-nine-nine, heavy, we have a new emergency."

"Go ahead, Freestyle three-nine-nine!"

"We've had a catastrophic failure of the number two-engine and are losing number one hydraulics–"

A muffled yell from the cargo bay interrupted Richard's transmission. The first thought in Richard's mind was: *Now what*!

Richard turned. "Jeff, see what happened to Dan!" Jeff released his restraints and ran towards the back. Richard, meanwhile, pulled back on the yoke and corrected the aircraft, pulling the nose out of a slight dive.

"Freestyle three-nine-nine, you cut out! Restate your emergency!"

"Seattle," Richard began, "we've lost the number two engine and we're losing number one hydraulics."

The #1 engine started. "You've got number one engine back online," Mitch said. "The number one hydraulic pumps are off."

Shouting between Jeff and Dan reached the cockpit, dampened by the closed door. *What are they arguing about?*

"Jeff, what's the problem?"

Jeff entered the cockpit and secured the door, locking Dan out. Before Richard or Mitch could protest, he said, "He found the hydraulic leak!"

"Where?!" Richard said, his annoyance coming through. Get him up here–"

"No! First, put on your smoke goggles!"

The two pilots reached down and grabbed their goggles. As they placed them over their eyes, a faint pungent smell stroked their sinuses. They donned their oxygen masks.

Jeff clicked the mic to his oxygen mask. "The number one system hydraulics vaporized under system pressure in the cargo bay! One of the fan blades must have cut the hydraulic line under the floor when it came through the hull!"

Mitch's voice sounded muffled in his mask, "Can't he come up front?"

"Didja ever get that stuff in your eyes?" Jeff asked sarcastically. "Mitch, the guy walked into a cloud of hydraulic fluid! He can't see a thing; he's stumblin' around back there. If we let him back in then the mist comes with him." Jeff snapped his fingers, looking up at the overhead panel. "Oh! He said to isolate the cockpit! That stuff 's atomized! If it gets in the air vents, we'll be as blind as he is!"

Mitch reached up, flipped a selector switch to shut off pneumatics and isolate the cockpit.

"Freestyle three-nine-nine heavy, turn right heading zero-nine-zero, maintain altitude and speed."

Mitch responded back.

"The rudder isn't responding full deflection; look at the gauge," Richard said, turning the aircraft manually to the new heading. The rudder was showing limited movement, only a degree of deflection. "Looks like the rudder's jammed. All right people, let's get options!"

"Computer assistance is out of the question, Richard," Mitch offered. "Unless the Brainiacs who designed this flying colossus programmed some way-out scenarios into the flight command computers, you're going to have to fly this thing manually ... all the way to the scene of the accident!"

"Let's try to prevent that, shall we," Richard suggested.

"You have number two and three hydraulics–" Jeff began to say.

"Wait a minute," Richard said, cutting Jeff off as he came out of the turn. "Mitch, release the yoke." Both pilots took their hands off the yokes; the nose slowly began pitching over. "Why is she nosing over again?"

Jeff thought about it and said, "Well either the elevators were damaged by the number two break-up or the translatin' cowl hit one of 'em," he suggested, switching gears, "Look, you got two and three hydraulics working, which means you've lost half your hydraulic power on the elevators and ailerons, but your rudders and spoilers should have two systems each."

"What about stab trim?"

"That's number one and number three systems; you can trim with the stab, but it'll be slow. Ya also got full flaps, but your brakes are under the number one and three hydraulics, so yer pretty limited, stopping-wise. You're down to number two hydraulics for gear extension, so I suggest we drop 'em with the manual release and the weight should lock 'em in place. If not, bump with pressure and they'll lock." Jeff paused for a few seconds, but the hesitation advertised bad news, "Oh, and Cap'n?"

Richard sighed, "What now, Jeff?"

"Ground steering is number one system," he mentioned calmly, "you can't steer with the rudder pedals or the tiller. A hydraulic fuse'll prevent the steering actuators from depressurizing, but you can't move them."

"Three-nine-nine heavy, you are sixty miles out. Descend to eight thousand."

"But," Jeff continued, "you can steer by alternating pressure on your left and right brakes. I just can't promise you won't shimmy the nose gear apart."

"Seattle, copy; descend to eight thousand," Mitch answered back. "We're going to need to turn on final early; we have limited rudder deflection, Three-nine-nine heavy."

In Seattle, a group of controllers gazed at the screen; the stress on the room was already adding to a particularly long day. One controller shook her head and said to a muted microphone, "Can you make this anymore fun?"

Jeff pulled his oxygen mask down and sniffed the air. Satisfied there were no traces of hydraulic fumes he pulled the mask completely off. "The hydraulic fluid has vented out, but I'd keep my goggles on just in case."

Tentatively the two pilots removed their oxygen masks. Convinced the cockpit was hydraulic fume-free they stowed their oxygen masks. They took a moment to adjust their goggles and fix their headsets. Mitch looked over at Richard. "We can pull a Sioux City."

Richard's left eyebrow rose. He said, nodding. "Just what I was thinking."

In 1989 a DC-10 lost all hydraulic pressure and the #2 engine during a standard flight. The flight crew maneuvered the aircraft using the two wing engines to steer; increasing and decreasing thrust alternately to turn the jet side to side and as a result directing it with limited flight control input.

"Do you want–" Jeff began to ask.

"No!" Richard anticipating the question, he replied emphatically. "I think you're capable, but we've done the training. We can use you to help with other duties though."

As Flight 399 slowed, buffeting of the tail became more pronounced. The #2 engine loss was causing a challenging amount of inefficient drag on the jetliner and the loss of thrust was starting to be a problem at the lower speed. Visions of the tail ripping off occupied everyone's mind as the shimmying worsened. Time slowed as ground speed appeared to crawl. Richard and

Mitch were fighting the aircraft which was depriving them of accomplishing their other tasks.

Jeff looked up on the overhead panel at the fuel gauges in order to check quantity. "Captain, you're losing fuel out of the tail tank."

Richard glanced up. "Just pump it all forward, Jeff."

"Freestyle three-nine-nine heavy, turn left heading three-four-zero, descend to four-thousand. Contact Approach on one-two-five-decimal-nine. Good luck gentlemen!"

Mitch repeated the last directions. Richard turned the aircraft employing alternate engines; he advanced the throttle for #3 engine while retarding the #1 engine.

"Three-nine-nine heavy, Southwest seven-two-two. There's an engine cowl sticking out of your left tail feathers; looks like it knifed itself perfectly into your stabilizer's underside."

"There's where our translating cowl ended up," Mitch said. "No wonder she's pitching over."

Richard eased the disabled jetliner left while nursing the engine throttles along with the unresponsive rudder; it made the turn excruciatingly sluggish. He had to work through the turn to avoid overcompensating, the result of which would be a forced go around – or worse – a total loss of stability. As Flight 399 maneuvered through the center of a wide arc, Richard brought it back. Again, the jet was lethargic as he fought not only the rudder, but the damaged horizontal stabilizer.

As Richard brought the airliner out of the turn he called, "Flaps two." Mitch put the flap handle in the two-degree detent and watched the gauge to track. At first the flaps started to move together, but then the left inboard flap trailed the other three; the aircraft began to roll left.

Mitch moaned when a red 'ASSYMETRY' lit up on the status page.

"It rains, but it pours," he said tiredly. "We have no flaps, Richard." He put the flap handle back in the zero detent and keyed the mic, "Seattle Approach, Three-nine-nine heavy, we have to come in fast because we have no flaps."

"Copy, Freestyle three-nine-nine heavy. You are lined up on three-four-right, our longest runway at eleven-nine."

"Copy Seattle Approach, we need the trucks. We've got limited brakes and reversers but no ground steering."

"Three-nine-nine heavy, the trucks are standing by. Descend to one thousand. Field conditions are dry at three-seven. Winds are zero-three-zero at three-zero knots, gusting to four zero."

"Nice cross wind, Richard," Mitch mumbled. "That should make it interesting."

Jeff asked, "What about Boeing Field?"

"We can't. Their longest runway is thirty-one left at ten thousand feet; the cross winds would be worse at about ninety degrees. Besides he's lined up; to change direction now isn't easy."

"Man, I need a vacation!" Richard said.

Two news helicopters hovered several miles to the east; two local channels were ordered away from traffic duty to bring the cameraman as close as possible to the sensational story taking place south of Seattle. Another news chopper was making way after it was diverted from a factory fire, but would probably miss the window of opportunity.

Several news vans, whose occupants had also been monitoring the airwaves, were already deploying their boom equipment on the south end of the field; the reporters were taping introductions for the feeds and practicing their looks of shock or dismay.

Across the nation, television broadcasting was being interrupted to allow the minute-by minute drama to play out for those stations clear to the east coast. Images of the wounded KR-450C were transmitted to every news affiliate and subsequently displayed on every tuned in television. The hole in the right side of the #2 engine yawned for the cameramen who employed zoom lenses to get all the footage they could gather. Flight 399 waved its wings as Richard struggled with an aircraft battling his every command.

In Virginia, Megan Tenace was doing something she never did: watching cable news while nursing a cup of coffee.

"Mom," Patrick said angrily, "turn off the news. If anything happens with Max, you don't want to hear it there."

"Patrick, I need to see what's going on."

The anchorman cut in on a story about gas prices to announce that they were going live to their Seattle affiliate where a ... what kind of plane is it? There was a muffled dialogue off camera before the anchorman continued, saying that a Freestyle Airlines KR-450C is losing the battle to stay airborne. They warned viewers that these images could become too graphic for children.

Megan, who now had leaned forward to the edge of her couch, dropped her coffee cup and put her hands to her face. The cup fell and spilled hot coffee over a section of the beige carpet, staining it permanently.

Richard eased the -450C right slightly to catch the runway centerline; the wings rocked unsteadily as the airliner continued to fight his commands. The buffeting increased as winds drove into Flight 399 from starboard; the wings dipped sporadically to the right to compensate for the crosswind's effects.

As they flew over South 216th Street, housing receded below while they passed over wooded acres that were mostly unpopulated. Tree lines, that had months before sacrificed their foliage to the oncoming winter, stood by helplessly as the injured jetliner swiftly flew overhead.

People from neighborhoods to the east glanced skyward at the unusual spectacle; an aircraft of odd design was passing overhead. Some were excited; assuming they saw what they thought was Boeing's new model before anyone else. As it crossed the airspace four landing gears slowly emerged from their wells and sluggishly extend. It was not until they realized that there was a gaping hole in the tail with the Freestyle logo painted proudly on the side, that the observers figured something was amiss.

But by then it was too late as Flight 399 flew past their field of vision.

"One hundred ..." announced the digital voice in the cockpit. Richard was still fighting the crosswinds as N901FS screamed over a golf course; its wing dipping more frequently to the right. As they cleared the airfield's perimeter fence, he allowed the plane to sink faster towards the deck, aiming to flare just past the threshold to give himself as much stopping room as possible.

Richard eased the nose up to flare, but it was then that nature played its last nasty trick: a forty-knot gust of wind caught the -450C as it settled towards the runway. To counteract the effect, Richard rolled it right, but the gust ebbed quickly and he was caught rolling too hard; the right wingtip scraped the ground one hundred feet down the runway. Pieces of the damaged winglet and shattered navigation light lens scattered, littering the runway with small debris.

The aircraft was no longer lined up on the centerline; Richard gave left rudder and nursed the #3 engine forward. The jet coasted above the deck while the nose slowly lined back up on the centerline.

"You've got about eight thousand feet left!" Mitch said.

Richard again cut the throttles, the nose now several degrees left of the centerline. As he pitched up to flare, the aircraft sunk until the gear barely touched. Richard was closing in on the runway halfway mark when the translating cowl half imbedded in the stabilizer caught the ground; it dug in, snapping the left elevator clean off. Both the elevator and the translating cowl spun out of control, obliterating a lighting stanchion at taxiway Papa.

Richard let the -450C settle on the mains, keeping the nose up as long as he could. Mitch deployed the spoilers manually; this interrupted airflow over the wings and decreased the lift. Both pilots stood on their upper rudder pedals, applying as much wheel braking as they could. Richard could not get the nose to cooperate; he found himself veering off the centerline again.

"Get off the brakes!" He yelled.

Crowds of onlookers awaiting their flights in the terminals gazed open-mouthed at the scene playing before them. Some quick-thinkers were filming on their various handheld devices, looking like concert attendees, arms outstretched, inciting their favorite artist to return to the stage.

The speed was bleeding off the airliner as the far end of the runway rapidly approached; the nose started to settle and both pilots anticipated the upcoming change in direction. As the nose ground sense switch activated, the #3 reverser flew open causing the nose to swing further right. The nose gear now bearing its designed weight rattled violently as the unpressurized steering cylinders refused to dampen the shimmying; vibrations thumped through the airframe; it felt as if it would shake apart. The rudder pedals pummeled Richard's feet, transmitting painful shock waves into his ankles. Still moving at sixty knots and just past taxiway Hotel, the three in the cockpit watched helplessly as the -450C departed the runway and drove onto the sod at the right.

Two and a half days of heavy rains had softened the grassy area; properly saturated, the ground was unable to carry the weight of a multi-ton jet before allowing it to sink into itself. As the right gear entered the grass and dirt, the forward wheels on the gear's truck burrowed into the ground; the inertia of the aircraft's heavy mass contributed to the forward momentum, which was too much for the gear to restrain. The right gear snapped at the mounts and the fuselage continued forward, leaning heavily to the right.

The #3 engine hit the ground while at idle; the large angle forced mud and dirt through the still turning engine, passing through the engine's core; debris spewed out the back, showering metal and earth one hundred feet back before the engine suddenly seized. The continuing forward momentum of the airliner broke the #3 engine free at the pylon, leaving it with its insides ravaged, inlet down in the dirt.

The jet spun to the right, whipping around on the pivoting #3 engine pylon. The right wing dug in, rending the fuel tank open and showering fuel in all directions as the jet continued to die. Though reserving enough energy for one last shock, the massive aircraft ended its drama by ripping the right wing off entirely; fuel from yet untapped sources poured out of the ruptured wing tanks and formed growing lakes of flammable Jet A. Having had enough stress laid upon it, the left and center gears too gave up to the enormous side stresses put upon them; the left gear collapsed within its own well, while the center snapped free, pointing towards its departed brother to the right.

Though the fuselage's integrity remained intact, sparks thrown up during the death throes of N901FS caught the fumes of the newly spilled fuel. Within seconds, enormous flames shot up along the side of the fuselage that came to rest in an almost wings-level attitude.

Close by fire trucks approached at high speed within seconds of the last movement; sirens wailing announced to all to stay clear. From fifty feet away, one truck was already spouting flame retardant from a cannon onto the inferno, even before it rode up alongside. Seattle airport's fire brigade could not have made it any faster; already they were forcing back the flames which licked hungrily at the fallen airliner.

The Air Crash Files: Jet Blast

BOOK FIVE

CONCLUSION

The Air Crash Files: Jet Blast

CHAPTER 32
SUNSHINE MEETING

June 22

The NTSB Hearing room was brightly lit. A majority of the seating reserved for accident parties, witnesses or subject matter experts is now unoccupied; this is to be the Sunshine meeting; the culmination of months of work to be presented to the Board Members as the official Blue Cover Report.

This blue cover report had been paraded in front of the NTSB editors for weeks, taking numerous facts, statistics, interviews, and analysis from all the investigators and forming an intelligent narrative that speaks to the common man without sacrificing technical accuracy. The Board Members have had two weeks to read and absorb the contents before holding court in front of industry and the media.

The Sunshine meeting is unmistakably different from the Investigatory Hearing, in that, there is no further need for speculation or expert testimony. Questions are restricted to those posed by the Board Members and are aimed at the staff. Conclusions have been reached. The Members will accept the final report's probable causes for the accident and vote in the numerous recommendations authored by the staff.

To the Board Members' right are the only seats used outside the audience and are occupied by the NTSB staff. In the front row, sit those whose specialty most affected the report's outcome; each seat has a nameplate in front of the investigator, his or her name boldly written in large font with their specialty below it. Presently seated in this row are Ronald Gebbia, Philip Tulkinghorn, Jim Hughes, Christopher Wilkerson, and George Slade.

The seat between George and Chris is empty, the microphone is turned down. 'Daniel Tenace, Aircraft Maintenance' is written on the nameplate.

As the audience chamber continues to fill, the Board Members slowly make their way to their assigned places. Chairwoman Ellen Potter does not look happy; she is not presently basking in the attention she normally commands. Her dress, normally ostentatious, is plain grey as if she desires to blend into the background. She avoids contact with the media, instead sliding into the Hearing room unnoticed. She walks in at a fast pace, head down reading her notes before practically leaping into her center chair.

In contrast Vince Scalia is in the center of the gallery between the Members' table and the audience. He basks in the attention brought by the media; they have been closely following the information coming out of the Freestyle accident in Seattle. Vince's arms are animated as he drives home that facts brought out by the doomed Freestyle flight were made possible through his intercession. He has been practicing all night the dramatic discourse which tells how the cause of the accident was discovered, not by the guessing of others least qualified, but by the foresight and dedication to safety by only those who truly understand the industry.

As soon as everyone was seated and at exactly 9 o'clock, Ellen Potter began the meeting with a hard rap of her gavel. Potter welcomed all observers and explained the origins of the Sunshine meeting; she delivered a speech in a monotone voice heavily peppered with gratitude to Philip Tulkinghorn, who led his capable staff in pursuit of the truth; that the facts, though hidden, were brought forth by Phil's steadfast 'can-do' leadership. She added that it was in large part the guidance of the Board Members that made the success of this accident investigation a shining example of the Board's position as the Monument of Safety.

She hesitatingly turned to her co-Members and asked if there was anything to add. Vince raised his hand and Potter reluctantly surrendered the floor to him. At once Vince dismissed all the backslapping and self-congratulatory bloviating Potter just accomplished, rendering it all ineffective amid flashes from cameras and the aggressive reporting of events from the media. It was apparent to all, who commanded the room.

Vince went on for ten minutes, moving the staff front and center while pushing Phil further and further back, to the equivalent of the broom closet. Vince further trivialized Tulkinghorn's naïve contributions as irrelevant and controversial. All the while, Vince's eyes flicked back to the empty chair where the Aircraft Maintenance Investigator would normally sit.

"But before we continue with our obligation," he stated, gesturing to the gallery, "I would like to recognize Freestyle Airlines' Captain Richard Grace, First Officer Mitch McNally and Mechanic Jeffrey Harper. They agreed to testify to vital findings from the Freestyle accident in February as these facts pertain to the

Gyrfalcon accident. I would also like to take a moment to acknowledge," he continued, gesturing to the empty seat next to George, with a hitch in his voice, "the ... late Daniel Tenace."

Chatter carried over the room as it was inundated with flash units going off, like strobes set to music; the empty chair sat bathed in alternating shots of illumination. George and Chris looked at each other, unsure of how to react to Vince's acknowledgement of the vacant seat between them.

As if on cue, one of the back doors opened and Dan, still expertly wielding crutches, entered the room to nervous laughter and more flash units. Blinded temporarily by the surprise assault, he made his way with difficulty to his seat under full attention of the entire room. Unsure of why everyone was staring at him so intently or why his image was so popular to the lenses, he sat between his co-investigators, a look of confusion very evident to all.

"As I was saying," Vince said to sporadic laughter, "the *very* late, Daniel Tenace."

Embarrassed, Dan's eyes moved between Vince and the audience area. "I'm sorry, Madam Chairman, I wasn't able to make my normal train and the later ones were delayed for switch problems on the line. The other trains from Fredericks–"

Potter sighed loudly. "That's fine, Investigator Tenace," she said, cutting him off, greedily reclaiming the floor from Vince.

Dan spun in his assigned chair, maneuvering his legs under the table. Though he had shed some of the plaster and metal that were used to put him back together earlier this spring, he was still experiencing difficulty accomplishing simple tasks. He opened his binder and searched for the proper presentation.

That day in February came back to Dan in bits and pieces as he flipped through several pages, preparing for his presentation. He was sightless; efforts to open his eyes resulted in astonishing pain, intense chemical burning and blurred vision in the dark. Hampered by the unusual aircraft movements and a floor that rocked beneath him, Dan could not assure his footing. Blinded, he had been crawling forward, attempting to get near the ballast pallets. Then he recalled the mains touching down during the landing – if one could call it that.

A sudden sense of urgency took hold of him. Suspecting the pallets were close, he stood up to move faster, get a hold onto them or become a projectile. At that moment, Richard broke hard. Unrestrained, Dan was launched at his targets ... and that was the last he remembered.

In the hospital, Richard filled Dan in on what he missed. When the aircraft came to rest, Richard and Mitch began making safe the systems; all three engines had come to a sudden stop: #2 engine in the air and #3 engine in the dirt. #1 engine stopped suddenly when the left landing gear collapsed; the weight of the wing and fuselage crushed the bottom of the engine and irreparably destroyed the pylon, while the blades ground into the engine shroud. The engine itself seized after littering the ground about with metal fragments.

Since the aircraft was no longer in danger of inadvertent movement, Richard wasted no time in ordering Mitch and Jeff to the emergency exits; one glance out Mitch's window dispelled all doubt as to which side to egress. Mitch made a joke about going out the right side to avoid paying the bill for scratching the airliner. Despite himself, Richard guffawed.

Jeff tried to rush out the door to get to Dan and get him out of the aircraft, but Richard stopped him. He ordered both men down the slide; getting Dan out was his responsibility. Mitch inflated the left entry door slide and ordered Jeff down before hesitating himself.

"Richard, I can help."

"No," Richard replied calmly, "let's keep casualties to a minimum."

Mitch went to argue, but one look from Richard sent him down the slide as well.

Richard, still wearing his goggles, crossed into the cargo area. Visibility was close to zero as smoke hung trapped by the ceiling. Dark grey images seeped through the cabin as red shadows played against the left walls from the fire outside. Richard listened for a second for coughing, but Dan – wherever he was – remained silent.

Not good, Richard thought. He flipped on his flashlight, sending the beam down the length of the fuselage, but Dan was nowhere to be seen. He stepped carefully over a pallet, which sat askew on the aircraft's right side. In the background he could hear the firefighters fully engaged in laying down a thick coat of foam anywhere they could.

He swept the beam along the left side and found Dan wrapped grossly around the thick bars of the left-hand ballast pallet, pinning him painfully against the wall. His left arm was entwined desperately around the metal bars; it was this arm he used to stop any further momentum.

His left leg was at an awkward angle, the bone sticking out at a point in his mid-thigh.

After assuring himself that Dan was breathing, Richard ran to the doorway where Mitch and Jeff had disappeared and signaled for a stretcher. Two medical technicians clambered up the slide with Richard's help, bringing a come-along to move the pallet. After being freed and treated, Dan was maneuvered out the doorway and down to the waiting ambulance.

A camera many yards away managed to zoom in on Dan's features and the injuries played clearly for the general public. Thanks to the miracle of satellite television, Megan Tenace received an unobstructed view of her husband, live from Seattle.

The first thing Dan remembered, he was waking up in a hospital in Seattle two days later; his injuries were extensive. Pins were placed in his left leg and broken bones in his right arm were set with casts. Painkillers coursed through his system leaving him in a hazy dreamlike state. Gauze patches on his eyes prevented him from seeing anything.

The voices of Richard and Mitch seemed to hover in his conscious as they explained the end of the flight. Jeff, his southern accent heavily drawled, made no sense as he ate the gelatin from Dan's tray.

Still riding a pain-killer roller coaster, Dan noticed the room became uncomfortably quiet. His three colleagues from flight 399 managed empathetic pats on his shoulder as they left the room without a word. And then Megan was next to him, holding his hand; Freestyle flew her and Patrick in on their Challenger.

Patrick excused himself from the room. After assuring herself Dan was okay, Megan began verbally eviscerating her husband. Dan lay there quietly for twenty minutes, unable to escape.

"And if you think that your–" She continued, suddenly cut off.

"Megan!"

"What?!" She yelled, louder than planned.

Dan, his left leg throbbing despite the painkillers, asked, "What about Max?"

"Madam Chairwoman," Richard Grace humbly pleaded, "I wish to make a statement." The room quieted; Potter felt rather than saw Vince Scalia's piercing gaze boring into her skull. She could not escape the consequences of letting Captain Grace make a public statement that vindicated Tenace's theories, thus condemning her stonewalling.

"Yes, please proceed."

Richard Grace softly cleared his throat and held his breath for a count of four. When he spoke, his voice was low and even. "Madam Chairwoman, Board Members, my name is Richard Grace. I'm the captain of the ill-fated Freestyle Flight three-nine-nine that was destroyed in Seattle last February.

"I was also the captain of Freestyle Flight one-fifteen on June twenty-ninth of last year. On that flight my aircraft was almost lost off the coast of California when we experienced an uncommanded number two reverser deployment in flight. Mister Tenace and Mister Wilkerson insisted on looking into our emergency. When consideration of our–"

"Captain Grace, is it your intention to chastise the NTSB for past decisions?"

Richard allowed the question to settle on the entire room before responding.

"I'm not aware of any rebuke, Madam Chairwoman. I'm simply recognizing the efforts of two of your own."

Potter rubbed at the headache that was cropping up inside her forehead. "Please proceed."

"Thank you. Whether anything could have been changed to prevent the tragedy in Memphis of last September, I will not speculate." He paused again for several seconds to allow those words to settle. "However, when approached, Daniel Tenace did not hesitate to fly with us to test his concerns against the findings of the Gyrfalcon accident–"

"Captain Grace–"

"Madam Chairman," Vince Scalia readily interrupted Potter, "I respectfully recommend we allow Captain Grace to finish his statement."

Potter fumed; special interest groups and their lobbyists were watching these proceedings with great interest. Her effectiveness to them was very much in question. She reluctantly nodded to Scalia and motioned for Richard Grace to continue.

"Thank you, Madam Chairman," Richard continued, giving a slight wink to Vince. "I commend the NTSB for hiring professionals who have the experience to back them up. It is encouraging to see this is the direction the Board has taken in hiring investigators; qualified detectives who are proactive, not reactive."

"Thank you for those supportive words, Captain Grace. I'm sure your inten–"

"Madam Chairman, I'm not finished."

Potter pursed her lips. She wordlessly gestured for him to continue.

"But one true cause of Gyrfalcon's accident cannot be tested for or modified to fix it." Richard cleared his throat again. "Complacency."

"Captain Grace," Potter barked, letting her pride take over, "I'm sure you consider yourself qualified to make recommendations, but I assure you ... this organization – under *my* leadership, mind you – has our investigation processes well under control."

The cameras' timing was incredible; it caught Potter's pretentious scolding long enough to broadcast it onto the two big screens; they panned away just before she could suck the words back in her mouth. The cameras went right to Captain Grace's face as he reacted with a wounded expression. From the angle of the cameras, all anyone saw was the Chairwoman – an inexperienced Presidential appointee – berating the professional pilot, unequaled in his field.

"I assure you, Madam Chairman, my point is well proven. What Dan found was the physical problem with the aircraft. What I am suggesting ... I'm sorry ... demanding," he emphasized with a pound of his fist, "is that the Board and the FAA start to take some serious looks at how the technology is outpacing our pilots and mechanics.

"These machines are the zenith of man's engineering ability. They can outpace, out troubleshoot, and out fly, the most talented airmen I know. The industry's economics are dictating that we let the computers manage more and more; assume total control during the most vulnerable stages of flight.

"What we end up with are pilots who are out of practice; they're becoming no more than trained circus acts, limited to pushing buttons or flipping switches just so the airline can save a few dollars."

"Captain," Vince said, in a tone that sounded rehearsed, "doesn't the airline train you to anticipate mechanical errors?"

For the first time Richard hesitated – not out of theatrics, but out of true concern. "Lately, when I train, emphasis is on flying the computer, not the aircraft. We get the simulator up to a set altitude and then spend the rest of the test flight turning knobs. The airlines don't want us flying the aircraft, they don't want mechanics troubleshooting, and now they don't want air traffic controllers routing planes. They want the computers to do it all."

"But can't the computer fly the plane out of a problem?"

"Yes," Richard replied, "but it can't work through something the programmers didn't teach it. With Gyrfalcon's accident and our near-death experience, the computer reacted the way it was programmed to because," Richard paused to look at each member individually, "it didn't know any better. It simply had no one to turn to."

"What are you suggesting will happen?" Vince asked.

"I'm not suggesting anything, Member Scalia," Richard said quietly. "I'm telling you, there will be more accidents where the pilot won't react, simply because he doesn't remember how. Furthermore, the NTSB will call it 'pilot error' and nothing will be fixed."

Vince allowed a silence to blanket the room.

Member Carol Sanford cleared her throat and switched on her mic, "Captain Grace, you make a strong case. I, for one, would not trivialize anything you say or your experience for that matter."

Potter fumed, but remained quiet.

"I move," Sanford continued, "that we task staff with putting Captain Grace's suggestion into words as a recommendation for the blue cover report. Do I hear a second?"

Vince raised his hand, "I second."

Potter slapped her gavel down, taking control back from Carol Sanford. "It is so moved. Thank you, Captain Grace for your insight."

"Thank you," Richard said. As he rose in his chair, Vince barely gestured a thumbs-up; Carol Sanford caught the gesture and gave Richard a knowing wink.

"Thank you, Inspector Slade," Chairwoman Potter conveyed quietly. "Do any Members have questions for Inspector Slade?"

The presentation George provided was succinct and technically comprehensive; it was unchallenged by the Board. Dan knew that George did these types of presentations on purpose, so they would not ask him questions. It was, George often quipped, his superpower.

"You're next," he whispered at Dan.

"Inspector Tenace, please introduce your findings," Potter said with little enthusiasm.

Dan opened up a binder he kept before him. He glanced at the technicians who were operating the computers that fed the two big screens; one of them gave him an OK-sign. Dan nodded, sliding his reading glasses on. A picture of the accident aircraft, taken months before the accident by an aviation enthusiast, jumped on the screen. The picture was of N374GY rotating during a takeoff roll; the nose pointing towards the sky.

"This is the accident aircraft," Dan started, reading partially from the binder. "N-three seventy-four G-Y was a K-R dash three-fifty-Y owned and operated by Gyrfalcon Airlines.

"What really happened to cause Gyrfalcon four-twenty-seven to crash? To answer this, we need to look at the new Satellite Positioning and Airspace Restructuring, or SPAR, system approved for the aircraft, particularly the Saturn Digamma-six Ground Tracking Computer." As he said this, pictures of the items projected off the two screens.

"SPAR is not yet online, meaning the FAA hasn't fully activated the system. Most SPAR systems are still being tested, so technically this accident shouldn't have happened ... yet. Furthermore, the Digamma-six isn't a cruise phase navigation computer. Its intent is to display ground traffic status during low visibility approaches to prevent runway incursions. Otherwise, it has little use in flight.

"In the situation with Gyrfalcon four-twenty-seven ..."

"Excuse me," began the deep voice of Member Dick Baier, "Inspector Tenace, you said 'yet.' I believe the statement was: 'the accident should not have happened yet.' Are you saying the accident should have happened, as if planned?"

"No, no, Member Baier. I didn't mean to suggest the accident should have happened at all, but that the equipment was used in a non-test environment. Captain Fedow may have jumped the gun. I – I mean to say that if he hadn't been using the device, the accident would not have happened."

Baier pressed, "Are you suggesting it was his fault?"

"No, it isn't my place to judge. He was using equipment he'd been trained on that was installed in the cockpit. He wasn't instructed *not* to turn it on. Perhaps, the airline should have disconnected it to avoid inadvertent use of the system.

"Now," he began again, "in the situation of Gyrfalcon four-twenty-seven, as I just stated, Captain Fedow was employing the Ground Tracking Computer during the flight. What is unusual is that the Digamma-six doesn't work above ten thousand feet. From physical evidence and interviews with the surviving first officer, Dayton Chamberlain, we determined that Captain Fedow was using it, that his screen was on, and before he could shut it off, he became engaged in landing procedures.

"But," Dan said, pausing for effect, "the computer itself didn't bring the aircraft down; it had help." Dan hesitated for a moment to allow the last statement to sink in. "A faulty landing gear ground sense switch on the left main gear was partly responsible for the deployment of the reversers."

"And you know this because ...?" asked Member Ira Goldberg, co-Chairman; his large bloodshot eyes displaying doubt.

"A faulty switch was found on the main gear of Gyrfalcon four-twenty-seven." Dan said, shooting a glance at Phil, who stared at his hands. "And a similarly faulty switch was found on Freestyle one-fifteen in June of last year."

"Are you referring to the Freestyle flight Captain Grace–"

Chairwoman Potter cut Goldberg off. "We need to let Tenace finish." She waved her hand disdainfully at Dan. "Go on, please."

Everyone in the room noticed, on some level, the absence of the title 'Investigator' in Potter's rebuke. The tone of voice with which she cut Goldberg's legs out drew more attention than the omission of the title. Across the room, reporters wrote quickly.

"The faulty switch *was* discovered on Freestyle one-fifteen after the mid-air deployment of the number two reverser last June," Dan replied. "When the engineers tested the switch, it was found to have the same design flaws as the Gyrfalcon switch."

Ignoring Potter, Goldberg asked, "Was the FAA made aware of this?"

"Yes sir, Aaron Campo and I talked about it and he worked the problem from within the FAA. They were in the process of redesigning the switch when Gyrfalcon crashed. Also," Dan added, "the switch is a different part number for the Gyrfalcon jet. The fault was never found anywhere else beforehand, so there was no reason to question the Gyrfalcon jet's ground sense switch."

"Dan, explain how you know it's the switch," Vince said into the microphone.

Dan pressed his lips together, trying to figure a way to explain this. Throwing caution to the wind, he plowed on. "The faulty switch from Freestyle's incident last June was placed on the accident aircraft this past February, before it was flown to Seattle."

"Let me understand this," Potter interrupted, leaning forward, "you knowingly installed a broken switch on an aircraft to force a reverser deployment?" Potter's eyes were practically sprouting from a red face as she shook her head in disbelief. "What did you hope to accomplish by doing something so irresponsible, Investigator Tenace?"

"Some of my fellow investigators were not convinced that the findings of the Portland tests were conclusive. The main reason being that, the Systems and Maintenance groups were prevented from using a comparable aircraft for the test.

"Captain Grace and I were trying to duplicate the conditions in a controlled environment. Richard Grace and Mitch McNally? They're test pilots for Freestyle. In addition, Captain Grace also was present during the reverser deployment last June."

"You didn't answer the question; what did you hope to accomplish, Investigator Tenace?" she asked, her teeth grinding out the name.

"Well, for one, it would appear to me that they may have saved lives in the future," Member Carol Sanford said from the Chairwoman's right. "If the original Gyrfalcon tests hadn't been corrupted, then by double-checking the results they prevented another accident, possibly with more passengers on board. Furthermore, I would ask Philip Tulkinghorn why the tests were not properly carried out."

"That is not a topic of dis–" Potter began.

"Not today," Sanford insisted, "but believe me, I will find out!"

"If I may," Member Dick Baier interrupted. The former Air Force colonel had no patience for tangents. He turned to Dan. "You said only the number two reverser deployed last summer. I'm familiar with the K-R-four-fifty; it has three engines. Why did you have three reversers deploy in February, if the tests were duplicated?"

Dan turned to Chris, who turned on his microphone. "That's a really good question, Member Baier. There was an unforeseen problem: the nose gear ground sense switch was also faulty on the Seattle airplane, just like in Memphis. That switch will tell engines one and three to deploy reversers because it thinks that weight is on the nose gear. The switches' cases were most likely compromised, allowing moisture into the switch. We found heavy corrosion in the damaged circuits."

"Per an Emergency Airworthiness Directive, the FAA required both switches be redesigned last August after Gyrfalcon four-twenty-seven," Chris added. "The FAA had expanded on their original directive to include all AeroGalactic airliners – not just the dash-three-fifty. It dictated that *all* operators of *any* AeroGalactic airliner replace both switches with modified switches before the next flight. In addition, the deactivation of all Autoland systems for AeroGalactic aircraft was still in effect from the Gyrfalcon accident, so there was no chance of repeating Memphis."

"But if the FAA had ordered the changing of nose gear switches last October," Baier pursued, "why wasn't Freestyle's nose switch changed before February?"

Dan replied, "Because N-nine-oh-one-F-S was not active in the fleet at the time. In fact, we were flying it to a maintenance check in Seattle to catch up its maintenance."

"I'm not sure I understand: why didn't the number one inboard reverser stow?" Vince asked, making the planned question sound like a true query.

Dan took a deep breath. "Parts from the number one reverser were cannibalized while in the desert. In other words, parts were removed – *cannibalized* – from nine-oh-one to put on another aircraft." He pulled out some pages from his binder.

"Chris Wilkerson and I went to Cleveland last month and found the hard copies for nine-oh-one's maintenance logs. Some of the cannibalized parts from the reverser, specifically the number one inboard upper reverser track, were not in the computer records. Plainly put, the records were lost."

He took a breath. "You see ... when the aircraft was taken off the operations specifications for storage, parts tracking became inaccessible to the mechanics and Freestyle's data entry group. Chris and I think that's why the problem occurred; the reverser's upper track removal was never properly recorded."

Member Carol Sanford leaned forward, gazing left and right to assure herself she would not interrupt anyone. Potter sighed loudly, knowing that Sanford would prolong the presentation. Carol Sanford ignored her.

"Investigator Tenace, though I do appreciate your talent for putting such prosaic information in a format that even simple minds like mine can grasp, I feel that you're holding back."

Of all the Members – aside from Vince – Dan liked Carol Sanford the best. Always shooting from the hip, she never professed to be more knowledgeable than she was.

"Member Sanford," Dan said faltering, "I was not aware I was–"

But Sanford just shook her head to gently dismiss the apology. Vince smiled as she removed her glasses. "You said the gear switch was only *partly* responsible; in the report, you talk about a NAND Gate." She leaned forward. "My questions are: what is a NAND Gate? And most importantly, what possessed you to fly to Seattle in the first place?"

Dan shifted nervously in his seat. "To answer your second question, I was out of options. Captain Grace offered me a chance to prove there was something beyond a simple reverser rigging gone awry. The Gyrfalcon mechanics never did anything wrong, but the true culprit was getting lost in the finger-pointing.

"To your first question, the defect in the ground sense switches only allowed a signal to pass through to the flight command computer. The redesign only postponed another event, anywhere from a day to maybe a decade in the future. The true cause was more involved." He tried to explain the computer logic but was met with blank stares, even from Vince. Instead he decided to break it down to the basics.

"Digital logic aside," he began, "let's put this in laymen's terms. Captain Grace was speaking before about computers being smart enough to fly the airplane by itself. But as advanced as it is, a computer still follows commands. The SPAR systems installed in Gyrfalcon's and Freestyle's AeroGalactic jets were originally designed for Boeing and Airbus airplanes. In those airliners, the ground sense switches *close* on landing. If you want to turn on the mic in front of you, you *close* the switch and the mic works.

"But AeroGalactic's ground sense switch *opens* on landing; AeroGalactic designed their computers to work this way. With the ground sense switches shorting out, the command computer made a mistake. It mistook the signal coming from the DATTAM ground tracking computer for the ground sense switch signal."

Dan paused. "It thought it was on the ground."

Chris sat next to him nodding his head. Vince grinned while the other four members sat aghast. Dan sat back and waited for the flood of questions, but none came; the Board Members understood.

"Board Members, that concludes my report and presentation. If you have any further questions, I am available to answer them."

Member Baier spoke up, "First, let me say to those attending that the Board Members normally don't interrupt an Investigator at the Sunshine meeting, but this case is unique in many ways; I'm sorry if we confused your presentation in any way.

"I just wanted to ask two questions. First, do you believe that this information would have been found if you hadn't embarked on that Seattle test flight?" Vince went to object to the term 'test flight,' but Baier interrupted him. "I'm taking liberties, I understand. So, please, just answer the question."

Dan looked at Vince and then at Captain Grace. "No, Member Baier, I honestly believe we would have suffered another accident with the limited information we had."

"I agree," Baier said. "Do you credit the impressive technologies we supposedly have here at the NTSB for finding this?"

"I think," Dan replied, smiling stupidly, "we've become a sensationalistic society. We watch T-V and think what we see is true; that there are C-S-I groups with these wonderful means to solve anything. I believe the Board's greatest breakthroughs are with stone knives and intuition. The greatest technology I used was a highlighting marker."

Dan thought for a second before adding, "There are no experts here."

The Board Members voted unanimously to adopt the report as written and to endorse the recommendations. As the people in the room dispersed to the exits or towards the Board Members for statements, Dan sought out Richard Grace. A group of reporters almost caught Dan, but Chris deftly blocked their approach and led them to Vince.

"Richard, I haven't had the chance to thank you again, face-to-face, for coming to get me," Dan said, shaking Captain Grace's hand. His accident-mates stood before his table to limit his crutch use.

Richard laughed at the memory. "Well, seeing how your wife reacted when she saw you, I think I would have put my own life in danger if I hadn't got you out."

Dan smiled at the remark. "Well, she seems to have gotten over it."

Richard turned serious. "How is your son in Afghanistan?"

Dan hesitated, unsure of how Richard found out about Max. "The day after the accident in Seattle," Dan explained, "Max called Megan on her cell and told her that he was the one who was supposed to make the news and not me. Apparently, they saw footage of the accident all the way over there.

"But in answer to your question, his unit got cut off. He's the medic, so he had his hands full with wounded. Anyway, he went to help this one guy who was hit in the middle of a firefight." Dan's voice checked; he shook his head as he tried to get it back. "This guy Grabowski, who, according to Max is as stocky as a rock cliff, protected Max while he worked on this kid; I mean, Grabowski used his body as a shield. Max stopped the bleeding, Grog – that's what they call Grabowski – threw the kid over his shoulder and the three of them take the scenic route back to the unit."

Richard smiled. "That's good news, Dan. We need guys like your son."

"Thanks Richard."

"Dan, let me give you some advice," Richard said, his face getting serious. "There's a story in this ..." He smiled at Dan's confused look. "Seriously, you need to write this down. I know you may not be able to now, but someday you could use this experience to sell a book. Think about it."

"I may be out on a limb here, Dan," George said, "but are you and Megan working out your issues with Max?"

They were making their way to the elevators for the ride up. "You know how Megan is, George. She wants me to convince Max to leave the Army."

George looked skeptically at his friend. "Are you going to?"

Dan pressed the UP button. "No. When we lost Tyler, our second son; God, it's going on two years now ..." Dan shook his head at the realization. "You see ... when I tried to tell *him* what to do, it resulted in him taking off –

no note, no call ... He died four days later in a car collision."

"You can't blame your–"

"You're right, George, I can't. And yet I do," Dan said as the doors opened. "I'm constantly wondering: what if I'd done things differently, would he be here today?"

As the elevator rose, George smirked, easing into a new subject. "You're going to ignore Captain Grace's advice, aren't you?"

Dan snorted a laugh. When they arrived at Dan's office, George stood out in the hall while Dan maneuvered around his desk. "You gotta give it some thought; at least write it down. Who knows, you may get the chance to author something someday."

"Well, I'll think about it," Dan said, laughing off the thought. "I'd have to be careful 'cause I doubt Phil would be too thrilled with that type of story."

George looked both ways down the hallway before leaning into Dan's office. "Well, whatever you need; let me know."

Dan played with the thought in his mind. He was tired and truly did not have the strength to catch the train home, so he was opting for a later train, maybe at 7:00 PM. George did not move, anticipating that his friend was seriously considering it. "Don't put it on the common drive. Phil may find it." George said, after a brief pause, "Yeah ... don't do that."

Dan pulled a memory stick out of his computer bag. "I could keep it on my hard drive and on a stick."

"Are you going to use a pseudonym?"

Dan's right eyebrow rose. "I could use my Grandmother's maiden name. How does Sheridan sound?"

"Yeah, Daniel, with your Italian looks," George chuckled, "Sheridan would be perfect." He smiled, taking a quick glance at his watch. "Well, as Johann Sebastian once said, 'I'll be Bach,'" He went back down the hall towards the elevators; he placed his fedora on his head and cocked it to sit rakishly over his left eye.

Dan started his computer. As he waited he called Meg and told her he was taking a late train to avoid the crowds. He told her how the meeting went and she told him to get home soon; she would pick him up at the station. As soon as the computer warmed up, Dan opened a Word document and stared at the pulsing tempo of the cursor playing on a blank page. Finally, he typed in:

NAND Gate

Which he quickly deleted. He then typed:

Jet Crisis
By Dan Sheridan

He wrinkled his nose in disapproval. *Sheridan won't do,* he thought. *And I've gotta work on that title.* Several images played in his head as he typed:

Above the earth, a myriad of stars shows brightly. Constellations normally bathed pale by city lights are out front and on display, their patterns so obvious to the keen-eyed astronomer taking advantage of the dark Midwestern sky. Hercules stands ready for battle; the globular cluster M13 shows clearly in ...

THE END

ABOUT THE AUTHOR

Stephen Carbone has been actively involved in the commercial aviation industry for over thirty years. While working for the airlines he pursued and received his Masters Degree (2001) in Aviation Safety Systems. Bringing experience from the airlines in both labor and management, he joined the NTSB where he investigated major accidents, both domestic and international. For several years, Stephen worked as an aviation safety inspector for the FAA, where his experience and education played important parts in his success.

Stephen resides on the East Coast with his first love, his wife of thirty-five years. He continues to write articles about his second love – aviation, while working on other works of fiction like *The Air Crash Files: Jet Blast*.

Manufactured by Amazon.ca
Bolton, ON